TIME FLASH: ANOTHER ME

FIRST EDITION

Printed in the United States of America
ISBN 978-0-9970834-5-3

Cataloging Information: 1. Ayers, Lana; 2. Time Travel Fiction;
3. Science Fiction; 4. Women's Fiction.; 5. Action and Adventure. 6. Romance.

Cover Art: *Cat Nap* (acrylic on canvas), by Marie Fox
http://mariefoxpaintingaday.blogspot.com/

Author Photo: Andrew E. Ayers

Layout/Design/Cover Concept by Andrew E. Ayers
Created with Vellum

Night Rain Books / Night Rain Press
PO Box 445
Tillamook, OR 97141

Night.Rain.Press@gmail.com
http://NightRainBooks.com

I saw huge buildings rise up faint and fair, and pass like dreams.

— H. G. WELLS, THE TIME MACHINE

This book is dedicated with gratitude and love, across the dimensions, to my brother, Alan Hechtman (1956-2010), who being older, controlled the TV and turned me into a science fiction geek, thereby gifting me the universe.

TIME FLASH: ANOTHER ME

LANA AYERS

Night Rain Books

ORIGINAL TIMELINE

YEAR 2000 — THE PRESENT

Of all the words of mice and men, the saddest are, 'It might have been.'

— KURT VONNEGUT, CAT'S CRADLE

Let your life lightly dance on the edges of Time like dew on the tip of a leaf.

— RABINDRANATH TAGORE

CHAPTER 1

SARA, AGE 37

Monday, April 3, 2000, 6:50 AM
Sara & Jon's condo
Bayfront, Long Island, NY

$\mathcal{M}$y life has been a series of deprivation diets. The only time I ate until I was full was when I was pregnant. Now, after ten days on this Plain Grains Granola diet, I'm so ravenous I could eat my own shoes. But I've been good. *So good.* Not even a single cheat. And I know all about my husband Jon's secret stash of chocolate truffles in the cupboard just behind his assortment of novelty accountant mugs. We don't own a scale. So, I'll settle for losing just enough weight to be able to slip that red satin dress over my hips and turn Jon's thoughts to lust.

This natural cereal diet promises twenty pounds off in a month, as well as rosy skin and perkier breasts. The menu is simple—granola three times a day and little else. Not only am I starving, my teeth feel brittle and my eyeballs are crunchy. I was hoping the twenty pounds would slide off all at once, like a snake shedding skin, or in my case, fat.

My smiling reflection in the walk-in-closet mirror appears a lot more confident than I truly am. I should wait until after Jon leaves for work to try on the dress. But I read somewhere you weigh the least first thing in the morning, right after stepping out of bed. Which means now is the absolute best time.

Smooth and silky as a kiss. That's how the satin feels beneath my finger-tips. I bought this little red cocktail number to set Jon's passions aflame. Marked seventy-five percent off, the best bargain at the mall, gorgeous without being gaudy, it's a once-in-a-lifetime dress. The luscious shade of red complements my tawny skin. The cut is curve conscious, perfect for our fifth anniversary. Ideal in every way—except for being two sizes smaller than what I normally wear.

"Wish me luck, Gallo."

"Mrow," Gallo says, rubbing his cheek against my ankle. It sounds like "luck." The matted, black, mewling shelter kitten covered with scratches grew into our handsome, big-furred cat. With his affectionate nature, uncanny knack for stealing pens and carrying them off in his mouth, and abundant vocalizations, he's our sweet baby. Our only one. *"Mrow, mrow mrow, mrow,"* he says, as if impatient.

I slide the dress over my head and maneuver my breasts into place one by one. The V-neck makes a nice display of my cleavage without being too risqué. I shimmy the garment the rest of the way down. Before I can take a look at myself, the doorbell rings. *Who could be at our door this early?*

Jon must be thinking the same thing. "Who's there?" he calls out.

His question is answered by a syrupy Southern drawl that echoes all the way down our condo's railroad-car-length hallway. "It's *moi,* Jon darling."

Moi is Candy Starr from apartment ten. *Holy molé salsa!* Candy has been trying to catch Jon's eye since we moved into this building. Except for her red hair, she's almost a clone of his ex-girlfriend from college, with the same wasp waist and legs up to her neck. A regular Rita Hayworth. At the elevator, in the hallways, and in the parking garage, she cozies up to him, oozing sexual innuendo. Her scent, a suffocating honeysuckle cologne, lingers on his clothes after those encounters.

Candy has never had the nerve to come to our door before this.

I throw my terry robe over the cocktail dress and hurry to the living room.

Gallo runs alongside me.

Shruuuuup.

My amazing dress shreds open at the hips and down the sides. No time to stop and assess the full damage, I tie my robe tight and keep going. And in a moment, I can't believe what I see.

Candy is wearing a coral silk baby-doll nightie that perfectly comple-ments her creamy complexion. She leans over the granite breakfast counter.

She's toying with the ribbon bow in the center which seems to be the only thing preventing her bouncy breasts from exploding the rest of the way out.

"You've got all the right equipment," she licks her lips and adds, "for the task I have in mind."

"And just what is that?" Jon says. He's standing there with nothing but a towel wrapped around his waist. His muscled torso glistens, as taut and toned as the day we met in the accounting department of Domestic Global International.

Gallo springs onto the counter and lets out a loud *"Grrrowwwl."*

Candy straightens, stumbles back a step.

"You knocked on the wrong door, Candy" I say. "Our building super lives down on the first floor."

They both turn to me. Gallo flicks his tail.

"Hey, neighbor." She struts closer to Jon. "I came to borrow your man."

Even her breath reeks of honeysuckle. *What does she do, gargle with cologne?*

"No can do," Jon says, holding up both hands like an air traffic controller. He's a man who talks with his hands, and with the five digits of each, he can say things to my body not translatable into words. *At least he used to.*

"Oh, sugar snap peas, pretty please." Candy stretches out her sharp-nailed hand as if to claw Jon's bare chest.

My husband, good man that he is, sidesteps her reach. He bumps into the back of the sofa and nearly loses his towel. "I've got to get ready for work."

She frowns. "I guess I'll find someone else to turn my mattress upside down."

I grab her arm and lead her out.

"You do that, Candy."

"Bye now," she says stopping at the threshold to look past me and give Jon a wink. She sashays down the corridor, then turns and x-rays me with her eyes. "Nice frock, Sara. What's left of it, that is."

My robe must have come open while I was helping her leave. I slam the door on her smug expression.

"Sorry about that," Jon says coming to me. Premature patches of silver-gray in his wet, black hair match the shine of his dark eyes. "That woman is a pest."

"We should hire an exterminator," I say.

"I was looking for you when Candy barged in. My deodorant ran out. I know you bought more. Where the *bejeezus* is it?"

Even perplexed, my husband's voice penetrates my muscles like deep tissue massage. But how is it that after five years of marriage, the man I love still has no idea where we keep anything?

"Have you tried the yellow pages?" I cross my arms. "You know, you didn't have to let that woman in here."

"Listen, Sara." He twirls his fingers through my long curls. "'Listen to me as one listens to the rain.'" He's quoting from his favorite Octavio Paz poem, like he does all the time.

Gallo, somehow no longer on the kitchen counter, launches from the back of the sofa with the grace of a gull and lands inches from our feet. "*Mrow, mrow, mrow.*" He bolts down the hall toward the bathroom, where his litter box resides.

"Gallo will show you where your deodorant is," I say.

"And I'll show you," Jon says. "Come here." He strips off the towel from his waist, throws it around my shoulders, and pulls me against him. He smells like soap and coffee. He sucks at my earlobe.

Tingles ripple below the surface of my skin.

He blows lightly in my ear. "Deodorant's not in there," he says. "Where should I look next?"

I grab his hand and guide it to my breast. I want to take this affection all the way. I kiss him hard on the mouth, and send my own hand south, between his thighs. This is how it should be between us, how it used to be— us making love at any hour, in any room, across any surface.

Like all those times he said, "Hey baby, what'cha doing?" in the middle of dinner. He tore me from my chair, pressed his hot chest and hotter groin against me, worked a hand into my jeans, making me wet and wanting more. Finally, the unbuttoning sliding, rising, riding, right there on the table, to hell with the dinnerware. We had to buy three new sets of dishes the first year of our marriage.

Jon's thumb tickles my nipple. His lips kiss a trail across my throat. Suddenly, he wrenches away. He's glaring at me, his cheeks wind-burn red.

"What's the matter? Is it the dress? It's a mess, but—"

"What's that on your neck?" He prods the spot.

"Ow." I stop his hand with my own. "Nothing. Bug bite I guess."

"That's not from any insect," he says under his breath. He snatches his towel from my shoulder and re-secures it around his waist.

"It can't be that bad. I've always been a mosquito magnet. Maybe it just got infected. Should I see Dr. Gentry about it?" While Jon probes the sore spot, I crane my neck.

A web clings to the overhead light, but there's no web-maker in sight.

"Maybe it's a spider bite," I say.

He lets go of me. "Don't bother with Dr. Gentry. He'll just tell you to use antiseptic cream." Jon smiles, but not quite all the way.

"I'm sure you're right, *mi sol*. Let's just pick up where we left off." I move to kiss him again.

He turns his head and my lips graze his cheek. "Sorry. I can't be late for work. Morning meetings. The antiseptic is probably near my deodorant. Which is where?" He flexes both hands to emphasize the question.

"Right where we always keep it. Third shelf in the bathroom linen closet."

He stomps off for the bathroom. Partway down the hall, he reverses direction and returns to retrieve his favorite novelty mug from the counter. It's the one that declares *Accountants Do It Between the Spreadsheets* in faded red letters. "Hey, sorry, *mi luna*." He flashes a half-smile again. "I've got to get going. Everything will be okay with your neck, I promise. And don't forget my mom wants us to have Easter here."

My mother-in-law, María García, is a bleached-blonde, hot-pants-wearing version of my own mother. Her idea of a compliment is telling me "At least you'll float if you ever fall off a boat." Mrs. García is the only reason I thought twice about marrying Jon.

"Easter is the day before our anniversary," I say. "It's wood for five years." It's his wood I want.

"Great, we can celebrate both." He lays a hand over his heart. "Invite your Dad too."

I don't even have a chance to say *bueno* before he clops off. Nothing is going to happen now. Once again, he's found a reason not to make love. At least he started. That feels like progress. But I am not a light switch he can flip on and off. I'm a candle—once I'm lit I burn for hours. I'll have to drown my sorrows in coffee.

At least the earthy aroma of brewing French roast overpowers the fake honeysuckle stench Candy left behind. Jon must have finished the first pot and started a new one for me. *He can be so sweet.*

Over the years, I've gone from a one-cup-a-day drinker to three. Sometimes even more when my tax clients get persnickety. Plus, the caffeine helps revive me from nightmares.

Some people see their loved ones in dreams, have encounters with famous people, or even fly. I haven't been that lucky. I have exhausting dreams often filled with funerals—and wake feeling more drained than when I went to bed. Last night, I dreamt I was in a hospital being operated on while wide awake. I tried to scream, but no sound came from my mouth.

I drain my first cup of coffee in a few gulps.

"Mrow, mrow," Gallo says from the top of the fridge.

I never even saw him leap up there. Add stealth to his list of talents.

"Okay, your turn." I pour kibble into the gold-rimmed, chipped white saucer. This dish is the one piece of Grandma's wedding china that survived my mother's bad temper. At least Gallo can make use of it. "Come and get it, boy." My destroyed dress splits open some more as I stoop to set the kibble on the floor.

Gallo launches to land beside his bowl. His ears twitch at the Doppler sound-effect of my husband's *thwapping* footsteps approaching from the back bedroom, but he keeps gobbling.

Jon, exceedingly handsome in his navy suit, strides past, practically a blur. He's more rushed than usual, and he's already talking to someone on his mobile phone. He covers the mouthpiece with his hand and says, "Love you," without the slightest romantic inflection. The door snaps shut behind him.

"I love you too," I say to the space his body occupied a moment ago. I hurry to our balcony, too narrow for anything but pacing. *If Jon really loves me, he'll look up as he leaves the building.*

The dark outside the living room windows feels portentous. A steely haze hangs over the neighboring buildings, like sheet-draped furniture in a closed-up summer home. I half-expect an enormous flash of light, after which everything will be different and Jon will want me again. Maybe a dazzling solar flare that paints the New York sky with aurora and forces the jaded masses into a state of awe. Or a massive solar wind that brings down the power grid and returns us all to huddling around home-stoked fires. Half-expect, half-wish. I suppose it's the science fiction lover in me wanting the fantastical to come for breakfast in my kitchen.

My husband exits the building moving at a rapid clip. He heads left without a nod in my direction.

That doesn't mean anything, right?

We never eat breakfast together anymore. Or any meal, for that matter. His job is all he has time for. We live in different worlds. Maybe I never should have stopped working with him at Domestic Global International. At least we saw each other in the car on the way there and back.

Then again, most of the women I worked with at Domestic are divorced, some twice over. That place strains relationships. But five years of marriage hardly feels like an accomplishment with Jon and I living like roommates. Our lovemaking consists of broken-off starts like this morning. Nights, he says he's too tired from work. But that isn't the whole story. We both know I'm not exactly the woman he thought he married.

I hear my mother's voice in my head saying, *He's cheating on you right this minute. Why would Jon want you when he could have a thin woman?*

I know nothing is going on with Candy. Jon wouldn't go behind my back and he would never lie to me. But he comes home late every night and the first thing he does is shower. Not even my obsessive-compulsive college boyfriend washed that much. Jon says the warm water helps him unwind.

So at two in the morning, when he's still not home, my mother's voice in my head wakes me with doubts. I hear her say, *Lose weight or you'll lose him for good.*

I change out of what remains of the red threadbare disaster and pull on comfortable sweats. My private tax clients don't care what I wear to balance their books.

Second cup of coffee in hand, I stroll over to my leather reading chair. I always like to start the day off with a good book. Today, I really need someone else's story to distract me from the awful reality of my morning. I turn to the last section of Kurt Vonnegut's autobiographical collage, *Fates Worse Than Death*.

If I were to write the story of my life, I might title it *Table for One* or *A Steady Diet of Solitude*.

CHAPTER 2

JON, AGE 43

… I travel your forehead like the moon …

— OCTAVIO PAZ

Monday April 3, 2000, 7:20 AM
Office of Joanne Vento
Senior Investigator, Department of Justice
Special Undercover Operations Bureau
Little Village, Queens, NY

I *should have seen this coming. How could I be so stupid?* These thoughts play over and over in a loop in Jon's head. Distracted by his fury, he manages to smack his right side into a file cabinet as he turns the corner to his partner's office. The DOJ's covert headquarters are cramped and musty. Nothing like the plush digs at his usual weekday location, his undercover job at the corporate office of Domestic. He steps inside Joanne Vento's office and shuts the door harder than he intended. The entire translucent glass clinks.

Piles of papers on the dented steel desk flutter, but do not scatter.

Vento looks up, her expression more confusion than annoyance. "García, what are you doing here?" With reading glasses attached to a chain that rests against her high-neck purple dress, plus her hair up in a bun, she reminds him of a scolding librarian.

"You can't be serious. I'm out of there today. They messed with the wrong guy's wife." He pounds his fist on the desk, but the wood-grain Formica deadens the sound.

She remains calm. "You have to keep up appearances," Vento says. "I explained all this to you on the phone. You should be at Domestic." She comes around the desk, sits in one of the folding chairs intended for the occasional visitor, and motions for him to sit in the other. "It may not be exciting work, but the financial paper trail is how we close them down. The DOJ needs you undercover there. Aren't you the one who told me 'a little more time and I'll hit pay dirt'?"

He drops into the matching chair. "I feel like a glorified accountant, but that's not the issue. This is personal now. I saw the syringe mark on Sara's neck. Those bastards are experimenting on my wife."

She snaps a knife-hand blow to his wrist. "Language, mister."

He shakes his arm to diminish the sting. *My partner can single-handedly take down a cadre of subversives with karate, but she can't abide a cuss word.*

"Frank and John Sullivan are good men," she says. "I assigned them to protect your wife right after you called. No one will get within five feet of Sara with those two working surveillance. The brothers are on alternate shifts starting this morning. No need to worry."

Is she serious? Not worry? She's not married, she has no idea. "Let's take Sara to the safe house now and get the experimental crap out of her bloodstream. What do we gain by keeping her in play?"

"I want you to understand how invested I am in keeping Sara alive. There's something I never told you." Vento uncrosses her legs. "A secret about my past."

Jon's stomach clenches. Vento's never shared anything personal before. She's always played it close to her vest.

"A secret about your wife," she continues.

"What do you mean?" he says. "Sara and I don't have any secrets."

Vento whistles like a sailor. "Except she thinks you're an accountant."

He stands and stuffs his hands in his pockets to keep himself from shouting. "Whose fault is that? Bureau policy punishable by dismissal."

"Covert means covert. Besides, I told you during the interview this job isn't conducive to relationships."

"Right. If you mean lethal, I see your point. Was that crispy corpse Joe's girlfriend? Are the dental records a match? I'm not—"

"Stop," she says, stamping her feet. The loafers wheeze against the concrete floor. "Sara was my best friend. I love her too."

"What? You've never even met my wife."

"Sara and I grew up next door to each other in Woodward. We were best friends until a boy came between us."

"Why the hell didn't you tell me this before?"

"It had no relevance. Besides, I thought you'd figure it out on your own. Didn't she ever mention me to you? I taught her everything she knows about rock-n-roll and baking."

He snorts at the thought of Vento in an apron, but searches his memory. "That was you—the girl with the playhouse in her parents' basement?"

"Our friendship ended a long time ago, but I think of her as family, like a kid sister."

"You tried to get me to stop dating her as payback for some boyfriend you two fought over years ago?"

Vento shakes her head. "I was a lovesick adolescent, the boy in question a juvenile delinquent. Not worth losing my best friend over. Hindsight is a killer."

"Why didn't you get back in touch with Sara when you saw her name on the Domestic employee roster?"

"Too risky. I might have let my emotions cloud my thinking. Just like you are doing right now. I'm not proud of it, but I was horrible to Sara. She doesn't want me back in her life. The important thing is that we protect her and find out who gave her the injection and under what circumstances."

"I told you," Jon says. "It has to be Candy Starr. She's slept with half the guys in the condo, including the super. Stealing keys from him would be a breeze. And she had the nerve to show up at our door this morning. I'll tear her place apart tonight if I don't get a confession out of her."

"Dana Kevin is running the investigation on Starr. He hasn't found any evidence of serum at her place or in her possession. You will not compromise his operation. Is that clear?"

"Do you know what you're asking? Sara is my whole life."

"Stay on the job at Domestic. Get the evidence of illegal fund transfers. Let the other agents do their jobs." She clutches her heart. "If there is a whiff of danger, the Sullivans will whisk Sara to the safe house immediately. You have my word."

He studies Vento, the set of her jaw and her cool hazel eyes. She's composed and confident, but he knows all about her poker face. She fleeced him out of fifty bucks last week at the bureau game night with only a pair of deuces.

Heading out, with one hand on the doorknob, he says, "I'm holding you responsible if anything goes wrong." As he utters the words, he's aware they're meaningless. *Even Vento can't make guarantees, especially when a company as devious as Domestic is involved.* But then again, she comes through when it matters most. Vento had saved his bacon more than once. He can trust her to be true to her word.

She stands and faces him. "Go crunch some numbers, García. I'm on this."

"Yeah, I'll do that. And why don't you go bake me some cookies. I'm partial to chocolate chip."

Vento cracks a smile. "Maybe for your birthday, but don't hold your breath."

He leaves, just as troubled as when he went in, but he manages to avoid crashing into anything or anyone. *No matter what Vento says, I'm going to do everything in my power to protect my wife.*

CHAPTER 3

SARA, AGE 37

Monday, April 3, 2000, 8:00 AM
Sara & Jon's condo
Bayfront, Long Island, NY

a phone ringing at this hour of the morning sounds more like an alarm. Usually bad news. The same could be said of a doorbell. Like Candy earlier.

"This is Sara García," I say, in case the caller is an anxious tax client.

"Do you want to change your life?" a woman's voice says.

I hang up without waiting to hear what she wants to sell me.

Every one of the diets I've tried over the years started with that appeal. The cabbage soup diet, the fifteen-day fast, the green-food diet …. I've lost track of them all. Instead of transformation and an astounding number of pounds dropped, I got bad breath, indigestion, acne, cramps, or migraines. For me, like many women over thirty, trying to lose weight is like trying to force a tuba through a paper shredder.

I never should have bought that red dress.

At least, I don't have to worry about my wardrobe since quitting Domestic. Sweats or jeans are fine for working at home. My clients don't see me most of the time. I only have to look presentable when I pick up or deliver paperwork. Tax preparation isn't brain surgery, but January and April are crazy busy.

I use music as motivation. For the day's initial soundtrack, I select and load a CD. The bright, brassy sound of *Sergeant Pepper's Lonely Hearts Club Band* never fails to lift my spirits. The vinyl version was the first record album I ever owned, a gift from my first best friend Joanne. I lost them both.

My mother smashed the album with her stilettos after she found a cupcake wrapper in my junior high gym bag. She said, "You broke your promise to me, so you deserve what you get." I'd worn down the grooves playing it over and over on my toy phonograph anyway, and Jon has his own copy. But losing the gift still hurt. I never actually promised to stick to any of the diets Mother foisted on me since the age of eight. I only followed them to make her happy.

Losing my best friend Joanne was another instance of opening my big fat mouth, not to eat, but to tattle to her boyfriend.

My stomach grumbles when I hear the line about marshmallow pies from "Lucy in the Sky with Diamonds." I can't believe I forgot to eat. Candy's visit really threw me for a loop.

I go to the pantry cupboard and stare inside at the same boxes of cereal I puzzle over every morning. Jon and I argued over his never sitting down to breakfast once he started leaving for the office at the crack of dawn. Then we argued over his missing dinner because of all his late nights. Those disputes didn't help things any between us. My grandma used to say *pick your fights*. I can't even pick a cereal from the lineup on the shelf. Not quite as extensive as Seinfeld's collection, but close.

Berry Beary Crunch with chocolate marshmallow cubs is my husband's favorite cereal, not to mention the number one choice of children across America for over thirty years. The artificial fruit flavor of those bear-shaped bits, in combination with the powdery marshmallows, makes me want to gag. The box shows a purple cartoon bear, dressed in circus attire, juggling smaller marshmallow bears in shades of brown. *Odd way for a bear parent to treat his or her offspring.*

Next to the Berry Beary Crunch, a bright green box depicts an innocuous and pristine golden field with a cloudless sky. Plain Grains Granola announces it comes one hundred percent from nature. *More like one hundred percent from Satan.*

Beside the granola, the ever-popular corn flakes box displays the stylized graphic image of a cow in blue and yellow. *Corn-flakes with honey sounds yummy.*

Gallo's whiskers tickle my ankles. *"Mrow."* he says. It sounds like "No."

Is he reading my mind again? "You're right, kitty," I say. "I should give the granola diet at least one more week. And maybe I can fix my dress."

Decision made, I shove the Berry Beary Crunch aside to reach for the Plain Grains. My arm tingles. Bright lights fill my vision like flickering flashbulbs.

TIME FLASH 1

YEAR 1975 — THE PAST

The past is as easy to travel into as turning the pages of a book ...

— S.R. FORD, MIMGARDR

CHAPTER 4

SARA, AGE 12

Wednesday, June 25, 1975, around 4:30 PM
Wauldsons Supermarket
Woodward, Queens, NY

I had that feeling, the one where I'm just about to fall and I pull myself back in the nick of time. Except I wasn't about to fall. I was standing perfectly upright, studying the cereal boxes on the shelves.

From a speaker somewhere overhead, a female voice announced, "Malcolm, clean-up in aisle three. Malcolm to aisle three."

At eye-level, the Berry Crunch Bear slimmed down and elongated looked more like Scooby Doo—my brother's favorite cartoon. He juggled bear cubs resembling Fred, Velma, Daphne, and Shaggy. Plus, my brother loved Beary Berry Crunch. My mother told me I couldn't eat it because "it would just go straight to my hips." I wondered if my mother had already picked up a box of the cereal.

I spun around to look for Mother, but she wasn't anywhere in sight. I glanced at my watch. The bumble bee second hand buzzed around the daisy dial. My grandmother gave that watch to me for my tenth birthday, one of my best gifts ever. It was late. 4:30 already. My mother liked to be home from shopping excursions well before 5:00 to start cooking dinner. My heart beat hard inside my chest. She couldn't have left without me, could she? *Not again.*

My rainbow-striped jeans swished between my thighs as I ran. I felt light-headed, or at least light on my feet. No one in the pasta and sauce aisle. I hurried up and down the aisles—frozen foods, canned goods, condiments.

Near the toilet paper, a woman sporting a monolithic beehive hairdo pushed a grocery cart with a wailing toddler in the seat. As I got closer, the boy stuck out his blue tongue at me. What was left of the blue lollipop had adhered to his white shorts. I kept going.

By the dish soap, an old man in a wrinkled, stained gray suit smiled at me. His front teeth were missing. His grin gave me the heebie-jeebies.

I didn't see anyone I knew. Nobody who would be able to help me find my mother.

Tears streamed down both cheeks by the time I spotted someone who worked at the store. Tall with red, curly hair and a pointy chin, the young man wore a white coat emblazoned with a Produce Clerk patch.

"I can't find my mother," I said.

"Don't be a crybaby. You're a big girl. Too big."

My cheeks burned.

He shook a bony finger at me. "Check with the service desk. The lady there can make an announcement. Be grateful she didn't fly Eastern."

What the heck did that mean? I wiped my wet face with the back of my hand and headed to the front of the store. Cash registers made noisy clicks and dings. Far off to the right, I spied the sign for the service desk. A woman I knew stood at the counter. Not my mother as I'd expected.

Grandma.

My whole body prickled with chills. It was all wrong—all of it—everything, everyone, including me and my table-top flat chest. Where were my breasts? They ballooned to size Ds right after I turned thirteen—practically overnight. And Mitchell Katz broke the crystal of my daisy watch in a co-ed high school volleyball game. And what about those horrible pants? I would have had to lose a bet to wear them now.

The most wrong of all was my grandmother. I hadn't seen her for twenty years. Not since she died. And there she stood, a few feet away. I had to be dreaming.

I thought of the expression *pinch me, so I know I'm awake.* I did. *Holy molé salsa,* that stung. But I remained in the store, in the dream, or hallucination, or whatever this was.

My grandmother wore a pink cotton shift printed with a rose pattern, my favorite dress of hers. The service manager handed her a sheet of green stamps. Grandma slipped them into her carpetbag of a pocketbook, then managed to hoist the two paper sacks. She headed toward the exit.

I wanted to call to her, but I had a terrible fear. What if she vanished before my eyes? Worse, what if she transformed into a monster, the way people sometimes did in my nightmares?

My sweet Grandma, the only person in my whole life who ever loved me unconditionally, was walking out of my dream, leaving forever. I bounded after her, my legs wobbling like Jell-O.

Outside the supermarket, a salty bay breeze that felt and smelled absolutely real fluttered against my skin. I spotted Grandma at the corner, about to step off the curb.

Didn't she see the crosswalk signal that read *Don't Walk*?

Probably not. She was nearsighted without her glasses, and she was always misplacing them.

A Volkswagen Bus minivan careened toward my grandmother.

Despite my awkward legs, I leapt, latched onto Grandma's shoulders and pulled her back with all my might.

The vehicle's driver laid on the horn and missed hitting us by inches. We tumbled backwards to the pavement, a tangle of limbs. Groceries spilled and scattered. An orange rolled into the sewer drain and vanished—a déjà vu moment. I was dreaming about the time I saved Grandma's life, exactly this way, back when I was twelve years old.

"*Oy vey*," she said. "I could have died, *amorcito*. I'm lucky you grabbed me. You saved me for sure." My grandmother's cataract-clouded eyes reminded me of sunrise marbles, and tears flooded my own eyes.

We helped each other up.

"I didn't see you in the store. I thought you went home without me, *bubeleh*." She put her arms around me. "You are the best little girl ever."

I hugged her a long time, leaning into her scent—so vivid—baby powder with a hint of vanilla extract. I felt like Dorothy in *The Wizard of Oz* when she returns to Kansas. More than my mother or my father, Grandma meant home to me.

I stroked her gray hair, coiled like mine, then touched her face. I didn't remember her furrowed skin being marshmallow soft. I'd forgotten about the tiny black hairs on her chin like a line of ants.

Grandma let go of me and held a finger to her lips. "*¡chis!* Your mother will put me in a nursing home faster than you can say *kasha varnishkes*. Let's not tell her I almost got run over."

In real life, I never told anyone about my grandmother's near miss.

"Our secret." I helped collect up groceries. When the walk light came on, I led her safely across the busy boulevard. If this dream neighborhood matched the actual Woodward, we would cross only smaller, less trafficked streets to reach my childhood home.

I'd always been very strong for my age, so I easily managed the heft of a grocery sack filled with canned beans, canned fruit cocktail and jars of applesauce miraculously unbroken. The weight of the bag in my arms felt actual, not dreamlike.

The warmth of my small hand in my Grandma's was wonderful, if greasy. She'd always slathered on petroleum jelly because she believed it cured everything—warts, nail-biting, dandruff, bad breath. My dad nick-named her "Dr. Vaseline."

We passed South Bay Pizza and my mouth watered at the smell of wood-oven baked crust, tomatoes and oregano.

Everything was incredibly, precisely real, down to the last detail—the sights, the smells, the sounds. Maybe this was what was meant by a lucid dream? Being with my grandmother, I had no desire to wake up.

Nostalgia for my old neighborhood overwhelmed me. Maple trees and yew bushes lined the streets. Yew berries crushed into the pavement reminded me how we kids waged goo-bullet wars with them. In the dappled light of a summery afternoon, Woodward shone with immaculate sidewalks and neat islands of grass.

Women strolled by in hot pants and chunky platform shoes or thong sandals. Most of the men wore extra-long side-burns, striped polo shirts and belted shorts. The area could double as a set for *The Partridge Family*.

Grandma walked at glacial speed because of her aching bunions. She sang the line, "It's later than you think, we are in the pink," over and over. I recognized the clipped, mangled lyrics from her favorite Guy Lombardo tune.

Jet planes overhead and oversized Cadillacs, Buicks and Pontiacs with behemoth engines drowned out her singing at times. The original VW Beetle and the wide-bodied AMC Pacer rumbled at a quieter octave. Those vehicles, on the less congested roads of the past, zipped along faster than their more fuel-efficient year 2000 counterparts.

Though the cars moved faster, the people walked at a more relaxed pace, without the distractions of the future's mobile phones and Walkman music players. Even strangers smiled and said hello.

Growing up here must not have been as bad as I remembered. But not too many others in Woodward looked like me— a mixed ethnicity, multiracial, dual religion, chubby girl with kinky curls. If chunky boys got bullied or called names, they could threaten and intimidate with their size. Despite my strength, I wasn't a fighter. I ran to the girl's bathroom to cry whenever kids teased me.

The sensation of sun on my shoulders made we wonder if I could wake from this dream with a tan. I ran my fingers through my thick, big, natural hair. I wished I'd never started straightening it. I endured the expensive process that burned my scalp and thinned my hair to get closer to a non-ethnic, Caucasian beauty standard. Before those harsh chemical treatments, I tried crème rinses, conditioners, oils, rollers, and ironing— time-consuming and temporary.

The racist name-calling started when I went to junior high. I inherited my looks from my half-African, half-Sephardic Jewish Grandma. After years *of fatso, tubby, butterball, rhino*, and *pig-face*, racial slurs felt like a novelty. For a short while, anyway. At the mall with paler friends, store security guards watched my every movement as if I'd been furloughed from prison. In the world's eyes, I went from fat slob to no-good thief. My size and skin color branded me an affront to society.

It disgusted my mother, a slim, fair-skinned, straight-haired Argentinian of noble descent, that I didn't inherit her looks. I tried to ignore Mother's constant put-downs of my appearance, but my self-esteem ended up battered.

"Let's take a rest," Grandma said.

We stopped at a bench in the middle of the block.

A black Firebird Trans Am honked as it passed us and screeched to a stop at the corner. A tall, male with dark-blond hair cut like David Cassidy's stepped out. In his tight, white muscle shirt, sun backlighting him, he gleamed. He waved at us, then cupped his mouth. "Hey Sara," he called. "Hey, Granny Bloom." He motioned for us to come to him. "I'll give you a ride home."

With the sun in my eyes, I couldn't tell who it was. Why didn't he back his car up to save Grandma from having to walk all the way to the corner? As I went to him, my heart palpitations answered who and why.

Daniel Astrella—my brother Adam's best friend. Crush-worthy cute, but Danny never had much common sense. My mother used to say, "That boy is dumber than a box of hammers," even to his face.

I was nine the first time I saw him. He swooped up the front stoop, banged on the screen door, and let himself in. At the kitchen table reading a book on Greek mythology, I thought the god Apollo had appeared before me. From that day on, I believed with every fiber of my being, that if Daniel Astrella loved me, then my life would be perfect.

I started keeping a diary to document my feelings for him. I wrote in it every day for many years. I stopped because the things I fantasized about, the *me* I tried to become for my mother, never materialized.

What ever happened to Danny? I last saw him at Adam's funeral, when I was just shy of sixteen. He zoomed off in the same Trans Am before I could thank him for being good to my brother.

"Hey, let me take those." Danny grabbed our bags, jogged back to his car, opened the trunk, dropped them inside, and slammed the lid.

"*Dios mio,*" Grandma said. "Watch you don't get a hernia."

He beamed his good-natured smile.

It wasn't hot out, but my temperature was rising.

The car radio blasted ABBA's "Mama Mia." Danny opened the driver's side door, flipped down the front bucket seat for me to squeeze in the back. "Get in, squirt."

Once we were on our way, I stared at his face in the rearview mirror.

His eyes were the color of clover, of hope.

How could I have forgotten those eyes? But I knew his smell—like gasoline and the seashore. A smell I associated with arousal. I experienced my first orgasm fantasizing about Danny. Four years younger, I was a *squirt* to him. He never showed the slightest interest in me.

Grandma, and now my first crush—this was some dream. I sat back to enjoy the ride. My hand brushed a copy of David Gerrold's *The Man Who Folded Himself.* I read the book, about a man who time traveled and met other versions of himself, right after my brother borrowed it from Danny. I picked up the hardcover and flipped through the pages. The text seemed to be completely there, with every page filled. How was this level of detail even possible in a dream?

Danny and my brother traded many books and comics. My brother, being older and sickly, got to decide what we watched on TV—reruns of *Star Trek, The Twilight Zone,* and monster movies. Danny, my brother, and me, unalike in most ways, shared a deep common bond—we were Science Fiction nerds.

"You look pretty today," Danny said.

My heart soared until I realized he was talking to my grandmother.

"Pink brings out the roses in your cheeks," he said.

Where did he learn to be charming? And why didn't girls fall all over themselves to be with him? He hung out with my brother and their crew of misfits all throughout their junior high and high school years. I never saw them with any girls except me and my best friend from next door, Joanne, who attended an all-girls Catholic school.

I idolized Joanne. Four years older than me, she was easy going, funny, pretty, and lean, with long, wheat-colored hair and hazel eyes that changed hues in different lighting. As the youngest child of five in her family (with two pairs of twin sisters), she appreciated having me to order around. Her bossiness felt more like parenting, and she was so much kinder than my own mother. I'd be lucky to see her in this crazy dream of mine, too.

Danny screeched the Trans Am into the driveway of my childhood home, a square, red brick ranch, even smaller than I recalled. How did our family of four live there without killing each other? If my brother had remained healthy, there would have been a murder for sure with my mother's steady derision of my dad and me. Or not. Dad never lost his temper or seemed to notice her insults.

Danny let me out of the car on the driver's side and rushed around to help Grandma. "I've got the groceries, Granny Bloom."

"I'll take a bag," I said.

He mussed my hair. I hated people touching my hair, but Danny's hand on any part of me was fine.

"No, little darling," he said, "I got it."

Little darling. My heart fluttered. I held open the side screen door for him, which squeaked like someone saying "ouch."

I entered the dark kitchen cramped with pine cupboards. Even during the daytime, light fixtures needed to be switched on because the east-facing window let in limited, filtered light.

Danny set down the grocery bags on the Formica countertop decorated with teal and pink boomerangs. He mussed my hair again, then strode out of the kitchen, down the hall toward my brother's room.

I wanted to chase after Danny to say one more thing to him. Something like, "I love you." Too shy in real life to have done it, maybe I could in this dream.

Or, I could run next door to see Joanne and make her promise to never stop being my best friend, no matter what stupid thing I did. How could I know that telling her boyfriend Ronald Gott she said they'd have pretty children together would drive him away? Only a kid, I had no idea teenage boys didn't romanticize fatherhood. My dad told me Adam and I were glimmers in his eyes from the moment he met our mother at the Woolworth's lunch counter.

"What's all this?" my mother said. There she was—alive and beautiful as ever in a crisp white sleeveless, button-down shirt and navy-blue shorts, with her tar-black hair styled in a flip. Fuchsia lipstick brightened her lips. She could have graced the cover of *Vogue*. She told me herself a thousand times, if she had been tall instead of five-foot nothing, she could have been a high-fashion model and become a globe-trotting bachelorette. Seeing her this young and lovely and alive made me ache knowing how her life ended.

I unpacked the first grocery bag, setting each item next to the sink. I fumbled the deli container of pickled herring and it tumbled to the linoleum.

"Butterfingers," Mother said.

Grandma said, "Just like me."

The container didn't break. If it had, my mother would have unleashed a tirade of insults. Good luck like this was only possible in dreams.

Mother took stock of the contents of the ancient Norge refrigerator, a tractor of an ice box. "Why did you buy all this?" An unlit cigarette dangled from the corner of her mouth. She flicked her special sterling silver lighter engraved with the words *Miss Congeniality* and puffed the Kool to life. The dream kitchen soon filled with menthol smoke. "Where are we supposed to put it?"

The lighter, a prized memento from when she competed in the Miss Bronx, USA beauty pageant, was the only thing I kept of mother's after she died. Dad buried her with her few pieces of good jewelry.

Mother's golden eyes glittered with annoyance. She shoved the herring into the fridge and thumped the door shut. "This is the last time I let you two go shopping without me."

"Be glad we're in the pink," Grandma said. "Think of the starving children in Europe."

"Does my daughter look like she's starving?" Mother said. "Little miss pudgy has already outgrown her summer clothes and it's only June."

Mother's cruelty about my appearance never wavered. On her deathbed, she nagged me to flat-iron my hair, powder my skin, and lose weight. Two of the last words she ever uttered to me were "gastric bypass."

"Growing up is a good thing," Grandma said.

"Growing out isn't," Mother said.

I hid my face and flicked my fresh tears away before my mother, like the produce clerk earlier, could add "crybaby" to her insults.

"I'll put away the other stuff." I grabbed the cheese crunches and opened the cupboard under the wall oven. Not snacks as I thought, but cereal boxes, all lined up.

I reached into the grocery sack and pulled out a box of Berry Beary Crunch. My arm tingled, my head throbbed, my legs buckled.

The room swirled before my eyes. Grandma, Mother, and the entire scene transformed into a fading Dali painting.

REDO 1

YEAR 2000 — THE PRESENT

… you can't get back to the universe you started from …

— EVERETT ALLEN & THOMAS ROMAN, TIME TRAVEL AND
WARP DRIVES

CHAPTER 5

SARA, AGE 37

Monday, April 3, 2000, 12 noon
Sara & Jon's condo,
Bayfront, Long Island, NY

The clink of metal against ceramic startles me awake. I'm seated at the breakfast counter in my kitchen. The clock over the sink reads a little past noon. My brother's Easy Reader Timex, in its constant place on my wrist, concurs. *What happened to my morning?*

Rain pelts the living room window. Staring into the gray haze, my dream comes back to me. Grandma, Mother, and Danny. I didn't even have a chance to see my brother alive, make Joanne swear her friendship, or hug Grandma one last time. I scrape grit from the corners of my eyes. My right forearm is numb. I must have been lying on it. How could I have fallen asleep sitting up?

My legs teeter as I stand. I feel fuzzy-headed and achy all over, the way I used to back in college after a night drinking Tequila. I massage the back of my neck.

"Mrow," Gallo says and leaps up to the counter. He nudges the spoon around the rim of the bowl, then laps up the little bit of milk and soggy cereal bears.

Did I just eat that stuff? I must have been sleepwalking, or worse, sleep-eating. I would need to be unconscious to choose the cloying, artificial sweetness of Berry Beary Crunch. Even with my sweet tooth, I'll take honest to goodness bee honey over those chemical marshmallows.

The motor hum of the refrigerator is the only sound disrupting the condo's quiet. Didn't I put on *Sergeant Pepper* this morning on repeat mode? The stereo is switched off and the CD remains in its case. *That can't be.*

My heart pounds like it wants out of my body. I clap my hand over my chest and realize my comfortable sweats are gone. Instead, I am wearing a white eyelet blouse and black slacks. I don't recall putting on these fancy clothes. Why would I?

What is the last thing I do remember?

Staring into the pantry cupboard.

I go back over there. The cereal boxes face out on the shelf as always. The beans, rice, and condiments still occupy the lower shelves. Nothing is disturbed or out of place.

A person doesn't just lose four hours of her day. The dream couldn't have been that long. "I must be going crazy," I say aloud.

Gallo's ears twitch, but he refrains from comment and goes back to licking the cereal bowl.

Maybe I should call Dr. Gentry after all. Something has to be wrong with me to forget so much.

The phone rings and the sharp sound echoes.

I trip going to answer it, but grab for the edge of the sink and somehow manage to stay upright. I get to the receiver before the answering machine clicks on. The caller had better not be another stranger promising to change my life.

"Everything okay there?" Jon says.

I want to say, *No, I'm going crazy.* I want to say, *I am scared out of my wits. Help me, please.* Instead, what comes out of my mouth, like an LP caught in a groove, is "You're calling to tell me you'll be late again, right?"

CHAPTER 6

JON, AGE 43

… you close my eyes with your mouth of water …

— OCTAVIO PAZ

Monday, April 3, 2000, 12 noon
Domestic Global International Office,
Valley Way, NY

*J*on downloads yet another concealed database he discovered after breaking through the company's firewall. *How many more of these hidden files are there?*

His co-worker, Rick Pokorny, knocks and steps in.

Jon switches his monitor to the annual reports in an instant. Even though no one can see through the back of the computer to the screen, he can't take any chances.

"Leiter's pitching this afternoon." Pokorny is a Mets fan and a decent guy —a worker bee who clearly has no involvement with the illegal operations. "With the boss's blessing, a couple of us decided to skip out early and head over to Shea. Want to join us?"

"Barely have time for a sandwich," Jon says. "Maybe next time."

"Your loss." Pokorny is on his way out the door when he says, "Say hello to that pretty wife of yours. You know Sara would have been mine if I got to her first."

Jon's heard this from him before. "Not a chance, Rick. She has good taste." With all the men after her at Domestic, he was damned lucky she fell for him.

Pokorny turns down the corridor, out of sight.

Jon hesitates flipping back to the download screen. The nagging feeling about his wife's safety returns. *This case isn't worth Sara's life, not even after all the time I've logged.* This morning, when he saw the injection site on her neck, he knew he could lose her.

But I've been losing Sara for years. After their baby died, he threw himself into the job and clocked overtime with Vento to distract himself from the pain. It doesn't make any sense, but he can't touch his wife in bed without thinking about her being pregnant with their little one. The vision of her perfection at four months pregnant—naked and glowing—is with him still.

He needs to confess what he's been up to for the five years of their marriage. Hell, the whole time they've been together. Once she's safe and the responsible parties are locked up, he can come clean. *I'll beg her forgiveness. I'll show her how much I love her.* He'll apply for a job on the Bayfront force, and then they can dive into the adoption process.

All morning, something in him has been saying, *go home to her.* He fought the urge, but now he picks up the phone. He wants to hear her voice to convince himself that she's all right. With each unanswered ring, his pulse quickens.

She finally answers after the seventh ring.

"Everything okay there?" he says.

There's a noticeable pause before she answers, "You're calling to tell me you'll be late again, right?"

She's given him an opening and he takes it, out of stupid habit. "Yeah, sorry. The audits. You know, bad time of year. Don't wait up." He wants to stop lying, but he can't. Not yet. First, he's got to deliver the evidence against Domestic.

"Used to it," she says. Her voice sounds more sardonic than sympathetic. "Don't wear yourself out, *mi sol.*"

"You either, *mi luna.* Staying home all day to work on clients' tax filings, right?"

"Sheep to the slaughter. Oh, I've got another call coming in. Gotta go."

The line clicks off. "I love you," he says to dead air. *I'm such an idiot.* He wants to call her back right away to spill his guts.

He will do just that—in time. The Sullivans are good men. They'll keep his wife safe.

This case has swallowed up years of his life. The end can't come soon enough. The DOJ take-down of Domestic Global will stop their illegal mind-control experiments. No one else will get hurt, especially not Sara.

CHAPTER 7

SARA, AGE 37

Monday, April 3, 2000, 12:35 PM
Sara & Jon's condo
Bayfront, Long Island, NY

*M*y plan to call Dr. Gentry to make an appointment, despite Jon's wanting me not to, is prevented by the phone ringing. No one answers when I speak my name, but I hear heavy breathing on the other end. Great, an obscene caller. Just what I need. I slam the receiver. Now, I'm sorry I rushed Jon off the phone. I ache for him to my core. Nothing like the silly puppy love I felt for Danny in the dream.

Maybe I should have steered clear of love and focused on my career. That's what I swore I'd do when my college boyfriend Steve dumped me right before graduation.

But Jonathan García came along and swept me off my feet. I noticed him the minute he walked into the accounting office at Domestic, with his chestnut skin and those intense autumn eyes. There was such an air of mystery about him. He never revealed too much about himself, but wanted to know everything about me. The few words he spoke reverberated in a sexy baritone. He could be reading from an accounts payable ledger and I'd swoon. All my female co-workers did. I was the lucky one he chose.

The first night we made love, he said to me, "I can't tell where you end and I begin." At the time, I thought he meant the two of us being together was predestined. What a romantic goof I was. He probably just noticed our skin tones matched.

My mother threatened to disown me over Jon being Mexican. She wanted me to marry up, which entailed someone lily-white with an Anglo name and a business suit.

At least I got the suit part right.

Jon and I had no real first date, no courtship. In less than a month, we were cohabiting. Natural as breathing. Now, he's distant and we hardly talk at all. No wonder I couldn't find a way to tell him about my crazy morning. I wouldn't know where to start.

I stare at the number pad wondering whether to call the doctor. Maybe I just need to hash out my crazy dream with someone. I lost touch with my college girlfriends and didn't keep up with my friends from Domestic after I quit to start my own business and try to get pregnant. So, I dial the only person I can. After ten rings, I'm ready to hang up.

"*Hola*," Dad says, his breath ragged.

"You sound like you ran a marathon."

"Just got back from the cemetery. You know, your mom loves the yellow tulips I brought her."

He talks about Mother as though she's alive even though she's been gone almost five years. It isn't healthy to put all his energy into someone who's gone. "Dad, listen, we're having Easter at our place again with Jon's mother and probably her latest boyfriend. Come for a change. I'll make *borrego*, your favorite."

"I hate to disappoint you, Sara, but I'm no good at social events without Reya. I'll come another time when you don't have company."

"Jon's mother is family, not company. You need to get out more than to the gravesite. Mother would want you to."

He calls me on my white lie. "She may not be here, but we both know she would hate being left out. Besides, 'Solitude is the profoundest fact of the human condition.' If that's the only reason you called—"

My father, instead of bedtime stories, read me Octavio Paz. Oedipal or not, I married a man like Dad, even down to his profession.

"Dad, you've quoted that *Piedra de Sol* line a hundred times. You don't have to live alone. I've told you over and over to move in with us. Anyway, I didn't call to argue. Something weird happened to me today, and I'm scared."

"*Mija* ... what is it?"

I twist my finger through a curl of my hair. "One minute I am trying to decide what to have for breakfast, and the next I wake up over an empty bowl of cereal four hours later." I lean in and brace my arm on the counter. "I don't have any memory of eating or feeling sleepy."

"You work too hard. You're over-tired. You shouldn't have become an accountant like your old man. What does your husband think?"

I blow out a breath. My dad won't like the answer. "I haven't told him yet but—"

"All I ever wanted was for you to find the same happiness Reya and I did. This has gone on too long. You two need to talk to each other. Or do you want me to give that husband of yours a piece of my mind?"

"I'll tell Jon. Don't worry." Dad's no dummy. He can sense things aren't right between Jon and me. I need to change the subject. "But listen. I had this vivid dream when I was asleep. Grandma was there. I held her hand and smelled her skin and heard her singing."

"Well, that doesn't sound so bad."

"It was lovely, actually." I don't mention I saw Mother too. "We were grocery shopping together in Woodward Park."

"I wonder how the old neighborhood is doing. I haven't been back in a while."

"In my dream, everything looked like it did when I was a kid. But, Dad, I'm worried. I mean, I've never had black-outs or memory problems. Didn't Mother lose her memory right before she went crazy?"

"*Ay dios mio!* Reya never went crazy. She had a difficult change of life."

"But she had hallucinations she thought were real. Remember she was always smelling garlic. What if that's what's happening to me, Dad?"

"Dr. Gentry said your mom's waking dreams had to do with estrogen levels. She was fine after hormone therapy. Are you having other symptoms?"

"Just going cuckoo today."

"Get yourself to the doctor's office right away. You're a strong woman, Sara. Just like your mom."

I know what he means—she and I both survived the loss of a child. But I don't have anything in common with her except for that. At least I cried. Mother was dry-eyed when Adam died. Refused to let any of us talk about him.

"Sara, you still there?"

I switch the phone to my other ear. "Yes, Dad."

"Promise me you'll go see Dr. Gentry."

"Okay."

"Good. Ring me up after you see him to let me know what he says."

We exchange *I love you*s and say goodbye.

An unfamiliar female voice answers Dr. Gentry's phone. The strange woman tells me the doctor left the office on personal business and won't be back until the end of the week.

What happened to Elise? She's been the doctor's office assistant for decades longer than I've been going there. She gifted me lingerie when I told her I was getting married. She handed me a teddy bear when my pregnancy was confirmed. And I wept in her arms after the baby died. Elise has as much to do with patients' mental health as the doctor does with their physical well-being. Maybe she just took a day off.

I insist on the next available appointment, which happens to be 3 PM on Friday. *Fine, as long as I am not in the nut house by then.*

I need to get to work. Maybe I've already started and can't recall. It would be great if several of the dozen personal tax returns I have to prepare are already completed. After all, the IRS waits for no man. No woman either.

Sometimes I miss the social aspect of working in the corporate world. My office is the bedroom that would have been our nursery. Sixteen weeks into my pregnancy, I miscarried. Our little baby boy died. Soon after, the doctor told me that I'd never be able to bring a fetus to term because of an endometrial condition. We donated the crib and clothes to Goodwill. There may still be baby gifts tucked away in the closet. I can't bear to look.

The office space is outfitted with an old school teacher's desk, bookshelves, a couple of used file cabinets, and a brown corduroy sofa from Jon's bachelor apartment. A little awkward to make love on, but we found ways back then. Those cushions haven't seen any action in a long time, not unless my mother-in-law sneaks in her male friends when she stays over.

I put on Santana's *Supernatural* album. The walls between apartments are well insulated, so I can crank up the volume on the living room stereo and hear the music in my office.

I'm ready to settle into the comfy desk chair Jon gave me last Christmas when I notice the client folders' basket on my desk is at an angle. Files are spilled out and papers have scattered over the edge of the desk onto the carpet. I can imagine only one culprit.

"Gallo!"

"Black cats are bad luck," Jon said when I picked him out at the animal shelter. I pointed to the white tuft of fur on his neck. "See, he's black and white," I said, "like me." My husband relented. Bad luck or not, Gallo is mischievous.

"Mrow." Gallo peers down at me from on top of the bookcase.

Though toppling things over is his special talent, appearing out of nowhere is his forte as well. I could have sworn he wasn't there a second ago.

I keep begging Jon to make sure he closes the door after he uses the office computer. But like his trail of socks and underwear on our bedroom floor, old habits die hard.

On my knees collecting the errant records and receipts, something silver under the desk catches my eye.

Holy molé salsa—it's a hypodermic needle, the plunger pushed all the way down, the tube empty.

My mother-in-law likes to say she's diabetic because she's too sweet. Nothing could be further from the truth. But even she wouldn't be careless enough to leave an insulin needle on the floor.

Or would she? Maybe this is another way for her to test me, prove my poor housekeeping skills. Even if I could pass the white-gloved dust test (which I can't), she will never think me good enough for her son.

Not knowing how to dispose of the hypo, I enfold it in paper, apply duct tape, and drop the package in the bottom drawer of the file cabinet. I can deal with it later.

"Mrow," Gallo says from the back of the sofa.

I didn't see him bound from the bookcase. "How did you get all the way over there, boy?"

His swishing tail is no answer.

Maybe my kitty is simply magical.

CHAPTER 8

SARA, AGE 37

Wednesday, April 5, 2000, 3:20 AM
Sara & Jon's condo
Bayfront, Long Island, NY

*T*he shriek of bed coils rouses me from a recurring dream—a surreal scene of bawling babies in a hospital nursery on fire.

Jon tugs the cover to his side of the bed.

When did he get home? The digital clock reads 3:20 AM. I lean into him. His damp body smells of soap.

Did he shower to wash away Candy's scent? The pre-dawn hours breed paranoia. I know better. *"Mi sol,"* I say. I kiss his shoulder.

"Go back to sleep. Didn't mean to wake you." *He never does.*

There's been no late-night lovemaking for us since before I was pregnant. Still trembling from my dream, I want him to hold me. "I was having that nightmare again."

"Sorry, *mi luna.*" He kisses my forehead. "There. Now you will have sweet dreams." He turns onto his stomach, but wraps his arm around me.

"At work all this time?" I bite my lip, tell myself to stop acting like a suspicious cow.

"Brews with the boys," he says into his pillow.

Not the kind of pillow talk I have in mind.

"And watched a replay of the Mets game," he says.

"Are the in-house audits done?" I hope that sounded reasonable.

"International accounts are a mess."

I wriggle out of his hold onto my side. I never got the chance to tell him about losing hours Monday. I didn't wake when he got in last night and he left before I was up this morning. "I need to tell you something," I say, massaging his back. "Or I could let my fingers do the talking."

"Sorry, love, I'm dead," he says.

No surprise there. He already gave at the office. *Or maybe at Candy's.* No —I have to stop thinking like that. That's my mother's voice alive inside me, still taunting. Jon wouldn't give Candy the time of day. Or if he did, he'd be too tired to give her anything else.

"Let's get some rest, love," he says. *"Por favor."*

I've never had an aptitude for sleep. Once I'm wide awake, it's hard to get back. My thoughts shift to Monday's happy dream. To Daniel Astrella, specifically. I am imagining what it would be like to be in his arms. Except it isn't this me, but a younger, skinnier, more Caucasian version of myself with naturally straight hair.

Danny whispers in my ear. "Hey, beautiful."

But it's make believe. I can't smell his scent of seashore and gasoline. And I feel guilty fantasizing about someone else. I haven't done that since the night Jon first kissed me. From that moment on, he was the only man I ever wanted.

I get up, wiggle my feet into slippers, maneuver around Gallo sleeping on the rug, and pad down the long hallway. My footfalls make no sound. I am a ghost in my own home.

There's enough glow from the microwave and clock radio for me to steer to the fridge. Door open, the kitchen fills with aquarium-like light. I examine a take-out box I don't recognize filled with something resembling barfed-up noodles. It smells like cat pee. Jon never eats leftovers. *Why does he bring this stuff home?* Maybe it is his way of sharing meals with me even though we're apart.

I don't have an appetite, but I go and stare into the pantry. The Crunch bear sports big floppy shoes, a red wig and nose. I've never been a fan of the circus. Clowns are scary.

What if? I reach around the box of Berry Beary Crunch and grab the Plain Grains Granola. I wave the box of granola in the air. Nothing happens. No flashbulb light going off and no tingling in my fingers.

I set the granola back on the shelf and reach for it again. I'm not transported to the dream world of Grandma and Danny. I really must be *loca* to think it possible.

I settle for the solace of my reading chair in the living room, like I do whenever sleep eludes me. Tonight, the last chapter of Vonnegut's *Timequake* awaits.

CHAPTER 9

SARA, AGE 37

Wednesday, April 5, 2000, 12 noon
Sara & Jon's condo
Bayfront, Long Island, NY

The phone's been ringing nonstop since eight. I wish there were two of me to answer all my clients' tax questions. Maybe then, one of me could sneak breakfast. With my lack of sleep, I'm running on coffee and fumes by noon when I say goodbye to Mrs. McFligh, who wants to know if her author husband can write off the cost of his lucky socks. I could write a book about all my quirky clients. I need to get away from my desk and get a change of scenery.

Gallo, luxuriating beside the computer keyboard, stretches to situate himself in a ray of sun. As he moves, the letters "lk ndr bd" appear across the spreadsheet on the screen.

"Are you trying to tell me something, boy?"

"Mrow," he says. He rises and rubs his head against my chin.

I delete the rambling from the document.

"Mrow, mrow," he says and cavorts across the keyboard. The phrase *Look under bed!* materializes on the screen. He steps off the keys.

The odds of a cat typing real words—an actual meaningful sentence— must be astronomical. I should call *The Tonight Show with Jay Leno* and get my little miracle kitty on TV.

"*Mrow, mrow, mrow,*" Gallo says. He swats at the computer screen with his paw. It's like he's pointing at the words.

"You want me to look under the bed, boy? Did you lose your mouse?" This is ridiculous, a crazy coincidence.

"*Mrow,*" Gallo says. It sounds like "now." He hops down and chases his tail.

Look under bed—just random keys. Nothing more. Unless I really am going nuts. Maybe there is nothing on the screen but gibberish. I rub my eyes and check again. *Look under bed!*

It isn't good to sit so long. I need to get up and stretch my legs anyway.

Gallo trots beside me as I head down the long hall.

I stop mid-way. "This is just silly."

"*Mrow, mrow, mrow,*" he says. He dances circles all the way into the bedroom.

I follow.

He scoots and squeezes himself under the dust ruffle.

I didn't make the bed this morning. The imprint of Jon's form is still evident in the white sheets like a concave apparition. I lay face down into his pillow. The case smells like coffee and soap and a hint of his perspiration. *I love you, mi sol.*

"*Mrow, Mrow,*" Gallo says from under the bed.

I bend over the edge of the bed and pull back the fabric. Too dark to see anything, I reach around. Nothing but cat-fur dust bunnies and Gallo's fluffy tail. I move to the other side of the bed and try again.

A metal object rolls away. I stretch and reach further under. *Ouch!* Something pricks my finger.

Gallo would never claw me.

To extract the prickly thing, I first grab a few tissues and wrap them over my hand for protection. Out comes another hypodermic needle like the one I had found in my office, and then a gold cylinder of lipstick. There's a tiny bit of fluid left in the hypo—lime green, like science fiction movie plutonium.

My mother-in-law is getting on my last nerve. *Why would she be this careless?* She may hate me, but she has nothing against my kitty. She has a cat of her own. If Gallo played around with the needle, he could get hurt, maybe even die from the insulin.

I swaddle the hypo in more tissue and set it aside so I can examine the lipstick. Not my brand. I'm partial to the kind that comes in the rectangular silver cases. The shade is called Orange Crush. I open it, try it on my hand.

Nothing I'd ever use. It could be Mrs. García's, but I've never seen her wear anything but purples that make her mouth appear bruised.

Gallo comes flying out from under the bed, jumps over me and onto Jon's pillow. He settles down and licks his hind quarters.

"What do these mean, boy?"

Gallo has no comment. He continues grooming. For him to know, and me to find out, I guess.

I'm rubbing off the lipstick smear when it occurs to me—Candy wears orange everything. But there is no way that woman has been in my bedroom. This has to be María's stuff. My mother-in-law is more than nosey enough to poke around in our bedroom.

He's probably with that redhead right now, my own mother's voice in my head warns. In psychology class at college, we learned about the idea of the internalized mother. It's a daily effort to gag my inner maternal figure. She's always causing havoc. *Your husband's been sleeping around for months.* My mother's been dead almost as long as I've been married. I can't let her make me doubt Jon. I won't.

My blood sugar must be low—that's why I'm having these crazy hallucinations and seeing infidelity under the bed. A little snack will help me think more clearly.

~

There's not much in the fridge. A few gherkins swim placidly in green brine and a couple more of Jon's leftovers—congealed macaroni salad and a saran-wrapped hunk of ham that resembles burned skin. It's like he's leaving unappealing food as nonverbal communication. I don't even want to venture a guess at what it means. I toss the inedible food into the trash and go back to the pantry.

None of the cereal in the cupboard appeals to me. Even though there's no more red dress to fit into, nothing can change what I am—what I always have been—a woman on a diet. Technically, the cottage cheese and canned tuna I ate yesterday qualify as cheating. In fact, I haven't eaten granola since my blackout on Monday. I push aside the Berry Beary Crunch to get to the box of Plain Grains Granola. Pin pricks travel from my fingertips all the way up my right arm. *Am I having a heart attack?* Flashing light obliterates the room.

TIME FLASH 2

YEAR 1994 — THE PAST

A lot like yesterday, a lot like never.

— TIM O'BRIEN, THE THINGS THEY CARRIED

I loved you backward and forward in time. I loved you beyond boundaries of time and space.

— DAN SIMMONS, ENDYMIONREDO

CHAPTER 10

SARA, AGE 31

Saturday, May 21, 1994, 11 AM
Shop More Supermarket
Floral Gardens, Queens, NY

"*E*arth to Sara," Jon said. He snapped his fingers.

Feeling like I was about to keel over, I grabbed the grocery cart handle to steady myself.

"Huh?" I said. The market was lit up like a stadium. I squinted at my husband. There was something different about him. But God, he looked good. He had on his favorite number seventeen Mets jersey and a pair of loose-fitting jeans. I loved the way only I had carnal knowledge of the sexy body hidden beneath all those clothes.

"What's wrong?" Jon said.

"The ammonia smell must be making me lightheaded," I said. "I guess they just cleaned the floor."

"I don't smell anything. But you have a nose like a bloodhound. Let's get the cereal so we can skedaddle." He tapped his watch. "Did you forget I'm going to Rick's house to watch the game?"

His words gave me a weird feeling, like we lived this exact moment before. "You pick," I said, not knowing what else to say.

Jon tilted his head like he didn't quite understand what I'd said. He pulled at his mustache.

That's what was different—he hadn't worn a mustache in years. He had shaved it off for our wedding at his mother's command and never grew it back.

I felt suddenly cold all over. *I had to be dreaming again.* None of it was real —not the supermarket, not my husband, not the cereal boxes, not even me. But the lights, the smell, my sense of being in my body—my normal adult body—felt absolutely authentic.

"Okay, gorgeous, I'll choose." Jon barely finished getting the words out when "Lady in Red" started playing on the store's loud speakers. A male voice spoke over the lyrics, "Lady in Red brand canned tomatoes on sale, five for a buck. Get 'em while supplies last."

Our first dance together was to "Lady in Red" at The Wishing Well Pub.

Jon moved toward the Berry Beary Crunch display—the bear sported a blue, pinstriped baseball uniform. He reached out for a box, but it was a ruse. He pulled me into a dance hold instead.

A pins-and-needles sensation in my right leg made me fall against his chest after he swirled me around in a turn. His mustache tickled as he kissed me. I gave into the passion I ached for in my waking hours. I deepened the kiss and felt it all the way to my toes.

"Get a room," a male voice shouted.

I opened my eyes, but kept right on kissing Jon.

A redheaded grocery clerk, dressed in a white coat, scowled. He was an older version of the mean clerk from my other supermarket dream.

A room wasn't a bad idea. I would have settled for a dream of making love to my husband if I couldn't have the real thing.

The clerk stalked away down the aisle right as a peroxide-blonde wiggled toward us. She looked familiar.

"Hello, Johnny," the woman said. She pressed her fingers into Jon's shoulder.

He broke our embrace to look at her.

How infuriating that even in dreams, Jon never followed through. This blonde bombshell with big hair and skinny jeans had to be another instance of my mother's voice in my head working overtime.

"Misti," Jon said. "What a surprise."

"Told you yesterday, I go by Mist now, as in mist—erious. You shouldn't be surprised. We're neighbors." She tittered like a cartoon character.

She had to be Jon's ex-girlfriend from his college days. I never saw Misti in real life. We had our first big fight over his photos of her. I thought it was only fair of him to toss them away. I'd torched all my photos of Steve before I moved in with Jon.

He didn't even tell me that Misti lived in our neighborhood until after she moved away.

Jon wiped the sudden sweat from his brow.

"Who's she?" Misti pointed an arrow-sharp, red fingernail at me.

"This is …" He bit his lip as if he'd forgotten. "This is my fiancée, Sara."

I checked my ring finger. No wedding band, and Jon never gave me an engagement ring. We chose to be practical and save up for a condo. He didn't need to spend money on jewelry to prove his love. Of course, my mother said it meant he thought I didn't rate a diamond.

"What a shame," Misti said. She tossed her teased mane in my face.

The plastered hair smelled like mosquito repellant.

"You're missing out on all this, Johnny." She slid her free hand up and down her nonexistent hips, removed her other hand from Jon's shoulder, and wiggled away. As she rounded the corner, she pivoted and blew him a kiss. "Call me." She tittered again and slinked off in the direction of the baking aisle.

"I know." Jon held up his hands to prevent me from interrupting him. "I was going to tell you I ran into her on the subway. I forgot because she doesn't matter to me. Only you matter, *mi luna*." He had started using that endearment the first night he kissed me. Any time he called me that, my heart melted.

I took advantage of the dream, and pretended to be the 100-percent self-assured girlfriend I never was. "Doesn't matter, *mi sol*," I said.

Jon lowered his hands. "Don't be upset. She means nothing. I wanted her to know how serious we are. That's why I said fiancée."

"I'm not mad. Actually, I'm glad I got to meet her. She's a disaster." That was true. If my dream-conjured version of his girlfriend was anything like the real one, I couldn't believe my husband was ever attracted to someone who wore that much make-up and hairspray.

Jon raised his eyebrows. "I meant what I told her. You're everything to me."

"I know," I said. "You are going to marry me."

The corners of his mustache turned up. "What did you do with my jealous Sara, the one who'd be flipping out right now?"

"That's another me. I left her in the past." I smirked. "Or maybe, in the future."

Jon shrugged. "Okay, then, let's do this." He knelt on one knee in front of the Berry Beary Crunch display and took my right hand in his. "Sara Rodríguez Bloom, will you do me the honor of becoming my wife?"

That wasn't how Jon proposed in real life. He had asked me on my birthday in September over a candlelight dinner of red beans and rice in our old apartment in Floral Gardens. Though things hadn't been right between us for a long time, I loved my husband with my whole heart. I would marry him all over again.

I should have reached out to Jon after I lost the baby. Instead, I languished in my own guilt and grief. I shut down. Maybe this dream was a sign we could repair our relationship and get back the incredible intimacy we once shared.

Jon pulled on my hand. "Don't leave me hanging. *Te quiero.*"

"*Sí,*" I said. "Yes, yes, yes."

Applause rang out. Shoppers in the aisle gawked at us. An old man in a crumpled, light gray suit smiled at me, toothless.

Gooseflesh rose on my arms. He was the same old man from my other vivid dream. My mind must have been recycling the extra characters. First the grocery clerk, now him.

Jon stood and kissed me.

Heaven again. As I surrendered to his embrace, my elbow nudged the cereal display. Berry Beary Crunch boxes showered down around us. Without thinking, I reached to catch one.

My arm went numb.

A white flash washed everything away except a sound like wind whistling through trees.

REDO 2

YEAR 2000 — THE PRESENT

It isn't necessary to imagine the world ending in fire or ice. There are two other possibilities: one is paperwork, and the other is nostalgia.

— FRANK ZAPPA

Within a science fictional space, memory and regret are, when taken together, the set of necessary and sufficient elements required to produce a time machine.

— CHARLES YU, HOW TO LIVE SAFELY IN A SCIENCE
FICTIONAL UNIVERSE

CHAPTER 11

SARA, AGE 37

Wednesday, April 5, 2000, 3:03 PM
Sara & Jon's condo
Bayfront, Long Island. NY

My head bangs against the desk, and I startle awake. Whirling stars rush across the computer screen. Gallo snores atop the printer. Johnny Cash sings "Folsom Prison Blues" from the living room stereo.

I jiggle the mouse. There's a half-completed tax spreadsheet for the Eloys on the screen. I don't recall entering any of the data. The computer shows the time as 3:03 PM. Last thing I remember, it was just before 9 AM.

I've lost six hours of my day sleeping. I've never been one to doze off in the morning, even after a sleepless night. Most of my life, I've functioned adequately on four or five hours sleep. Maybe I've developed narcolepsy. My appointment with Dr. Gentry can't come soon enough. Something is seriously wrong with me. I don't feel well at all. My stomach lurches.

～

After a long time with my head bent over the toilet, I get up, run some cold water, and splash my face.

The woman who stares back at me in the mirror looks drained. *No.* Looks wrong.

I take inventory. Large brown eyes, check. Wide nose, check. Plump lips, check. Dangling, white gold *pi* symbol earrings Jon gifted me our first year living together hang from my ears. He could think of no other way to express how *irrationally* important I was to him. I tried not to take it the wrong way, after all, love isn't logical.

My mirror image bears a scar below her right ear from the childhood swing incident with Adam that required stitches.

The woman looking at me is me. Except for one thing. The Sara in the mirror is a blonde. *That can't be.* My hair is dark brown. I've never bleached it.

I heave into the sink. Nothing but bile until my stomach relents. I wilt to the floor.

Gallo dashes into the bathroom and onto my lap. *"Mrow."* He nuzzles my chin and purrs.

As I run my fingers through the horrible mess on my head, a scene flashes in my mind. Mrs. García hands me her beautician's card, adamant that the wedding photos would look better with the two of us dyed *Blonde Bliss* to match.

That never happened.

But my memory says Jon asked me to marry him in the Shop More supermarket on May 21, 1994. Says my mother-in-law to-be made me change my hair. My memory insists those are the events of my real life. Not dreams—my actual life.

Jon's original red beans and rice proposal in September feels like a hallucination now.

I am losing my mind, just like my mother did for a while. But she got better with estrogen treatments. Maybe that's all I need. Some hormones, plus an expert beautician to make me look like me again.

CHAPTER 12

SARA, AGE 37

Friday, April 7, 2000, 2:45 PM
Dr. Lance Gentry's Office
East Neck, Long Island, NY

*W*hy can't things just stay the same, reliable? I miss Elise. She was practically family. "What happened to Mrs. Wells?" I say. "You know, Elise Wells, the doctor's long-time assistant?"

A *tisk tisk* sound escapes Doreen's lips, but she keeps on reading *Biochemistry Monthly* through thick glasses. The name plate on her desk reads Doreen Chen. She looks to be in her twenties. Guess she's not going to answer me.

At least nothing else is different in the office. Behind Doreen, on the paneled wall, hang dusty, framed medical degrees and certificates for Lance Gentry. The molded black plastic waiting room chairs are as uncomfortable as ever.

And there's the piped-in music, like always. Tori Amos's "Cornflake Girl" begins as I browse the wicker caddy of magazines— news, cooking, decorating, and fitness. Buried at the bottom of all the popular stuff, I discover a single issue of *Next Wave Physics*. The smudged yellowed address label prevents me from seeing the subscriber's name. Pragmatic Dr. Gentry wouldn't read this. *Next Wave Physics* must belong to Doreen.

Three years out of date, the January 1997 issue boasts a cover story of

"Time Travel Secrets," with the subheading "'Easy as Instant Oatmeal.'" I flip to the article to find the byline name is Stephen Ranger. That's too much of a fluke. It can't be my college boyfriend. Unless Asimov was right and coincidence is everywhere.

Our school friends dubbed Steve and I *doppelgangers* because we wore matching all-black outfits, down to the motorcycle boots. He dressed in black because of "the sadness of the world." It suited his poet-rocker persona. Mother advised me to wear black for the slimming effect. Steve's moonlight-pale skin and dyed-white hair sharply contrasted my sun-bronzed flesh tone and ash brown tresses. I was more his shadow than he was mine.

A thoughtful lover, he always brought me to orgasm first whenever we spent the night together. I expected to marry him. But he broke up with me to go to Sweden to participate in a revolutionary, intensive therapy for obsessive-compulsive disorder. He said he didn't want to be unfair by asking me to wait for him. He swore if I wasn't dating anyone when he came back, he would be mine. I never heard from him again.

He'd aspired to become a writer. But math and science were his weakest subjects. Without a photo or bio of the journalist, there was no way of knowing if he was my Steve.

The first line of the article cites Einstein as the father of time travel because of his special theory of relativity.

That leads easily to the idea of visiting the future. Not as easy, the conception of traveling to the past, but with the finesse of newly discovered Quantum Ionic Hierarchies, also known as Penrose waves, feasibility increases exponentially.

"Mrs. García," Doreen says. "The doctor will see you now."

I shove the *Next Wave Physics* into my tote bag and head down the hall. The future will have to wait.

The doctor's exam room is a study in sun and shadow. I'm hoping for illumination.

"Sit by the desk," Dr. Gentry says, which is in the shadier part of the room.

He always has me climb right up on the examination table. I thought the fancy mahogany desk was just there for show. And Nurse Randall usually joins us.

"Doreen tells me you're having some trouble." His bristle-shaped brows knit together. "What's been going on?"

Normally clean-shaven, the lower half of Dr. Gentry's stroke-disfigured face is covered in stubble. His hair is greasy, and his wrinkled lab coat looks slept in. Maybe he's having some trouble too.

I sank into the molded plastic chair in front of him. I open my mouth and everything spills out at once. "I have this infected bug bite on my neck. Someone's leaving hypodermic needles in our condo. I've been losing hours. My husband's proposed to me in a supermarket instead of over red beans and rice. And now I have this new blonde hair. Blonde hair! This isn't me."

Dr. Gentry rubs his enormous hands together as if they're cold. "That's a lot of mumbo jumbo, dear. I don't know what you mean by most of it. You've been married a while. Five years, is it?"

I'm winded, so I just nod. I started seeing Dr. Gentry before Jon and I were married. I wanted to go on the pill. In retrospect, I never should have gone off it. My getting pregnant was the best and worst thing that happened to Jon and me.

"As for your hair, well, you've been blonde for a long time. You can tell it's not natural, but it looks nice enough."

How can his memories be wrong too? "I've never been a blonde. Ever. I am a brunette. I've always been brunette."

"Well, if hair color's the issue, you're in the wrong place. Betsy's Babes Salon is down the street. My wife Claire—"

"But doctor—"

Dr. Gentry shushes me.

I want to jump out of my skin. Why won't he let me talk? He's always been such a good listener.

"Let's start with your neck," he says.

I unbutton the top buttons on my blouse and pull the collar away to show him.

The doc gets up, bends over me. He examines my wound, sniffs it, and presses it with his thumb.

"That hurts," I say. "I wanted to see you about the sore spot on my neck. Then I started having these vivid dreams and sleeping through mornings.

Now my memories are wrong. I feel like I'm going crazy. Could it be my hormones—like my mother?"

He puts a finger to his lips and taps hard, as if to say *Shut up, you moron.* Not like him at all. He's never shushed me before. He ambles back to his desk chair and sits. "Looks like a black fly bite. Needs some antiseptic."

"That's what Jon said. He made me swear not to come here."

"Smart man. Did you say something about needles?"

"I didn't tell Jon about them." I search my tote. I know I put the wrapped hypos in there. That's why I brought the tote and not my regular purse. But the packages are gone. All I seem to have in there are my wallet, keys, the stolen *Next Wave Physics*, and my mother's prized silver cigarette lighter from her pageant days. I've kept the lighter with me since she died. Better to light a single flame than curse the darkness of the condo building parking garage and entryway.

"The needles are missing," I say. "One of them still had fluid in it. Someone must have taken them from my bag."

"Maybe you forgot them?" he says.

"I've been confused lately. Maybe."

"Good, good," he says. "Probably your mother-in-law's insulin needles. No harm there. I recall you telling me she's a diabetic." He pulls on his chin with his hand, exaggerating a nod. He looks as insane as I feel.

Does he want me to agree? "Yes, I'm sure you're right." I shake my head up and down for emphasis, not sure of anything. "But why would Mrs. García be so careless? I would ask her, but she might take it the wrong way. Think I'm criticizing her. She doesn't like me as it is."

Dr. Gentry smiles too widely. "Wait a minute, won't you?" He sits there and braids and unbraids his extra-long fingers.

According to my brother Adam's Timex, two minutes pass like this. *Holy molé salsa*, first I go nuts, now the doc. Crazy must be contagious.

At last, there's a knock.

"Enter," Dr. Gentry says.

Doreen pokes her head in the door. "If you don't need me, I will be going."

"Fine, fine." Dr. Gentry waves her off. After the click of the outer office door closing, he says, "Okay, I am going to give you a prescription."

"For antiseptic?"

"A mild antibiotic to stave off infection. Hold off your inquisition until I finish." The doctor's hand hastens across the paper.

Inquisition? The land of strange keeps getting stranger. Dr. Gentry is definitely not himself. He always encourages questions.

He hands me the prescription, which turns out to be a note instead.

Don't say a word. The office is likely bugged. You know you can trust me, but there are very few people you can trust now. I am certain the blood I collect from you will prove that you have been injected with an illegal, experimental serum. Someone probably took the needles to cover their tracks. I have seen cases like yours before. You are being experimented on. I will do what I can. Please follow my instructions.

As soon as I look up, he snaps the paper away from me. He writes some more and shows it to me.

Please just nod or shake your head to answer questions.

Confused and frustrated, I want to scream, *What the hell is going on?* Instead, as directed, I nod.

He writes and shows me the paper.

Any idea who is injecting you?

I shake my head no.

"How is Jon?" he says, writing again.

"Working all hours," I say.

Have you had any break-ins at your home?

I shake my head no.

He writes some more.

"What happened to Elise?" I say. "I miss her."

"Retired. She's taking a cruise around the world."

Does anyone besides me and the receptionist know you are here?

I shake my head no because I'm sure my Dad has forgotten about me going to the doctor. Mother is the only person on his mind.

More scribbling from the doctor.

Ask me aloud about allergy testing.

I feel like I'm starring in an episode of *The Twilight Zone.* "I was wondering if I have allergies." My voice shakes. "Maybe you can test me."

"Yes, dear, we can develop allergies as we get older even if we never suffered them. Allergies can cause drowsiness, confusion, double vision," Dr. Gentry's voice sounds wooden. "I can show you the allergy panel options. There are almost a thousand items you can be tested for. Let me show you."

He hands me a typewritten sheet.

"You'll see items such as meats, dairies, grains, fruits, nuts, spices and so forth." He offers me his pen. "Check all that you wish to be tested for based on the foods you currently consume."

Instead, the directive at the top of the sheet urges me to mark all symptoms that apply.

Dizziness
Confusion or disorientation
Dry mouth
Loss of appetite or forgetting to eat
Infected or swollen areas on skin
Memory loss or new memories
Unaccounted for blocks of time
Hallucinations
Vivid, life-like dreams
Feelings of unreality
Sleepwalking
Waking up in unusual places or positions
Elevated libido
Nightmares
New phobias

I check everything on the list except the new phobias and dry mouth. I add "Scared out of my wits" and "please tell me more," then hand the page back to him. I want to know what this experiment is all about.

He looks it over. "Uh-huh." He stands and ushers me over to the examination area. "Okay, let's get some blood."

I climb up on the table. "Where's Nurse Randall?" He doesn't touch a female patient without her being present.

"She had to leave early. Emergency at home." Dr. Gentry easily locates a vein in my arm. He hums something that sounds like Grandma's favorite Guy Lombardo tune "Enjoy Yourself." The doc fills and labels two vials, then places a cotton ball over the needle puncture, puts pressure on it. He removes a small slip of paper from his lab coat pocket, waves it under my nose and positions it atop the cotton ball. Using medical tape, he secures the paper and cotton ball to the crook of my arm. "You need this so you won't get a nasty bruise."

~

Sensing I'm going to want to be sitting down when I read the paper the doctor stuffed under the adhesive on my arm, I race to the bookstore up the street. I pass Betsy's Babes Salon, where dye jobs are half off.

The bookstore smells, not surprisingly, like books and coffee beans, two aromas that usually bring comfort. "Flying," an instrumental song from The Beatles' *Magical Mystery Tour*, plays in the relatively empty café. At one table, a couple of teens pass a graphic novel back and forth. At another table, a white-haired woman spoon-feeds a toddler some chocolate cake.

I'm so rattled, I nearly drop my cup of coffee as I make my way to the back-corner booth. Seated, I rip the tape from my arm, and crumple it, along with the cotton ball, into a napkin. The tiny note folded over four times, has even tinier print. As I read, my heart is a wasp nest that's been kicked. I can't seem to manage a sip of my coffee without spilling it.

Strange things are happening to you and many others because you are the subject of a mind-control experiment. Your life is in danger. Do not trust those closest to you. They are most likely responsible for what is happening. Call the phone number below as soon as you are alone. An answering machine will thank you for contacting Paradise Time Shares. Leave this exact message, "Hi, I am (say your name) and I want to buy a time share with an eastern exposure." A special agent will return your call. Do exactly what the agent tells you to do. This agency is your only hope now for survival. Godspeed.

A phone number is penciled in by hand. The exchange is local. Dr. Gentry has been my doctor for years and he's always been a straight shooter. I don't want to believe this is real, but what choice do I have? I need answers. I hope Paradise Time Shares can give them to me.

As soon as I get home, I'm going to call Jon and tell him everything. Despite the doctor's note, I know I can trust my husband. There is no way Jon can be responsible for what's happening to me. *Then again, why did he try to prevent me from seeing Dr. Gentry?* Peculiar, but everything this week has been odd.

I could make the call right away if only I'd taken Jon up on his offer to get me a mobile phone for my birthday. It seemed such a waste of money since I work from home. I run out of the bookstore, wasps swarming inside my chest.

CHAPTER 13

SARA, AGE 37

Friday, April 7, 2000, 5:05 PM
Sara & Jon's condo
Bayfront, Long Island, NY

I open the door and call out for Jon. Of course, it's way too early for him to be home.

Gallo rushes to greet me and circles my legs three times before jumping up on the sideboard, jostling our wedding photo. I grab the frame before it hits the floor. The glass is dusty. When was the last time I took a good look at this picture?

Jon and I decided in April to cancel the wedding bonanza scheduled for August and get married as soon as possible at City Hall. Mother was bedridden with breast cancer that had metastasized to her organs. She died the week after we were wed. Despite the fact that she disapproved of Jon not being Anglo, she was relieved to know her "obese offspring" was not going to be an old maid as she'd predicted.

In the wedding photo, I'm wearing the cream lace tea-length dress I shopped for with Mrs. García. Jon stands a half foot taller than me in a gray suit. Our hands are clasped around each other's waists. We're on the steps of the Queens County courthouse. The day is as I remembered it before Jon's proposal changed. But there is one difference—my light hair. I would never

LANA AYERS

dye it blonde. And yet I did, or rather that other Sara did, the one beaming from the photo.

As anxious as I am to call the agents who can help me, I'm terrified of what they might say. I dial the number anyway. I can call Jon after I find out more.

An answering machine picks up. The message comes on, as the note said it would. It's a woman's voice, familiar, but I can't place it.

I wait for the beep, say my name, express my desire for a time share facing east, and hang up the phone.

"*Mrow,*" Gallo says. He bounds into my arms.

I cradle him. His purr coordinates with the rhythm of my pacing as I wait for an agent to return my call.

When the phone rings, Gallo toasters about a foot into the air, before landing on all fours on the wooden floor. From there he vaults over to his favorite spot on the back of the sofa.

"*Be at the pay phone outside the Green Apple Market on Hill Forest Avenue in 30 minutes,*" the familiar female voice says.

"Who is this? Do I know you?"

"*No questions. Be at the pay phone in half an hour. Bring only the essentials. You will be gone overnight.*"

"How do I know I can trust you?" I say. "I need to know who you are. What's happening to me?"

"*All your questions will be answered soon. Tell no one else.*"

"*Mrow, Mrow,*" Gallo says from the living room. It sounds more like *no, no.*

"Not even my husband?"

"*No one. Your life depends on it.*"

"Please—." The line clicks off. I need to tell Jon.

But if I want to get there in thirty minutes, there's no time to waste. I'll have to call him from the payphone at the store. The market is twenty minutes away, plus I have to pack.

And just what are the essentials when your life is in danger? Toothbrush. Change of underwear. Concealed weapons. We don't own any firearms. Too bad I didn't ask for a Glock for Christmas instead of that comfy desk chair.

CHAPTER 14

JON, AGE 43

… the doors that open into an empty room …

— OCTAVIO PAZ

Friday, April 7, 2000, 5:20 PM
Joanne Vento's car, Corona Clearing Park
Queens, NY

*J*on could be here all night on surveillance. Better than having to go home and face Sara with all he's keeping from her. Vento offers him these extracurricular details to placate him. She thinks his joining her on field missions will prevent him from bailing on Domestic's accounting office and going rogue. He won't make her any promises. Not as long as his wife's in danger.

He's worked the night detail with Vento going on two weeks, with little to show for it. The intel about Ranger being Domestic's lead contract killer has to be horseshit. *Vento's about ready to pop an artery, she's so fed up.*

The guy they're watching seems like a pussycat. At the very least, a neat freak. His hands in latex gloves, he's picking up cigarette butts and gum wrappers. Keeping the park clean. Lucky guy lives in the apartment building behind Corona Meadows Park, the north end, where the merry-go-round spins from May to September. The carousel stands empty. The horses haven't come out of dry dock yet for their annual repairs. He and Sara picnicked there all the time before they were married. *So long ago, it feels like another lifetime.*

"Incoming," Joanne says, opening the driver's side door. She hands him the Dunkin's cup before situating herself behind the wheel. She dribbles coffee down the front of her brown pantsuit. "Sugar," she says. Her curse word for *shit*.

Not that the stain will be noticeable. Someone ought to tell her excrement is not a flattering shade. She masquerades as a clothing sales rep. Hardly a believable cover the way she dresses. Not a bad-looking woman either. Tall and slim—well, bony actually—but with a pleasant enough face. Either she doesn't like men or doesn't want one.

He takes a sip of coffee. "Hot and dark," he says to annoy her, "just the way—"

"Just the way I like my women," she recites, finishing his sentence.

The mark of a good partner. She knows him well enough to know how he thinks.

"Yeah, heard that one before, García," she continues. "What's our boy Ranger up to?"

"Cleaned up the park. Now, our pussycat appears to be reading the newspaper. Better cuff him before he gets to the sports section."

"Must be waiting for someone," Vento says.

"More like waiting to watch the sunset. Tracking nature boy here is about as fascinating as watching grass grow."

"You know Parsons is going to nix this detail if we don't get anything concrete soon."

"Vento, I don't mean any disrespect, but there's as much chance of Ranger being a sociopathic killer as there is me being elected President of the United States."

Laughing, she chokes on her coffee. "Like America would let a *beaner* like you run the country."

Payback for my coffee remark. "You're the only person who can call me that to my face and not end up with a black eye or worse."

"I've put in a recommendation to director Parsons to move you up to field detail permanently. Once you've closed Domestic."

Vento's got years of seniority over him, but she's always treated him like an equal. "So you can get a new flunky? Seriously, I appreciate your confidence in me. But to tell you the truth, once this case is done, I might clear out. Sara being attacked makes me rethink my priorities."

"You going to go back to accounting for real?" she says.

"Right. I'd rather have a simultaneous root canal and proctology exam. I might try to get into law school, and if they won't have me, there's always the force. A nice desk job."

"Come off it, García. You'd miss me too much."

He's about to say he would when her mobile phone rings.

She answers. Her face blanches. "Holy Mother of God," she says into the receiver.

It's serious if she's invoking Jesus' mom.

"When? ...Who? ... Any leads? ... What about the bird? ... No, can't ... on surveillance ... with me ... I'll fill him in." She hangs up and crosses herself.

Must be very bad news.

"García, it's Frank Sullivan. Twenty minutes ago, a passerby saw him slumped over in his vehicle outside your condo building and called it in to the cops. Investigating officers determined Sullivan was shot in the head at close range. Dead. The witness reports seeing a stranger, a tall, thin, red-haired man jogging away down the street."

Jon's heart might explode out of his chest. "What's happened to Sara?"

"Lorentz is on the scene, cooperating with locals. He reports no evidence of forced entry. Your wife isn't at home. Where would she go at this time of day? Errands?"

"I don't know, but Sullivan would have followed her," Jon says. "Whoever killed him prevented that. I've got to go."

"We don't know anything yet." Vento lays a hand on his arm. "I need to keep watch on Ranger. You go home. Just don't do anything rash."

CHAPTER 15

JON, AGE 43

… and the silence covered in signs …

— OCTAVIO PAZ

Friday, April 7, 2000, 5:35 PM
Jon & Sara's Condo
Bayfront, Long Island, NY

*J*on flashes his badge and the uniformed DOJ investigators let him into his own apartment. Lorentz fills him in on what they know, which is nothing new.

And it's true. There's nothing to see in the condo. No sign of a disturbance. Sara is just gone. *God, if only I'd bought her a mobile phone for Christmas instead of a new office chair, at least I could call her.* She could just be out shopping. But something else is wrong.

Where is Gallo? His cat always comes to greet him at the door, gets tangled around his ankles. After a quick sweep, he notes the cat's food and water bowls are missing.

Why would Sara take Gallo with her? *Maybe the cat was ill.* He checks every closet and cupboard looking for the cat carrier, but he can't locate it.

Jon searches by the phone for their veterinarian's number. He dials. A recording tells him that the office is closed for the evening. He hangs up without leaving a message.

Could Sara have left me?

After they lost their baby, Sara was diagnosed with a congenital endometrial disease that prevents her from being able to carry a fetus to term. She offered to leave, to let him out of the marriage. He wouldn't hear of it. He assured her he was fine with adopting.

But the loss hit him harder than he expected, and things got complicated at the bureau. His lies escalated to keep her from finding out what he really did for work. Secrecy and grief erected a barrier between them.

She loves me. She wouldn't just go. Not without talking to him about it first. *But when have I given her the chance to really talk lately?*

Maybe someone grabbed Sara and Gallo both. What kind of perp takes a cat? An animal lover. *Well, that's a good sign, right?*

To be thorough, Jon checks under the false bottom in his bedside table drawer where he keeps a spare gun, his journals, and a photo of *Papá* and him at Shea Stadium.

Only the books are missing.

He started keeping a journal in junior high, not regularly but whenever something major happened in his life. He wrote about girls he dated, various events at college, his father's death, his time at the police academy, falling in love with Sara, his proposal, their wedding day, and her pregnancy. He hasn't written anything since they lost the baby. And he never wrote a single word about the bureau. He knew that could compromise his Domestic investigation.

How long have the books been missing—weeks, months, years? If Sara found them, she would mention it. Or at least put them back.

The uniform in charge asks if anything appears to be missing from the apartment.

Jon says, "Just my wife." *No sense telling them about the journals or the cat.* They'll assume she did leave him, poor sap, give him pitying looks. That's the last thing he needs.

After he bids goodbye to the investigators, he notices an outline of dust on the sideboard by the door. *Didn't our wedding photo used to be there?* And though he hasn't smoked a cigarette since high school, he has the urge to light up.

CHAPTER 16

SARA, AGE 37

Friday, April 7, 2000, 5:40 PM
Green Apple Market
Grand Neck, Long Island, NY

I pull up to the supermarket and a parking space opens in the front of the lot. Maybe this is a good omen. I'm usually lucky to get a spot in the boondocks after circling a dozen times.

I can't fully wrap my mind around the note from Dr. Gentry. I take out the paper and look at it again, as if the words could say something different this time. *Why me?* I am a lowly accountant. There's nothing remarkable about me.

I roll down the car window. The dusk air smells like hyacinths. The market's doors swish open and closed as shoppers come and go.

A couple of young men stand off to the side of the entrance, engaged in a heated debate over last week's "Star Trek Voyager" episode. From the bits I can make out, their argument has something to do with what defines a person's true character. If I were just here to shop, instead of waiting to get help from some secret agency, maybe I'd join them. I'd say the way a person acts when there are no consequences defines her character.

But there are always consequences, aren't there? My life has gone from boring to bizarre in just a few days. I want to jump out of the car to call Jon before the agency contacts me, but the payphone is in use.

A stoop-shouldered man in a rumpled, gray suit starts shouting into the receiver. He gesticulates wildly, and then grabs the base of the payphone as if he means to rip it out of the wall. He slams the receiver instead and turns around.

Holy molé salsa—he's the old man from my dreams, the one with no teeth —somehow transported into the real world. *No, that can't be.* Maybe I've seen him here before, and my subconscious used him as a character.

The old man shouts an obscenity at a woman exiting the store whose cart just misses running over his foot.

The woman flashes her middle finger and stalks off to the minivan parked next to me.

The old man hobbles into the store, dragging his left leg.

I dart to the payphone as it starts ringing.

"Sara Bloom?"

I know the voice. My toes curl. "Yes, but it's Sara García now. Who is this?" I ask to be sure.

"I'm hurt you don't remember me, Rosy," Steve Ranger says.

Rosy is the nickname he gave me when we were dating in college. He came up with it because my last name was Bloom and he thought me, in his stilted, Shakespearean way of speaking, "more Rose than thorn." The endearment pleased me at the time because Grandma's name was Rosa, and I wanted to be more like her than my mother. I never gave him a nickname though. "Ste—"

"Shush. Don't say my name. We don't know if this line has been compromised."

"Then why did you use this phone?"

"Stay where you are. I'll be right there."

I haven't seen Steve since before college graduation. Now he's coming to pick me up. *How am I going to explain all this to Jon?* "I need to call my husband," I say, but the other end of the line is just static.

Steve's hung up.

My temples throb.

"Hey, Sara."

I turn around and find Candy standing behind me. *Not her again.*

She's a vision in a slinky orange dress that perfectly matches her carrot-color, Farrah-Fawcett-style hair.

I try not to dwell on the fact that her lipstick shade looks a lot like the tube of Orange Crush I discovered under my bed. "Candy, I don't mean to be rude, but I need to make a call."

"I won't keep you, Sara. Please let Jon know he left his sweater at my place. The dark blue one with those pretty pewter buttons." She pronounces pretty as if the *e* and *r* are reversed.

I gave Jon that sweater for his birthday last year when he turned forty-three. He proclaimed it his favorite and wears it all the time. My internalized mother says *he's sleeping with her.* "When was Jon in your apartment?"

"Johnny was helping me relieve a little pressure …" She pauses to twirl a lock of hair, "… in my pipes."

Innuendo instead of answering *when.* "What are you talking about?"

"Every time I got into the shower, I heard a whistle." She shakes her lioness mane. "I expect whistling when I'm out walking, not when I'm home by myself."

"Our building has a super. He takes care of those things. Not my husband. I told you that on Monday when you barged into our apartment."

"Well, he's been a sweetie to me." Candy pronounces sweetie like it's southern iced tea. "He's always offering to help. Such a honey bear."

So Jon has been seeing her. *Why would he help her behind my back?* "He's always working. When does *honey bear* find the time?" I can't believe I said that last part out loud.

"I see Johnny all hours. He's always dropping by to help me with this and that."

I hear my mother's voice say, *I told you so.* Is she why Jon comes in late and takes showers before bed? Pain travels down my face to my jaw, making every word hurt to speak. "When did he leave his sweater?" *What I really mean is why did he take his sweater off?*

A black convertible drives by and honks.

Candy waves to the bald man driving. "Hey, Arthur," she says. She watches him drive by, then turns back to face me. "Art's a sweetie too. Now what was it you wanted to know?" She looks at me with doe-eyed innocence.

I wish I was dreaming right now. I don't want this conversation to be real. "Jon's sweater?"

"He must have forgotten it after the shower."

I lace my fingers together so I don't try to turn her face into an orange crush. "Why the hell was he in your shower?" Blondes are supposed to have more fun. If I've been a blonde the last five years, like my new memory tells me, how come I am not having more fun?

"He gave my pipes a good going over." Candy bats her eyelashes. "The shower was wet and steamy from me just stepping out. Johnny didn't want to ruin his sweater, so he took it off. I got him to take off all his good clothes."

What's a little homicide between neighbors? I can take the insanity defense. Blame everything on the mind-control experiment. "Is something going on between you two?"

"Don't get your panties all bunched up, honey pie. Tell Johnny he can come by to get his sweater any time, day or night. I'll be waiting."

"Tell him yourself," I say. "Or better yet, I'll come get his sweater tomorrow." I turn to go. But I have an idea and pivot back. "By the way, Candy," I say, "have you noticed anything different about me?" I run a hand through my spiraled, crazy blonde hair.

Candy eyes me up and down. "Oh," she says, then pushes her clawed-nails into my belly. "You're with child."

I pry her fingers off me. "I'm not pregnant. I'm blonde."

A car horn beeps.

Another guy for Candy? An older model white van with dark tinted glass stops in front of my car. The driver's side window rolls down enough for a hand to motion.

"Sara, come with me." It's Steve's voice.

"I've got to go."

"Try the Berry Beary Crunch diet," Candy shouts from behind me. When she raises her voice, the southern drawl vanishes. "And Betsy's Babes Salon. Betsy does a great platinum." Her unaccented voice reminds me of something. Maybe the voice from the sales calls about changing my life?

I retrieve my suitcase and Gallo's carrier from my car and hurry to the passenger side of the van.

Steve lowers his sunglasses. His pale eyes gleam. "Come here often?"

The bad pick-up line throws me for a loop, and I flash to the day he left me. The sad look in his watery eyes. How sorry he said he was but that he had to go for treatment. Something he needed to do on his own.

"You are as lovely as ever, Rosy. Climb in."

I hand him my suitcase and the cat carrier loaded up with food dish, food, water, and disposable litter pan, plus his favorite stuffed mouse. Gallo does not travel light.

"*Mrow*," my kitty says.

Steve's nose wrinkles. "You brought a cat?" He sets everything down behind my seat, in the back of the van. "We do not need a chaperone."

Chaperone? Weird thing to say. At least he didn't proclaim felines are dirty animals like he used to. He avoided our friends' cats because of the germs.

"The woman on the phone told me to bring the essentials. My cat Gallo and my husband Jon are all I have in the world. And I was pretty sure I couldn't bring my husband." I clutch my tote bag, get in, and close the door. *Am I doing the right thing?*

The van is immaculate inside, outfitted with oversized, dark gray bucket seats. The vehicle smells faintly of ammonia. A tub of sanitizing wipes is tucked into the dashboard cubby hole. Either he has children or his Obsessive-Compulsive disorder remains a problem. A black briefcase peeks out on the floor from behind the driver's seat. Up front, a couple of thermoses occupy the cup holders.

"You didn't tell your husband anything, did you?" He clutches my hand too tightly for comfort.

"Didn't have a chance. I was going to call him when I ran into an annoying neighbor."

"Excellent." He lets go of me. "You may phone him from the safe house if you still think it the correct course of action. Buckle up."

"Why can't I call Jon now?"

"We have to go right away. Agents have been monitoring you. They are at your house right now. I need to get you to safety."

I snap the seatbelt. "I feel helpless. Please, just tell me what's going on."

Steve eases the van out of the parking lot. "I will tell you everything you want to know, in time. Scout's honor."

To my knowledge, Steve was never a boy scout. "Why not now?"

"At the safe house. For now, no questions, okay?"

"Safe house? I feel like I am going crazy. I need answers."

He strokes my thigh.

His touch is electric. My body remembers him, but I can't have that. I push his hand away.

"Blonde looks good on you by the way. Anything would, but I am curious as to why you'd trade in your raven locks?"

"My life's in danger and you want to talk about my hair? Anyway, long story." I rub my temples.

"If you have a headache, give my vitamin infusion a try. Here, Rosy." He holds up the red thermos. A vein on his neck twitches noticeably.

I take the thermos and set it back in the cup holder. *Why does he keep calling me Rosy?* He gave up the right to use a pet name when he broke things off.

"It has been too long since we have been together," he says. "A dozen years." He turns on the headlights. "Where does the time go, Rosy?" The van merges onto the interstate.

"Please, just call me Sara. And by the way, it's been over sixteen years."

"You did miss me." His smile dazzles. "I knew it."

That mouth made me go all puddle-y inside back in the day. Not now. "Did you sail off the edge of the earth, Columbus?"

He still wears our uniform from college—black leather jacket, black jeans, a black t-shirt, and motor cycle boots. He's sinewy and sexy as ever. *Damn him.*

"European cognitive therapy is not for the faint of heart. The Swiss are supposed to be mild. Not so. An excruciating and extensive procedure, but I am very much cured." The neck vein twitches again.

"I was sure you told me you were going to Sweden, not Switzerland."

"You know, I remember that day on the campus quad as if it happened yesterday."

"The day you dumped me?"

"Sara, you know we agreed to take time off from our relationship while I sought help." He touches my thigh again.

I push his hand, but he grabs mine instead. I wriggle free.

He sighs. "The day I am speaking of is the day I told you I loved you."

"If you are not going to answer my questions, can we at least stop this drive down memory lane?"

He ignores me and goes on. "February fourteenth, 1981. You were worried about a calculus test."

He said he loved me on Saturday night to be exact, right before a school Valentine's Day dance. Steve was my first love, my first everything includ- ing, my first broken heart. "I never got nervous before math tests. Just tell me, how is it that you are the agent sent to help me? What's your involve- ment? Who's experimenting on me? How are they doing it?"

"Slow down, Rosy. It may have been an Anthropology test. You were headed to meet me at Gunpowder Hall. I saw you coming toward me from across the quad. Sun backlighting you, you looked like an angel. My dark angel. When I called your name, you almost took a tumble."

"Hard to be graceful in Harleys half a size too large." Steve gifted me those black motorcycle boots identical to his own. Neither of us ever rode hogs. "You're not answering my question. Why you?"

"I knew in that moment how much I cherished you." His skin appears iridescent in the dusk light.

Cue the violins. "This is all very touching, Steve, but if you are not going to give me answers, you can just pull into the breakdown lane and let me out."

"I asked to be your contact because I thought you would trust me more than an agent you did not know and ...." His neck vein twitches a third time as he trails off.

He didn't have any tics in college. Maybe it's a result of the obsessive-compulsive disorder cure.

"... and because you and I meant something to each other once." He turns to me, his eyes damp. He was always so sensitive to my feelings and felt everything so deeply himself—a big part of what I loved about him.

"I don't mean to sound callous." I touch his shoulder. "This is all too much. I had these vivid dreams, found needles in my house, my doctor told me I am being experimented on, and just now, my neighbor implied she might be having an affair with my husband. To top it all off, I am being whisked away by my ex-boyfriend to who knows where, who knows why."

He takes my hand and brings it to his lips for a quick kiss, then lets it go. "I swear to you, I will not let anyone hurt you, Sara. I wanted to be back in touch much sooner. Circumstances beyond my control intervened."

"Like what? Are all Swiss phones made of chocolate and melt when you try to use them?"

"Please do not be angry with me. My time in Switzerland—long story— as you said earlier. I will tell you later, if you want to hear it all."

He obviously isn't going to tell me much of anything right now. Remembering the article in *Next Wave Physics*, I try another tack. "Speaking of stories, are you still writing? You were such an amazing writer."

"You are the only person who felt that way about me," he says. "Rejection after rejection broke my spirit."

"I read somewhere *Gone with the Wind* was rejected about thirty-eight times." My headache flares from me talking too much.

"How about a drink? It really will fix what ails you." He pushes the thermos into my hand. "I use my own blend of vitamin infusions."

I take a few swallows. It tastes like lemonade.

"I make a lot of health drinks to stay in shape. I see you have kept your figure, same dangerous curves."

How can Steve look at me and not see how much I've changed? I want to tell him to stop flirting, but it comes out as a yawn. Followed by another yawn. I can't stop yawning. The headlights from oncoming cars on the other side of the interstate blur. The road is a blur. "Everything's fuzzy," I say. My voice sounds far way.

"Go ahead and get some rest, Rosy," he says.

My eyelids, heavy as cinder blocks, close under the weight.

CHAPTER 17

SARA, AGE 37

Friday, April 7, 2000, 8:45 PM
Grok's Groceries
Boykill, NY

I wake to my body pitching forward and for a moment have no idea what's happening.

Then Gallo meows and I realize I'm still in the van with Steve, my rescuer.

The loud staccato of singing frogs fills the night air. A red neon store sign for *Grok's Groceries* looks doubled, like bad three-dimension.

"Wake up, sleepy head?" Steve tousles my hair.

"Don't," I say. My mouth is cottony.

"Did you get up on the wrong side of the van?"

I try to wipe drool from the corners of my mouth. I swipe at the air the first couple of times and miss my face entirely.

Steve comes around and opens my door. His four eyes take on a demonic glow in the store's neon light.

I attempt to get out on my own, but my body acts like a sack of wet laundry.

Steve maneuvers me out of the van.

I fold at the knees.

He hoists me up and steadies me.

"What was in that thermos?"

"Take a few deep breaths," he says. "You are just disoriented from being roused from a deep sleep."

I breathe in and out a few times. It does make me feel better—much better. The scent of pine fills my lungs. My vision returns to normal. "Did you drug me?"

"Some of the vitamin infusions are alcohol based. Possibly I overdid the vodka this time.

"Right, one-hundred proof vitamin drinks. You should market them. You'll make a fortune. Where are we, anyway?"

"Boykill," he says. "Up North."

"Better than Girl kill," I say.

Steve doesn't crack a smile. He used to laugh at my jokes.

"I have not eaten dinner," he says. "You must be starving as well."

It feels like the middle of the night. I look at my watch. A quarter to nine. "I could eat." *Should I mention the granola diet?* Actually, I've been off cereal since Wednesday and the blonde hair debacle. I've been subsisting on canned tuna for the last couple of days.

He guides me to the store, but stops just short of the door and whispers in my ear. "Before we go in, I should ask you if you know your triggers."

His warm breath on my ear makes me tremble like old times. "Triggers?"

"Sorry about the cold." He enfolds me in his arms.

He no longer smells like Old Spice cologne. His scent is more like basil mixed with something medicinal.

"Before your vivid dreams began, what consumer goods did you handle?" Steve says.

"What difference does that make?"

"Strange things are happening to you and many others."

"That's what the note from Dr. Gentry said."

"Dr. Gentry has been in touch with us about your case. Tell me what you were doing right before you had those dreams and lost hours of your day."

"Breakfast cereal," I say. "I reach for cereal, then I'm lost in a dream world that feels exactly like the real world in every way."

Steve frees me from his embrace.

"So no cereal," he says. "We will likely sleep in anyway." He winks.

Is he making a pass at me? His attention has to stop. I love my husband even if .... I change the subject before I start obsessing about Candy again. "Do you think they *grok* Spock here?"

He wraps his hands around my neck, mock chokes me for a moment. "You used to be funnier," he says.

"You used to have a sense of humor."

He frowns. When he opens the door, a bell tinkles.

I can't help myself. "Another angel got its wings." Steve and I both loved *It's a Wonderful Life.* We must have watched that movie together a dozen times.

He plants a quick kiss on my cheek.

I shudder again.

He scoops up a shopping basket, takes my arm, and leads me back to a glass butcher case.

"What do you fancy?"

I'm so starved for a real meal, I could probably eat every one of the steaks, chickens, and pork chops in the window. The man wearing the apron gives me a start. He resembles the nasty supermarket clerk from my dreams. Same angular face. Only this man's hair is gray, not red. Could be the mean grocer's father. *Another coincidence? Like Gallo typing a message and Steve being my rescuer?*

"Steaks look yummy," I say, just to give an answer.

He drops my arm and makes a peace sign with his right hand. "Two of the rib eye, please."

While the butcher readies the order, I scan the shop.

The small store has a little bit of everything. A Berry Beary Crunch cereal display looms at the end of one of the aisles.

When I turn back to Steve, his brow is furrowed. "You are going to be fine now that you are with me." He takes hold of my hand, squeezes it.

"I'm okay." The headache I had earlier is gone. Maybe his vitamin drink cured what ailed me after all.

We finish the shopping. I stay far away from the cereal. Actually, Steve won't let me touch anything. We don't speak much except for his asking me if I want this or that. He selects Worcestershire sauce, olive oil, a few lemons, broccoli, butter, eggs, cheddar cheese, bacon, milk, coffee, tea, a bag of sugar, three bottles of Merlot, and a loaf of French bread.

Dinner and breakfast? The woman from Paradise Time Shares did say I'd be gone overnight.

At the checkout, Steve requests a bunch of red carnations, my favorite flower. When he pulls out his wallet to pay, a photo of a blonde-haired woman flashes by too quickly for me to see. He takes out a few bills.

"I can chip in," I say, then realize my tote bag and wallet are still in the car.

"This is a business expense. I can write it off."

I'm relieved I'm just business to him despite his harping on our past relationship.

~

Back in the van, Steve switches on the radio, which is set to the oldies station. He sings along to Steve Miller Band's "Abracadabra." The next song to come on is Heart's "Tell It Like It Is." His lips are sealed.

Steve steers the van off the main street onto a dirt road that seems to go on forever.

It feels like we've been driving an hour. This safehouse must be on another planet. We don't pass any houses, other cars, not even deer. The van lurches over bumps.

"Mrow," Gallo says.

"Sorry about the poor condition of the road." Steve turns off the radio. "We are almost there."

There is in the middle of a forest. It's pitch dark until we come to a small wooden cabin with a dim porch light.

Steve grabs his briefcase, my suitcase, and gets the groceries out of the van.

I gather up Gallo's carrier and my tote.

Despite being saddled with stuff, Steve manages to unlock the deadbolt and waves me inside. "If my hands were not full, I would carry you over the threshold," he says.

"Maybe you're trying to make me laugh, but trust me, that isn't funny." Jon did carry me over the threshold of our condo even though we'd been living together a while by the time we bought the place.

"Voila," Steve says and flips a switch. "Welcome to my humble abode."

Steve's cabin is a study in cedar—cedar walls, cedar floors, cedar cupboards, cedar ceilings. A sweet-smelling tinderbox. Good thing neither of us smokes. At least he didn't smoke when we were dating, not even pot. His van didn't smell of cigarettes, but how much do I know about him now? Sixteen years is a long time. This place reminds me of Red Riding Hood's grandma's house. Maybe Steve thinks he's the wolf.

The big main room is sparsely furnished with old but solid pieces. A stone fireplace dominates the living room area on the left, where framed prints of red barns cover the walls. No television in sight, but a large portable radio hogs the end table by the sofa. An old-fashioned corded phone hangs on the wall next to the refrigerator in the L-shaped kitchen area on the right. An oval dining table with four chairs occupies the center of the room with a wagon wheel chandelier hanging above.

The cabin seems homey, but I can't help feeling something is off about it. Still, I suppose we are safe in the middle of nowhere.

Steve closes and double locks the front door, then carries everything to the kitchen.

I set the cat carrier down on the dining table and let Gallo out.

"Please wipe down the table after you are done with the animal," Steve says.

Gallo emerges, sniffs the air, then leaps over to the sofa and perches on the back of it.

I grab my things and try the door on the left behind the table.

The bathroom is fitted with bead-board walls, a pedestal sink, an octagonal tile floor, a pull-chain toilet, and a combination tub shower. Everything is immaculate and white, including the towels and the terry robe on the back of the door. The clear shower curtain decorated with goldfish offers scant privacy. A mirrored medicine cabinet hangs over the sink. I set out Gallo's litter box between the sink and shower where it won't be stepped on. The door, which I notice has no lock, gives a high-pitched squeak when I close it to use the facilities.

When I'm done in the bathroom, I try the other door and discover a small bedroom with a queen bed, nightstand, and dresser. I toss my suitcase and tote onto the white crochet bedspread, then store Gallo's carrier and toys next to the dresser. With only one bedroom, Steve had better be planning to sleep on the sofa.

The lit lamps and overhead chandelier lend the main room a warm glow. Steve is at the kitchen counter cutting up the broccoli.

I fill a bowl for Gallo at the sink.

As soon as I set it down, Gallo strolls over and laps up some water. He looks at me and blinks his yellow iridescent eyes. "Mrow," he says, then flies through the air to his sofa perch.

"Making yourself at home?" Steve has on a white apron with the Carl

Sagan quote, *If you wish to make an apple pie from scratch, you must first invent the universe.*

"I need to call my husband. I don't want him to worry." I realize now that in my rush to get to the supermarket, I didn't even leave Jon a note. In truth, with all his late nights, he probably won't even be home yet to notice I'm not there. But Steve doesn't need to know that.

"I am sorry, Sara. You must not let him know where you are," He sets down the knife and comes to me. "This is a crazy situation." He lays his hands on my shoulders. "Allow me to serve dinner first. Once we have food in our bellies, I will tell you everything, Rosy." He kisses my forehead. "If you still wish to call your spouse after what I tell you, you will be free to do so."

"You've been putting off giving me any information since I got into your van. Why should I trust you now?"

He presses his left hand to his heart and holds his right hand in the air. "I will tell you what you want to know, on my mother's heart." His mother died when he was sixteen. His father left when he was a baby, so she was everything to him. He always spoke of her with deep affection and admiration.

I believe he would not sully his mother's honor with a lie.

"Wash your hands after you wipe the table, please." He used to obsess over cleanliness. He could scrub his hands for ten minutes straight. And he'd insist I do the same.

I find cleaning spray under the sink and oblige his wishes.

"The broccoli is steaming, and I am about to put the steaks in the pan. You can open the wine and set the table. Everything you need is in that cupboard." He points.

The dishes and glasses are simple, unadorned, and functional. I locate a wooden cutting board and slice the French bread. I open the wine and pour two glasses. This is the first hot meal I've had since going on the granola diet.

What did Jon do for dinner tonight? *Maybe he had some Candy*, my mother's voice in my head taunts. I sip the wine that smells a bit like violets. It tastes fruity and earthy. Jon and I used to drink wine with dinner. We stopped when I got pregnant and never went back to it.

The aroma of caramelizing meat fat fills the room. In a few minutes, Steve brings the food to the table.

"A toast," he says. He tops off my wine. "To first love." He clinks.

"To answers," I say.

We clink again.

"Try the rib eye," he says. "It is just as you prefer it."

The steak is cooked medium rare and seasoned to perfection. "Wonderful." I give a thumbs up. *To hell with the granola diet.* "Now," I say, my mouth full of delicious meat, "tell me everything."

"Domestic Global International has been attempting to find ways to induce customers to purchase more of their products, such as breakfast cereal. They began with an investigation of food additives to enhance the effects of subliminal advertising. The experiments have escalated over time. The dreams, as you call them, are a result of what has become a full-blown mind-control experiment."

"Mind control? That's certainly unethical, not to mention illegal. But what has Domestic's research got to do with me? I never volunteered for any research study. I used to be an accountant there and Jon still is."

"I am truly sorry to tell you we have reason to believe your husband is one of the corporation's biggest operatives in the experiment's illegal testing."

The buttery broccoli slides off my fork. "Jon has nothing to do with this."

"Dr. Gentry messengered your blood to our agency. I received a call while you were in the bathroom. Our lab confirmed you have been injected with the experimental serum. Who else would have access to you in your home besides your spouse?"

"He wouldn't do this to me." I swallow the rest of my wine to calm myself. "And who exactly is the *we* who all think this?"

Steve refills my glass. "While in Switzerland being treated at the clinic, I was recruited by an organization that covertly monitors corporate research for any improprieties. I have been assigned to the Domestic case for a while now. They discovered and tracked your husband's movements."

"Movements? Jon works in accounting. He has no movements, except with a calculator."

"Accounting is Jonathan García's cover story. He is assisting the corporation with unlawful activities."

"I don't believe you." My appetite soured, I push my plate aside.

His neck vein twitches double-time. "What reason would I have to lie to you?"

He dumped me. *Reason enough.* "I don't know," I say.

"I am prepared to answer all your questions. Just ask. But I warn you, the answers will be painful to hear." He takes my hand.

"*Grrrowwwl.*" Gallo bellows a deep, continuous growl from his perch on the sofa.

Steve releases my hand.

Gallo's growling relents.

That's my good watch-cat! Even though I'm not sure I want to know the answer, I ask what's been on my mind thanks to Candy and Mother's voice in my head. "Do you know if Jon's cheating on me?"

"García is teamed with a female operative. Perhaps he is doing more than working with her. I am not privy to that." Steve empties the rest of the wine into my glass.

My stomach gurgles. *I need to stop drinking before I can't think straight.* "Jon loves me. Who is this woman?"

"I have never interacted with her. Her code name is Red Cross, and she is very dangerous."

I gag on the wine. "Red as in red hair?"

"Who knows? Most test subjects suffered permanent brain damage, compromised motor function, and even permanent paralysis as a result of the experiment. Some have died. But those Red Cross deals with apparently meet a more violent end. Rosy, you are lucky to get away. Especially since your husband is a part of all this. His code name is The Auditor."

Of course it is. "Why would Domestic Global want to experiment on me?"

"All the most recent test subjects we identified grew up within a mile of a 1960s model electrical transformer station that leaked a certain type of radioactive compound." After that mouthful, he chews a forkful of broccoli.

"There was a big transformer station four blocks away from my childhood home. But what does radioactivity have to do with mind control?"

He dabs the corners of his mouth. "Radioactivity affects brain development. Specifically, the amygdala."

"So I have a mutant amygdala?"

"The amygdala is linked to emotional states. Domestic tried to chemically manipulate the brain organ to create a sense of bliss in the minds of consumers when in the presence of their products and advertisements for such."

"So that buying Berry Beary Crunch will make me feel like a Zen master?"

Steve laughs. "Now there is the hilarious Sara I remember." He tears a crust of bread. He still eats like a linebacker, but has the physique of an ice-skater.

"My dreams didn't make me feel like buying cereal."

"The experiments produced unexpected side effects."

"Tell me about it." I run my fingers through my hair.

"I believe you saw the article with my byline in *Next Wave Physics?*"

The broccoli I was pushing around my plate falls into my lap. "How did you know?"

Steve frowns at my mess. "Not important. But the speculations about time travel as described in the article turn out to be far more than speculative. You should know better than anyone."

"What do you mean?"

"I am not authorized to reveal certain details, but if you have already discovered them for yourself, I am permitted to clarify."

The back of my neck prickles. "My dreams felt real, more real than any dreams I've ever had before. Are you telling me I actually traveled back in time?"

"Mrow, Mrow, Mrow," Gallo says.

"Phrase that as a statement," Steve says.

"I went back in time for real. But how?"

"The amygdala is also the receptor for electromagnetic pulses called Penrose waves, as well as being responsible for the human perception of time."

"How can I travel back to be inside my pre-pubescent body, knowing what I know about my future, about now?"

He sets down his fork. "I would have liked to have known you back then."

I shoot him a look that could freeze the Atlantic Ocean.

He clears his throat. "Domestic Global International stumbled upon a monumental discovery which redefines human consciousness, or the soul if you will, as electromagnetic."

"My soul is a bunch of charged particles?"

"You are as brilliant as ever."

"So, my consciousness went back in time, to an earlier me?"

"Bravo." Steve gets up, moves behind me and begins to massage my shoulders. "Your brain is like a radio tuned to receive your consciousness, no matter from where the signal is being sent."

The way to a girl's heart is through her sore muscles.

Gallo hisses, tries to swat Steve away from me, but the sofa is too far for his paws to reach.

"It's okay, boy," I say to Gallo.

He stops hissing, but his ears flatten.

Steve's fingers haven't lost their magic in sixteen years. "Could you rub my back too?" I lean forward in the chair. "But what happens to the consciousness already in that body in the past? Where does she go? The *me* at that age can't just disappear."

"Good question. Our scientists believe the consciousness may be suppressed somehow. Off the air, so to speak." His finger kneads down the center of my back. "Can you tell me exactly what you experienced?"

"The first time I left my kitchen, I ended up in a grocery store with my Grandma. Such powerful smells. My grandmother's skin and ...." I stop myself before I say Danny Astrella's name or mention his gasoline and sea musk scent. Steve is already acting like a love-sick fool.

"Did anything seem different to you when the time displacement ended and you returned to the present?"

"Not really. Except I seemed to have eaten a bowl of vile Berry Beary Crunch. The second time I dreamed—went back—I was with Jon at a grocery store and he proposed to me right there. But that's not the way it really happened. I woke nauseated. I ran to the bathroom, threw up a bunch, and then saw I had blonde hair. I never had blonde hair."

"Did you do anything differently during your experiences in the past?"

"I told Jon I wasn't jealous of his ex-girlfriend."

"And you were jealous previously?" He stops rubbing my back and drops into the chair next to me.

"He held on to photos of her. I never met her. Yet there she was at the market."

"What about your blonde hair?"

"I have these new memories of dying my hair to match Jon's mother's for the wedding photos. And then keeping it blonde because of all the compliments." I slap the table. "But I would never dye my hair blonde."

"And yet, you did. Or a version of you did."

"But how do I have memories of both versions of Jon's proposal?"

"Somehow you changed your past, and now the present version of you is different. Another Sara."

"What about the paradox thing? You know, you can't go back in time and kill your own grandfather?"

"There is something called the Context-Dependent proof which invalidates the Grandfather Paradox as a viable argument against time travel. And there are a multitude of multiverse theories, offshoots of Hugh Everett's ideas."

"You sure sound like a science geek. Are you saying I could go back in time and change anything I want, create parallel worlds?"

"All I can say is that you now have two competing memories of how your husband proposed and a hair color you do not seem to be happy about."

"You're a lot of help."

"I want to help, Rosy. Let me." He leans in as if he's going to kiss me.

I shove my hand against his chest to hold him back.

His heart is racing.

I deflect him with a question that pops into my head. "Hey, we both come from Woodward. How's your amygdala?" Actually he only lived in the neighborhood until he was five, and we never met.

"Only this one universe for me." The corners of his mouth turn down.

"Do I know these other time travelers, are they people I grew up with?"

"I am not authorized to divulge information about other test subjects."

I have a million questions. "Can I control the time travel by touching cereal? Can I go back to any year I want?"

"These experiments have put you in grave danger." He gazes into my eyes. "I could not abide losing you again, Rosy. We belong together."

I ignore his assertion. "Did my husband inject me with the serum, knowing it could harm or kill me?"

"I am so sorry. It would appear that way, my love." Steve moves in and throws his arms around me.

Gallo screeches, bounds onto the table, and swats at Steve's head.

"Some cat," Steve says. "Your knight in shining black fur." He distracts Gallo's gallant efforts by dangling a strip of rib eye in front of him.

My kitty seizes the hunk of meat in his jaws and swoops back to the sofa. *Some defender.*

Steve, safe from cat attack, presses his lips to mine.

CHAPTER 18

JON, AGE 43

I grope my way through corridors of time ...

— OCTAVIO PAZ

Saturday, April 8, 2000, 8:00 AM
Jon & Sara's Condo
Bayfront, Long Island, NY

*a*bandoned cups and glasses litter every surface. A half-eaten sandwich molders on the breakfast counter. Jon gathers what he can and shoves it into the sink before Vento's knock at the apartment door.

"I never thought I'd see you here," Jon says. He steps aside to let Vento enter. For secrecy's sake, she's never been to his place.

"Nice to see you too. I take it you've still had no word from Sara. You look like mildewed cardboard."

Whatever that means. "None. Did you come here to flatter me or do you have information about my wife?"

"First, coffee, light," she says. She hands him a small plate wrapped in foil. "I baked these for you."

He lifts the aluminum wrap. Cookies, thick and bursting with chocolate chips. They look amazing, but he has no appetite. "It's not my birthday."

"I figured you could use something sweet right now."

The card shark has a heart after all.

She proceeds to the living room like she owns the place, relocates the stack of books on Sara's chair, and sits. Vento's got on another god-awful brown pantsuit that blends with the color of the leather.

He fixes her coffee and pours himself another cup, his sixth or seventh of the morning. He ought to be bouncing off the walls, but everything feels fuzzy, surreal. He should have followed his instinct Monday and confessed everything to his wife. If he had, maybe she'd be here right now.

As if reading his mind, Vento says, "None of this is your fault. Sullivan's death. Your wife's disappearance. Domestic is getting desperate. We're too close, coming at them from all angles."

Jon sets his cup down on the end table. "What've you got for me, Vento?"

She bites her lip, as if she's still deciding what to say.

"Joanne, please spit it out. I'm going crazy here." He never uses her first name, but this is an exceptional situation. He needs her to tell him everything she knows.

"After you left the stakeout, our boy Ranger got a call on his mobile, sped off in a turbo-charged white van. I lost him in Flushing, near the college. I ran the plate. Turns out it was stolen. The number belonged to a black Mustang convertible registered to an Arthur O'Keefe in Fishburg Falls, about four hours upstate if you're Mario Andretti. The registration expired three years ago, and the given address turned out to be an abandoned soybean processing factory."

"And this has what to do with Sara?" He runs a hand through his hair to disguise his impatience with her.

"Last night, Ranger was observed upstate at a market accompanied by a woman matching your wife's description. We checked the store's security cameras—"

"That sociopath took my wife—why?" He leaps to his feet. "Where is he now?"

"He's a pussycat. Your word, remember?" She slurps from the mug. "And by the way, I was never here."

"Got it. Give me the recon."

Vento motions for him to sit back down.

He obliges. *She's a true friend, breaking protocol for me.*

"Starting today," she says, "you are on personal administrative leave.

You know the only reason I am disclosing any information is because I care about you and Sara. And because I'd want you to tell me if the situation were reversed, and it was my family. I trust you to do the right thing."

"Of course. I'm not going to jeopardize Sara's life. Any more than it is already." But Vento can't expect him to twiddle his thumbs or else she wouldn't be telling him any of this. He would do the same for her.

"Good." She finishes the coffee in a long swallow. "The van was last seen outside Grok's Groceries in Boykill, New York. No bead on where it is now. We'll have a report from the DMV later this morning on all white vans registered in the vicinity. But since he switched plates, the van may be stolen too. If we come up with anything ..." She stands before finishing the thought.

"Thank you," Jon says.

"Pretty good coffee." She hands him the mug. "Bureau might be in the market for another office assistant. You could put in for it since you want a desk job." She heads to the door.

"Wait," he says. He throws his arms around her. "I mean it, thanks."

Vento pats him on the back. "Keep it together, García." She pushes his arms off, steps out into the hall, and closes the door behind her without another word.

He rushes to the computer to locate Grok's Groceries. In a few minutes, he's ready to leave for the area where Sara was last seen.

On the way to the stairs, Jon passes Candy Starr's condo. The orange plastic roses tacked above her buzzer are mangled. *Someone must have been mad at the flowers—or at her.* He'd pounded on her door last night wondering if she'd had anything to do with his wife's disappearance. There was no answer then, but the decorations were intact. Now the apartment door is ajar. *Foul play?* He doesn't want to delay getting to Sara, but maybe the same person who took his wife is in cahoots with Candy. He knocks, calls out. "Candy, you home? It's Jon."

There's no answer. He doesn't hear any movement inside.

Jon calls her name again and pushes against the door. It groans open.

The honeysuckle air freshener chokes him. *Like someone sprayed an entire can.* Mismatched floral pillows belonging to the studio's daybed are scattered all over the rug. The bed cover and sheets are a tangled mess. *A struggle or wild sex?* He has no idea about her sexual habits. But from previous visits, he knows Candy, like Sara, keeps a tidy apartment.

His wife hates the way he leaves a trail of clothes from the bedroom to the bathroom. But he can't remember the last time she gave him hell for doing so. Or complained about anything else, for that matter. All he recalls is the ache in Sara's voice when she wanted to make love a few days ago and all he wanted was sleep. He'll pin her to the mattress next time. If he ever sees her again, that is.

Candy's bedsheets are cool to the touch.

Rooting around the mess on the floor, his toe catches a pair of orange lace panties. That underwear was the only stitch she had on her body the last time she invited him over, ostensibly to fix her toaster. He feigned interest, but cleaned the crumb tray and kept his hands off her. Everything about her is bogus—her Southern accent, massive breast implants, and stripper-sounding name. Nothing about Candy is the least bit appealing.

If Sara suspects something's going on between them, she's never brought it up. He wishes he could have told his wife that their neighbor is a suspect in the Domestic investigation. Nothing more than a job, and a damned unpleasant one at that.

Jon calls Candy's name again and knocks before entering the bathroom.

He has to cover his mouth to keep himself from fouling the crime scene. The odor is something like rancid bacon.

Candy naked, bloated and blue, face up in the tub, eyes wide, breasts perkier in rigor mortis. He's no forensics expert, but he knows the colorful bruises around her throat indicate strangulation.

When he saw his father's dead body at the funeral home, he bawled. Seeing Candy, his eyes tear from smell alone.

Back in the main room, he phones Vento using his mobile.

She tells him not to touch anything else and to wipe his prints. She'll be back in fifteen minutes to "discover the murder scene" herself.

At least she doesn't give him hell for sticking his nose into the Starr investigation.

He tells her he'll wait to buzz her into the building. That will give him a chance to look around some more. If Candy juiced his wife, there must be evidence.

He appropriates the pair of dishwashing gloves by the kitchen sink, dons them, and heads back into the bathroom.

Nothing unusual in the medicine cabinet. Aspirin, toothpaste, and the like. Under the sink, spare toilet paper. He lifts the toilet tank lid and fishes out a large, sealed bag containing books of some kind. He undoes the plastic and discovers his missing journals. Proof positive Candy violated his condo beyond just barging in the other morning. She had to be the one who injected his wife.

Jon continues his search in the main room. He unzips pillows and finds nothing but stuffing. He checks under the bedding and daybed—nothing. He rifles through her chest of drawers and closet. The extensive variety of lingerie—see-through, netting, leather—doesn't surprise him at all.

The freezer resembles a liquor store, while the fridge is full of diet orange soda. In the oven he finds every flavor of uppers and downers, and even some antipsychotics. Candy played vapid to the extreme but didn't seem the type to use drugs. *Maybe she doped her victims before injecting them.*

Under the sink, there's the usual cleaning supplies. But when he picks up an unlabeled bottle to sniff the clear liquid, he notices a loose plywood panel. He uncovers her stash below it—a case of hypodermic needles filled with a neon-green fluid and a ring of keys. He matches one of the keys to his own condo door deadbolt key.

If she wasn't already dead, he'd consider killing her. He doesn't really wish her dead, though. He can't interrogate a corpse.

He leaves the sink cabinet and oven doors open for Vento. She'll be peeved he touched anything else, but she'll get over it. She's always called him incautious, but she can't scold him this time. Not with Sara missing.

Waiting by the open window to watch for his partner, he stuffs the dishwashing gloves in his pocket and thumbs through one of his journals. A passage highlighted with a yellow marker catches his eye.

I knew right away—SRB is the woman I want to wake up to every
   day. Not because of her excellent taste in music, but that is a bonus.
   Not because she is amazing in bed, but, oh, yes she is. I know because her
   eyes say there is nothing more important than me in her world. When she
   looks at me, she sees the man I always dreamed of becoming—
   courageous, empathetic, generous, kind, good. And I am all those things,
   everything my father was (or at least, I can be), with her at my side.

Why the hell would Candy highlight this passage? A car door slams. Vento sprints to the front entrance. He lays on the buzzer with his elbow to let her in, then flees the apartment, journals in hand. Eager to leave the cadaver behind, and get on the road to Boykill where Ranger took his wife, he bounds down the stairs two at a time.

CHAPTER 19

SARA, AGE 37

Saturday, April 8, 2000, 12:30 AM
Steve's cabin
Boykill, NY

*S*teve's lips are insistent.

I lost myself in his kisses back in college, but I won't now. I can't. I have a husband I love, whether or not he still loves me. I push Steve away. "I need to go to bed."

Steve's face is flushed.

"You read my mind."

"I'm sorry. I'm a married woman."

"We are not as different as you think," he says, venom in his tone. "Your Jonathan and I have much in common."

I don't ask what he means by that. I have no desire to start comparing my first love with the love of my life.

He stomps off to clear the table.

"Steve, please don't be mad."

He lets out a long sigh. "I was being foolish," he says, his back to me, "thinking we could just pick up where we left off. You need time to absorb everything that is happening to you."

"This whole experiment and time-travel thing is beyond confusing," I say. "It's surreal. Let me help you with the dishes."

"No need. You should sleep in the bedroom," he says. "I will take the couch. Go ahead."

"I'd like to feed Gallo first. Then take a hot shower." *Steve's kiss makes me feel unclean.*

Instead of responding, he turns on the radio. The station touts a summer tour for The Who and Jimmy Page & The Black Crowes.

Gallo eats all his kibble, even after the big piece of steak he consumed. At least the chaos of traveling and being in a strange place hasn't put off his hearty appetite.

~

Waiting for the water to heat up, I stare at my reflection in the mirror. "Jon loves you," I say aloud. "Believe in him." It could be the wine talking. My eyes are bloodshot. My hair looks like an albino squirrel curled up on my head and died.

To prevent the bathroom from getting too steamy, I crack open the window.

Cool night air seeps in, along with Steve's voice.

Is he calling me? I open the door a smidge.

"I thought you said ten ... what then?" He must be on the phone.

I snoop a little while longer on his one-sided conversation.

"Yes, I can ... naturally ... no, not yet ... okay ... not a problem ... of course ... will do." He stops speaking for a while. Dishes clink. He must have hung up.

The hot water can't wash Jon from my thoughts. How effortlessly we fell in bed together the first time. The amazing sex. How happy we were—before the baby. But we managed to stay together after losing our child, more than most couples do. We said we'd talk about adopting some day when the pain lessened. That day hasn't come.

Maybe Jon is cheating with Candy, but what Steve told me is worse. *Much worse.* My own husband experimenting on me for Domestic. *No.* Steve has to be wrong. Even if Jon has stopped loving me, he wouldn't do something so gruesome. Someone else had to inject me. Possibly Red Cross, the female operative, whoever that is.

I try to quiet my mind by singing The Beatles' "All My Loving." Not the best choice.

The door squeaks open. I cover myself with a washcloth.

"*Mrow,*" Gallo says. He climbs into the litter box.

"Letting the cat in," Steve says from behind the door. "I thought you might like some company."

Does he want me to invite *him* in? *Not gonna happen.* "I'll be out in a minute, Steve."

He closes the door without another word.

A new litter box aroma is added incentive to finish quickly.

There's no lock on the bedroom door either. I search my suitcase and realize I didn't bring anything to sleep in. "I guess I should just put on clean clothes, huh, boy?"

"Mrow," Gallo says and hops onto the bed. He circles and settles at the foot.

Steve leans his head in. "Feeling better?"

Does he even know how to knock? I grab the top of the towel to make sure it stays on.

"I made us some tea," Steve says. "Should we have it in here?" His tone is friendly once again.

"Give me a sec. I'll be right out."

He pouts, but closes the door.

How can he think I would just rush into his arms after all these years? I can't turn back the clock on what happened. Well, maybe if I were time traveling, I could. If only I could just move ahead in time enough to travel past all this craziness and uncertainty. Can I travel to the future as well as the past?

I dress quickly, with my back to the door. As I fasten Adam's watch, I notice the time— 1:15. Jon probably still isn't home. Maybe he's with Candy and doesn't know I'm gone.

I pet Gallo's velvety fur. Anywhere my kitty and I are together can be home.

"We are going to be okay, boy," I say, wondering which one of us I am trying to convince.

The kitchen area is spotless. A tea kettle burbles on the stove, and a fire crackles in the hearth. Steve sure gets a lot done in a short time. The room is as cozy as can be, but something still seems off about the cabin. I can't put my finger on it.

From the radio, Rod Stewart sings "Forever Young."

Oldies are a kind of time travel too, I suppose.

Gallo follows me into the living room and reclaims his perch atop the sofa back.

Steve places tea bags into the mugs and pours steaming water over them.

I sit in the wing chair closest to the fire. "Who was on the phone earlier?"

"My superior at the agency. A special team will be here tomorrow afternoon to evaluate you for the proper medical protocol. We can keep each other entertained until then."

"Why didn't you take me to be checked out?"

Steve's neck vein pulses. "I am not supposed to know the location of the medical facilities. An added level of security. If I am captured by the bad guys and tortured, I will not be able to compromise the location. Our agency thought of all possible futures."

"I doubt that with the crazy things that have been happening to me. Changing the past and the present. Speaking of which, do you know if time travel into the future is possible?"

"I do not. We have right now, Rosy." Steve flashes his killer smile again.

I am suddenly weepy, but I manage to hold it together.

He brings me a mug. "Chamomile, plus some extra herbs to help you sleep. You always had such a hard time."

His fingers linger on mine as I accept the tea.

"I appreciate all your kindness." I sip the soothing lemony sweet brew. I feel sorry for both of us, not having the love we want.

CHAPTER 20

SARA, AGE 37

Saturday, April 8, 2000, 8 AM
Steve's cabin
Boykill, NY

I wake to the buzzing of a razor. The room is dark, with a hint of sunlight glowing through the window shade. There is a sharp odor of wet clay in the air.

When I become less cloud-headed, I realize the droning sound is Gallo purring, his head tucked next to mine. I feel rested, but not quite ready to get out of bed.

"Good morning," I say to my kitty.

"Good morning."

I bolt upright.

Gallo startles alert at the sound of Steve's voice. He jumps to hunker over my legs.

Steve stands by the foot of the bed.

How long has he been here watching me sleep? And how could he have snuck up on my cat too?

As if he's reading my mind, he says, "I just came in to check on you. You always rose before the sun."

"Back in the days of eight AM classes," I say. "Is there any coffee?"

"High-test, no additives, correct?"

"You got it."

Dressed in all black again, he looks gloomy instead of cool. His puffy eyes make me wonder if he's been crying. He comes to me and sweeps some hair off my forehead.

Gallo bounds over and whacks at Steve's hand.

"I have not forgotten a single thing about you. I never will." He leaves and closes the door behind him.

Never will—that has an ominous and final ring to it.

Speaking of rings, I have to call Jon, hear his voice, and let him know where I am. I want him to tell me he didn't inject me, that Steve is wrong. I need to hear my husband say he loves me.

I pull on my jeans, slip on my shoes, and go to put on my Timex. It isn't on the nightstand where I left it. I check under the bed. Nothing there, not even dust bunnies.

Steve still keeps everything immaculate.

Could I be misremembering? Maybe I left my watch next to my toothbrush.

When I get out of the bathroom, I am greeted by the aroma of fresh coffee. Light streams in from all the windows. The kitchen clock shows ten after eight.

"Have you seen my watch? I know I had it before I went to bed."

A gray sweater now breaks up Steve's solid black attire. He pours coffee into two travel mugs. "You look bright-eyed and beautiful this morning." He sounds more chipper than he looks. There are lines on his forehead I could swear weren't there yesterday. Maybe he didn't sleep well on the couch.

He removes his leather-banded watch and comes to me. "Maybe your cat made off with it in the night. You can borrow mine." He fastens it to my wrist. "Time has been getting away from you lately."

I don't laugh at his pun. "It was my brother's watch. It means a lot to me."

"Adam's Timex, I remember. I promise to turn this entire house upside down after our walk. Unless you want to enjoy breakfast right away."

There can't be a lot of hiding places in a place this small. "Exercise will do me good," I say. "But first, let me at the coffee."

Steve offers the red travel mug.

I sip—rich, dark ambrosia. "Tastes as good as it smells."

"My pleasure to serve you." He bows, then retrieves a flannel-lined jean jacket from the coat hook and holds it out for me.

I switch my mug from hand to hand to slip it on. The coat smells like wood smoke.

Gallo, perched on the back of the sofa, licks his paw, and then uses it to wash his head.

"You stay here, boy. I'll be back soon." Hopefully, with more information from Steve about what is happening to me.

My lungs fill with pine-scented morning air, and I feel much more alert. All I want to do is keep moving forward.

Steve steers me toward a wide path at the side of the cabin. He loops his arm through mine.

It feels natural, which is weird, because a few minutes ago I was disturbed by his watching me sleep.

Serenaded by birdsong, sipping coffee, we walk for a while without talking. It feels wonderful to stretch my legs. Steve and I used to go for walks in all kinds of weather back in college.

"Remember our campus promenades?" he says.

Is he reading my mind again? "I was thinking about that too."

"Rather ironic," he says, "you traveling to the past and me wishing to be back there with you."

"The past is the past," I say. I hope I don't sound bitter.

Several birds dart across our path.

"Cerulean warblers," he says.

When did he get this knowledgeable about wildlife? There's a lot I don't know about him. Maybe I should ask. "Ever marry?" I regret asking the moment the words leave my mouth. I could have inquired after his new favorite bands—at least something innocuous.

"Never been married. No serious relationships either. Work has been all-consuming." The vein in his neck pulses. "No one could hold a candle to you anyway."

What about the blonde in his wallet? "Steve, I didn't mean to snoop, but I did notice a photo of a woman when you were paying for groceries."

He smirks, stops walking, balances the travel mug under his chin, and produces the wallet from his pocket. He flips it open to the photo.

Holy molé salsa—a picture of me with my blonde hair. "Where did you get that?"

"The agency has been keeping tabs on you for a while. I pulled this photo from a surveillance file. It astonished me to discover one of the test subjects is the woman I love."

Love. Present tense. Not *loved.* I return the photo and we start walking again. "But if your agency knew I was in danger, why didn't someone rescue me sooner?" I say. "And why did I have to come to you?"

"I am not privy to all the agency stratagems. I requested to be your contact as soon as I became aware of your involvement. Rosy, when this is all over—"

"What's going to happen to me now?" I say, as much to change the subject as out of true curiosity.

"The agents are coming after breakfast, as I told you. They will make sure you are medically safe."

There's a loud bang from somewhere in the distance.

Hunters? "If I'm all right, do I get to go home?"

"That depends on the whereabouts of your husband. There are agents working on his capture."

"What will happen to Jon? He won't be hurt, will he?" I'm going to have to distract Steve when we get back to the cabin so I can call Jon and warn him. My husband may be a bad guy, but I don't want anything bad to happen to him.

"You need not worry about García. He will be turned over to the proper authorities for processing. The important thing now is to keep you in the right hands." Steve stops once more. "In my hands." He looks like he wants to kiss me again.

I won't allow that. "Jon is a good man. Please, promise me that he'll be unharmed." I hurry ahead, but he gains on me.

"Our agency would never cause unnecessary injury."

"Who decides what's necessary?"

"I need you to know how sorry I am I never contacted you before all of this began. I have never loved anyone else but you."

I want to reassure Steve, but not encourage him. "I forgave you a long time ago," I say, even if it isn't true. "Then, I moved on with Jon."

"I am not a bad guy," he says, his face half in shadow.

I can't see his eyes but I would bet anything they have tears in them. "I know you're a good man." He was, once. Wrote me odes. Never flirted with other girls. Read me books in bed. "You were always very ..."

Suddenly, I realize what's off about the cabin. *No books*. None. Not even a magazine. Back in college, Steve would never leave home without two or three volumes in his backpack. Could he have changed that much?

"Everything okay?" he says. "You stopped talking mid-sentence."

I don't know why, but I am afraid to ask him about the lack of books. What if the cure for obsessive-compulsive disorder took away one of his greatest pleasures? "I guess I'm hungry," I say avoiding the subject. "How about breakfast?"

"This path circles back to the cabin," he says. "It will be shorter to keep heading in this direction."

We pick up the pace.

Then again, maybe the absence of books doesn't mean anything. Maybe he just carted off all his books to a library sale. I could ask Steve what he's been reading lately.

"You know," he says, "I envy you. If I had the opportunity to go back in time knowing what I know now, I would do quite a few things differently."

I bet Steve wants to tell me he wouldn't have left me. What good does it do either of us now? He did leave. "I had no idea I could change things. I don't even have a clue how getting proposed to in a different location turned me into a blonde. Besides, the first time I went back, I was an adult in a kid's body. Kids have no say."

"Adults do not have complete control over their lives either." His expression is glum.

I don't know how to respond to this. Instead, I try to get information from him. He must know more than he's telling. "How does time travel work exactly?"

"I am far from an expert."

"But you wrote that magazine article. And you are aware of other time travelers. While my consciousness is off somewhere else in the past, what is my body doing in the present? Am I slumped over, dead weight?"

"It is difficult to say. Perhaps the version of the present the traveler leaves ceases to exist."

"No, I can't destroy the whole world simply by leaving it."

"My world's never been the same without you," Steve says.

Oh, no, I'm not letting him distract me. "What do you know about other experiment victims?"

"Our agency has secured evidence that the serum induces a change in brain waves, much different than REM. The altered phase could be construed as a coma while the consciousness leaves the body."

"So my brain is basically the time machine?"

Steve laughs. "A good way to put it. The science is very complicated for a layman like me. There is an equation which presupposes that the brain's Penrose wave transmissions travel outside the speed of light, but always remain connected to their point of origin. In your case, your brain in the year 2000."

"Nothing travels faster than light," I say. Didn't Einstein prove that?"

"Nonlocal action at a distance accounts for instantaneous communication. Einstein disputed it, dubbed it *spooky*, but never disproved quantum mechanics."

"So why don't some other connected brain waves come from the future faster than the speed of light and take over my body in the present?"

"Our scientists have not explained that."

"What happened to my real life, the one where I am, and have always been, a brunette?"

"The theory, as I understand it, is that the universe favors certain patterns. The Penrose wave travel you experienced shifted your life into a new pattern, an altered timeline."

"Can I go back and change things again to be the way I want them?"

"A very dangerous proposition. The serum needs to be reintroduced every ten to fourteen days to keep the Penrose wave center active. If you are trapped in the past when wave functions return to stasis … and remember this is merely scientific conjecture … the brain dies, and the time traveler with it."

"Thanks for not sugar-coating it. But why only the past, why wouldn't I die in the present too? And how would anyone in the year 2000 remember me if I die in the past?"

"A conundrum to be sure."

We arrive at the cabin's front stoop.

Steve takes out his keys, but doesn't unlock the door. "Sara, promise me two things. First, if at all possible, stay right here, right now. But if you cannot, and you happen to travel back to a time to when we were together, stop me from going to Switzerland. Use any means necessary. Do not let me leave."

Isn't he happy about being cured of his disorder? "Steve," I say, unable to prevent the sharpness in my voice, "I made a fool of myself begging you not to go. I don't know what more I could have done."

"Get pregnant," he says. "I could never leave you then."

My cheeks burn. I go to slap him, but he catches my hand before it connects.

I don't know if it's grief over the baby Jon and I lost, or sorrow over not being able to ever bear children, or my fury at Steve, but I can't hold back the tears.

Steve takes me in his arms.

I sob into his neck.

CHAPTER 21

SARA, AGE 37

Saturday, April 8, 2000, 10:05 AM
Steve's cabin
Boykill, NY

*a*s soon as I step inside the cabin, Gallo greets me with a shin-rub dance and loud purring. I feed him his breakfast like everything is normal, and he obliges me by eating.

Steve turns on the radio. "Yellow Submarine" plays. He sings along off key while prepping another pot of coffee. I imagine he's hamming it up to make me smile, and it works.

It's all too easy to recall how much I loved this man once. And for a moment, I wonder if this is what things would be like if he and I never broke up. *A lazy weekend getaway in the country with our cat.*

But Steve would never allow a cat. Gallo is Jon's and mine.

"Breakfast will be ready in a jiffy," Steve says. "Better go wash up."

I should call Jon right away, but I have to get Steve to leave the room since the only phone is in the kitchen. "Wouldn't you feel better having a shower first?"

"Let's eat first. We can shower after."

Wherever Jon is, I just hope he's safe. I hurry to the bathroom as I feel another cry coming on.

~

I splash my face with water. My eyes are much less red than I imagined. My hair looks more like a bird's nest after being blown about. I check the medicine cabinet for any kind of hair balm, as I forgot to pack mine.

I find toothpaste, toothbrush, razor, deodorant, talcum powder, a ton of first-aid stuff, and a single prescription. I can't quash my curiosity. The bottle labeled *Thioridazine* was prescribed by Dr. Gentry. I've heard the drug name associated with mental patients, but I don't know exactly what it does. Probably something for his obsessive-compulsive disorder.

Steve pokes his head in the door. "Breakfast is served."

I fumble to hide the bottle behind my back. "Just a second," I say, trying to conceal the evidence that I've been spying.

"Remember, 'I have measured out my life with coffee spoons,'" he says, quoting T. S. Eliot.

That is his fancy way of saying he's tired of waiting on me. I wet my frizzy mess of a hairdo and smooth out my curls.

~

A vase of red carnations graces the center of the table.

Where did he keep those flowers overnight? Maybe he has a hiding place after all, and that's where my Timex is. Or maybe I'm being paranoid. He must have stored the carnations in the fridge.

Steve brings over steaming plates of scrambled eggs, bacon, and toast, and sets down a cup of coffee. "Bon appétit." The vein in his neck pulses. Perhaps the tic is a side effect of that medication he's taking.

I gulp the coffee, expecting the same rich brew of earlier, but it tastes bitter. I set it aside. *Is he trying to drug me—again?*

"Something wrong?"

"Coffee tastes bitter. What did you put in it? Hopefully not more of your hundred-proof vitamin infusions."

He seizes my coffee and takes a prolonged gulp.

I'm surprised he doesn't instantly go to the bathroom to gargle away my germs.

"You are correct," he says, setting down the empty cup. "The beans must have been burned. I am terribly sorry. I can fix a fresh pot." He goes and empties the entire coffee carafe into the sink.

"No, no," I say, "don't trouble yourself. I drank enough earlier." A slice of crisp bacon cleans my palate wonderfully. The food tastes better than it smells, and it smells glorious. But after a few bites, my body itches everywhere, like there are ants crawling all over me. Serves me right for breaking my diet again.

"Steve, I feel weird." I can't seem to prevent my head from falling into the eggs.

CHAPTER 22

SARA, AGE 37

Saturday, April 8, 2000, 12:45 PM
Steve's cabin
Boykill, NY

*M*y vision is blurry, as if my eyes are coated with Vaseline. I can make out the shape of the window, shade partially drawn, the light coming in.

"Are you awake, Sara?" Steve is lying next to me. He straightens the blanket over me, and I feel his fingers brush my midsection, skin on skin.

Holy molé salsa. I'm not wearing my shirt. *Did we sleep together?* I can't remember. I sense coarse fabric beneath my fingertips. At least I am still wearing my jeans. And, thank goodness, they are zipped.

Steve's t-shirt undulates. It is made of live snakes.

I blink. No—it's a Billy Idol t-shirt. *What did you do to me?* I try to say, but my mouth doesn't seem to be working. My words come out as grunts.

Steve strokes my cheek. "Don't strain yourself. Do you remember me carrying you to the bedroom?"

I try to shake my head but I can't sense whether it is moving back and forth.

"You passed out at breakfast," he says. "Eggs soaked through your blouse and undergarment. I removed them and your shoes before I laid you down." His entire neck quivers this time, not just the vein.

The bitter coffee … Steve drugged it after all. Why would he do that? No … wait … he finished my cup himself, and he wouldn't do that if it were drugged, would he?

Steve says he still loves me. But I thought Jon loved me, and he's the one who probably injected me with experimental serum. I don't know who to trust anymore. I need to get out of here.

I try to sit up, but can't. My elbows are rubber, my legs, Play-Doh. Maybe Steve is worried I will try to run before his fellow agents get here. *Where would I even run to?*

"I called our medical team to confer. Dr. Luciente said the best thing for you is rest." Steve kisses my forehead.

My kitty hasn't let him get this close to me before without complaint. *Where's Gallo?* I try to say, afraid something might have happened to him. My words emerge as more grunting.

"Hush, Rosy. Everything will be okay, I promise. Let me go fix you some herbal tea." Steve leaves the bed.

Seeing him fully dressed is a relief.

A blur of fur leaps onto my chest. Gallo must have been shut out of the room.

I try to pet him, but somehow my hand keeps missing his body.

Gallo licks my nose.

It tickles a little and somehow puts me more at ease. I feel myself drifting off to sleep again.

CHAPTER 23

JON, AGE 43

… I follow my raving, rooms …

— OCTAVIO PAZ

Saturday, April 8, 2000, 2:00 PM
Steve's cabin
Boykill, NY

Overcast and humid, a gray pall hangs over the afternoon. Jon checks the final address on Vento's list of white vans registered in the area. He parks off to the side of the road and heads parallel to the long dirt driveway through the wooded lot. *Sara has to be there. She just has to.*

After a couple of minutes of hiking, he spots an older Ford van parked in front of a cabin. The plate matches the stolen one. Worn, wood shingles give the building the appearance of something out of a fairy tale, the one where the big bad wolf eats Grandma and Red Riding Hood.

There's a sudden tightness in his gut. *Did that psycho hurt Sara?*

Jon peers in the curtained window on the right side of the cabin. Beyond the kitchen area, a man sits on a sofa, his back to him. The blond buzz cut says it's most definitely Ranger. No one else occupies the small, square room.

He phones Vento to inform her of the correct location.

"You've got twenty minutes before our agents get there," she says. "Don't do anything stupid, García. Only fools rush in. Wait for the team."

He agrees. But he's already at the dwelling. *Couldn't hurt to look around outside some more.*

He goes to the rear of the cabin. There's a window, partly open, screen in place, with the shade drawn most of the way down. Through the bottom third, he can make out some furniture in the room, part of a dinged dresser, and the end of a bed. On the pilled blue blanket lies a familiar fluffy black lump—Gallo. The bumps under the blanket, next to his cat, have to be Sara's feet.

He calls to his wife.

No response from her, but his cat runs toward the window, stands on his hind legs. *"Mrow, Mrow, Mrow,"* he says.

"Quiet boy," Jon says. The window frame doesn't want to budge, probably old paint. He puts his weight into it. The window groans, but goes up. *Hope Ranger didn't hear that.* Using his pocketknife, he cuts away the screen.

Gallo flies out the opening, a flash of black fur.

"No, Gallo, come back," Jon calls.

But his cat disappears in the brush, running in the direction of the road.

Sara's going to kill me if I lose him. But he has to get his wife out first. He climbs in.

She's lying face up, her body at an odd angle.

"Mi luna," he says, leaning over her.

"Bad guy," she says. Her speech is slurred.

"It's me," Jon says. "I'm going to take you away from the bad guy. Are you hurt?"

It sounds like she says, "Wet noodles."

He pulls back the blanket and sees her bare breasts. "Shit, where's your shirt? Never mind. Everything's going to be okay now."

The bedroom door bursts open.

"Everything is already quite fine, Agent García," Ranger says. He trains his gun on Jon's face.

"Let's be reasonable, man. All I want is my wife."

"You had your chance and frittered it away. She wants to be with me now. Right, Rosy?"

"Who the hell is Rosy?" Jon says.

Sara says, "Cat attack," her speech fuzzy. Her eyes open and blink rapidly, then close.

"What did you give her?" Jon says. "If you hurt her, if you touched her, I'll kill you."

"You are in no position to threaten. I have a firearm pointed at your temple." Ranger cocks the piece for emphasis. "I assure you I am a skilled marksman. Join me in the other room, please. Hands over your head."

Jon has no choice. He raises his arms.

Steve steps back over the threshold into the main room and motions for Jon to follow. "Wait. Close the door behind you," Ranger says. "My lady needs her rest."

His lady—crazy bastard. He lowers his hand as if to close the door, but instead reaches back for his gun.

Ranger fires before Jon can take aim.

The bullet rips through Jon's right shoulder. He drops his gun, and it goes spinning along the polished floor into the kitchen area, out of reach. Adrenaline pumping, he hardly feels the wound as he lunges for Ranger's weapon.

Fighting to hold on, scrappy Ranger demonstrates impressive strength.

The gun goes off again. Wood dust rains down from the ceiling.

Jon bends Ranger's arm backward.

Ranger drops his weapon. It skitters under the couch.

While Jon watches the gun, Ranger gets a chokehold on him from behind.

Jon elbows Ranger in the solar plexus and stamps on the man's foot, breaking the hold.

As soon as Jon pivots to face him, Ranger lands an upper cut to his left cheek.

Man must be a prizefighter. Jon gouges Ranger's eyes, then boots him in the knee.

Ranger goes down screaming.

Jon wallops him with a few well-placed kicks.

Ranger's out cold.

Jon removes the double-density cable ties from his jeans pocket and binds his opponent's hands and feet. Battered and bloodied, the man's pale face seems angelic. *Bullshit.* This bastard abducted his wife. He stomps on the man's ribs once to teach him a lesson.

After he secures both his own and Ranger's weapons, he attends to his gunshot wound as best he can with the first-aid supplies he locates in the bathroom. At least the bullet went clean through.

~

Lips parted, wild hair fanned out, Sara, half-naked in Ranger's bed, looks vulnerable but sexy. *God, I'm a lucky man.* To think, he almost lost her.

He wraps Sara in the quilt. With difficulty and a fair amount of pain, he hoists her fireman-carry style. "I've got you, *mi luna*," he says.

She doesn't answer.

Whatever drug she's on must be a doozie. He'll rush her straight to the medical center.

~

Ranger's still on the floor, unconscious.

If Jon wasn't a professional, he would shoot the creep in the crotch for good measure. But he'd have to set Sara down to do that, and he doesn't want to let her go. Anyway, the bureau team should be there in no time. They can deal with this pussycat. *But where is my real cat?*

He strides through the woods with his wife hoisted over his good shoulder like a rolled-up carpet. "Gallo, here kitty, kitty." There is no sign of the cat.

Sara is going to be pissed when she finds out. But right now, he's got to get her medical attention. There is no time to spare.

CHAPTER 24

JON, AGE 43

… all crumble inside my blind skull …

— OCTAVIO PAZ

Saturday, April 8, 2000, 2:35 PM
Jon's car, County Road 17
Boykill, NY

a hard rain falls, slowing their escape. Jon is grateful he cleared Ranger's dirt drive before the sky broke open. He keeps checking the rearview mirror to see if Sara has woken up.

"Steve?" she says from the backseat. She sits up, rubs her eyes. The blanket slips down.

"Sara, thank God," Jon says. "Are you all right?"

She tugs the blanket up to cover herself. "Where's Steve?"

Great, I risk my neck rescuing her and she wants to know about the kidnapper. At least, her speech is clearer. "Your boyfriend put up quite a fight, but you're with me now. Don't worry."

"He's not my boyfriend. Not for a long time."

Jon's gunshot wound throbs. "You've been dating Ranger behind my back?"

"No. I'm not the one hiding things. Steve was my college boyfriend. I told you about him."

"You mean your Billy-Idol-wannabe boyfriend is Ranger? Well, that's quite the coincidence. You went with him willingly?"

"Asimov called it the 'Laws of possibility,'" she says. "But you've been playing me for a fool."

She has every right to be mad. He's been lying about being an agent, about his interactions with Candy, about his late-night and weekend stakeouts with Vento. But his jealousy gets the better of him. "What about you being half-naked? You've got some explaining to do."

"That's all you have to say to me?" She enunciates each word as if he is hard of hearing.

He sighs. *She's right.* "I have a lot to tell you, but not now. First, we have to get you medical attention."

"Medical attention? Is that your euphemism for shooting me up with experimental drugs?"

"You think I injected you?" he says.

"Who else? Stop the car and let me out." She smacks the back of his head over and over.

"It wasn't me." In the midst of her attack, he spies a navy-blue vehicle coming up fast. Too fast. *Damn it, Domestic's on my tail.* "But I'll tell you everything when I get you to safety. Stop hitting me. I've got to focus now."

She lays off for a second. "And what did you do with Gallo? You didn't put him in the trunk, did you?"

"Gallo, ah … sort of … ah … ran off. Don't worry, he'll find his way home."

"*Holy molé salsa,* you lost my kitty! How could you?"

"I had to move fast. Anyway, he's our kitty. Mine too."

The blue car zooms by, cuts him off.

Jon wrenches the wheel to avoid rear-ending the vehicle. His car screeches into oncoming traffic, missing a collision with a motor home by inches.

"Are you trying to kill us both?" Sara says.

"Got to get away from these guys." He slows way down to ready for a quick U-turn.

A second navy blue car comes up from behind. Rams them.

Jon holds tight but Sara slams into the back of his seat. "You okay?"

"No thanks to you," she says. Her lip is bleeding.

Before he has time to get out his handkerchief for her, the blue car rams them again. The force of the impact sends the car skidding across the road, doing donuts. *Shit.* He steers into the slide, but can't gain control. They careen into a gigantic oak. The passenger side folds in around the tree. The car's windows shatter on impact.

Jon staggers out, dazed and bleeding. "Sara." She's on the floor of the backseat, face down, broken glass all over her back. "Sara, *mi luna.*" She's not moving.

"Hey, cowboy," someone shouts.

A tall, skinny redheaded man barrels toward Jon from the blue car.

At least Bozo isn't armed. Jon reaches for his gun. Not there. He must have lost it in the crash.

The redhead bulldozes into him.

Winded, his shoulder blazing with pain, he can't raise his right arm to block. He punches with his left.

The redhead pummels his face.

This guy must be Ranger's sparring partner. Jon knees his attacker, but it doesn't stop him. *I have to save Sara.* He elbows the redhead's throat.

CHAPTER 25

JON, AGE 43

... better to be stoned in the plaza than to turn /
the mill that squeezes out the juice of life ...

— OCTAVIO PAZ

Saturday, April 8, 2000, 2:57 PM
Jon's car, County Road 17
Boykill, NY

*J*on, supine on the ground next to his smashed car, opens his eyes. His jaw aches, an open gash on his cheek stings, and his sore gut makes it difficult to breathe. He manages to stand.

Where is Sara?

The car's back door hangs open. The blanket is there, but she isn't.

The blue car that crashed into them is gone.

He tries to call out but his lungs don't cooperate. He coughs. *The redhead has her.* He failed Sara. *Again.*

CHAPTER 26

SARA, AGE 37

Sunday, April 9, 2000, 1 AM
Gentry Research Laboratory
Fishburg Falls, NY

The room, lit with buzzing fluorescent bulbs, smells something like pea soup with ham, but there is no food in sight. Nobody else is around either.

When I first woke, I thought I was in a real hospital. But my arms and legs are strapped to the bed, and an IV feeds neon-green fluid into my arm. It looks like the same stuff left in the hypo I found in our condo. My body feels battered. My mouth tastes like copper. *How did I get here, wherever here is?* The last thing I recall is Jon driving me somewhere for medical attention. *Holy molé salsa, how could my own husband do this to me?*

As if to answer, the Plain Grains Granola theme, the 'Call to the Cows' section of the "William Tell Overture," plays from a loudspeaker above my head .

A searing pain tears into me, akin to a dentist's drill hitting a nerve.

After the Plain Grains Granola theme ends, the *Berry Beary* jingle blasts. "Berry Beary knows the way, Berry Beary brightens your day …"

My body tingles all over. A pleasant sensation—oddly arousing.

The room pixilates like a bad TV signal.

TIME FLASH 3

YEARS 1994 & 1995 — THE PAST

Then I quit trying to phrase it, realizing that if time travel ever became widespread, English grammar was going to have to add a whole new set of tenses to describe reflexive situations—conjugations that would make the French literary tenses and the Latin historical tenses look simple.

— ROBERT A. HEINLEIN, THE DOOR INTO SUMMER

CHAPTER 27

SARA, AGE 32

Saturday, December 17, 1994, 8:45 AM
Shop More Supermarket
Floral Gardens, NY

"Clean-up in aisle three," a man's voice announced over the loudspeaker.

Clutching the handle of the Shop More grocery cart, I stumbled inside my body, as if I were falling— an odd, but familiar sensation, like vertigo. I pushed forward and stopped just shy of plowing into the Berry Beary Crunch display.

The Crunch bear wore a red *Star Trek: The Next Generation* command tunic and bore a striking resemblance to Captain Picard. All the cubs he juggled had Captain Kirk's face.

Distracted by the box, I couldn't remember what I'd come to the store to buy. I rifled through my down jacket pocket for a list, but came up empty-handed. Mother was an ardent list-maker, and I'd picked up her habit. Something felt wrong, something more than just forgetting my list. But what?

I scanned the shelves hoping to jog my memory. I saw something that stopped me dead. A short way down the aisle, a red-haired clerk in a white coat slit open a carton. I knew I'd seen that man twice before—when I thought I was dreaming.

So either I was dreaming again, or, as Steve had told me, I was actually traveling in time. How could I tell if any of this were real? And where in time was I?

A shopper in a white-collared, blue buttoned-down shirt turned into the aisle and stopped to stare at the shelves of breakfast cereal. "They all look the same to me," he said. "I don't know which to get." He looked a bit like the actor Kurt Russell. "What do you prefer?" His caterpillar brows knitted. Not only did he look like Kurt Russell, but he also resembled someone I knew. This man possessed the same sandy hair and strong jaw.

"Are you related to Dr. Gentry?" I said.

He smiled and wiggled abnormally long fingers as if playing air piano. "Well, my wife is a doctor too, but she works in clinical research. Do I know you?"

The resemblance—down to the huge hands—was striking. Only this man's face had not been distorted by a stroke. "You look like another doctor I know."

He smiled wide, revealing his enormous sparkling white teeth. That made me think of the wolf in Red Riding Hood. *The better to eat you my dear.* "My new ad is in this month's *PennyGiver*," Dr. Gentry said. He indicated a circular dated December 1994 in the child seat of his grocery cart.

A wave of nausea rolled in my belly. *It was April 2000, wasn't it?* I had just been in a laboratory with neon-green fluid being forced into my arm. The fluid must have made my consciousness travel back in time, to 1994 again, this time December instead of May. "You're Dr. Lance Gentry, aren't you?"

"You know a lot of people ask me for my autograph thinking I'm Kurt Russell," Dr. Gentry said. "You're the first person to ask me if I'm me. Nice, thanks." He held out his giant hand and I reciprocated. He glommed on. "What's your name, dear?"

"Sara," I said, when he finally let go.

"Well, Sara," he said, wriggling his thin fingers in the air again, "help me solve this cereal dilemma. What's good for me but 'tastes so good it shouldn't be'?"

Without thinking, I spun around and pointed to the Berry Beary Crunch display. My body moved as if not under my control. Dr. Gentry went over, took down two boxes, and held one out to me. "Brilliant choice!" he said. "You'll be wanting a box too, no doubt."

A sensation of pleasure, like a mild orgasm, washed through my body as the doctor thrust the cereal into my empty cart. Steve said cereal was my trigger. Shouldn't I have been beamed forward to my own time once I'd chosen to buy the Berry Beary Crunch?

Nothing happened. The scene didn't fade. I remained in the market. Maybe because I hadn't physically touched the cereal? Without saying goodbye to Dr. Gentry, I backed up my shopping cart, made a U-turn and sputtered around the corner. I had no idea why I was running, or where.

I glanced back and Dr. Gentry waved. The red-haired clerk, box cutter in hand, ambled toward me.

I abandoned the cart and made a beeline for the exit. My trusty Keds, the pair that eventually fell apart in the washing machine, carried me out through the parking lot onto Continental Street. Piles of sooty snow flanked the curbs. I zipped up my jacket against the nip in the air. Out of the corner of my eye, I spotted the redheaded clerk sprinting toward me.

I took off as fast as my legs could go. The apartment I shared with Jon before we'd bought the condo was six blocks up, four over. We didn't own cars then. We walked or took the subway everywhere. Life was simpler, happier.

When I arrived at the locked lobby door of the apartment building, I instinctively reached into my left pocket and pulled out a set of keys. Three flights of stairs to go. The redhead was nowhere in sight. I scrambled up the stairs.

CHAPTER 28

SARA, AGE 32

Saturday, December 17, 1994, 9:08 AM
Jon & Sara's first apartment
Floral Gardens, NY

I slammed into apartment 3-G winded, but relieved my thirty-two-year-old body wasn't as out of shape as I had always believed. I had to make things right. I thought of the line from *Slaughterhouse-Five*, "Everything was beautiful and nothing hurt."

Except things did hurt. What I was about to do to Jon. No Gallo to greet me. We didn't adopt a kitten until we moved to the Bayfront Long Island condo. Jon said Gallo had run away. I hoped my kitty would be okay. I'd have to search for him when I got back to my own future. That is, if I didn't wake up still strapped to a bed in a laboratory.

Our former apartment smelled like coffee and oranges. Jon's brown corduroy sofa occupied one wall and our bed another. Against a third wall, opposite a six-foot expanse of windows, stood tall bookcases and a small computer desk.

The vocabulary-a-day calendar hanging over the desk displayed the word *inculpate* for Saturday, December 17, 1994. The main definition: *blame*. The only person I blamed for the mess I found myself in was me. I chose to marry a man who put my life in danger. He couldn't love me anymore. *Maybe he never did.* I knew what I had to do, despite the fact that my last time flash to 1994 was what prompted Jon's early marriage proposal.

I switched on the Macintosh computer. It took a long time to boot up compared with its year 2000 descendent. I opened the word processing program, and the note seemed to write itself.

Dear Jon,

I can't marry you. I'm sorry but I know for certain we are not right for one another. Please don't try to find me or contact me. I am going far away to make this less difficult for both of us. I hope you never forget that you are a good man.

The printer huffed away for a while. I looked over the page and wondered whether it would have been kinder to hand write the note. What did kindness have to do with anything? I was making a new start, undoing my connection to a man who had betrayed me. I located a pen and automatically signed, "Love, Sara."

I had to leave Jon, quit my job at Domestic and get out of town fast. Since I couldn't recall my old office number, I picked up the corded phone and called information. The operator put me through to a recorded voice saying to leave a message or call back Monday after eight AM. After the beep I said, "Mr. Rosewater, this is Sara García—I mean Sara Bloom. Sorry to be doing this with no notice. I have a family emergency and need to leave town for a long while. I won't be coming back."

Not knowing how long I'd be able to stay in the past, I checked my wallet for cash. Only twenty-three dollars and some change. Without enough money to afford three meals a day, I'd be on yet another weight-loss plan—the penny-wise diet. *Unless ...* In the top desk drawer, I found my bank book.

I gathered up my toiletries from the bathroom. *Holy molé salsa.* The Sara I saw in the mirror seemed to smirk at me, her hair already dyed blonde—months too early.

I grabbed my suitcase from the closet shelf and began packing for the second time in as many days. *Why did I own so many striped sweaters?* Maybe to defy Mother, who always said horizontal stripes made me look wider.

In addition to the necessities, I added my love-worn copy *of Dr. Futurity.* Philip K. Dick was a visionary. Or maybe a time traveler.

Over the bookcase that held all my favorite titles hung a framed photo of

Jon and me from the day I moved in with him. Surrounded by my packing boxes, looking frazzled, our smiles beamed optimism. My chest tightened. Who can I trust if not you, *mi sol?*

I didn't want to believe Jon was capable of harming me, but he did. He took me to some research lab and dumped me there. And my rescuer Steve had drugged me. *Why?* Maybe to prevent me from calling Jon and giving away the location of the safe house. But my husband found us anyway. Nothing made sense. I didn't know if it ever would.

I had to stop thinking in circles and get out before the Jon of my past came back from wherever he was.

Down on the street, I checked for the redhead. He was nowhere in sight. I hurried anyway along the four blocks south to Continental and two blocks up to the bank. I withdrew all but one hundred dollars from my account. *A little something for a rainy day,* my grandma used to say.

Ready for my getaway, I scurried to the taxi stand by the subway exit. "Penn Station, please, and make sure no one is following us."

The driver regarded me in the rearview mirror. His eyes were dark as espresso beans.

"What did you do, that someone is chasing you?" The livery license listed his name as Tannen Libya.

"I'm undoing something, Mr. Libya," I said.

"Harder to undo than do," Libya said, "but not impossible." He sped along the boulevard. "A great philosopher of my people once said, 'Set not the chain of Fate upon thy foot. There is a way beyond this rolling sphere.'"

"What does that mean?"

The driver arched his eyebrows. "For you to ponder," he said. His Cheshire smile reminded me of Steve's.

CHAPTER 29

JON, AGE 38

… my shadow shatters and I gather the pieces …

— OCTAVIO PAZ

Saturday, December 17, 1994, 10 AM
Sara and Jon's first apartment
Floral Gardens, Queens, NY

The radiator hissed on but did little to keep up with the cold from drafty windows. Jon shivered as he removed his pea coat and tossed his gym bag into the corner. He'd showered at the sports club to save them from tussling over bathroom space. If they didn't get moving, they would be late for the matinee of *A Christmas Carol*. Seeing the Broadway musical had been her idea. *The things you do for love.*

Not many places to hide in a studio apartment, Sara had to be in the bathroom getting ready. Still in bed when he left to work out, she probably slept late.

She'd woken up at two AM, screaming in one of her nightmares, but couldn't explain the dream in any detail. Said she was running from a red-haired man who wanted to harm her. Sara had the oddest nightmares. Fortunately, they occurred less often the longer they were together.

His comforting Sara turned into lovemaking, slow and tender. Their passion for one another kept growing since they had first made love. He believed it always would.

He called to Sara and opened the bathroom door.

She wasn't in there.

He tried to remember their earlier conversation.

She hadn't mentioned any errands.

He checked the fridge door and found a to-do list tacked up under the *Yes, Way!* magnet. One item remained uncrossed—polish boots. Her knee-high lace-ups slumped in their usual spot by the entry.

So where could she be?

The red dress she planned to wear hung on a hook outside the closet. He appreciated how the slinky fabric hugged her curves.

She couldn't have forgotten about the play. They'd been planning this for weeks and had dinner reservations at Barbetta's, her favorite Italian restaurant.

He inspected the desk area. Sure enough, a printout had been taped to the frame of the Mac.

He swallowed hard as if that would make the words easier to digest. No matter how many times he read it over, the note didn't make sense. His confusion gave way to anger. *How could she up and leave him?* Maybe she had cold feet about getting married. The wedding planning involving his mother overwhelmed her, and she hadn't been keen on changing her hair color. But that was no reason to walk out. *With no discussion, no goodbye.*

This had to be a mistake. Or a bad joke. Or maybe, somehow, she'd found out about him lying to her about his work. She told him from the get-go that honesty was the most important thing to her in a relationship. But telling her the truth hadn't been an option.

He rummaged through papers on the desk. Nothing else of importance.

He checked all around. Her suitcase wasn't in the closet. He surmised from the disarray in her otherwise tidy drawers that clothes had been removed in a hurry. *Where would she go?*

He dialed her parents. *Thank goodness, Mr. Bloom answered.* Sara's mother, even sick with cancer, would have given him the third degree. "Hello, sir. It's Jonathan. Have you heard from Sara today?"

"No, son. She hasn't phoned. And I've told you, you can call me Dad or *Papá.*"

His *Papá* was gone and no one, not even Sara's wonderful father, could ever take his place. "I thought she might be stopping by to see you."

"If she is, she hasn't told us. And you know how Reya dislikes unexpected visitors, especially now."

"Well, if you hear from Sara, please give me a call." Jon hoped he sounded calmer than he felt. He didn't want to worry her father.

"There's something you're not telling me. You two had a fight, didn't you?"

Jon played it down. "A minor disagreement." But her not wanting to marry him, or be with him at all, qualified as major.

"And she's walked out, right? Learned that habit from her mother. She'll be back. Give her time to cool off."

"Okay sir ... I mean, Dad. I will. Can you think of anywhere she might go?"

"Reya gets herself a suite at the Ritz whenever we have a tiff. Relationships are give and take. You give, and you let her take. Buy Sara some carnations. Red. You should know they're her favorite. Begging her forgiveness wouldn't hurt either."

Jon was prepared to do more than plead. He would give her whatever she needed to stay—even reveal the truth about his undercover operation, if it came to that. "I'll phone you when she gets home. Or call me if she does drop by."

He hung up and immediately dialed information. "Ritz Hotel in Manhattan, please."

CHAPTER 30

SARA, AGE 32

Saturday, December 17, 1994, 10 AM
Penn Station
Manhattan, NY

Could I really change my past in a big way? I was going to find out.

The driver, Libya, remained quiet the rest of the cab ride, and traffic was mercifully light.

With Christmas a week away, the cold city streets bustled with shoppers. A Salvation Army Santa Claus jingled his large bell over a mock chimney donation box. Running away from my loved ones during the holiday season was far from ideal, especially with Mother in the final months of her life. But I needed a chance to get away and think about my options. What was possible with time travel?

The cab pulled up in front of the railway station. "Nobody followed us," Libya said. "I made sure."

Along with the fare, I added a generous tip. I'd have to watch my spending.

"One more piece of advice you should know," he said. "Same philosopher. 'Be not entangled in this world of days and nights; thou hast another time and space as well.'"

Gooseflesh rose on my arms. *Did he just allude to time travel?* Maybe he worked for Domestic. *No.* I was being paranoid. Tannen Libya was just another intelligent, over-qualified New York cabbie who had probably been a professor of philosophy in his own country.

~

The crowded rail station thrummed like a colony of ants with appointed undertakings.

I seemed to be the lone straggler wondering where to go. *Somewhere Jon couldn't find me.* Someplace no one would think to look for me.

The Maine coast was my favorite location on Earth. Did anyone know that in 1994? My brother Adam knew, but he died in 1978 and had never met Jon. Our family vacationed on the coast whenever Adam was well enough to go. The ocean waves rejuvenated us all.

That's why I had suggested Maine for a honeymoon trip with Jon when Domestic Global International surprised us with a week of paid leave after we eloped. He wanted to go to Hawaii, but booking a trip to the islands with only a week's notice proved impossible. We boarded the train for Rock Beach two days after we said *I do* at the courthouse. I felt like I was living in a fairy tale with my perfect prince of a husband, on my way to happily-ever-after.

The departure board updated with numbers cascading like somersaulting Chiclets. It just so happened that a train to Rock Beach via Boston would leave in fifteen minutes. I should have been amazed, but I was getting blasé about coincidences.

I looked around after I bought the ticket, wondering if Domestic could trace my Penrose wave signature into the past. I should have thought to ask Steve when I had the chance. *Too late.* Or too early depending on your vantage point. It was becoming impossible to keep all my timelines straight.

Maybe Mr. Libya wanted me to believe I had another destiny. Had I forged a new fate the moment I made a different choice—decided to leave that note and not marry Jon? Was I making a huge mistake? Time would tell. Or it wouldn't. All I knew was I still missed Jon, fool that I was. He would always be the love of my life.

I boarded the train and settled into a comfortable seat by a window. The car was clean, but smelled faintly of sour milk. Four other people, a family with two young children entered the car. They sat at the far end. I was relieved not to have to make idle chit-chat with strangers. I stared out as the urban landscape became more suburban, letting my mind disappear into the passing scenery.

~

I am at a party in someone's home, the living room lit with many small tea lights hanging from lanterns. I sit in the corner by a window. It's dark outside. I see my face in the glass. My dark hair is swept into a messy up-do. I have on a red satin cocktail dress.

I can see the party reflected in the window as well. A man who resembles John Lennon stands near me. His face is painted with a yin-yang symbol, but instead of black and white, it's yellow and white. I turn my head to get a better look, but he isn't there.

Instead, I glimpse my childhood friend Joanne Vento across the room. She is still pretty despite her short gray hair and the lines around her eyes. I call her name, but she doesn't hear me over the din of the guests.

I try to make my way to her, but it is difficult to maneuver through the crowd, which like a snake keeps twisting into my path. I lose sight of Joanne and spend hours wending my way through various rooms of the house searching for her.

Someone begins to sing in a language I don't recognize. His back is to me. He is tall, with short, dirty-blond hair and he wears blue jeans and a white shirt. The melody reminds me of Air Supply's "Lost in Love." I can make out two words—"Rock Beach." Someone taps my arm.

CHAPTER 31

SARA, AGE 32

Saturday, December 17, 1994, 7:30 PM
Rail Station
Rock Beach, Maine

"This is your stop, ma'am," the conductor said, nudging my arm. "Rock Beach, everybody off."

The strange dream ended, and I gathered my belongings and exited the train.

Already dark out, the sodium vapor street lamps glowed yellow. The salt air stung me to alertness. I trekked from the train station nearly a mile up the beach to the Low Tide Inn, where Jon and I had spent our honeymoon in my original past. The two-story building looked more decrepit than I remembered. I squeezed my way into the motel office cluttered with file cabinets and stacks of tourist brochures.

The desk clerk, an old man with bloodshot brown eyes and pointed chin, reminded me of pictures I'd seen of my paternal grandfather. He'd died long before I was born.

"Ever stay here before?" the clerk said. "You look familiar."

I couldn't give him the real answer. *I would have stayed here a few months from now, which is actually five years ago from my present, but since I changed my past I won't be coming then.* The answer, technically yes and no, I just shook my head.

He informed me that since all the single rooms were closed for remodeling, I'd get a double at the single rate. "And how long will you be with us?"

I wished I knew. "Till the day after Christmas," I said. It sounded reasonable. I paid cash for two nights in advance, grateful the clerk didn't ask me for any more information. I accepted the actual room key, not a plastic swipe card. Somehow, the metal object made everything feel more real.

In my room on the second floor, I unpacked my things. The decor appeared to be the same as the room I stayed in with Jon—coral-colored walls, floral bedspreads with matching curtains, and a leaning television set that looked like it would fall over if you sneezed. I felt lost, even though I knew where and when I was.

Could I really go through with this attempt to change my past? Questions about the man I love whirled in my head. *Had he seen my note? Was he looking for me? Did he hate me for leaving? Did he ever love me, and if so, when did he stop?*

To distract myself from unanswerable thoughts, I switched on the TV and flipped through the channels. On the three stations that came in I had my choice of a *Columbo* rerun with Jack Cassidy, news, or a show about making gingerbread houses. I couldn't pay attention to any of them.

I woke at twenty past nine. No dreams this time. I went in the bathroom to freshen up. The rumpled, blonde-haired Sara blinked back at me in the mirror. I had no idea what to do with this younger self, but I suddenly recalled Quinn Mallory's line in the TV show *Sliders*. *We have a plan—we just don't know what it is yet.*

In the coming days, if I really went through with this, I'd need to change my name and look for a new job. I wondered what it would take for the Social Security administration to let me change my number. At least Maine should be far enough away to keep Jon from tracking me down.

He could find another test subject to marry. Maybe I knew some of the others who'd been experimented on. Perhaps kids I went to school with, or even my ex-best friend Joanne. For a second, I pictured Jon getting together with Joanne. It did not compute. She was too hard-edged for him, bless her pure heart.

What is my next move? I could eat. I'd lost track, with travel across years, how many actual hours it had been since breakfast with Steve in my present. I knew of a reasonably priced diner three blocks up the street that served terrific lobster bisque. Jon and I ate there almost every day of our honeymoon.

Maybe coming to Maine wasn't the brightest idea since it would constantly remind me of Jon.

I wonder what would have happened if my husband hadn't kidnapped me away from the cabin. Steve, like Jon, turned out to be someone who betrayed me. *How could he drug me, not once but twice?* I cooperated with him. And he acted like he still loved me. He seemed genuinely sorry for giving me up in order to fly off to Europe for experimental treatment. We all have regrets. I just hoped changing my actions in 1994 wouldn't earn me any new remorse.

On the walk to the diner, my head crowded with more questions and fears about Gallo, Domestic Global, Jon, and Steve. I barely had the capacity to relish the crisp, star-filled sky and the swoosh of ocean waves. I'd walked a block past the restaurant by the time I discovered I'd gone too far.

The Rock Beach Diner's wall décor consisted of life preservers and lobster traps, as I'd recollected. The seasonal green plastic vases of fake holly that topped the tables were new to me.

A tall waitress approached. She had her silver-blonde hair done up in a high ponytail and wore a simple gold crucifix around her neck. Her name-plate pin read *Barb*. She may have waited on Jon and me during our honeymoon. I couldn't recall.

"One for dinner," I said.

"I've been there, hon." Barb pouted. "Don't worry, I'll treat you right. Who needs those bastards? We don't."

She sat me at a table for four behind the salad bar, but next to a window.

Possibly, she believed I'd appear less pathetic there than I would at a table for two. Or perhaps she thought the salad bar would deflect the pitying eyes of the couples who occupied the restaurant.

Grateful to be by the window, I observed the rushing whitecaps, visible under streetlights. I could lose myself staring at the water.

"Honey," the waitress said, breaking my reverie. "Give me a holler when you're ready to order." Despite her weather-beaten skin, she maintained a youthful, slim figure. With her short skirt and long legs, it was easy to picture her as head cheerleader back in high school.

"I already know what I want, Barb," I said.

She beamed. "Good girl. I like a woman who knows her own mind."

I waited for her to get out a check and start writing. When she didn't, I went ahead and ordered.

In less than a minute, she returned with a glass of house white wine and a bowl of bisque.

The soup, as delicious as my memory of it, likely totaled a thousand calories. *Take that, granola diet.* I no longer needed to diet anyway—no more anniversary dress to fit into. *No more anniversary.* So why did I still feel guilty about eating?

Barb brought a second glass of white as soon as I took the last sip of the first. "Two for one." She winked and bounced away before I could protest.

Twice the calories. Yet, Steve wanted me the way I was. *The way I am.* The way I will be. *Oh, hell.* I gave up trying to figure out tenses and swilled the wine.

Barb plopped a dessert topped with a generous dollop of whipped cream right in front of me. "Best sweet potato pie you'll ever eat," she said. "We make everything fresh here on the premises." She winked again. "Free pie after nine."

The universe conspired to give me bigger hips. "Thanks, Barb," I said, "but I'm stuffed."

She frowned. "Watching your figure?" She didn't wait for my answer and plowed on. "You don't need to worry about weight. You're like Sophia Loren. Voluptuous. And that gentleman over there has been watching your figure since you came in." She swung her ponytail, and I followed its trajectory to a table by the restroom sign.

A man sat alone at a table for two, his profile masked by the oversized coffee mug. He was tall and clean-cut with sandy, close-cropped hair.

"He's a cutie," Barb said. "Fix you up?"

"A guy is the last thing I need right now."

She struck her hands to either side of her waist, elbows out. "A little flirting never hurt anyone."

Before I could protest further, she strolled across the room and tapped the man on the shoulder. She pointed to me.

I wanted to slide under the table.

The man rose and lifted his bomber jacket off the back of the chair.

Dressed in blue jeans and a white buttoned-down shirt, it was as if he'd stepped right out of the dream I had on the train. He headed toward me.

My heart pounded the way a landlord's does on rent day.

I knew him.

CHAPTER 32

JON, AGE 38

... I fall to the depths, invisible path ...

— OCTAVIO PAZ

Saturday, December 17, 1994, 6 PM
Wishing Well Pub
Manhattan, NY

*A*t his booth in the corner, Jon downed his second double shot of scotch, then signaled to the bartender for a third. *Where was she?*

The 34th Street Pub, just down the block from Macy's department store, bustled. Patrons bellied up to the wooden rail with two or three shopping bags. The jukebox had been belting out Christmas music for the entire half hour since Jon arrived.

Vento galumphed through the door as "Fool on the Hill," Jon's pick, came on. Her puffy, white winter coat made her look like a polar bear. "What am I doing here, García?" she said, nostrils flaring. "I finished my Christmas shopping before Thanksgiving."

That didn't surprise him. She came from an enormous Italian family with lots of kids, little cousins, nieces and nephews to buy presents for. His partner was the picture of efficiency. "What did you get for me?" he said.

"Same as last year. Soap on a rope. You didn't drag me across three boroughs to ask me that." She rocked up and down on her boot heels.

"Would you mind standing still or at least sitting? You're making me dizzy."

Vento shrugged off the polar bear coat and sat. "How many of those have you had?"

The bartender delivered the new drink and scooped up several dollars from a pile on the table. He asked Vento what she wanted.

"Iced tea, no lemon, no straw," she said.

"Thanks for coming," Jon said. "You're a pal."

"All your Brooklyn drinking buddies have prior engagements? Never mind. I'm here. You look like soggy paper towels."

Jon had no idea what that meant, but it didn't sound pleasant. He handed Sara's note to his partner. "My girlfriend's gone," he told her. He studied Vento's bland expression as she read. She had the best poker face he'd ever seen. He and the other guys always lost their shirts to her at bureau card game nights.

True to form, her face gave away nothing. Without saying a word, she pushed the paper across the table, through a puddle of condensation.

Jon rescued the note and waved it in the air to dry it. "Well?" He hoped Vento could shed some light on the workings of the female mind.

"Tough luck," she said.

The bartender arrived with her tea, lemon wedge on the rim, straw poking up out of the ice.

Vento lifted the yellow fruit as if removing a dead mouse and set it on her napkin.

"I'm buying," Jon said, indicating the stack of dollars next to his glass.

The bartender took a dollar and left.

"But why would she do this to me?" Jon said. "Everything was going well. My mother's already invited all our relatives to the wedding."

Vento extracted the straw from her drink and looked at Jon through it. "Those two words— 'my mother'— could be a clue."

"Sara and my mother aren't chummy. No woman would be good enough for me in *Mamá*'s eyes. But that can't be the reason."

Vento discarded the straw next to the lemon. "Maybe your fiancée ran off with another man. It happens."

"Jesus!" *So much for reassurance.*

"Holy Mother of God," Vento said, smacking her palms together. She looked up at the fissure-tile ceiling and said, "Forgive this blasphemer for taking your son's name in vain."

"Sorry," he said. "But what am I supposed to do? I could ask Dan Davis in the 110th to put out an APB. We went to the academy together and he owes me a favor."

"She's not an escaped convict or a missing person. She left of her own accord. Are you telling me you had no warning?"

Jon thought for a moment, but came up empty. Her parting words as he went off to the gym had been, 'I miss you already, *mi sol*.' "We had sex this morning."

"I didn't need to know that." Vento gulped half the iced tea. "I don't see how I can help."

"But you're a woman. Have you ever walked out on a man?"

"Never let it get that far. I told you when you joined the bureau, undercover work kills relationships. All the secrecy destroys trust. Besides, you told me you were a confirmed bachelor. It's better that way, with the work we do."

"That's how I felt until I met Sara. Do you know why I came here?"

Vento tapped her fingers on the tabletop, but didn't ask the question.

Jon answered anyway. "This is where we first kissed. Right outside that door."

"García, you're a hopeless romantic, emphasis on hopeless."

"Sure, kick a guy when he's down," he said.

"Look, I'm not trying to make you feel worse."

Could have fooled me. "Maybe I shouldn't have bothered you." He stared into his shot glass as if it were a crystal ball. No visions came.

After Jon's jukebox selection ended, Bing Crosby crooned "White Christmas." Several patrons sang along at top volume, off-key.

Vento craned her neck to watch some drunks muddle through the song. "Ruining a classic," she said. "Maybe Sara discovered you've been lying to her about your job."

"I don't see how. Nobody knows outside the bureau. Unless you told her."

"You haven't introduced me to your girlfriend."

"Fiancée." He downed his drink. "Haven't you ever been in love, Vento?"

"We weren't talking about me," she said. "But, in fact, I have been in love, a couple of times."

"What happened, if you don't mind my asking?"

"I do mind. One died. The other never seemed to notice I was alive."

"I didn't mean to bring up bad memories."

"Seems to me that's all love is." She wiped her hand on the edge of her napkin.

"Could you … I mean, you are a woman … please help me figure out a way to get her to come back?"

"Be realistic. She said it was over. Besides, you have a job you can't tell anyone on the outside about. Your life could be in danger every day. She doesn't need your kind of trouble." Joanne squinted at him. "My friend, spare her."

"I never take my gun out of its holster," Jon said. "The biggest danger I've faced since starting the undercover operation at Domestic is a paper cut."

She glugged the tea. "You're missing my point. If you want to get married, go get an actual desk job. Your girlfriend fell in love with an accountant."

"I'd walk away from the bureau in a heartbeat if that would bring her home."

Vento patted his arm. "You've got it bad. I'm sorry, García. I really am. Maybe she'll change her mind. But if not, you need to let her go. You can't force someone to love you." She extracted her wallet from the puffy polar bear coat. "Let me reimburse you for the drink."

"Nah, I got it." It hadn't been the pep talk he expected, but at least she listened. "I appreciate your coming all the way here for me."

"You're welcome," she said, "but now you're leaving with me."

"Where to?" A new case would at least be a distraction.

"The movies. I have two tickets to a private preview screening of *Mixed Nuts* with Steve Martin. My cousin's a friend of one of the producers."

"But what if Sara tries to call the apartment? Or comes home, and I'm not there?"

"A couple of hours won't make any difference. If she wants you, she'll wait."

Even funny man Steve Martin wouldn't be able to lighten his heart, but he went with Vento. *Might as well kill some time until Sara comes back.*

CHAPTER 33

SARA, AGE 32

Saturday, December 17, 1994, 10 PM
Rock Beach Diner
Rock Beach, Maine

From across the diner, my brother's best friend, the boy I had a crush on all my teenaged years and then some, sauntered toward me. My pulse fluttered at the sight of his exotic green eyes.

"Sara Bloom," he said. "The squirt's all grown up. And gone blonde."

"Daniel Astrella," I said, "I would know you anywhere."

His thick, shag hairstyle was no more. The forehead creases hadn't been there a few days ago, when I time traveled to my childhood. Maybe the years were not as kind to him as they could have been.

Danny pulled out a chair and sat next to me. He combed his finger through his crew cut. "I'm surprised you recognized me."

"You look the same," I said.

"You look different. Last time I saw you was at our high school graduation—I mean mine and your brother's. How old were you then, thirteen, fourteen? Well on your way to becoming a babe. But now, I mean, holy shit."

Being given a compliment by the cutest boy in the world made me feel thirteen again. But he was wrong. "Adam's funeral was when we last saw each other."

"That's right." He rested a hand on my arm. "Sorry … thinking of happier times. I still miss him. Always will."

"I never got to thank you for being such a good friend to my brother. Especially when he was so sick. I don't know how he would have gotten through any of it without you."

"Adam was a good friend to me too. The only one I had who didn't expect me to be someone else, ya know. I was far from being a brain and too damn clumsy to be a jock. Adam accepted me for me—a shy, dumb klutz. Everyone else thought I was stuck up or something."

It never would have occurred to me, with his good looks and impressive physique, Danny was introverted or unathletic. Or that he felt self-conscious about his intelligence.

His leg pressed into mine.

On purpose? Every cell of my body enflamed. I hoped it didn't show on my face. "You're a long way from Woodward," I said.

"So are you, Blondie." He smiled.

I felt my face flush at the new nickname. "What brings you to Rock Beach?" I tried to sound casual.

His smile evaporated, and he took a moment to answer. "I worked as a salesman. Office equipment. Down East was my territory."

"Was?"

"A long story. Maybe I'll tell you some time." Danny took his hand off my arm.

I noticed his wedding band and felt unexpectedly bereft. "I'm surprised to see you out alone on a Saturday night. Where's your wife?"

Danny coughed. "Did you hear I got married?"

I tapped his ring.

He twisted the gold band for a few seconds.

"Well, that's done with," he said, "but the ring is stuck. Divorced. No kids. Then I relocated up here from Queens. Wanted to make a clean start of it, ya know. How 'bout you? Why's a babe like you all alone, hiding behind the salad bar?"

I had to look away from his smile for fear of melting. I could have been truthful, said I traveled back in time from the year 2000. Said that I undid my marriage because my husband worked for an evil corporation doing experiments on me in the future. But I didn't want Danny to think me a whacko.

"I'm newly single too," I said, and as I did, a deeper sadness washed over me. Even sitting next to the beautiful guy I had a crush on during my formative years, I couldn't stop missing Jon.

"Tough break," Danny said.

Barb came over with two mugs and poured us each some coffee. "Let me get another fork. You two should share the pie." She patted Danny on the shoulder.

"Sounds good," he said and poured some half and half into his coffee.

I watched the ribbons of cream swirl until they blended in.

Barb returned with the fork and a third wink. I was beginning to think she had a nervous tic like Steve's.

Danny scooped up some pie on his fork and held it out in front of my lips. His eyes glinted. "Give it a try, Blondie," he said.

Feeling awkward, I took the bite.

Danny set down the fork. His face tensed as he watched me chew and swallow.

His scrutiny made me nervous.

"Okay?" he said.

"Delicious."

His face relaxed, and he stuffed a gargantuan piece into his mouth. "Tell me about you," he said, chewing. "Are you working here? Odd time of year for a beach getaway."

Not wanting to lie, I tried to give an answer that was at least part of the truth. "My fiancé and I worked in the same office in New York. Since I broke off the engagement, I had to quit my job. Came here for a change of scenery, and to figure out what to do next. In fact, I arrived a couple of hours ago."

"Lucky for me," Danny said. "I could use a friendly face."

"Such a coincidence running into you," I said. "I'm thinking of a line from *Casablanca*, 'of all the gin joints, in all the towns, in all the world ....'"

"Coincidences mean you're on the right path. Someone famous said that."

I wondered who he meant. "There have been other coincidences in my life too."

Danny's green eyes lit up like go on a traffic signal. "Oh yeah, like what?" He shoveled more pie into his mouth. "Name some coincidences."

Holy molé salsa—he ate like a horse chomping oats and still looked sexy. "I crossed paths with my college boyfriend the other day, and today I'm running into someone from my childhood." *Not just someone—my first crush.*

I kept that to myself. And the fact that he was dressed exactly like the man with his back to me in the dream I had on the train.

Danny frowned. "I hope you kept running from the college boyfriend. But you can stay put now that you found me."

I laughed.

Barb returned. "Looks like you two are hitting it off," she said. "Call me cupid."

"Cupid," Danny said.

"We knew each other when we were kids," I said.

"Well isn't that something!" She slapped her thigh. "Small world. Now, I'm not trying to break up this reunion, but can I get you anything else?"

"No thanks," I said.

"The check," Danny said. "Put hers on mine. I'll take care of us both."

"A true gentleman," Barb said before she went away.

"I can't let you buy me dinner," I said.

"Least I can do to thank you for keeping me company for dessert. Besides, I ate all your pie." He grinned.

I told him the pie was a gift from Barb.

She returned, set the check next to Danny and refilled both our coffee cups. "Take your time," she said. "Life is short and love is long."

"My Grandma used to say that too," I said.

One more wink at me, then Barb disappeared into the kitchen.

"What do you want to do now?' Danny said. He rubbed his leg against mine again.

He had to be stretching his long legs, not coming on to me. My skin tingled. "I worked as an accountant in New York. I guess I'll stick with that or bookkeeping."

He laughed. "I meant, what do you want to do with me right now? But I'll bite. Tell me more about being an accountant."

"Know what's more boring than an accountant?" I said.

"What?" he said.

"A talkative accountant."

He chuckled. "Okay, let's go back to your place. We don't have to do any talking."

I almost fell off my chair. Daniel Astrella, the cutest boy in the world, grown up impishly handsome, just made a pass at me. Joanne would have been jealous. She too pined for him long ago.

"My place is a room at the Low Tide Inn."

"Perfect." He stood, dropped two twenties on the table and grabbed his jacket. "Let's go."

He helped me put on my coat before he donned his own. As we headed for the door, I glimpsed Barb giving me two thumbs up.

～

Outside in the frigid night, Danny put an arm around my shoulders to direct me through the parking lot.

The evening seemed more like a dream than real life. But there was no denying the sensation of his closeness. Things felt even more surreal when he stopped in front of a white Ford Escort.

What happened to the Firebird Trans Am? He must have seen the question on my face.

"Need to keep a low profile," he said. His words rose in the cold air like smoke.

Maybe he was running out on alimony. "My motel is only a few blocks." I pointed. "We could walk."

"I need to keep my wheels close by. In case I have to make a quick getaway."

He had to be the love 'em and leave 'em type. "Quick getaway from me?"

He smacked his forehead. "Oh, sorry. I didn't mean I'd run from you. You're the first person in a long time I can really talk to."

But what if he wanted to do more than converse? I needed to be honest with him. "Thanks, but I don't want to lead you on. I just got out of a …" I paused to keep myself from saying marriage. "… engagement. I'm not ready for—"

"Don't worry." He patted my shoulder. "I'm not that easy."

Someone's mucous-y cough covered up the hyena-giggle that escaped my throat.

Danny spun on his heels to see who it was.

An older man, bundled in a puffy brown coat, lumbered by smoking a cigarette. He kept walking and hacking.

"Could have been me," Danny said. "I quit smokes for good." He unlocked the passenger side door and ushered me in.

I sat down on top of something rigid, then lifted it out from under me. Another book I knew, like the one in his car the first time I traveled to the past.

Danny started the engine. The radio blasted a few bars of Nirvana's "About a Girl" before he lowered the volume.

"I read *In Search of Schrodinger's Cat* years ago," I said, holding up the tattered hardcover.

"Oh, I'm done with it. Not much new there. Toss that in the back, but if you see something you like, grab it." He switched on the overhead light.

I turned to toss the hardcover. The rear bench, stacked high with books, looked like a library return cart. I recalled Steve's cabin in the woods without a single volume. It suddenly occurred to me Jon might have killed Steve before he kidnapped me. But if Steve was right about the way time travel worked, maybe that version of 2000 had already vanished. I needed to keep moving forward. Nothing else I could do. Though *forward* meant back in time for me.

"Something wrong?" Danny said. "It's a mess. Sorry."

I studied the titles. "Are those all physics books?"

"Most of them. A few on sports and the stock market. But time travel is a special area of interest for me."

I felt the blood drain from my face. Maybe Domestic sent Danny back in time to capture me. Before I could decide whether to bolt from the Ford, the car peeled out of the parking lot.

He drove like lightning. *So much for his low profile.* We arrived at the motel in seconds.

CHAPTER 34

SARA, AGE 32

Saturday, December 17, 1994, 10:30 PM
Low Tide Inn
Rock Beach, Maine

anny squealed the tires turning too fast into the Low Tide Inn. He parked the car in a dark corner of the lot and hopped around to the passenger door.

Was Danny a bad guy too? Would I ever be able to fully trust anyone again? Even people I thought I knew? But if ever I needed a friend it was now.

"Hey, you look like you've seen a ghost," he said. "You okay?"

"Too much wine, I guess."

"I can carry you to the room," he said. "I'm stronger than I look."

He looked damned strong. I told him I could walk and led the way up the stairs to my room. If he planned to kidnap me like Jon did, he could have kept on driving past the motel. I hesitated outside the door to the room. *Should I let Danny in?*

"I'll go in first and make sure it's safe," Danny said.

"Why wouldn't it be safe?"

He took the key from me. "I'm going to leave the door open, but you wait out here till I give the word." He flipped on the light. He checked under each bed and between the drapes. He examined the lamps, television, and mini-fridge. He perused the wastebasket. He unscrewed the phone then put it back together. He opened the dresser drawers, one by one. He rifled through my underwear and clothes. He went into the bathroom. When he came back out, he waved me into the room.

"All clear," he said. "Sorry to make you wait in the cold. Come warm up." He held his arms open.

I stepped into the room and into his embrace. He being so much taller than me, my face pressed against his chest. I inhaled his gasoline and seashore scent. A second before I had wondered if he was a bad guy working for Domestic Global. But in his arms, my chaotic thoughts calmed. The world became his fragrant skin, his heartbeat, our breathing.

He rubbed my back up and down as if trying to start a fire.

It worked.

"Better?" he said.

"Um hmm."

He helped me out my coat. "Two beds. Are you staying here alone?"

What would Jon think of me being with Danny? Jon would never know because he was out of my life forever. "Just me." I dropped to the bed near the window.

Danny plopped on the opposite bed. "Good. Nice place."

"What were you looking for?" I said.

"Bugs," he said.

"Cockroaches?" I said, disturbed by the notion.

"The listening kind of bugs. I needed to be sure."

Danny was more paranoid than me. "Are you in some kind of trouble?"

"Maybe, but nothing illegal. At least not on my end." He sighed. "I should be okay here for a while. I didn't find anything."

"What kind of trouble?"

He scratched his chin. "Hard to talk about. Maybe I'll tell ya tomorrow."

"Why tomorrow?"

"If you don't mind, I'd like to stay here tonight. I'm currently between digs. Been going through hell these past few weeks—years—weeks."

I wanted to tell him I'd been going through hell too. He seemed genuine. But then so had Steve. And I never caught on to Jon's betrayal and lies. "I'm sorry," I said.

"I don't know who to trust anymore," he said. "I can trust you, Sara, can't I? I mean I watched you grow up."

"I hope we can trust each other. I could use a friend right now myself."

The truth of my own words caught in my throat. I felt like sobbing again, but managed to hold it off.

Danny patted the pillow.

I moved to the foot of his bed, instead of next to him. If he took me in his arms again, I would have broken down.

"Don't be shy, squirt. I don't bite." He wiggled his eyebrows up and down. "Much."

I stayed put.

"Hey, I've got some brews in the trunk. I'll be back in a sec." He grabbed his car keys and went out without his jacket.

I could have locked the door and been rid of Danny. But if he had some evil plan in mind, would he run out for beer? Maybe. Common sense was not his strong suit.

Before I made up my mind, he was back. He secured the door behind him, set the chain, and snapped the drapes shut.

After I declined a can, he helped himself to one from the case and stowed the rest in the mini-fridge. He popped open the beer and took a long swallow. "That's better," he said.

If Danny were involved with Domestic, I needed to know. I screwed up my courage. "You mentioned you've been reading books on time travel. How did you get started on the subject?"

"Long story." He raised one eyebrow. "Why do you ask?"

"I'm kind of into the subject myself," I said.

"How so?" He squinted as if he needed to concentrate on my answer.

"This is going to sound crazy, but I traveled back in time from the year 2000."

Danny slammed the can down on the nightstand. Beer sprayed out. He stood and pointed an accusing finger at my face. "Who are you working for?"

His anger took me by surprise. "I'm an accountant like I said. I work for myself. But I'm being experimented on by Domestic—"

"Domestic Global Tobacco?"

"Domestic Global International. My husband works there. He injected me with a mind-control serum that caused me to travel back in time."

Danny sank to the bed, deflated. "Wild story," he said in a low voice.

I leaned forward. "I thought I was going insane myself. But it's true. This is the past for me. I've lived 1994 before."

Danny gulped some more beer. "You're married? I thought you said you broke the engagement."

I had just told him I was a time traveler and he wanted to know about my marital status. *Strange priorities*. Like Steve wanting to know about my blonde hair. "I am, I was married in my present, the year 2000." I said. "But I traveled back here to this time and broke up with Jon." My voice cracked. "We won't be getting married now."

"I see," Danny said, not looking at me. "Any kids?"

A pang of pain. "None." I didn't mention the baby I had lost. No point.

"Me neither. I wanted kids, my wife didn't." He held the beer can chest high but didn't drink.

"Danny, do you believe me?"

He looked up at me. "If you are working for Domestic, either I can take you out, or I'm screwed. And I've already been pretty screwed."

"How do you mean?"

He swigged from the can, then crushed it. "I've been back and forth in time like a friggin' boomerang."

If he was a victim of the same experiment, he had to be a good guy. I felt a surge of hope. "Domestic experimented on you too?"

His forehead lines deepened. "Had to quit smoking."

"What does smoking have to do with anything?"

"Every time I reached for a pack of smokes, boom, off I went, back in time."

"Oh, the same thing happens to me with breakfast cereal. Hey, you didn't smoke back when we were young."

"Hid it well. Never smoked in the Firebird, or around parents. And your brother Adam gave me a hard time. He hated your mother's cancer sticks and didn't like mine much either. Once he got really sick, I stopped smoking around him altogether."

"Thank you for doing that. You know, I almost saw Adam when I first time traveled. I would have liked to say some things I never got to as a kid. But I did see you."

"Yeah, what was I doing?" Danny smiled again, and his wrinkles disappeared.

"You gave me and my grandma a ride home from the grocery store."

"A regular boy scout," Danny said.

My thoughts flashed to Steve swearing scout's honor back at the cabin and then drugging me. I'd be more careful around Danny. "What happened to you, when you went back in time?"

"Which time?" he said. "This is my eleventh ... no, my twelfth trip."

"Wow. This is my third, I guess."

"It took me three trips back to make the connection between the smokes and the time travel. Once I figured it out, I tried to quit smoking cold turkey in the past. I was a mess."

"But if you quit at a younger age, when you returned to your present, weren't you a nonsmoker?"

"Nah. Always went back to the smokes. What can I say? I'm weak." He kicked off his shoes and swung his legs up onto the bed.

I fought the ridiculous urge to take his feet in my lap and rub them. "What year is it in your present?"

"Two thousand, same as you. This is my last trip back though. I am going to stay here and live my life over all the way through."

"Can you do that? I mean, won't someone from Domestic come after you?"

He tossed me a pillow. "Get comfortable. Lay down by me."

Is he avoiding my question? I crossed my legs under my body and hugged the pillow to my lap. "You said you'd been pretty screwed. What did you mean?"

"What do you know about Domestic Global?" he said.

"I worked as an accountant at Domestic Global. That's where Jon and I met. When I left to start my own business, he stayed on. I suppose he secretly helped with their illegal research all along."

Danny slapped his thigh. "That's rough. I'd like to beat the crap out of your ex-husband."

"I don't want to believe Jon did this to me. But he's the only one who could have given me those injections in our own home. A special agent rescued me and confirmed Jon was working with Domestic's illegal research team."

"Sara, how do you know your so-called rescuer wasn't lying? What if he was a Domestic flunky too? That company has more tricks than a five-dollar hooker."

His analogy startled me. It must have shown on my face.

"Sorry. Excuse my language."

"My rescuer was someone I knew back in college. Actually, the ex-boyfriend I mentioned earlier. And he told me everything he knew about the experiment."

"The best way to fool someone ..." he paused and looked away from me at the crushed beer can on the nightstand, "is to tell him the truth."

"What do you mean?" I wondered if I should tell Danny about Steve drugging me.

"The third time I went forward to 2000, I ran into an old girlfriend. She told me she'd come to rescue me and keep me from getting my brain fried." He massaged his temples.

"Do you have a headache?"

"Nah. Anyway, the chick was a corporate whore. She slipped me a Mickey and dragged me back to a lab. They did some *Clockwork Orange* shit to me with cigarette ads and jolted my nuts with electricity." He laid a hand on his crotch. "That's how I figured out the experiment had to be a cigarette brand thing."

"The last time I saw my husband, I ended up in a lab too. I had to listen to cereal jingles while my jaw felt like a giant walnut getting cracked."

"Sorry you had to go through all that, Sara. But how do you know for sure your college boyfriend was on the level?"

"Everything he said made sense. Like that the drug was supposed to make buyers feel good when they bought Domestic products. And how the Penrose waves were activated in certain brains because of radiation leaking from power transfer stations. Like the one where we grew up."

"Yeah, I've been trying to read up on the science behind it. Candy told me stuff along those lines too."

The hair on my arms stood on end. "Candy? I've got a neighbor named Candy Starr. In my present, I mean."

"Candy Starr, my old girlfriend, that's the corporate whore." He whistles. "You know her?"

"Red hair, huge boobs, wears clothes that would be tight on a toddler?"

He laughed. "And a southern accent that comes and goes."

"I wondered if my husband was having an affair with Candy. But I never imagined the two of them worked together. She didn't seem smart enough to be a spy."

"Good actress. And she would screw a fly if it had a big enough dick. Pardon my French. What about your college friend, Steve? Are you sure he wasn't playing you?"

No sense holding back. "I think Steve drugged me a couple of times. Once on the way to the safe house, and once there. I thought I could trust him."

"Don't feel bad." He leaned forward to put his hand on my knee. "I got taken in too. It's just corporate America fucking with us, finding new ways to force us to buy more of the shit they want us to buy. And years earlier too, thanks to time travel."

Instead of feeling comforted by his words, I was spooked. He could have been lying to me with the truth too, like Steve. "Danny, how on Earth can we trust each other? I mean, maybe you're telling me you're a time traveler to trick me."

"I think we need to decide to believe in each other or not. And I have a good feeling about you, Sara. You're genuine, ya know. So am I."

"I've been fooled before. It scares me how easily."

"I would never do anything to hurt my best friend's kid sister." Danny removed his hand from my knee. "But if you want me to leave right now, say the word, and I'm gone."

Looking into his ocean eyes, I felt lost at sea. I couldn't make up my mind.

He got up and went to the bathroom. The sound of water followed.

I stood and paced.

Danny came out and grabbed his bomber jacket. "Nice seeing you," he said in a low voice. "Good luck doing this on your own, Squirt."

My indecision hurt him. Maybe I was making the wrong choice, but I didn't want to be on my own. "Don't go," I said.

Danny turned toward me, moved in close.

If he wanted to kiss me, I didn't know if I would stop him.

He mussed my hair. "Two heads are better than one. Maybe we can beat this thing." He went to the door. "I'll get my bag. Be right back."

Why didn't he get his bag when he got the beer? I watched him propel downstairs, go to his trunk, and then run back up.

"Presto," he said, "I came back before you changed your mind." He held out the bag to me. "You can search it if you want."

"I have a good feeling about you too," I said. "I don't need to rifle through your undies—even though you gave mine the once over."

He dropped his duffel on the desk, then put his arms around me. His seashore-gasoline smell hypnotic, he stared into my eyes. He really was going to kiss me—the kiss I wanted long ago, the kiss that would have changed my life.

"You're a good kid," he said. He let go of me and went for something in his bag.

Holy molé salsa—kid! At the restaurant, he called me a "babe."

"I'm gonna get ready for bed, unless you want to go first," he said.

I couldn't let him go without asking. "Why do you keep traveling in time if you know your trigger is a certain brand of cigarettes?"

"You'd know if you were ever a smoker."

"Why not stick with the Domestic Global brand, stay planted in your life?"

"Domestic's brand tastes moldy. And quitting smoking's a bitch." Danny tapped his forearm as if he were feeling for a vein. "I was afraid I'd get addicted to something harder than nicotine. Plus those damn smokes are everywhere. Every time I bumped into a butt or an empty pack, zip, off I went into the past."

"But you've quit now," I said. "I haven't seen you light up. Are you on the nicotine patch?"

"Patch didn't work for me. But I've licked the habit for good now. Behavior modification therapy. The nicotine craving doesn't make me want to light up any more. It makes me horny."

"This is a nonsmoking room," I said, wondering if he understood my double entendre.

He smiled. "Guess you're safe." He went back into the bathroom.

I felt guilty for doubting his intelligence.

The shower came on.

I sat in the wing chair and tried to watch TV, but Conan O'Brien reminded me too much of the red-haired supermarket clerks. I had a terrible thought. Maybe Candy was *Red Cross* and she had stuck me with the hypos. Not Jon. What if Jon had no idea Candy did that to me, and he was innocent? But Steve said Jon worked with the female operative, so he had to know. Plus, Jon dumped me off in the research lab.

I felt like curling into a ball. I wanted Danny to tell me everything would be better from that point on. No more Domestic experiment. No more redheads. *If only Danny would hold me and help me forget.*

At the safe house in 2000, I kept avoiding Steve's affections. I never forgave him for dumping me. And I wasn't even close to being over my love for Jon. So why did I wish for Danny's kiss? It could only make things more complicated.

"Your turn in the bathroom." Danny had stripped down to boxers.

I tried not to stare at his Chippendale physique. "*Thanks,*" I said, but the word came out as an incoherent grunt. I tried again but my mouth couldn't say words—just like what happened when I was with Steve. Panicked, I motioned to my mouth and grunted some more. At least this time, I could move.

"Choking?" he said.

I mimed locked lips.

"I know what this is." He took my hands in his. "It happened to me. It's minor. A side effect of time travel."

It didn't feel minor. I wanted to scream, but couldn't. If this was a side effect of time travel, maybe Steve hadn't drugged me after all.

"This goes away." Danny guided me to the bed. "Happened to me twice and hasn't happened since. Remember, I've been at this longer. I'm peachy. You will be too."

Despite my fear of permanent brain damage, Danny's sureness calmed me.

He stroked my cheek. His skin was rough, but his touch gentle. "Don't worry, Blondie. I'm here for you." He kissed my forehead.

I felt tortured and adored all at once.

"Let's go to sleep. In the morning, you'll be good as new. Promise." He stood. "I'll be a couple of feet away in the other bed. Come wake me if you need anything."

I needed him to hold me, and maybe more. It was better I couldn't speak.

CHAPTER 35

SARA, AGE 32

Sunday, December 18, 1994, 10:30 AM
Low Tide Inn
Rock Beach, Maine

For once I knew exactly where and when I was. That had to be a good sign, right?

Danny, dressed in jeans and his bomber jacket, his cheeks reddened by the cold, strolled into the motel room holding a tray of two take-out cups of coffee. "How'd you sleep, Squirt?" His green eyes glowed like springtime despite it being winter.

After my panic had finally settled the night before, I tossed a while. Danny's snores soared over from the next bed. But I must have dozed off at some point. "I'm okay." I sat up and smoothed my t-shirt down to be sure my body was covered.

"You can talk," he said. "Told ya, you'd be fine."

"I can talk," I said, realizing it for myself. Domestic's experiment had not irreversibly fried my brain. Not yet.

Danny produced a bag from the jacket's deep pocket. "Breakfast," he said.

"You mentioned the muteness went away after a second time," I said. "What other fun impediments do I have to look forward to, Mr. Been-around-the-calendar-a-dozen-times?"

"Migraines my fourth go-round. Maybe from nicotine withdrawal. But nothing in a while." He patted his washboard abdomen. "How about we talk on a full stomach? I got us some bagels with cream cheese to go with the Joe." He tossed a bagel and a packet of cream cheese onto my bed.

Gallo loved to sneak licks of cream cheese out of the container when he thought you weren't looking. I missed my fluffy fur bag. He wouldn't be born for another few years, in some back alley on the mean streets of Queens. Could I be at the shelter to rescue him again when the time came?

Danny took a taste from each of the cups before holding both out to me. "Want you to know there's nothing funny in either one."

"Except your spit," I said.

He laughed. "Extra flavor."

I took a cup and sipped. "Ambrosia," I said, "but can you take the calories out of the bagels?"

"Why are girls with curves always trying to diet them away?" He didn't give me a chance to answer. "It's colder than a polar bear's pecker out there, but it looks like it's gonna be a clear day. After we eat, we can go for a drive up the coast."

"A drive sounds great," I said. The shoreline would captivate my attention and keep me from ogling Danny.

In the shower, instead of washing quickly the way I always did, and singing to distract myself, I went slowly. I made a serious appraisal of my body. With the diminutive bar of motel soap, I traced my generous landscape— shapely, cambered. Not *disgusting* as Mother claimed. Not *Gordota*, her pet name for me. Flesh in womanly places. Jon never once commented negatively on my weight. Neither did Steve. And Danny's assessment made it three to one.

Maybe if mother didn't have such a narrow view of what men wanted, she would have lived longer. She smoked four packs a day instead of eating.

CHAPTER 36

SARA, AGE 32

Sunday, December 18, 1994, 11:45 AM
Al's Gas
Rock Beach, Maine

*O*kay, so I hadn't actually worked out any kind of plan, but at least I wasn't going it alone any longer.

Sunlight glinted on the sea. The bracing salt air made me feel alive.

Danny stopped for gas at the first station we came to on the way to Cove Keep Lighthouse.

I headed for the convenience store to get us drinks for the drive.

"Hey, Blondie," Danny called.

When I turned, I saw a Greek god from my childhood picture book. Not Apollo this time, but Poseidon wearing shades by the seaside, gas pump hose his trident. "Get me some Twincakes, will ya." He lowered those sunglasses and said, "Pretty please."

No woman could have turned down those eyes. I was living another Sara's life, a different reality entirely, and for that second, it didn't seem bad at all. Maybe things would be okay.

The engine's exhaust sent cloud angels up into the frigid air. Sheryl Crow's

"All I Wanna Do" coursed out the driver's side window. I couldn't remember the last time I did something just for fun.

Danny ran around the car to open the door for me. He reached for the bag I held. "No smokes?"

"Nope. No cereal either." I climbed into the car as "December, 1963 (Oh, What a Night)" started.

Danny switched off the radio.

"Not into The Four Seasons?" I said.

He coughed. "That was our song. My wife and me. We danced to it at our wedding."

Odd choice for a wedding song. "Bad memories?"

"I tried to get it right, ya know. Our marriage. A few times." Danny drove out of the station and headed left, up route 1A. Unlike the previous night, he seemed to be in no hurry and observed the speed limit.

"You tried to change things when you time traveled?" I said.

"Yeah, I tried like hell."

"We should compare notes about our trips in time. Might help us figure things out."

He looked over at me. "You want to know about my wife, don't you?"

"If you want to tell me." *Hell yeah.* I wanted to know about the woman who won his heart.

"Carmen was the file clerk at the office supply company. We got married a month after we met. Love at first sight. At least for me."

"For Jon and me too," I said, already sorry I had gotten us on the topic.

"Carmen was tall," Danny said. "Almost my height. And exotic, ya know. Dark like you, with brown eyes." He glanced my way. "Take those off."

I lifted up my glasses.

"Your eyes are a lot bigger than hers," he said. "Sweeter, too."

It annoyed me being compared to his wife.

"Anyway, long story short," he said, "twice when I went back, I tried to prevent Carmen from cheating on me with my boss. I succeeded. But instead of sleeping with the boss, she screwed two other salesmen. Can you beat that?"

"I'm sorry."

"Wasn't meant to be," he said.

We passed a weathered sign announcing *Brain Freeze Ice Cream*.

I couldn't get Jon out of my thoughts. If he were the one time traveling, would he have wanted to marry me all over again? Danny must have really loved Carmen.

"Still with me, Squirt?" he said.

"Do you believe in fate?" I said. "I mean, that there are some things we can't change? Like milestones in our lives that remain fixed no matter what."

"Don't know," he said. "I mean I have changed a few things in my past."

"Like what?"

"Don't want to say." His neck reddened. "I don't want you to think less of me."

"Let's be honest with each other. I'm not going to judge you, Danny."

"Well, I told you about the smoke and horniness thing and you didn't bat an eye. So here goes. I changed stuff when I went to a whorehouse. My fourth trip back in time."

"When did that happen?" I tried to sound casual, but I never imagined he'd been to such a place.

"All the guys went there to celebrate high school graduation. You know what clods we were—all virgins."

Danny was a hunk. My brother and the rest of his friends were goofs. "Sounds nice," I said, but I couldn't believe Daniel Astrella had to pay someone to lose his virginity. I thought the girls would have been lining up for the honor. I would have, if I had been old enough.

"Your brother wouldn't go in, ya know. He stayed in the car."

"I'm not surprised," I said. Adam never showed much interest in anything but comic books, Star Trek, and Godzilla movies. Plus, he was ill. "So, you did something different when you time traveled back?"

"Yeah, well knowing what I knew, that Adam was going to die not long after ... I'm sorry for bringing up sad times again ...."

"We're keeping his memory alive."

"Always," Danny said. "Anyway, I forced Adam to go with a hooker. I kind of guilted him into it. I didn't want Adam to die without ever being with a woman, without that kind of intimacy."

Maybe he meant intensity? Sex with hookers didn't mesh with my idea of emotional intimacy. "Thoughtful," I said. As I patted Danny's arm to reassure him, a new thought occurred to me.

I would never be able to go back in time and save my brother from leukemia. Tears rolled down my cheek. Maybe there was such a thing as fate. I wiped my face. "Adam loved you. I bet even more so after you did that for him."

"Well, I wasn't only thinking of Adam, ya know. I was thinking of myself too."

"How so?"

Danny scratched his nose. "I went with a different hooker the second time. Lisa instead of Janet."

"Did anything change in your present when you got back?"

"Yeah, I never got the clap."

"Good thinking."

He took his eyes off the road to look at me. "You're crying. Does this change anything between us?"

What did he mean *between us*? We were two test subjects seeking safe harbor. "No judgment. I was just wishing this time travel could help us save the ones we love."

He didn't answer. Instead, he turned up the volume on the B-52's "Love Shack."

So many of the motels we passed posted *Closed for the Season* signs.

Lowering the radio, and finally breaking our silence, Danny said, "Want to tell me about your trips back in time, Squirt?"

"First time back, when I saw you, I was twelve years old, like I told you, shopping at the grocery store with my grandma."

"Granny Bloom was a sweet lady. Nothing like my grandmother. She liked to drag me around by the ear whenever I got on her nerves."

"Ouch," I said. "I thought I was dreaming. But it was wonderful to see Grandma again and feel her arms around me. We were walking home when you came by in your Trans Am and picked us up."

"I sort of remember doing that."

We passed the burned-out hull of a steakhouse.

He had been honest with me about the whorehouse. *Here goes nothing*. "I thought about telling you I had a crush on you. But I woke up in 2000 before I had a chance."

Danny scrunched up his face as if he'd smelled something rotten. "No way. I had no clue. You always seemed mature for your age. And a brain. All A's in school." He ran a hand over his gold-brown hair. "I wouldn't think you'd go for a dimwit like me."

"You read the same geek books Adam and I did. That qualifies you as smart too."

He smiled. "If I was smart I would have stuck around till you weren't jailbait. So, what had changed when you got back to the present?"

"Nothing much after that first time travel episode," I said. "Except I ate a bowl of Berry Beary Crunch. And I was sure something was wrong with me. I lost hours of my day."

"Yeah, I thought I'd gone crackers the first few times too."

We passed the sign for *Cove Keep Light & Beach Access—2 miles ahead.*"

"Hey," Danny said, "glad we're almost there. Nature calls."

Danny was waiting for me outside the port-a-potty. He rubbed his gloved hands together and bounced on his heels. "Ready to walk on the beach?"

Cold out as a penguin's butt—hell, as my own ass after sitting on the absolute zero toilet seat. The sun shone, the wind was calm, and I needed the exercise. "Onward."

He took my hand in his, grip firm but comfortable. I wished we weren't wearing gloves.

We hiked up to the tide line, then marched in the damp sand. Neither of us said anything. We had the beach to ourselves. The shushing sound of the waves calmed my nerves.

At the seaside with Danny, I felt like the heroine of a romance novel, strolling the tropical shore into the sunset with the handsome hero by my side. But the thermometer in Maine in December wouldn't pass for paradise, and a happily-ever-after ending was far from assured.

In fact, being the subject of a corporate mind-control experiment, danger seemed the more likely outcome. Or brain damage. Or death. But time travel changed me. I wasn't the Sara of yesterday. The new me, without Jon, for better or worse, stepped into uncertainty. I had to let go of my original life.

Breaking my reverie, Danny said, "What happened your second time in the past? Did you see me again?"

"Jon wasn't my husband yet. We were living together—"

"You should have looked me up," Danny said. "Anyway, go on."

"We were at the grocery store and ran into Misti, my husband's former girlfriend. That didn't happen before. I never met Misti in my real life. I mean, my life before the time travel. My first life. Damn! It's frustrating to try to talk about it. How do you keep track of all your trips?"

"Why I got migraines, probably. Too many opposing memories for one brain. I started thinking of my trips back as time flashes and whatever happened in 2000 as redos. Ya know, redo 1, redo 2, and so on."

"Wow, redos and time flashes. Very clever. Remember that book by Ken Grimwood, *Replay*? We're definitely not replaying. Domestic is dangerous."

"You were talking about your husband …. Go on."

"I was jealous of the pictures I'd seen of his hot blonde ex, Misti. But when I met her in the market, she seemed fake and ditzy. I didn't know I had traveled back in time—I mean, time flashed. I thought it was a dream, and I knew Jon would marry me, Misti or no Misti. So, I wasn't jealous at all. And—"

"Misti should have been jealous of you. You got nothing to worry about."

Danny was a charmer for sure, but was he right? Jon loved me back then, ample flesh and all. My heart sputtered. *Or else it was all an act.*

Jon might have married me just to use me as a lab rat, like Steve intimated. If I were just an experiment to him, he could have been with Candy all along.

A seagull cried out. It sounded like an infant.

But what about our baby? If not for my genetic condition, I would have been the mother of Jon's child. He must have loved me if he got me pregnant. Or was that an accident? No, he was happy—he wanted to be a father. My head hurt trying to make sense of things.

A couple of gulls dove for the water, came up empty.

"Hey, Blondie. Didn't mean to make you stop talking," Danny said.

I'd forgotten he was there. "Sorry, I lost track. Jon was impressed I wasn't jealous, so he proposed to me right there in the supermarket. But in my life before redos, he proposed in our apartment months later."

"And you said yes again?"

"Of course. I loved him." I still did.

Danny frowned. "So, did anything change when you got back to 2000?"

"Blonde hair. Like now. I dyed my hair for the wedding to please my future mother-in-law, who dyed her hair the same color. Weird. And I kept my hair blonde in redo two because everyone seemed to like it better on me. Jon too, I think, but maybe it didn't make any difference to him."

"I wondered why you'd do that to yourself." Danny stopped walking and faced me.

He ran his hand through my hair, tucked some curls behind my ear. He was going to kiss me. *Finally.*

My bones thrummed with excitement.

"Never went for fake blondes," he said.

I wanted to scream. Or, dye my hair back to brunette that very second.

He pulled a bottle of water out of his coat pocket, uncapped it and took a swig. He held out the bottle to me.

I guess his lips on the bottle was as close as I would get to a kiss. I took a sip.

A couple of men walked by us. Both wore green parkas, black suit pants with black dress shoes. The tall, skinny man had on sunglasses and a Red Sox baseball cap. He tipped his hat to me as he passed, revealing locks of wavy red hair.

Holy molé salsa—he looked like the grocery clerks I kept seeing. My stomach dropped to my feet.

Both men strolled on ahead.

"Danny, I have a bad feeling about those guys. Especially the one with red hair."

"Let's head back to the car," he said in a low voice. "Go slow. Act like everything's cool." He took my hand again, held it more firmly than the first time. He glanced back.

"Are they following us?" I said.

"Maybe."

A splat of seagull poop missed my face by inches. Grandma used to say *if a bird makes caca on you, it's good luck*. Perhaps the near miss meant the opposite, a bad omen.

CHAPTER 37

SARA, AGE 32

Sunday, December 18, 1994, 12:39 PM
Cove Keep Lighthouse parking lot
Cove Keep, Maine

"The suits don't seem to be coming for us," Danny said. "But's let's split anyway." A true gentleman, he unlocked the passenger door first and let me in. More than Steve had done.

As we sped south along route 1A, I kept checking the rearview mirror to see if those guys from the beach were following us. An old woman with a gray bun and huge glasses trailed us in a beat-up Cadillac.

"Granny get-up could be a disguise," I said, trying to lighten the mood.

Danny glanced in the mirror. "You think?" There was concern in his voice.

Before I could tell him I was joking, he lurched into a right turn.

The old woman kept going straight.

We drove a few blocks, passing a mix of pristine and dilapidated houses, most boarded-up summer rentals.

"Guess you were wrong about the old broad being a spy," he said. He circled back to route 1A. "Hungry? We could have a big meal now. Save the Twincakes for supper."

"Sure, I could eat." My stomach was in knots, but I didn't want to deprive him of a meal. He needed to feed all those muscles.

He rubbed the scar over his right eye. "Next place that looks good, I'll pull in."

"How did you get this?" I touched the faint pink welt.

"Tried to get rich off some bookies. Not a good idea. Should have stuck to the track. The few winning horses I could remember didn't have big payoffs though."

"That's awful." I hadn't known Danny was the gambling type.

"Not your fault. I studied up on stocks last couple of redos. I'm ready now. I'll invest in Rain City Coffee and Wiggy Search Engine, and then I'll be rolling in dough."

"I haven't had a chance to think about anything but trying to undo my marriage. Getting rich quick sounds too good to be true."

We passed a *Trust in Jesus* sign.

"Should work. But it will take a few years. I have to get a job soon. And I plan to sweeten the pot with a legitimate bet or two."

"What kind of job are you thinking of?"

"Used to work construction with my cousins, and I helped out at my uncle's garage. So, maybe boat repair. Seems to be in demand out here. I'd like to stay in Maine. Peace and quiet."

We passed a sign that said *Good Catch Bar & Grill. Open Daily Year Round.*

"Peaceful except between Memorial Day and Labor Day," I said. "It's a zoo here in the summer. But I'd like to stay too."

"Good. It's decided then." He turned to me. "We'll stay here in time and place."

"Can we do that? I mean, what's the longest you've ever stayed in the past?"

"About seventeen days, but I couldn't help smoking."

"Steve told me the serum kept the brain wave centers active up to two weeks."

"Dunno," Danny said. "Maybe since I've been injected so much, I have more staying power."

A crow picked at a squirrel carcass on the median.

"But aren't you afraid you might die when the Penrose wave center in your brain shuts down?"

"Nah. Those scientists didn't know they invented time travel until some lab rats went back and told them. They know jack shit about it. You and I are the experts."

I didn't feel like an authority. And I wasn't sure I was willing to risk my life trying to remain in the past. "What makes you certain you can stay off cigarettes this time?"

"I graduated the behavior mod class with honors." He licked his lips. "Plus, I have you to help me if I get a craving."

That Danny, all talk and no kissing.

CHAPTER 38

SARA, AGE 32

The Good Catch turned out to be a hole in the wall situated in a strip mall with a shoe repair business, a kite shop closed for the winter, and a tire store. The dim restaurant lacked ambiance. A fish net hung on the wood-paneled wall behind the bar. Ten white rectangular tables surrounded by black vinyl chairs that harked back to Dr. Gentry's office filled the square room. The scratched, red vinyl floor tiles bent up in places.

A bald man seated at the bar watched sports news on the corner TV.

"Sit anywhere you like," the bartender said in a pronounced Yankee accent. An older man with wavy silver hair, he reminded me a little of my dad.

I needed to get in touch with my parents. Jon may have called them looking for me after he read my note.

"Don't see any ashtrays," Danny said. "At least I won't go flashing forward." He pulled out a chair for me at the table by the wall, closest to the bar. "Haven't had lobster this trip yet."

"How long have you been here this time?" I said.

He looked at his watch. "Ten days. Spent most of it reading. And wandering around the coast. How 'bout you?"

"Wow, you must be a speed reader with all those books. A little more than a day for me. But I can't believe how much things have changed in a few hours. I unmarried my husband."

"Regrets?" Danny said, arching an eyebrow.

"Full speed ahead," I said, trying to sound flippant. My stomach grumbled. Whether from distress or actual hunger, I couldn't tell.

"What to drink?" the bartender said.

Danny asked for a beer on tap.

I chose seltzer water.

We both ordered the special off a blackboard propped up against the back of the bar—a bowl of clam chowder and a lobster roll. I was going to blow off my diet—again.

I sipped the seltzer, hoping to ease my tummy.

Danny drained half his beer, then wiped his mouth with the back of his hand, boyish and sexy at the same time. "Needed that," he said.

"Being with me driving you to drink?" I said.

"What do you mean?" He squared his shoulders as if readying for a fight.

Holy molé salsa, I put my foot in my mouth. Joanne had told me about Danny's father being an alcoholic. "A joke," I said. I reached for Danny's hand but he drew it back. "I can be hard to be around."

"Oh." He slouched. "I like being around you, Sara. I feel … like I don't have to be somebody else."

"I don't want you to be anybody else."

He lifted the beer glass and then set it back down without drinking. He looked into my eyes. "I want to be with you, too," he said.

I had to change the subject before I lost control and pitched across the table to kiss him. "Have you met other time …" I stopped myself, looked around. Only the bald guy and the bartender in the whole place. But Domestic could have spies everywhere. "I mean, have you met other travelers like us?"

He shook his head. "Not like us. But I could have sworn Joanne was."

"When did you see her?"

"I ran into her last time I was in Woodward to visit my mom. She lives at her parents' place. But I guess it's all hers now, with them dead and her sisters married."

"How's she doing? I wish we'd kept in touch." I should have kept trying to win back her friendship.

"Single, but she seemed happy."

"Did you see her in the millennium?"

Danny gave me a puzzled look.

I guess I should have said 2000.

The bartender brought the soups and sandwiches, asked if we needed anything else.

I asked for more seltzer.

Danny guzzled the last of his draft and ordered another.

A fragrant steam rose from the clam chowder. I stirred the soup to cool it. Sipping the seltzer seemed to settle my stomach. My heart was another matter. "I meant did you see Joanne in our present time or some other time?"

"Oh, millennium, 2000. Yeah, then." He plucked an intact piece of lobster claw meat from his roll and waggled it in the air before taking a bite.

I supposed his mother never taught him not to play with his food. But he could break every law of etiquette and still be adorable doing it. He was that cute.

"I wish I hadn't scared off Ronald Gott with my big fat mouth," I said. "She never forgave me."

"Nah, she's better off without him. That boy would have kept her barefoot and pregnant."

"Sounds good to me," the bartender said. He winked at Danny and set down another beer.

"Joanne's a pistol. No keeping her down," Danny said, lifting his chowder bowl to his lips for a slurp. "Anyway, I'm sure she's not upset any more. No one could stay mad at you."

"Maybe I could time flash to that day and keep my mouth shut for once."

"Nope. No more going back. You're staying here with me."

That wasn't up to him. Maybe not up to either of us. I started on the soup.

He pointed to my lobster roll. "Are you done?"

I hadn't begun, but the soup bowl looked bottomless. "All yours." I wondered about trying to make things right somehow. "Don't you think we could use time flashes to help people? I mean, prevent the bad events we know about from happening."

"I tried to help my mom. Get her to leave my drunk-ass dad. It didn't work. I don't understand it. Some things I changed really easy." He took a long swallow of beer.

"Maybe it's harder to change other people's decisions." But he'd changed my brother's mind at the whorehouse. *So why not me changing Joanne's mind?* "What made you think Joanne was a traveler like us?"

Danny stared into the beer glass. "I made a comment to her about having a hard time staying in the present. And she said she knew exactly what I meant. But when I pumped her for more information, she said something weird like 'people always regret what they didn't risk.' She had to run somewhere, and I didn't get to ask her more."

"What they didn't risk? I wonder if she meant you. I wasn't the only one with a crush."

"No way. Joanne thought I was a dolt. Not like I wasn't, but still."

"Joanne thought you were a hunk. What girl in her right mind wouldn't?"

He blushed.

I wondered why Joanne and Danny never got together. They would have made quite a pair—his loveable crudeness and her exasperating correctness.

After polishing off my lobster roll and his own, Danny said, "Adam was in love with Joanne, swore me to secrecy about it. But I guess it's okay to tell you now he's gone. I never could have dated her. Even after Adam died, it would have felt like a betrayal, ya know." His eyes misted over.

It touched my heart how faithful he was to my brother. And I wasn't surprised Adam had feelings for Joanne. She was lovely and they'd been friends since they were in diapers. "I believe Adam would have been happy for you to be with her."

Danny didn't acknowledge my comment. Instead, he studied the menu specials board and finished his beer. He turned to me. "Cheesecake?"

"Let's share," I said, certain he would consume the entire slice. Which reminded me of what happened at the diner. I had to ask. "Why were you spooked by the sweet potato pie yesterday?"

"My ex-girlfriend served me drugged pie. The way to a man's stomach and all. That's why I wanted you to take the first bite. I had to be sure you weren't another mole."

Dessert arrived, along with another beer. Danny dug into the cherry glaze with gusto. The way he ate and drank, he had to possess a gifted metabolism to maintain those outstanding abs.

As pleasant as being with Danny was, I wanted to do more than sightsee and eat out. We either had to get ahead of the bad guys or stop them somehow. "I feel like we ought to be on the offensive."

"We can do anything you like. I have enough cash to last us a while—as long as we're not too crazy."

"I mean, let's try to stop Domes ..." Paranoid, I kept myself from saying the name out loud. "... the corporation. We can locate others going through what we are and help them."

"How can two people stop a conglomerate?" he said. "Besides, we're a few years too soon."

"I don't know. I feel like we have to try. People were hurt. Some died."

Danny smacked the table with the heel of his hand. "The best thing we can do is get on with our lives."

"But what happens six years from now when they come after us again? Maybe for different products. For me, it could be yogurt instead of cereal. For you, it could be beer." I bit my tongue. *Another low blow.*

He pouted for a moment. "But we'll have a great six years, Sara. That's a lot of time. And they might not come at all. You won't be with your no-good husband, and I'll steer clear of my evil exes."

His calling Jon *no-good* stung. "I don't want to spend every day for six years looking over my shoulder." I said it in a louder voice than I'd intended.

The bartender arrived with a check. "Anytime you're ready, kids," he said. "No rush, and no fighting. You don't want to end up on Santa's naughty list."

"Too late," Danny said. "I'm a repeat offender."

"We weren't fighting." *Yet.* But it would be inevitable. I wanted to do some good, maybe even try to prevent the experiment from happening.

Danny seemed to live in the moment.

Was I too critical? Being with Danny was what I always wanted as a kid. Maybe I just needed to take a page out of his playbook and relax.

He scooped the final bit of cheesecake on the fork and held it out to me. "Last chance."

I ate the cake, hardly tasting it. No one deserved to be hurt by Domestic. There had to be something we could do.

"Don't look sad, Squirt," Danny said. "We'll figure things out." He drained his third glass of beer in one long pull.

Maybe the apple didn't fall far from the tree when it came to drinking.

He sucked the last clinging bits of cheesecake from the fork with child-like abandon.

I envied his simple joy of eating. I could have been that way if not for my mother's insults.

"No regrets," I said. I answered Danny's puzzled face by lifting the dessert plate to my mouth and licking it clean. It tasted sweet after all.

~

I phoned my parents, but no one picked up. I left a message that I'd broken up with Jon and needed to get away. I said I'd call them again in a few days when I was settled.

My mother would be sure Jon had left me for another woman. That was her problem.

By the time I returned to the table, the plates were cleared away, the check was paid, and Danny had donned his leather bomber. He declined to let me chip in for the meal, and helped me on with my coat.

"I could drive," I said, hoping he wouldn't be insulted.

"Takes a lot more than three beers to get me wired." He tapped his stomach. "Plus, I ate like a pig. And I would never do anything to put you in danger, Squirt."

Those green eyes looked like truth. He meant me no harm. And more, he wanted to take care of me.

But I needed to take care of myself first.

We were almost out the door, when the bartender shouted to us. "Hey, you two, look up at the ceiling."

Sure enough, high above our heads, a plastic mistletoe decoration twirled on a red ribbon. The Good Catch's one nod to Christmas.

Danny made the okay sign with his thumb and forefinger, then bent down and kissed me on the lips.

Holy molé salsa.

CHAPTER 39

SARA, AGE 32

Sunday, December 18, 1994, 3:48 PM*
Good Catch Bar & Grill
Cove Keep, Maine

G o figure. None of my teenaged fantasies of kissing Daniel Astrella ever included a dive bar in Maine called The Good Catch or the prop of mistletoe. Danny's lips on mine, wet and eager, definitely felt more than platonic.

So why wasn't I tingly all over?

He ended the kiss and stepped out the door, holding it open for me.

I had no words, but left a trail of breath ghosts in the late afternoon air as we walked holding hands. *Was being with Daniel Astrella supposed to be my fate all along?* That made Jon a mistake. I shivered.

In the car, Danny turned on the radio.

Fleetwood Mac's syrupy "Hold Me" played.

"Head back to the motel?" Danny said, his question almost too low to hear with the music blasting.

"Sounds good." I couldn't identify how I felt. The kiss was not at all what I had dreamt. I expected Fourth of July fireworks and marching bands.

Maybe the next kiss would be that way, and the first time was just a rehearsal. *Practice is a virtue*, Grandma used to say, mixing together two different adages. I liked her version better.

"I have to stop at a drugstore," Danny said. "Got to get a couple of things."

"Fine." Immediately, I thought one of those things had to be condoms. I left Jon less than two days ago. I wasn't ready to sleep with another man. Then again, if I was honest with myself, it had been a year or longer since Jon and I had made love. Maybe two years. I didn't want to tally time. As an accountant, that spoke volumes.

With the descending darkness and a full belly, my body craved hibernation, not sex. "Mind if I close my eyes for a while?"

"Sure thing," he said.

Was I a sure thing?

Danny lowered the volume on the radio as Louis Armstrong sang the first bars of "We Have All the Time in the World."

~

I lean forward in my wooden seat. A splinter grazes my thigh through my jeans. I seem to be alone in what looks like the assembly hall at Woodward High. But the place is too large.

"Just you then, love," a male voice says in a distinctly British accent.

The stage lights come up on a man tuning a guitar.

Although I've never seen him in person, from every TV show and photo, plus the accent, I know the man on the stage is John Lennon. A thrill flows through me.

"Love, this one's for you," Lennon says. He strums the guitar and hums.

At first, I don't recognize the tune. Then he sings the lyrics. It's Whitesnake's "Is this Love," a song from the late eighties. From after he was killed.

How is it possible he knows a song after his time? For that matter, how is he standing there on the stage? Unless we're both outside of time. Or both dead.

"Sing, love," Lennon says.

"Mr. Lennon," I say, "I don't mean to be rude, but do you know what's going on here?"

"Gravity, love, gravity." He stands and bows.

The stage lights dim, and the entire auditorium goes dark. "Imagine" roars from a distance.

I stand and try to feel my way to the source of the music. I trip over something and fall, but there is no floor to catch me. I keep falling.

CHAPTER 40

SARA, AGE 32

Sunday, December 18, 1994, 4:55 PM
Carry-all Store
Beachway, Maine

*M*y temples pounded.

The navy-blue night sky glowed and a star hung low enough on the horizon to see through the car's windshield.

"I'm going into the store, sleepy-head," Danny said. "You want anything?"

"Aspirin," I said. It hurt to speak.

"You don't look so hot. Migraine?"

It hurt to nod.

"Okay, I can help. Went through this myself. I'll leave the car running to keep you warm. Back soon." He kissed me on the forehead.

It felt more like he'd slammed me with a brick.

When he opened the door, the dome light burned into me as if I'd stared into the sun. Closing my eyes, I experienced the unique sensation of lead pipes beating my skull from within. I released the seat lever and laid back. The pain didn't ease, but at least it didn't get worse.

~

I am still falling, but then I start floating, up, up, up. My body is buoyant. I am an astronaut in a capsule, escaping Earth's gravity, leaving the world I know behind.

CHAPTER 41

SARA, AGE 32

Sunday, December 18, 1994, 6 PM
Low Tide Inn
Rock Beach, Maine

et cement filled my head and yet, I floated. *I must still be dreaming.*

Danny carried me up the flights of stairs at the Low Tide Inn. He maneuvered through the door and deposited me on the bed. The lamplight blazed brighter than a mushroom cloud.

"How ya feeling, Squirt?" He tousled my hair.

"Ouch." Every strand of hair prickled with pain.

"Let's get you under the covers. Dr. Danny will fix you up."

I wished Grandma, a.k.a. Dr. Vaseline, were still alive and there to comfort me.

Danny removed my shoes and coat but nothing else.

Steve had been more thorough.

Danny deftly rotated me side to side and rolled me under the covers. My dad used the same technique whenever I fell asleep during the car ride home from visiting the Brooklyn relatives. *Danny will make a great father someday.*

"I am going to whip up my special concoction," he said. "Gimme a sec."

A grenade went off inside my noggin with each word he spoke.

He tore open cartons, poured liquid, clinked glass, each sound a new *kaboom*.

I wished he would be quiet and let me die in peace.

Before long, he knelt beside me. "This helped with my migraines." He held out a glass of pinkish sludge. "Learned this recipe from Dad. Only perk of having a drunk for a father."

His words thudded inside my head like Godzilla stomping on Tokyo.

He propped my head up on the pillows. "You take this magic potion, you sleep a good long while, and you wake up a new woman."

I realized Danny was whispering. He had been all along.

"I'm already a new woman." My own voice exploded like cannon fodder in my eardrums. When I tried to push the glass away, my vision doubled— two Dannys with four smoldering green eyes and two glasses of horrible, pink puke.

One of the Dannys forced a glass to my mouth.

The pink stuff tasted like sweaty gym socks smell. I gagged, but got most of it down.

"That's a good Blondie," he said. He blotted my forehead with a damp washcloth, then cleaned the remainder of the gunk from my lips and chin. "I'll be back in a minute and join you."

Did he mean to sleep with me? It would have hurt too much to speak again. *I'll find out soon enough.*

The squelch of running water from the bathroom threatened to make my ears bleed. I squashed my face into the pillow to block out all the light and sound.

CHAPTER 42

SARA, AGE 32

Monday, December 19, 1994, 2:35 AM
Low Tide Inn
Rock Beach, Maine

*C*hainsaw snoring woke me. Whenever Jon slept on his back, I had to force him onto his side to stop the infernal noise. For some reason, Jon felt bigger, heavier than usual.

I switched on the lamp. Startled to see it wasn't Jon, I fell out of bed onto my ass. *Graceful as ever.*

"Hey, what are you doing on the floor?" Danny stumbled to a standing position, fully dressed.

"I forgot when I was." Using the bed as leverage, I pulled myself up.

"How's your skull?" he said. "Do you need another dose?"

My ass hurt like hell from landing on my tailbone, but my head didn't ache. I rubbed it to make sure it was still attached to my body. "Good as new."

Danny smiled. "Told you. But let's be sure. What's your name?"

I tapped on my noggin to demonstrate. "Sara García."

He frowned. "Try again."

He was right—no more husband. "Sara Bloom."

"I guess I fell asleep waiting for you to fall asleep," Danny said. Crushed beer cans covered the nightstand on his side of the bed.

Given the amount of alcohol he'd consumed, it came as no surprise he'd dozed off. "Thank you for the magic potion."

"Sorry if I frightened you. Waking up next to Frankenstein's clammy monster could scare the crap out of anyone." He looked delectable as ever, drool-stained chin and all.

"I feel like bride of Blondie." I patted my hair, which I could tell stuck out in awkward clumps.

"Glad, you're okay, Squirt." He wrapped me in a bear hug.

His warm body against mine made my libido want more.

He set me loose, then headed to the bathroom. From behind the closed door came the sound of the six-pack leaving his body.

"All yours," he said moments later, stripped down to boxers.

I needed a cold shower after another eyeful of him. I got my pajamas out of the dresser and headed for the bathroom.

"Wait," he said. He held out his arm to prevent me from passing. "Pay the toll." He pointed to my lips first, then tapped his left cheek.

I planted a kiss on his cheek.

He pointed to his nose.

I stood on tiptoes and kissed his Roman nose. I liked paying the toll.

He pointed to his right cheek.

I kissed the light stubble there.

He pointed to his forehead, then crouched even lower to allow me to reach.

I kissed there. I wanted to pay much more. I willed him to point to his lips.

He pointed to the bathroom. *All tease and no treat.*

By the time I came back into the room, Danny was in bed, once again sawing logs.

I wavered between relief and disappointment. "See you in the daylight," I whispered.

CHAPTER 43

SARA, AGE 32

Monday, December 19, 1994, 10 AM
Low Tide Inn
Rock Beach, Maine

*W*ith the sun glowing through the slit in the motel room's drapes, I felt a sense of hope. I'd changed my future. Mine and Jon's—on purpose. I had no idea what the year 2000 would look like when I returned there.

And just when would I? It was odd spending so much time in the past. Steve had told me about the danger of Penrose waves going dormant. I was in the Domestic lab, green fluid dripping into my veins, just before traveling to 1994. I probably could safely stay another week, but I didn't want to push my luck.

I had just finished the last bite of my egg sandwich when Danny said, "Let's get started."

Lost in thought, I'd nearly forgotten he was even in the room. But of course he was. He'd brought me breakfast in bed again. "Started on what?"

His eyes gleamed. "On this." He pulled off his shirt, let it drop to the floor, and sat next to me.

His gasoline and seashore scent made me swoon. He brushed the hair out of my eyes, then kissed me.

When I paid the toll last night, I wanted to keep going. Finally, he wanted that too, and I was scared. If I went down that path, my fate would be sealed. *No being with Jon ever again.*

I broke off the kiss with Danny. "Shouldn't we keep trading notes and figure out a way to keep Domestic at bay?"

"I'd rather trade kisses." He put his mouth on mine again and slid his hand down to my inner thigh.

His touch quickened my pulse. I kissed him, but I wasn't convinced Danny was who I wanted. I couldn't get my mind off Jon. *What was he doing at the moment? Had my break-up made him furious, sad, or worse, brought him relief?*

Danny stopped kissing me. "No offense, Sara, but your husband was wrong about the hair. You are enough exactly as you are, as you were."

I'd yearned to hear those very words my whole life. The right message, the wrong mouth.

He kissed me again.

I stopped kissing back. "I can't do this. What if Jon and I somehow get back together and I am married to him in 2000. Technically, this would be cheating."

"You're split up now. Anyway, you can't be with him if you marry me. Marry me. I love you, Sara."

"You want to marry me? You hardly know me. We've only just met—I mean, as adults."

"Think of it. What if all this wild time travel stuff happened so you and me could be together? We got rid of our bad pasts. Now we're meant to be." He looked dead serious.

The cab driver's words boomed in my head—*Set not the chain of fate upon thy foot.* "Maybe there is no such thing as destiny," I said.

Undaunted, Danny kept stroking my thigh. "But there's right now." He kissed me again, his lips as eager as his proposal. Before I knew it, he had my pajama top unbuttoned. His hands were all over me. His lips followed his fingers.

There was no denying my body responded to his touch, to him. But I couldn't afford to lose myself in the moment. Nor lose more of myself than I already had.

"I love how much of you there is to love," he said, after licking my nipples. "You're like a fleshy Salma Hayek."

Another me, a few days ago, would have heard him calling me a fat Salma Hayek. This me understood he meant it as a compliment.

He kissed and caressed all the way to my belly button. He lifted my hips and slid off my pajama bottoms.

I got caught up in the moment. I reached into Danny's shorts.

He was large and hard. He moaned as I stroked him. "Wait," he said. He ripped off his shorts, seized a condom packet from the nightstand drawer, tore into it, and rolled it on—one, two, three, four.

His preparedness gave me pause. I wondered how many women he'd bedded. Probably not many he asked to marry. But I didn't know for sure.

Danny swung on top, pushed inside me, hot as a torch. He lunged, thrusting fast. His eyes locked shut, his jaw clenched, hands braced the headboard as it banged into the wall.

Nothing like I'd fantasized years ago. All semblance of his tenderness vanished. "Slower, please. I want to feel you."

"Yeah," he said, but he didn't go slower.

I closed my eyes and focused on the friction. *Pretty good.*

Then gone.

He stopped moving, let out a loud groan, and collapsed on top of me.

When Steve and I lost our virginity together, the sex went on for a couple of hours. I wriggled out from under Danny's six feet of dead weight.

He opened his eyes, his expression sheepish. "Sorry, Blondie," he said. "I went like a shot. Been building since I first saw you in the diner."

"The first time with someone new always goes quickly." I didn't want to hurt his pride. And I had no idea what I was feeling. It all happened too fast to know.

"Next time, I promise, I'll make you come so hard, there'll be an earthquake on the moon."

Wouldn't it be a moonquake then? I recalled my first time with Jon. We kissed until our lips were raw. Then, he spent time caressing my entire body, inch by inch. He brought me to orgasm before he entered me. *No use thinking about Jon.* That was over. *Never again.*

Danny reached for a can of beer on the nightstand.

I trembled and pulled the blankets up to my chin.

"Cold?" Danny said. "I love when a girl wears my clothes." He reached down for his *Born to Run* tour Springsteen shirt.

Any girl? How special. His shirt smelled of gasoline and seashore. Like him. Like me at that moment. The scent of arousal had become the scent of disillusionment. I wore the shirt.

He got out of bed and stood there naked, smiling at me. Every inch of him sexy.

False advertising.

"Hey, Blondie," he said. "What do you say we find a judge to marry us, today." It wasn't a question.

How could he be serious? We'd only been together a couple of days. Marriage wasn't even on my radar. I had to get my head on straight. "How about we find some more coffee and go from there?"

"Anyone ever tell you how gorgeous you are in the morning?"

Once, Jon did, a long time ago, but I didn't say. I shook my head.

He dressed, then grabbed another can from the mini-fridge. He dropped onto the opposite bed and guzzled the beer. "Sorry. I should have offered you one."

"No thanks," I said. I didn't want to be with an alcoholic. Danny would need to address his drinking before I would even consider being his girl-friend, let alone his wife. *And the sex would have to get a whole hell of a lot better.*

I got up to go to the bathroom.

He seized the hem of the t-shirt and prevented me from going. "Nice shirt, but you look hotter without it."

Being there with my crush fawning over me should have been a dream come true. But my life felt less like fantasy and more like a Domestic mind-control nightmare. "We should stop playing and get serious."

He let go of the shirt. "About what?"

"Let's figure out a way to stop Domestic."

"Thought we went over this already. How the hell can the two of us do anything to stop an international conglomeration?" He raised his voice on the multi-syllabic words.

I kissed the scar over his right eyebrow. "Maybe we can stop Domestic from developing the experimental drug in the first place." I wondered if that would create some kind of paradox. If we prevented the experimental drug from being developed, how could we have traveled back in time to stop them? Circular thinking would give me another migraine.

"I'm dog tired, Sara. Don't you get it? I've been on the run from Domestic for too many time flashes and redos." He sighed. "We found each other. Now I have a shot at happiness. Can't we enjoy being together for a while? How about twenty-four more hours before we become Boris and Natasha, okay?"

"Deal." I didn't want to mention Boris and Natasha were the evil spies. I think he meant Rocky and Bullwinkle. For a second, I pictured Danny with moose horns. Still cute.

He yanked me onto his lap, clamped his arms around me, and started convulsing. I thought he was having a seizure. Then I felt the dampness on my neck. He was crying.

From all the times I tangled with my mother, I understood all too well what it meant to be exhausted from arguing so much you just broke down.

I held him tight. If he needed it, I would hold onto him day into night.

CHAPTER 44

SARA, AGE 32

Monday, December 19, 1994, 4 PM
Rock Beach Diner
Rock Beach, Maine

*T*he diner smelled of fresh-baked bread and clams. *I should just order a salad, eat light.* My stomach growled in defiance.

A dark-haired busboy clattered by with a tray of filled glass salt shakers. "Gotta switch these out. Barb will be with you in a minute."

"Well, if it isn't my lovebirds." Barb seated us at the same table we shared the other day. "Got fresh rolls cooking. And the shepherd's pie is the special."

After a lazy day watching television, kissing, playing cards, and more kissing without any further mention of time travel, neither of us wanted to venture far.

Danny grabbed my shoulders and told Barb, "I'm gonna make an honest woman out of her." He let go of me to shake hands with the waitress.

"Wait a minute," she said. She pointed to my finger. "Where's the ring, cheapskate?"

He looked hurt for a moment. "I'm going to let Sara pick it out." He winked at me. "A Christmas present."

"Okay, then," she said, "this calls for a toast." She disappeared into the kitchen.

The only other diners were white-haired couples. Jon used to joke he couldn't wait for us to grow old together so we could ride the bus for half price and eat bargain early-bird dinners. *Spoken like a true accountant.* Except he wasn't one—he was a bad guy.

Danny snapped his fingers in front of my face.

I looked up at him.

"There you are. And I meant it about the ring."

I didn't want to talk about the proposal and spoil his good mood. "Guess I'm a little out of it from the migraine yesterday."

"That's not it," he said. "I know you better than you think. You're upset over him, your ex. You had a far-away look. I was like that after Carmen and I split."

Barb set down a couple of champagne flutes filled with rust-colored liquid. "Not an ounce of bubbly in the place. Best I could do is this Promise Ale."

Danny raised his glass. "To the waitress who brought us together."

I clinked my glass to his. My hand shook with tremors.

Barb said, "You got a good one, honey." She took our orders.

When she was gone, I said, "I was noticing all the senior couples here. Guess we're early birds."

"That will be us in forty years," he said. "And by then, you'll know." His eyes were serene, a calm sea.

"Know what?"

"How much I love you. Don't ever change." He took my hand in his again. "Well, one thing you could change."

"What's that?"

"Go back to your real hair color."

I laughed. "But I was getting used to you calling me Blondie."

"How about hot stuff instead?"

I rolled my eyes.

"You know, I'm here for you. You can talk to me about Jon, if it helps."

"I don't want to think about Jon anymore." I leaned over and gave Danny a quick peck on the lips.

Barb set down our salads. "This is a family place." She wagged a finger at us, but she was smiling.

Salad accompanied the shepherd's pie, so I was half being good. I picked up my fork. It slipped from my fingers and landed in the plate. I tried a few more times. My fingers couldn't stay closed. Despite my panic, I attempted to sound calm. "Danny, I can't control my left hand."

His eyebrows shot up. "Are you sure?"

I demonstrated.

"Don't freak out. You're tired, like you said. Here, let me." He loaded up the fork with lettuce and tomato and held it to my mouth.

"You can't feed me an entire meal. What if this is permanent?"

"We'll get through this. Let's go back to the room. I'll tell Barb we want the food to go. She can see we can't keep our hands off each other."

CHAPTER 45

SARA, AGE 32

Monday, December 19, 1994, 4:26 PM
Outside the Rock Beach Diner
Rock Beach, Maine

anny helped me into the car and shut the door.
        We sped off in silence, no radio.
I kept trying to make my hand work to no avail.

As we pulled into the motel lot, I spied a couple of men in parkas and dark suit slacks heading up the stairs. One wore a Red Sox cap. *The same guys from the other day at the lighthouse.* My stomach churned. They had to be with Domestic. They traced me to the past after all.

Danny turned off the headlights, but left the car running. He had spotted the men too.

They stopped in front of my room. The tall, skinny one pounded. The shorter man shouted something I couldn't make out. The tall man pounded again. I thought they were going to kick in the door, but they moved on to a room ten doors down. The shorter man took out a key and let them both inside.

"This is what we're gonna do," Danny said. He sounded calm, authoritative. "I'll grab all our stuff, then we'll head north."

"But how did Domestic find us? I didn't use a credit card."

"We don't know they're Domestic. Could be Jehovah's Witnesses. Stay here, keep your head down."

"Jehovah's witnesses don't shout and bang on doors," I said. "I'm coming with you."

"Not with your hand the way it is. We don't have time to argue."

"I can be the lookout," I said.

He was out of the car and half-way to the staircase before I finished my sentence.

I got out and ran after him.

He took the steps, three at a time.

I couldn't keep up. When I got to the room, he had his stuff shoved into his bag and the fridge emptied of beer.

My things were more scattered. Nothing I owned meant as much as getting away. "Let's go," I said. "Forget my stuff."

"Almost done." He collected my things and packed like lightning, obviously familiar with being on the run.

A door slammed somewhere nearby.

I poked my head out of the room.

The Domestic guys headed toward us.

"Danny, let's go. They're coming."

"Run," he said.

I did.

So did he.

He made it to the car first and shouted, "Hurry up, Squirt."

Someone caught the back of my coat. I shrugged out of it and kept running all the way to the car where Danny had the door waiting open for me. I got in.

I turned around and saw the guy in the Red Sox cap still coming for me, waving my jacket. He looked like the grocery clerks from my earlier time flashes, but older, about fifty. *Were the redheads time travelers too?* Maybe Domestic's illegal research lab was staffed by a whole family of red-haired, look-alike relatives.

The sedan peeled out of the parking lot.

I was grateful for Danny's lead foot.

"'Let's make like a tree and get outta here,'" he said. "We should go *back to the future.*"

I appreciated his attempt at lessening the tension. But Danny's Ford Escort was no DeLorean.

CHAPTER 46

SARA, AGE 32

Monday, December 19, 1994, 4:41 PM
Route 1 North
Shipport County, Maine

$\mathcal{T}$he dusk sky clouded over as we made our escape from the redheaded man and his friend.

After Danny assured me we weren't being followed, I went to switch on the radio. The fingers of my left hand closed around the knob and made it work. My fine motor control had returned.

Danny didn't notice, and I didn't feel like making a big deal over it. I just wanted to be quiet and think, come up with a strategy. Instead of being on defense and running from the corporation, we should be on the offensive.

Boyz II Men sang the last few lines of "On Bended Knee."

"I'm not sure how to say this," Danny said. "I mean, after what we've been through …."

Madonna's "I'll Remember" came on next.

He lowered the volume. "I feel like you … maybe you're unsure about us … about me."

I didn't understand his priorities. How could he want to discuss our relationship when we had narrowly escaped capture? Perhaps he meant to distract me from the danger we were in. Neither one of us even knew where we could go to be safe. All we had been doing was heading north.

"I'm unsure about me," I finally said. *I might as well be honest*. This was a conversation that would have come up eventually. "I was with my husband over five years, and now I feel like I never knew the real Jon. My lack of self-confidence clouded everything. My mother drummed it into my head that I was too fat for any man to stick with me. I thought dieting was the answer to every problem."

"Your mother had a couple a screws loose," Danny said. "Sorry, but she did. For Pete's sake, she blamed your brother for the leukemia. Treated him like he was friggin' contagious."

My mother was cruel to me, but she doted on Adam. Could my perception of her have been so far off? "I don't remember it that way. It hurt her to see him suffering, and she stayed away. She couldn't—"

"Sorry to interrupt, but you're wrong. She did a number on you and Adam both. Reminds me of my dad's behavior. Let's get back to Jon. What happened?"

We passed a travel agency called *Trips R Us*.

Maybe it would help to talk about Jon, help get him out of my system. "We were married and in love. Or at least I thought so. Finally, I got pregnant after trying for a couple of years. I did everything I was supposed to do, read all the books, took all the vitamins, and avoided strenuous exertion. The baby died inside me. Jon got quiet, distant. He never cried, and I cried all the time. I felt like I failed him as a wife and as a woman."

We passed a sign for *Cut Your Own Christmas Trees*.

"Can't blame yourself." Danny brushed my cheek with his hand. "Those things happen. My mom lost two babies before she had me. If those babies didn't die, I wouldn't be here. Maybe someday we'll have a kid together. But kid or not, I'm going to love you all the same."

"You don't understand. It was my fault. My uterus is defective. I can't have children." At first the tears came one at a time, but soon, I bawled.

"Aw, Blondie, I didn't mean to make you cry."

"It's not you," I said between sniffles. But partly it was. Even if I could have, I didn't want to make a baby with Danny. I wasn't in love with him. Maybe after a while ….

"I'm going to pull off the highway next exit," he said.

I turned up the volume on the weather report predicting three to six inches of snow by morning. Then Richard Marx sang "Hold on to the Nights."

Off the highway, we passed a coffee shop called *Brewed Awakenings*. We followed a lodging sign for a place called *The Wander Inn*, which was six miles ahead.

I lowered the volume again. I wished I knew exactly what was ahead of me without Jon. "Ever time travel to the future, I mean after the year 2000?"

"That would be pretty cool," Danny said.

"In this article by my college boyfriend Steve, you know, the agent who brought me to the safe house, he said travel to the future should be easier than going back in time."

We passed a flower shop called *Eternally Irises* that had a sign shaped like a casket. I couldn't see how that would bring in customers.

I went on about Steve. "Funny thing was he had a hard time with science courses when we were in college. I couldn't picture him as a physics writer."

"In my experience," Danny said, "the more people seem to change, the more it's bullshit."

We passed a boarded-up hamburger stand covered with graffiti. In six-foot high, neon-green capital letters, someone had spray-painted *Repent*. How many sins had I already committed in the name of fixing my life?

CHAPTER 47

SARA, AGE 32

Monday, December 19, 1994, 5:12 PM
The Wander Inn
Rose Harbor, Maine

The Wander Inn turned out to be a sweet white colonial house with black shutters. Rose bushes, bare of leaves, but covered in rose hips flanked either side of the front door. A vacancy sign hung from a wrought iron post.

Were we going to be safe there?

Danny went to get us a room and came back a few minutes later. "I signed us in as Mr. and Mrs. Right. They didn't ask for identification."

He held out an old-fashioned brass skeleton key.

I snatched it from him.

"Your hand is working, Squirt. Probably nerves, earlier."

I didn't think so, but said nothing.

He removed his bomber jacket and draped it around me.

Thanks to the redheaded Domestic guy, I needed a new coat.

～

Navy blue ships sailed serenely across a cream background on the wallpaper. The wide pine floorboards groaned amiably under our steps. Our room was on the top floor at the end of a long hall. The placard told us we had the *Starboard Suite*. I made a mental note of the emergency exit a few paces away.

The nautical theme continued into the room, with a similar ship pattern to the fabrics and an actual ship in a bottle on the dresser. I suppose something about the nostalgia of sailing to distant lands must have captivated the decorator. A giant cherry mahogany sleigh bed took up most of the room. The other furniture consisted of a small bench, a writing desk with upholstered chair, and a full-length floor mirror. The open en suite bathroom held a pedestal sink and enormous claw-foot tub.

My leg suddenly numb, I slumped onto the bench.

"That tub looks big enough for two." Danny sat down and took my hand in his. "I'm going to keep you safe, Blondie. Don't worry."

I leaned into him. He was big and solid, but I didn't think anyone could keep us safe from Domestic or the deadly side effects of the experiment. An international conglomerate that large had endless resources. I felt more dread than fear. Not *if*, but *when*.

"Want to eat the take-out now?" he asked.

I'd lost my appetite when we fled the motel. "A bath sounds good to me, but you go ahead and eat."

"I can chow down while the tub is filling." He planted a kiss on the top of my head before walking away.

Shortly, I heard rushing water from the bathroom.

It was still a shock to witness those blonde locks in the mirror. My face looked drawn. I undressed in the middle of the brightly lit room, discarding my clothes one by one to the floor. I felt no anxiety about Danny seeing. Something in me had shifted. *Probably terror for my life.*

My breasts stood high, nipples rosy as they had been before pregnancy. My belly was stretch-mark free. I would have traded my unaltered body for a baby that made it to term. If I'd known about my defect before, I never would have tried to get pregnant. I could have spared myself and Jon the heartache, maybe saved our relationship.

But Jon was a bad guy. I had to keep reminding myself of that.

"Hello, hot stuff," Danny said, coming toward me in the mirror.

"Hold me," I said.

"Now you're talking." He pressed himself into me from behind, kissed my neck, and cupped my breasts.

I felt him getting hard.

We looked good like this. No, more than that. *I looked good enough to be with him.* "Bath," I said, before things took a different turn.

"Your wish is my command, Sara." He lifted me into his arms, carried me to the settee next to the tub.

He tested the water with his hand, then turned off the faucet. "Perfect, like you. Get in."

He held my arm as I entered the lavender-scented water. *Thoughtful of him to add bath salts.* I needed all the help I could get to de-stress.

His penis, at full attention, saluted me as he lowered his jeans and underwear. He joined me in the tub, took my legs into his lap, and rubbed the bottoms of my feet.

I closed my eyes. The foot massage felt better than anything that happened in bed at The Low Tide Inn. But if anyone deserved a second chance, it was Danny.

"You know," he said, "I did try to go to the future a couple times."

I opened my eyes. "What do you mean?"

"Well, I sort of focused on a date in my mind and grabbed for the pack of smokes."

"What year?"

"2001. Didn't want to get too ahead of myself, ya know, end up an old man."

"So, what happened?"

"Landed in 1975, the Quincy Mart on the other side of the high school bleachers." He squeezed my ankle. "But I was determined to see the future. So, I bought a pack of smokes there, you know they never carded kids, and pow, off I went again."

"Back to 2000," I said. "Was anything different in the present after such a short trip?"

He stopped rubbing my foot. "That's the odd part. I went from young to younger. Ended up in 1967. At a liquor store with my Dad picking up his breakfast." He let go of my ankle.

I moved closer and wrapped my legs around him. "You mean to tell me you traveled from the past into the past? How is that possible? Steve said the scientists determined that Penrose waves are linked to their point of origin, like a kind of homing beacon." I kneaded Danny's shoulders, eager for the answer.

"Scientists don't know jackshit," he said. "Oh baby, your hands are amazing."

"You were nine years old in 1967. What was that like?"

"Like I was squeezed into too small a space. I tried to act normal. Nothing about being with my dad was ever normal. He started swigging whiskey right there in the parking lot, before we got into his truck. Shoved the bottle in my face. I didn't want any." Tears welled in his eyes.

I stopped working his muscles and held him. "You don't have to go on. Let's enjoy the bath and each other."

He scooped up water and doused his head with it. "I have never told anyone about this, Sara. Not even your brother. But you deserve to know the kind of fucked up guy you're getting."

"You're not fucked up, Danny. Your dad was." I kissed him, hoping to quell his need to tell. I didn't want him to re-live the pain again, a third time.

He didn't kiss back.

I stopped trying to distract him and let him talk.

"We got in his pick-up. My dad grabbed me by my hair. Poured the whiskey down my throat. I almost choked to death on it." His voice got quiet. "Dad sat there laughing his ugly, half-toothless head off. He called me a pussy."

"That's unforgivable. He was horrible to you, deplorable." I whispered in his ear, "Don't dwell on it, darling."

"No. You need to know. You might not want me after this."

"Nothing can change what's in my heart." Truthfully, I didn't know how I felt about him, except sorry for what he'd had to live through with his dad. Twice.

Danny's eyes were open, but his vision turned inward. He wasn't seeing me, but a dark place of memory. "Then Dad said, 'If you're gonna be a pussy, you should have some dick.' He forced my face into his crotch. I threw up, but he kept making me suck him until he came."

The revelation of what Mr. Astrella had done to his son made me want to retch. I locked my arms around Danny.

Growing up with my mother had been hellish, but Danny's father was the devil incarnate. How any parent could hurt a child that way was beyond my comprehension. His mother should have gotten her family away from the torture.

We held onto each other until the bathwater turned cold and we shivered. We stepped out into the inn's plush terry robes.

I stood on my tiptoes and kissed Danny softly on the mouth. I vowed to myself I would see to it no harm would ever come to him again. Then, I looked into his sorrowful, beautiful, bloodshot eyes and said, "I love you Daniel Astrella."

And in that moment, nothing could have felt more true.

CHAPTER 48

SARA, AGE 32

Tuesday, December 20, 1994, 8 AM
The Wander Inn
Rose Harbor, Maine

*P*roud of myself for steering clear of all the cereal canisters in the breakfast area, I carried out a tray of fruit salad, apple muffins, and two coffees. I had to set the tray on the floor to get out my key to the suite.

I woke earlier in Danny's arms and slipped out of bed without rousing him. He had a hard night and needed all the rest he could get. We hadn't made love—only slept. It was the best night of rest since the time flashes began.

I opened the door. The bed was empty. So was the bathroom. Silly to check the closet, but I did. Sweat beaded the back of my neck.

Danny was nowhere.

We would have passed on the stairs if he went down.

The entire inn was nonsmoking, so he couldn't have time flashed. And if he had, wouldn't his body still be here, just not the consciousness I'd gotten to know? Or else wouldn't this timeline cease to exist?

I feared the worst—the pair from Domestic captured him. But why not me too?

I gathered up my things, readied myself to flee alone. But I'd need

Danny's car keys. I felt bad going through his personal things. On top in his duffel, I discovered a picture frame that held what might have been the last photo ever taken of my brother.

In it, Adam stood in the middle of, or rather was held up by, Joanne and Danny. The chemo and disease had taken their toll. Adam had no hair at all, no five o'clock shadow, no eyebrows. His face looked sunken in, and his height was diminished. And yet, he wore this enormous, goofy grin, as if it were the finest day in his life.

"What are you smiling about, bro?" I asked the photo.

I didn't know what went on in his head so close to death. I wondered how anyone as ill as he was could look foolish and relaxed.

As I was about to place the photo in my suitcase, Danny strode through the door. I almost dropped the frame.

"Goddamn you," I said. I smacked him on the arm.

"Hey." He tried to kiss me, but I backed away.

"Where the hell have you been?"

"Went to look for you. Thought maybe you forgot something in the car. Since I was out there, I sorted through my books for one you might like." He held out a copy of *Time Travel Primer*.

"I was terrified. I thought Domestic caught you."

"Aw, sorry, Squirt. C'mere."

Relieved, I let him kiss me.

"What have you got there?" he said when he saw I had something in my hand. He threw the book to the bed and took the frame from me.

"Packing for a quick getaway and looking for your car keys, I found this. When was it taken, do you know?"

"Snooping, aye?" He grinned.

"I plead the fifth."

He looked at the photo, tapped Adam's face. "Summer 1978, a few weeks before he died. I went back there and had to watch him die all over again." He sighed. "But Joanne looked smokin' hot in that crop top." He bit his lip. "Sorry. I didn't mean to say that out loud."

Joanne looked as good in a crop top as a flannel pajama top. His appreciation for her didn't sting. *What happened to my jealous streak?* "She's beauty and brains all in one."

"So are you," he said. "I wished we'd all stayed friends."

"Me too. Should we get a move on?"

"Why so soon?" he said. "We've got the bed till noon."

CHAPTER 49

SARA, AGE 32

Tuesday, December 20, 1994, 10:05 AM
The Wander Inn
Rose Harbor, Maine

*A*fter coffee, oral sex, apple muffins, and several orgasms, not necessarily in that order, I had an idea Danny wasn't going to like.

Showered and dressed in those delightfully snug jeans and a Guns N' Roses t-shirt, he said, "You ready to go, hot stuff?"

I sat with my legs crossed, browsing the *Time Travel Primer*. The book claimed paradoxes were self-preventative. "You know what I think we have to do?"

He sat next to me. "Have more sex?"

I leaned against the headboard, uncrossed my legs, and stretched them over his lap. "Try to time travel on purpose."

He leaned away from me. "Why?"

"We need to see how much control we have. Maybe it's more than the bad guys know."

"If we time flash out of here, I might lose you." He stroked my knees. "Remember, you love me."

"I love you," I said. The words left my lips like soap bubbles—pretty, but insubstantial. I wanted to love him like I did the night before. He was a good guy. *But he wasn't Jon.* "We have to do this to ensure our future. If we ever want to be safe, we have to take charge."

"So let's change our identities and get out of Maine."

"I'm tired of feeling helpless against Domestic. Those men in suits will find us. I want to try going further back in time, like you did."

"How would going further back help?" He pushed my legs off his lap and stood.

"I was in a lab before I time flashed here. Maybe being in a lab, they could track my Penrose waves or whatever. But if we went further back in time, it's possible they'd have no way to trace me."

He groaned. "I know what this is. You don't think I can protect you because I couldn't protect myself against my dad, right?"

"Danny, not at all." I didn't want him to regret telling me about his father's abuse. "It's not about you. I want—"

He poked himself in the chest. "Aren't I man enough for you?"

"You're more than enough man for any woman." I leaned forward and stroked his crotch.

Danny flung my hand off. "You don't trust me."

I got up to embrace him, but he kept me at arm's length. "Let's see if we can outsmart them. Wherever we travel to in time, we'll find each other and be together in an earlier year."

"You can't know that, Miss Psychic Hotline."

"My first time flash, I saw you. Here I am with you again in my third time flash."

His arms dropped to his side.

I placed a hand over his heart. "I believe we're drawn to each other, and we will be again. Let's put our trust in us."

His face sagged. "You're not going to let this drop, are you?"

"I can't."

"And what about too much time travel being bad for your health, like your buddy Steve said?"

"You've gone a dozen times and you're fine. I have a ways to go to catch up."

"If I agree," he said, "and we don't time flash, promise me that will be the end of it."

"One time flash and we'll go from there."

"Women. You can't live with 'em, you can't redo without them." He drew me to him. "Okay, Squirt, I'll do this for you. Consider it a wedding present for my bride."

CHAPTER 50

SARA, AGE 32

Tuesday, December 20, 1994, 11:25 AM
The Wander Inn
Rose Harbor, Maine

*W*hen we got back to The Wander Inn after braving the near foot of snow that had fallen overnight, we discovered an intruder, stretched out right in the middle of our rumpled bed.

I nearly fainted when I saw him hunkered there.

"Mrow," said the cat who looked and sounded exactly like my Gallo. But he couldn't be, since my kitty wouldn't be born yet.

"Gallo!" I said anyway and rushed to the bed.

Danny followed me. "What's a Gallo?"

The black cat leapt into my arms.

Danny took a step back.

I snuggled the kitty against my chest. "A couple of years from now Jon and I adopt a kitten who grows up to look exactly like this one. We name him Gallo because he reminds Jon of a fluffy rooster his uncle once owned."

The cat purred my Gallo's same baritone purr. I nuzzled his head with my face. He smelled of milk and white paste—exactly like my kitty.

"Must belong to the Inn," Danny said, and then sneezed half a dozen times.

"Allergic?" I said, wary of the answer. I couldn't be with a man who didn't love cats.

"Dander stuffs up my head."

Much as it broke my heart to do so, I carried the Gallo-alike to the door. "Thanks for the furry love," I said.

"*Mrow*," he said, and then shot from my arms, a cat-shaped cannonball. He raced down the hall, paused at the top of the stairs, spun around, and blinked his yellow eyes three times before descending.

I would have sworn he was my cat, but he couldn't have been. Unless Gallo time traveled too, like Gareth from the *Time Cat* books. *Wishful thinking.* I missed my baby.

"Are we gonna do this?" Danny said. He sat on the bed "You know we don't have to."

My back pocket held a pack of cigarettes.

We had agreed on a date to concentrate on. Thursday, May 28, 1984—the day before Danny asked Carmen to marry him. Also, the day after Steve broke up with me. It was another of those odd coincidences that our major life events coincided.

Danny married Carmen within a month of meeting her. I guess he'd always fallen in love fast. I wondered if he asked every woman he ever slept with to marry him, and she was the first one to say yes. Danny proposed to her at Lena's Lounge on Beachcross Boulevard when they were visiting his mother.

If Danny and I were destined to be together, we'd remember being in Rock Beach a decade before it happened. We'd find one another again, and hopefully, Domestic would be none the wiser.

Or else, something would go wrong and we might never see each other again. It was an insane theory, sure, but it was the best I could come up with. And worth the risk to be free of Domestic.

Danny didn't agree, but he wanted to prove he'd do anything for me.

We sat next to each other on the bed, our knees touching.

I concentrated on all the details I could recall of the rainy, raw day I visited Grandma's grave for the belated setting of the marker. Dad held my hand, both of us in tears. My stoic mother clutched her giant gator-skin purse to her chest. The rabbi prayed in Spanish and Hebrew.

"Whenever you're ready," Danny said.

I opened my eyes, and seeing the sadness in his, I wavered. Was my idea too absurd to work? "Too bad we can't hitch a ride on the Tardis," I said, trying to lighten the mood.

He didn't crack a smile. "Sara, we agreed to try this once. I know you won't forgive yourself it we don't. Let's be done with it."

"You're a good man, Danny," I said, then kissed him, aware it might be the last time. No fireworks, but the kiss was sweet all the same.

"Now or never," he said.

I held out the red pack of Stinsons, Domestic's best-selling brand.

Danny held out a box of Berry Beary Crunch, the bear sporting a lion's mane.

"Now," we both said at once.

I reached for the cereal at the same time Danny reached for the cigarettes.

An electric pulse shot through my body like lightning. The room blazed to blue-white nothingness.

CHAPTER 51

JON, AGE 38

… like the wind singing in a burning building …

— OCTAVIO PAZ

Saturday, April 8, 1995, 1 AM
Gentry Research Laboratory
Fishburg Falls, NY

*J*on, per Vento's orders, gathered preliminary intelligence on Gentry Research Laboratory. For two whole days, he tracked the daily comings and goings of various employees, including the security guards. One guard per twelve-hour shift. *One to one.* He liked those odds. Plus, those men did not appear to be in peak physical condition. And he doubted they had all the defense training he did. He could go in, get the proof he needed, and get out with no casualties.

The tip about illegal operations came from Mrs. Elise Wells, who said she was from five years in the future. She claimed an experiment at Gentry Labs had sent her back in time. Though it sounded totally loopy to him, Vento thought the lead had merit.

Examining the building plans the company filed with the county, Jon had decided the best course of action was to enter the lab through the back door. The whole Domestic conglomerate could go down once he gathered evidence of illegal human experimentation. Test subjects' lives at stake more than qualified as exigent circumstances.

He grew antsy waiting for Vento's go-ahead to move in. She had not returned his page or his multiple messages in the last six hours. She usually got in touch within minutes. Efficiency was her middle name. And she'd never blown him off. *Had something happened to her?* No, she was probably just tied up on her end of the Domestic investigation.

At one AM, a single car remained in the lot, the Ford pick-up belonging to the older guard.

It was the optimal time to go in. He couldn't justify waiting any longer.

Moths flickered around the low-wattage bulb that hung over the lab's back door. He worked the lock, cracked it in seconds.

Doors flanked the hallway inside, stretching as far as he could see in the red light of emergency exit signs. The soda and snack machines near the exit hummed.

He crept forward, gun at the ready. He hadn't discharged his weapon since joining the bureau, and he hoped to keep it that way.

The glass doors on both sides of the hall were locked. One room contained mainframe computers. He could break in and steal the tapes, but he needed to investigate the facility further. It was his duty to get the research victims to safety first.

A conference table with a dozen chairs filled the room on the opposite side of the hall. That door was unlocked.

The next set of glass doors revealed a doctor's examination room on one side and an operating theater on the other. He tried the door handles. Locked. He doubted any patient records would be stored there.

The next set of doors, made of steel, afforded no view. Behind the locked right door, a loud engine whirred. Through the door on the left came a repetitive thwapping sound. When he tried the handle, the door swung open.

He tiptoed into the dim, frigid room, making sure the door closed without making a sound. An eerie, blue glow emanated from steel cabinets that lined the walls. He side-stepped gurneys—all occupied—grateful for the smell of formaldehyde rather than decaying flesh.

When he reached the source of the repetitive sound, he couldn't believe what he saw.

The heavy-set guard, pants down, was pleasuring himself while staring at a naked female corpse.

Jon gagged.

The guard stopped moving. "Shit, Russ. Get outta here. Ain't your turn."

"Hold it right there," Jon said.

The guard guffawed. "That's what I been doing," he said. "Now, put your gun away and we can talk about this. Who the hell are you anyway?" He stumbled off the table.

"Kick your weapon to me," Jon said.

"Hard to do with my clothes around my ankles. Give me a minute." The guard pulled up his underwear and pants, then kicked his gun. It skidded across the floor past Jon toward the entrance. "Oops," he said.

"Next oops and you lose a testicle. Got it?"

"Yes, sir."

"Why did you call me, Russ? Is anyone else here?"

"I'm the only one on duty," the guard said. "When I heard you cough, I thought Russ—the other guard—had showed up. He likes the ladies too. You can have this one, I already warmed her up for you."

Disgusted, Jon fought the impulse to knock the guy's teeth down his throat. He directed the guard to keep his arms in the air and move to the exit.

"You want my wallet?" the guard said. The keys clipped to his belt jangled as he moved.

"I'm the one asking questions, on behalf of the Department of Justice. Where are the records for the experiments?"

"Anything like that would be in Dr. Gentry's office."

"Lead the way. And keep your arms up."

"My arms are getting awful tired, friend."

Jon prodded the man with his gun. "I'm tired of your voice, friend."

The guard kept his hands raised and his mouth shut.

The kicked gun lay on the floor ahead.

"You reach for the piece and you're dead before you make contact," Jon said.

The guard stepped aside, giving the area wide berth.

Jon pocketed the old, short-barreled Smith and Wesson. When the guard finally made it to the door, Jon said, "Open it slowly."

The guard obeyed.

Fluorescent light washed in from the hall.

Someone else had to be there to turn them on.

The guard took advantage of Jon's momentary distraction and dashed down the corridor.

"Stop," Jon said, impressed by how the heavy-set man sprinted like a rabbit. He fired and hit the man's thigh.

The guard screamed and fell flat on his face.

"Not so fast," another man said from behind Jon. "Drop your weapon and turn around."

Jon ignored the first half of the order.

The day-shift guard, a tall, big-eared man, stood a foot away, nine-millimeter Beretta poised. "You shot my best friend."

"He'll live," Jon said.

"He better," the thin guard said. "Now drop your weapon." When he adjusted his stance, his short shirt sleeve rode up, revealing the red "1" tattoo of the first infantry division.

Not on your life. His father got killed standing down. Jon fired.

Two things happened at once.

Jon's shot hit the big-eared guard in the chest, and the man collapsed.

The big-eared guard fired twice. The first bullet hit Jon in the throat, above the collar of his bulletproof vest. The second bullet went higher and entered his temple.

Jon flopped backward and fell to the ground. The warmth of his escaping blood covered him like a blanket. Breathing hurt like a knife to his lungs.

His vision blurred and everything went white.

Cold invaded his entire body.

Mamá, I'm sorry to leave you all alone.

REDO 3

YEAR 2000 — THE PRESENT

As if you could kill time without injuring eternity.

— HENRY DAVID THOREAU, WALDEN

There are years that ask questions and years that answer.

— ZORA NEALE HURSTON, THEIR EYES WERE WATCHING
GOD

CHAPTER 52

SARA, AGE 38

Monday, October 9, 2000, 2 PM
Pinebough Cemetery
Easthaven, Queens, NY

*T*he light breeze carries the scent of daylilies. Sunlight glints off the high-polished granite monument.

I have to squint to see. I am in the cemetery. *What am I doing here?*

I remember being with Danny in 1994, like it was a dream. And we were about to try an experiment. I clamp my hand over my mouth to cover my elation. *We did it! We went further back in time!* All I have to do now is go meet him at Lena's Lounge.

I should let my parents know I'm leaving. But I don't see them anywhere. In fact, no one is around. Not even the rabbi. *Oh no.*

Nothing is right for 1984. There are no clouds, and the day is warm enough that I don't have on a coat. So when in time am I?

What I see right in front of my face gives part of the answer. The space next to Grandma's plot is occupied. The headstone reads—*Reya Rodríguez Bloom, Beloved Daughter, Wife and Mother, 1932 – 1995.*

I slump to a nearby concrete bench in time to double over and throw up. My gut hurts so badly I half expect to expel rocks. Stomach empty, I check the tote bag I am carrying for a bottle of water. I notice my hand—no wedding band.

First thing I find in my bag is the *Queens Gazette* dated October 9th, 2000. I'm back to the present, not the past. Well, actually the future, since it was only April 2000 in my original life.

And today would be Jon's 44th birthday.

A bolt of pain explodes in my forehead. I close my eyes and new memories gush.

I reached for the cereal and didn't time flash. I remained right there, in the Starboard Suite of The Wander Inn. Danny, who didn't time flash either, insisted I marry him right away. We fought. He stormed off and drove away. I took a bus north to Warren, Maine. I never saw Danny again.

I open my eyes. That can't be. I did time flash. I traveled to here, to right now, to the year 2000. If I didn't time flash, I would have stayed with Danny and kept the promise I made to see no harm came to him.

But my memory insists that I stayed in the past.

How can both be true? I must be some kind of Schrodinger's cat paradox, having both time traveled and stayed in the past.

My memory says this new me is single and lives with Gallo in a cottage near the sea. My kitty and I like to garden. I called my cat Gallo even though Jon wasn't there to name him. I've been working as an accountant for Maine's Washington county school system for six years. I just visited Dad at his Hollymont, Queens condo then came to the cemetery to pay respects to the rest of my family before heading home.

I wonder if Danny understands what happened. But how do I find him in this timeline? I rifle through my tote. I'm grateful to see on my Maine license photo that I'm a brunette and look about the same as I did before all this chaos began. Apparently, I still don't own a mobile phone. At the bottom of the bag, I find a ring with three keys. I drive a VW Beetle, the same car as my original life, except in this redo the paint color is piss yellow instead of bird's egg blue.

Danny, wherever you are, hold on. Once I locate my car, I'm coming to find you.

CHAPTER 53

SARA, AGE 38

Monday, October 9, 2000, 3:30 PM
The Palace Saloon
Woodward, Queens, NY

*B*y the time I arrive in Woodward, my head feels like an over-inflated balloon about to burst.

I turn onto Beachcross Boulevard and look for Lena's Lounge, the place Danny proposed to Carmen. I spot the brick building. Still a bar, but now it's called The Palace Saloon. I park and go in.

The Saloon smells more like popcorn than sawdust. Outfitted in a sham western theme, saddles, horseshoes, and photos of cowboys adorn the walls. Instead of a mirror behind the bar there's a big sign notifying patrons to *Leave pistols with the barkeep, but hold onto your hats.*

Two men, a few feet apart, sit slumped on stools. One of them is broad shouldered and bald. The other is thin with red wavy hair.

Panicked by seeing the redhead, I bump into a wooden chair at one of the wagon-wheel tables.

The red-haired man turns toward the source of the noise.

Phew. Not a Domestic guy at all. This man's face is much rounder than all the look-alike clerks. "Sorry," I say to him.

The bald man looks in my direction.

I'm overwhelmed.

The scar over the bald man's left eye matches the one I remember over his right. And more scars cover his stubbly chin and cheeks. His checkered-flannel shirt gapes open over a bulging beer belly.

I trip over my own feet heading toward him. "Danny?"

"That's my name, don't wear it out." His eyes are the color of mold. "Sara Bloom." He chokes on my name as if it sticks in his throat. "What the hell do you want?"

I climb onto the stool next to him. "I want to know what happened to the two of us."

A bartender approaches, sets down a coaster in front of me.

I do a double-take. The barkeep looks like the Danny I remember from my time flash to 1994, but this younger version has dark eyes.

"What's your poison, pretty lady?" he asks. He's as charming as my Danny used to be. I order a cup of coffee.

"Gimme a sec. I'll brew up a fresh pot out back," he says and leaves.

"What happened?" Danny slaps the bar top with an injured hand. "You broke my heart, you bitch."

The word "bitch" is like a slap. "But I don't understand." I brush my fingers over his scraped knuckles.

He wrenches his hand away.

"Our experiment worked," I say. "But not how we planned. I think we can fix this."

"Fix what, you slut?"

I wasn't prepared for his anger. "Our destiny," I say.

Danny throws back a shot of whiskey and follows it with a long gulp of beer. He slams the mug on the counter.

I notice a plain gold band on his left ring finger.

He starts to stand, but falls back onto the stool. He's sloshed.

The bartender returns with a steaming mug and a bowl of creamers. "Sugar?"

"Maybe once," Danny says. "She hasn't been sweet for quite a while."

"No thanks," I say.

"Behave, Unc," the bartender says, wagging a finger at him. "Uncle Danny gets a little feisty with this much drink in him. Sorry if he's bothering you."

"No," I say. "We're old friends."

The bartender gives me a baffled look. "Okay, then. But give me a shout if he makes trouble. It won't be the first time I throw my uncle out on his rear." He heads back into the kitchen.

"Are you okay? Maybe you should drink my coffee."

"Can't you see my life turned out great, goddamned great?"

I ignore the sarcasm. "Your nephew seems like a fine young man. Reminds me of you."

"Yeah, fine boy," Danny says. "Better than I ever was though. What do you want anyway? I'm busy."

Drinking boiler makers in the afternoon is depressing, not busy. "I want to know what happened to us in Maine. I grabbed the cereal box and traveled here, to 2000. Did you flash forward to this bar when you grabbed the cigarettes?"

"Are you friggin' kidding me or are you completely out of your mind?" He shakes his head like he's trying to clear cobwebs.

"Please, I mean it. I need to know." I drain the coffee, hoping caffeine will relieve my headache. I massage my temples. "My brain hurts. It's telling me two different things. I can't make sense out of it."

"Hey, are you lost in time, hot stuff?" he says, the angry edge gone from his voice.

Hearing that endearment from him again makes my cheeks flush. "Lost as a blonde in a Barbie factory."

"Geez, okay." He blows a breath like he's trying to extinguish a birthday candle. "We did our little time travel experiment. I grabbed the cigarettes." He taps his breast pocket. "You grabbed the cereal. Nothing happened. No time flash. No redo. You wanted us to keep trying to fight Domestic. Said we should let the suits find us, then kidnap them, or some such bullshit. I wanted us to get married. You said no, not unless I agreed to your plan. So I made like a tree and got out of there."

As he talks, his words ring true. "My memory says that's the way it happened. But I didn't live it, Danny. That was another me. *This* me time traveled here. That other me who hurt you, stayed back in 1994. I'm not sure I know her." I lay my hand on his chest.

His heart is beating hard. He lays his calloused hand over mine, but doesn't answer. We both move our hands away at the same moment.

"I feel like I am living a paradox. Everything is wrong. I wouldn't have hurt you for the world."

"Are you trying to tell me it wasn't you who broke my heart in Maine? How could that be? Maybe you time flashed and I didn't. And the 1994 version of you took your place. But she wouldn't have understood what was going on. And you gave me hell—or the other you did, the year 2000 you. Man, this is confusing."

"You might be right. I came here, to the future, directly from the Starboard Suite in 1994. Well, to the cemetery like I tried for. Except years too late. But how did I end up with all these conflicting memories?"

"Like what?"

"My new memories tell me I didn't stop Domestic. They never came after me. Like a coward, I laid low. I skipped out to Warren, Maine and got a job. But this isn't me either. At least not the *me* I meant to be."

"Warren, huh? You were gone by the time I got back to the inn. I felt lousy. Never should have walked out. I called your parents to see if they knew where you went. Either they didn't or wouldn't say."

Danny came back for me. Guilt surges over how the *other* me treated him.

"So, are you married, Squirt?"

"No. It's just me and my cat, Gallo. Seems I haven't dated much."

Danny takes a hank of my hair in his hand for a moment. "Black suits you. Glad you went back to your real color."

The shade is more of a dark brown, but I don't mention it. "I see you're married. Congratulations."

Danny snorts. "I stayed at the inn a couple of days, hoping you'd come back. When you didn't, I went to Rock Beach to look for you there. After a while, I figured you were gone for good and got hitched to waitress Barb's niece. Met and married her a few weeks after I lost you."

Sure didn't take him long. The bitter words, "True love," escape my mouth before I can stop them.

The man on the other bar stool sneezes.

"Nah, she was like you," Danny says. "Couldn't stand by her man."

"I didn't mean for things to turn out this way. I'm so sorry."

"Don't be. I have a daughter, Kaylee. She turns five in a few months. She's a good girl, though her mother won't let her have anything to do with me." He pulls out a brown pack of Domestic brand Bozeman cigarettes from his shirt pocket.

"Hey, how come you don't time flash? You're touching cigarettes."

"I stopped getting flung around in time right after you ditched me" He shows me there's a photo tucked into the cellophane of the pack.

The pretty golden-haired girl reminds me of Joanne as a child. She has her dad's hypnotic eyes.

He kisses the picture before sliding the pack back into his breast pocket.

"We can fix this," I say. "Why don't we try?"

He looks me straight in the eyes. "Because you were lying to yourself when you said you loved me."

He's right. I was never in love with him. How did he get so wise? "I'm so sorry for what the other me did. Let this me do better."

"I may be nothing but a stinking drunk, but I have this wonderful kid. Even if I could go back with you now, what would I have?" His moldy eyes water.

Holy molé salsa. I don't want to, but I understand. He loves his little girl. If he goes back in time to be with me, she won't exist. And I can't give him a child. However bad his life turned out in this redo, he isn't willing to erase Kaylee.

I can't fix anything. My chest tightens with grief. "You're right. I shouldn't have come." I lay a couple of twenty-dollar bills on the bar. It doesn't make up for the damage I've done. It doesn't come close. I broke a promise. "Let me buy this round." I turn to go.

He tugs on my sleeve. "Wait. I haven't seen you for years. The least I can do is walk you out." He leans on me to stand.

We both stumble a bit, arms around each other's backs, and go out into the autumn dusk.

Danny taps a cigarette out of the pack. "I started smoking after you left me."

No sense reminding him that he walked out on me.

He lights up. "Here's to Domestic." He laughs, but his laugh becomes a hacking cough.

"We'll always have Maine," I say, as if it's a kindness.

"No more Blondie here." He kisses my hair, then whispers in my ear, "You're my beautiful Sara."

I swallow hard, trying not to break down. What a mess another me made of things. What a mess *this* me made of things.

"Either way," he says, "I'm here." He smiles a tobacco-stained smile.

I embrace Daniel Astrella.

He smells like beer and smoke and something else I can't identify. Maybe it's the scent of defeat.

I kiss his stubbly cheek, then go to my car.

As I pull out of the parking lot, I see him in the rearview mirror, waving goodbye. His cigarette sends unreadable signals to the sky.

After I drive a few blocks, I have to pull over. The tears come too thick to see where I'm going. And my head feels like it might explode.

It occurs to me, when I regain my composure, I could try on my own to time flash. Then I could find Danny and make sure he has a better life than this one. *Would he remember his daughter?* Maybe, maybe not. But I would, and that makes all the difference, to paraphrase Frost.

All I can do now is go back home to Maine. *Maine* and *home* in the same breath sounds strange. But what choice do I have?

CHAPTER 54

SARA, AGE 38

Tuesday, October 10, 2000, 2:40 AM
Sara's bungalow
Warren, Maine

*T*his redo me, initiated by walking out on my fiancé, is the very person my mother expected I'd be—an old maid with cats. Well, one kitty for the moment.

Memories of my alternate timeline guide me into the cracked driveway of my bruise-blue bungalow in the Little Beach section of Warren. Anemic path lights show a front yard planted with faded pink asters.

Gallo waits in a bay window. His fluffy black tail swishes back and forth to welcome me home.

My heart swells. I last saw my cat Gallo for sure upstate, in the cabin with Steve. Back in my original life, the one where I was Jon's wife. This Gallo never met Jon. He can't miss the daddy he never had. *But am I the version of me my kitty loves?*

As soon as I come through the door, Gallo leaps from the bay into my arms.

"Mrow," he says. He keeps nuzzling my cheek, purring his bassoon purr.

A cut-glass lamp illuminates the tight space. The oak floor creaks as I carry Gallo to the living room filled with a lumpy, slip-covered sofa and two beaten leather chairs.

Exhausted, I slump to the sofa. Such a long day. I've been awake since eight AM in 1994. I could fall asleep like this, kitty in my lap.

A painful twinge shoots down my right side, like red ants devouring my leg. I try to rub the agony away, but I can't sense my own touch.

Gallo scoots to the back of the sofa when I try to stand.

Steve told me about loss of motor function. First my hand, and now my leg. Maybe I'm going to end up a paraplegic.

To add insult, my stomach growls, reminding me I haven't eaten since breakfast six years ago. I had no appetite for rest-stop offerings on the drive home. I just drowned my headache to a dull roar with more coffee. Now, maybe the hunger pangs will distract me from the pain in my leg.

"Gallo, fetch me a tuna sandwich," I say.

"*Mrow*." he says, and rushes off down the hall.

"As long as you're up, make one for yourself too." Wait a minute, in this redo I've been gone for days. Gallo must be starving. My poor baby.

"*Mrow, Mrow, Mrow*," he says from somewhere in back of the house.

Next thing I know, feet are padding toward me. Not little cat feet either.

My blood pressure hits the ceiling. I lurch to a standing position, take a few tentative steps and manage to stay upright. As best as I can with a log for a leg, I rush to the coat closet and squeeze myself inside it.

"*Mrow*," Gallo says from outside the closet door. It sounds like *here*.

"What's the matter, you crazy cat?" a woman says.

I know the voice.

"I have a gun," she says. "Come out slowly or I'll start shooting."

"Joanne, it's me, Sara. Don't shoot." I push open the closet door.

Her hair in a bun, she's wearing blue-striped pajamas. She brandishes an impressive weapon, two-handed like an action hero.

I had no idea she owned a firearm. I guess a clothing sales rep needs protection out on the road.

"Oh, sweet Son of God." She lowers the gun. "Girlfriend, I could have killed you. What the hill of beans are you doing hiding in the closet?"

"When I heard you coming, I got scared. I didn't know you were staying here."

"Have you lost your mind? I'm cat sitting. Where else would I stay, on a lobster boat?" Joanne ushers me out.

"It's late. I guess I forgot. I'm done in." Knowledge comes to me with a pulse at my still-achy temple. I recall Joanne saying last week, "We old maids have to stick together," when I called to ask her to look after Gallo.

So, I lost a husband and a couple of boyfriends, but regained my best friend and my cat. This redo's not all bad. Except I might be paralyzed for the rest of my life. And I've turned Danny into a lonely alcoholic.

Joanne hugs me, then lets me go. "You look like the mystery meat in Gallo's canned cat food. Let me fix you some tea." She heads off to the left.

I limp along, the pain in my leg only stiffness now.

She doesn't notice.

The immaculate white kitchen smells faintly of lemons. This *me* appears to be a neat freak like Steve. *No, not me.*

Joanne cleans for fun the way most women shop. This is her doing.

She sets her weapon down on the butcher-block table and motions for me to sit.

Gallo leaps into my lap.

"You weren't supposed to be here till tomorrow. What the sugar shack made you come home in the middle of the night?" She goes to the counter and switches on the electric tea kettle.

"To avoid traffic?" My frightful lie sounds more like a question.

"I'm worried about you." She sits across from me. Her skin is creamy. Her highlighted golden-brown hair accentuates her hazel eyes. She could pass for being in her late twenties. She's forty-two.

"You're stunning," I say. "How do you manage to look so young?"

"Expensive cars and cheap men. Did you hit your head? You saw me a few days ago. I haven't changed that much."

She may be my best friend again, but whether she will believe me or not is another story. "I have so much to tell you. I've been going through some weird shit."

"Don't make me wash your mouth out with soap." Joanne never could stand cussing. The Catholic in her. "Begin at the start," she says.

"I reached for a box of cereal and—"

"Hold that thought." She jumps up and fetches a plate. "I baked for your homecoming. Eat." She pushes the oatmeal cookies under my nose.

I take one and bite into it. "Yum."

Shortly, the tea kettle clicks off. She pours two mugs of chamomile tea. Fussing in the kitchen, she moves with cat-like grace.

"Let's have it, now. Spill, and I don't mean this." She sets the steaming mug in front of me.

Gallo sits up and rubs his face against my neck.

Maybe the granola diet wasn't the best place to start. "Do you remember my fiancé, Jonathan García?"

Joanne cocks her head. "Fiancé? I have no idea what you mean. What's this García got to do with anything?"

"I married him."

She touches her hand to my temple. "You don't feel feverish. Did you hit your head? You ought to go to bed. I can sleep on the couch."

"I know how insane I sound. But I'm not bonkers, or at least not yet."

"Are you going to tell me what you're talking about?" she says. She chooses an oatmeal cookie, then immediately sets it back on the platter.

"In my life before this one, I married Jon."

Joanne rolls her eyes. "Are you talking about reincarnation?"

"No. Please, hear me out."

She plops back down in the kitchen chair. "I'm all ears."

"I time traveled years into the past. Three times now. And I changed things."

I can't read her expression. She doesn't say a word or even blink, so I keep talking.

"There's this corporation experimenting on people." I probe around my neck for the infected spot, but I can't feel it. "They inject people with a mind-control drug to coerce them to buy more of their products. But the drug caused some test subjects, like me, to time travel."

Joanne still doesn't bat a lash.

"Jon and I were about to celebrate our fifth anniversary when I went back in time and ended our engagement." I hesitate, weighing whether to tell her about my affair with Danny. *No need to hurt her.* "I ended up here, in this redo, this alternate present where I have never been married."

Joanne blows out a breath, sending her bangs momentarily airborne. "That's some story. What corporation did you say it was?"

"Really? That's the only question you have? You're totally buying the time travel? You're not going to send for the men in white coats?"

"Oh, Sara, I'm so sorry. Let me tell you. Domestic Global International. Right?"

"How did you know? Have they experimented on you too? Danny said he thought so from something you said." *Damn.* I didn't mean to mention him.

"Danny Astrella?

Time to fess up. "Danny's a lab rat like me. I met him when I traveled back to 1994."

"Oh, fudge," Joanne says. "My friends are victims. Both of you. Domestic seems to go out of their way to make their evil doing personal. Listen, what

I am going to tell you is top secret, but since you're involved …." Joanne trails off to gulp her tea.

"Don't keep me guessing here," I say, waving my cookie in the air. "Out with it."

"You must tell no one," she says.

"You sound like Dr. Gentry's note and the chick from Paradise Time Shares."

"Oh, sugar. You know about them too?" Joanne bites her lip.

"Yes, but go on already. You have my word. I won't tell." I sweep my fingers across my chest. "Cross my heart and hope to find a great sale at Bloomingdales."

Joanne smiles. She has the kind of face artists want to paint, well-formed cheekbones and porcelain skin. "I thought it was 'cross my heart and hope to lose ten pounds.'"

"Not anymore. I'm done with diets. Especially the granola diet. Staying put in this body. Now tell me what you know before I lose what little of my mind is still intact."

Gallo purrs against my chest.

"I work for an investigative branch of the Department of Justice. We are in charge of Corporate Crimes. Our operations are strictly covert."

"*Holy molé salsa.* That's why you have a gun. You're not a wholesale clothing rep. There go my free samples."

Her expression remains serious. "I have to travel a lot. Sales rep is a logical cover. I've been involved in investigating Domestic Global for seven years. Our agency nabbed them on all sorts of petty crimes. Nothing worthy of shutting down the whole business. We've been working the last few years to uncover their illegal human experimentation. They have something called serum H-88 they claim to be testing as a flavor enhancer. We believe it to be a mind-control drug."

"Steve Ranger told me about the mind-control research. When I called Paradise Time Shares, he came to take me to safety. But my husband Jon turned out to be a bad guy working for Domestic. He kidnapped me from the safe house and dumped me off in a lab."

"*Mrow,*" Gallo says. It sounds like no. He flies off my lap and bounds down the hall.

"Back up. Stephen Ranger. Oh, sweetie." Joanne pats my hand. "He's a Domestic operative known as *The Cleaner.* He doesn't bring subjects to a safe house. He executes them and disposes of bodies. We've been trying to apprehend him for the past eighteen months."

My blood goes cold. "That's not possible. Steve isn't a killer. He's afraid of germs. Yeah, so he cleans. He likes to have everything spotless, sure, but he wouldn't hurt a fly. We dated in college and he was totally sweet to me."

"You've never dated anyone by that name. Trust me, I'd remember. Ranger's disposed of at least a dozen subjects. Do you know how lucky you are to get away from him?"

"How does he kill them?"

"Are you sure you want me to tell you? It isn't pretty."

"I have to know."

"He gives them an overdose of drugs, then incinerates the bodies. We've found charred remains."

My stomach twists. "I can't believe it. Are you telling me I dated a serial killer?" I get up from the table in case I need to hurl. My right leg is still numb.

"Ranger's a hired killer, not a serial killer. There is a difference, but evil is evil." Joanne gets up to hug me. "I don't know what I'd do if I'd lost you."

"Oh, Jo, in my life before this, we weren't friends any more. Because of what I said to Ronald Gott about you wanting to have beautiful babies with him. I don't see how we could be friends now. I never undid my stupidity in a time flash."

"Time flash? Interesting expression. Our agency's consulting scientists refer to time travel as Chronotic Penrose wave modulation. Anyway, Gott's in prison for distribution of controlled substances. You saved me heartache." She latches onto my shoulders as if to brace me.

"There's something else you want to tell me. It's bad, isn't it?"

"Sara, there's more. But let's take our tea to the living room. Might as well get comfortable if we're pulling an all-nighter. Unless you want some rest."

"Are you kidding? I'm too wound up. But this slumber party isn't as much fun as when we were kids."

Joanne purses her lips in a pitying look.

CHAPTER 55

SARA, AGE 38

Tuesday, October 10, 2000, 3 AM
Sara's bungalow
Warren, Maine

*J*oanne's eyes pity me all the way to the living room. At least she doesn't comment on my stiff leg.

Gallo stretches out on the back of the sofa.

Having my kitty so close helps buoy me for whatever she is going to say. I sip my tea, then set it on the trunk that serves as a coffee table.

"Jonathan García was a fellow agent at the Department of Justice. He never mentioned you." Her hazel bedroom eyes appear gray in the dim lamplight. "And you and I never had secrets about men."

"Department of Justice?" I say. "That can't be. Jon worked at Domestic Global International's Long Island headquarters. We met when I worked there too."

"Listen, Sara. García and I were partners. I worked surveillance and background operations. He was an undercover operative, but he sometimes accompanied me on stakeouts. I can't imagine he could have been anything but a good man in your prior timeline. He would have been rescuing you from Ranger, not kidnapping you to bring you to a research lab. Maybe Domestic agents intercepted him."

Her words hit me like a sucker punch. The magnitude of my error is unfathomable. *My husband is a good guy after all.* I never should have doubted him.

"Oh no. I've made a terrible mistake. I thought Jon might have been cheating, but the late nights make sense if he was out spying. Still doesn't explain our neighbor Candy—"

"Candy Starr?" Joanne says. "Fake southern drawl, fake red hair—"

"Fake boobs," I say.

Joanne's smile fades quickly. "Starr works for Domestic. I don't imagine any version of García would ever crawl between her slimy covers. Maybe he was playing flirt to pump her for information."

The pun isn't funny in the least. "Jo, you have a way with words. But it's a relief to think Jon wasn't unfaithful. Did you know of a code name for Candy?"

"Red Cross," she says. "Why?"

Steve did lie with the truth. Just like Danny said. "Candy had to be the one who injected me with the drug in the first place, not my husband. But Jon still lied to me. Why wouldn't he tell me what was really going on with Domestic? His distance was torture—killing me and our marriage."

Joanne shrugs. "Bureau policy. We can't expose civilians to information that would put their lives in danger."

"You mean like you're doing now with me?"

"I couldn't tell you I was an agent before this. But now that you're involved in the case, I don't see a reason not to."

"Glad to know my goose is cooked."

She pats my arm. "No more than mine."

"But we're both making the assumption that Jon would be an agent in my original timeline as well as this one. And that Steve would be a bad guy in both."

"No mortal can fully comprehend the implications of alternate timelines." She sighs heavily, crosses herself.

What is she holding back? "I have to know, Jo, where's Jon now?

Joanne clasps her hands together. "Holy Father sustain us ..."

The answer must be bad—really bad.

"Brace yourself, sweetie. Agent García—Jonathan García—disappeared while working the Domestic case."

All the breath leaves my lungs. I don't want to believe it.

Gallo bounces into my lap, paws my chest, and kneads.

Joanne scoots up, promises to bring back Kleenex.

A dozen tissues later, I ask, "When did he go missing?"

"April of 1995. He's been gone a long time."

"We were married April of 1995 in my original timeline. What exactly was he doing?"

"Recon on a lab we believed Domestic used for experiments, likely the place where precursors to Serum H-88 were developed. He was supposed to wait for back-up—for me—before going in. He was too eager to crack the case. After he'd been gone six months, the agency assumed he had been killed."

My love died. He no longer exists in this timeline. "Did you ever find out who killed him?"

"By the time I arrived on the scene at Domestic, the lab was on fire. I went in looking for García, but there was no body. If there were any evidence, it went up in smoke."

"You've been trying get evidence against Domestic for all this time?"

"Domestic, the largest, richest, multi-national conglomerate in the world, has powerful allies and inexhaustible resources. But we're close now. We're going to shut them down for good."

"I can't understand why the richest company in the world needs to use mind control to get people to buy even more."

"In my line of work, you come to realize greed is responsible for more fatalities than heart disease."

"How can you sleep at night, Jo, knowing what you know?"

"I can sleep because I know when I wake up, I'm going to go after bad guys."

"I'm a bad guy. If I hadn't gone back in time and broken off our engagement, Jon would have been alive, like he was in my original life."

Gallo says, "*Mrow, Mrow.*" It sounds like *sorrow*.

"You are not to blame. If anyone is, it's me, my friend."

"Nothing I changed in the past accounts for why we're friends here."

"The scientists informed us that traveling into the past creates currents which move out in all directions. The slightest change, a sneeze or dropped gum wrapper, sends out quantum ripples that turn into tsunamis. They call it the Butterfly Effect."

"You're saying time isn't linear. But what happened to the original timeline where I started out? Maybe in some other dimension out there, Jon's alive."

"A comforting thought. Only our dear Lord knows." Joanne looks as heartbroken as I feel.

"Were you and Jon ever together, I mean romantically?"

"He was the best partner I ever had because he actually communicated. Most of the guys in the DOJ are tight-lipped, especially with female agents."

She didn't say no. "I remember my life with Jon even though it didn't happen in this timeline. The memories are fuzzier now, but there. And, Jo, I hated myself most of my original life for ruining our friendship. Do you remember us ever not being close?"

"You didn't spoil anything. You dedicated songs to me on the radio to say how sorry you were."

Wish the original me had thought of that. "Thank you for forgiving me."

"Come with me," she says. "You'll like this."

Gallo beside us, we shuffle down the hall and enter a tiny hospital-green bedroom.

This redo me has awful taste in paint colors. The décor is mismatched and shabby. Two overflowing wooden bookcases on either side of the bed serve as nightstands. On top of one, a lampshade glows with butterflies floating over high cresting waves—like a depiction of the Butterfly Effect.

"Look," Joanne says. "This section is all us. Do you recall any of it?"

Framed photos occupy an entire wall. A few of them are of family, but most are pictures of Joanne and me together through the years, a couple in exotic-looking places. "Some questionable fashion choices," I say, observing a few odd outfits.

"Even when we didn't look our best, someone, somewhere was wishing they were us," she says.

"How do you know that?"

"Because I've always wanted to be more like you, with your exotic bronze skin, long, coiled hair, and big brown eyes. And I've always admired how you bounce back from hurt. I mean, after Ronald broke up with me, it was hard for me to get serious about anyone."

"Oh, Jo, I've always wanted to be more like you, effortlessly beautiful and slim. And I always looked up to you, to your fortitude. You do what needs doing."

"Okay, we're both awesome." She points to a photo in which we're wearing red dresses, our necks draped with pink feather boas. "Our trip to Vegas Valentines' weekend. Remember the bucktoothed black jack dealer who kept following you around?"

I think a second. A pulse in my temple tells me all about it. "No, Harry who smelled like herring was your stalker, not mine."

"How about this one?" She indicates a photo of us in Halloween costumes. She's a tall, sleek Catwoman to my shorter, bustier Wonder Woman.

I try to recall the party. The pulse in my temple becomes a throbbing. Nothing comes. "This is from when we decided we needed new careers and gave streetwalking a try." I rub my eyes.

Joanne doesn't laugh. "You look like a slug kissed by a garter snake."

"Just a headache," I say.

She orders me to sit still on the bed while she fetches pills.

I obey and lounge against the headboard.

Gallo hurdles into my lap. He head-butts me, but his deep purr does nothing to assuage my pain.

It's been a while. Joanne must not be able to find the aspirin. I'd go help her, but Shakespeare-composing monkeys are flinging the typewriters around inside my skull.

A loud beeping sound from outside on the street only makes the ache worse. Must be someone's car alarm going off.

Finally, Joanne returns with the aspirin and a glass of water.

I swallow the medicine.

Joanne sits next to me on the bed. She looks grave. "Do you have any idea when you were last injected with serum?"

"I was in a lab hooked up to an IV serum drip before I time flashed to 1994. I spent three days there before I flashed forward here this afternoon. Does it matter?"

"Somehow the serum activates the Penrose wave receptors in the brain. That's what is supposed to make the transfer of consciousness possible across space-time. Receptors remain active for ten days to two weeks. People trapped in the past die when their receptors go dormant."

I did the math. "I must have between three and nine days left to time flash to the past again."

Joanne smacks her palm to her forehead. "Don't you understand the risk?"

"I don't get why I'm sick in both the past and the present. Shouldn't my body here in the present be unaffected when I come back?"

"Supposedly, Penrose wave activation affects the brain no matter where you go, backward or forward in time. The more you time travel, the greater effect there will be, and the more likely damage will be permanent. Enough said?"

"I've only gone back three times. Danny has time flashed a dozen times, and his brain is fine. He didn't die in the past either. His being bald, paunchy, and an alcoholic is my fault, not the Penrose waves'."

"What in Holy Heaven are you talking about? I think you better tell me everything from the beginning. If you can. How's your headache?"

The monkeys in my skull on hiatus, I tell her my story starting with seeing Grandma, to finding needles in my condo, to becoming a blonde, to Dr. Gentry's note, and Steve picking me up, to the redheaded clerks, all the way to meeting Danny back in time in Maine. I omit my affair with him to spare Joanne's feelings. Since I ruined our friendship once over a boy, I'm not about to chance doing it again.

"Thank you for telling me everything, Sara. Let's get some rest now," Joanne says. "I'll take the couch. After a good long sleep, we'll get your health checked out. First thing after we wake up, I'll take you into protective custody."

The hairs on my arm levitate. What she said sounds eerily similar to Steve, and he was allegedly a bad guy. I remind myself Joanne is my best friend, more like a sister. "Thank you for taking care of Gallo and me."

"You'd do the same. And once we make sure no serum remains in your system, you'll be tethered to the present, where I need you. After all, we're going to Acapulco for New Year's Eve."

"*Olé*," I say.

"Promise me you'll get some rest and stay right here, right now."

My best friend knows me too well. I bet she suspects I might try to time travel to the past to save Jon's life. "Will do," I say. But it's another promise I won't keep.

CHAPTER 56

SARA, AGE 38

Tuesday, October 10, 2000, 4:45 AM
Sara's bungalow
Warren, Maine

*M*y neighbors are likely calling animal control about Joanne's hyena-giggle snores. Her feet are hanging uncovered over the arm of the sofa. The racket she's making shakes the whole house. *How can she sleep like that?*

It's a good thing I never completely got rid of my headache from earlier or I'd develop a new one. The fact that the aspirin didn't nix it worries me. After I time flash again, my mental functioning might be toast. But I can't accept Jon's death and do nothing. Joanne will have to forgive me. Again.

Right leg dragging, I pass the sofa. I am about to make it free and clear down the hall to the kitchen when Gallo jumps on Joanne's chest. That has to wake her.

"*Mrow*," he says. It sounds like *now*.

She swats at him like a mosquito and— *Holy molé salsa*—keeps snoring.

~

I never should have told Joanne my trigger.

She took precautions to ensure I'd keep my word. There's not a speck of cereal anywhere in the house, not even an empty box. She must somehow have gotten rid of it all while I showered to try to ease my headache. *Damn.* I should have stayed in the living room and kept my eyes on her. I have no choice but to go to the grocery store.

~

My pee-yellow VW Bug is not out in the street where I parked it.

Joanne, being thorough, must have had her bureau tow my car away to keep me here. That's what the beeping noise was, and why it took her so long to bring me the aspirin.

I'll have to borrow her car instead. On tiptoes, I search the house for her keys and come up empty. Got to give her credit. My best friend is better at finding hiding places in my house than I am. I wish I'd paid more attention when criminals hotwired cars in the movies.

Nothing left to do but foot it to a nearby convenience store. From my new memories, I discover I often stop to buy lottery tickets at Quick Kat Convenience, a little under a mile away.

Before I go, I take Gallo in my arms. It's hard to say goodbye when I've just gotten him back. "I love you, boy. I hope to see you in my next life."

"*Mrow, mrow,*" Gallo says. It sounds like *you will.* He blinks at me three times.

As I sneak past Joanne, I blow her a kiss. Maybe we can be friends again, wherever I end up.

Thunder cracks.

I rush out the door into a downpour, and hopefully soon thereafter, into the indeterminate past.

TIME FLASH 4

YEAR 1982 — THE PAST

… we all lie to ourselves; we tell our own selves more lies than we ever do other people.

— PHILIP K. DICK, COUNTER-CLOCK WORLD

Time is a great teacher, but unfortunately it kills all its pupils.

— LOUIS HECTOR BERLIOZ

CHAPTER 57

SARA, AGE 19

Saturday, June 5, 1982, 2 PM
Wauldsons Supermarket
Woodward, Queens, NY

eeling like I was about to fall, I grabbed my mother's upper arm for support.

"Get off me," she said. Her permed, jet-black hair didn't flatter her narrow face or sallow skin. She flipped through a *Ladies Day* magazine without looking up at me.

The woman ahead of us in the checkout line had a cart piled high with dozens of cereal boxes and gallon jugs of milk.

Looking at all those boxes sent a shiver down my spine. Or maybe it was just the arctic blast of the air conditioning. I perused the racks for a fashion magazine to distract myself. The top periodical display held issues of *TV Guide* dated June 5, 1982, featuring "The Love Boat." Something about that felt wrong. I was about to pick up the *Ladies Home Journal* with Doris Day on the cover when someone tapped me on the shoulder.

"Hey, Sara," Joanne said. "Hello, Aunt Reya." She always called elders "aunt" or "uncle" out of respect. She had on tiny basketball shorts and a tight, white tank top. She looked both comfortable and sexy. Her bangs appeared to be freshly trimmed. She carried a bag of flour and a cash register receipt.

The sensation of vertigo washed over me, like I was falling through the ground. I knew what was wrong about the *TV Guide*—the year.

I'd just left Joanne in my Maine cottage in the year 2000. At the nearby Quick Cat convenience store, I grabbed for a box of cereal and a Penrose wave.

Joanne had somehow followed me back in time.

"Jo, I can explain," I said. "I couldn't keep my promise—"

"What promise?' Joanne said. "What did you go and do?" She patted her porcelain-skinned cheek. "Did you tick off that Shakespeare boyfriend of yours ... what's his name, Danger?"

Either she wasn't there from the year 2000, or she put on a great act.

"You expect her to keep a boyfriend?" my mother said to Joanne. "Just look at my daughter's hips."

Dressed in a pink tee and jean shorts, I appeared curvaceous, rather than obese. "Mind if I catch a ride home with Jo?"

"Tell your father you're abandoning me to go off with your friend."

"I'll send him up front to pick you up," I said, leaning in to kiss her cheek. Her yellowish skin smelled like grapefruit. I wondered if the cancer cells were already lurking in her breasts. Maybe I could get my mother to a doctor for early treatment, before the mastectomy she refused became a necessity, and before the disease spread to her organs.

Mother recoiled from the touch of my lips. "What's that for?"

We were never affectionate.

"Because I love you, mother," I said.

She picked at a nonexistent thread on her eyelet blouse. My declaration must have caught her off guard—but not for long. "Get lost, *Gordita*," she said.

I took Joanne's arm and strolled out of the store. At least my leg seemed to work fine.

The bright sunshine hurt my head. I reached up and found sunglasses nested in my wild hair.

Joanne surveyed the lot. "Where's Uncle Hector parked?"

I had no idea. I tried to recall which used car he drove in the eighties. Maybe the powder-blue, seventy-nine Caprice? I scanned the shady part of the lot. We never could afford air conditioning back then, even in a used vehicle. I spotted a rusted blue car with a dented right side and went toward it.

"What's the flour for?" I said to keep Joanne from asking me another question I couldn't answer.

"Sugar cookies. I'm sitting for the Morley kids tonight." It was just like her to bake for the children she babysat.

A newspaper blocked the face of the man behind the steering wheel of the Caprice.

"Dad?" I said.

He looked up. Less furrowed brow, but definitely, my dad. And not an ounce of perspiration on his face despite the heat. One cool character.

"*Niña*," he said. "And *hola*, Joanne."

"Hello, Uncle Hector," Joanne said. "You've got it made in the shade."

"Mother's in line. Your presence is requested." I kissed Dad on the cheek and said goodbye.

"You plan on telling me where we're going?" Joanne said, when we were a few paces away.

"To your car."

"It's all the way on the other side of the lot."

To be sure she wasn't from the future, I said, "Hey, Jo, I met this foxy guy the other day at the pizza place. Jonathan García. Do you know him?" I studied her face for a reaction.

She looked blank. "No. Should I?" Her response sounded genuine. "Tell me more."

"Six feet tall, medium build, lean but strong. Dark and dimpled."

No hint of recognition in her expression. "Sounds like a Hispanic Harrison Ford."

I laughed. "A Latin Indiana Jones." I never thought of Jon that way, but it fit. "You sure you don't know him?"

"No, but you can fix me up any time. Unless you want him. What about your boyfriend Danger?"

"You mean Ranger? Don't think it's going to work out with him." I sighed. I hadn't considered running into Steve again. If what the year 2000 version of Joanne told me were true, I had to find a way to stop Steve from getting involved with Domestic. They must have brainwashed him into becoming a killer.

"It sounds like you want the pizza guy," Joanne said.

"Absolutely." *I wanted Jon—more than ever.* It was a dozen years before we met. I had no idea where to find him. There had to be hundreds of Garcías in New York. Maybe thousands. I wanted to look for Danny first, since he should be in the area. I hoped I could help prevent his heartache with Carmen.

Joanne stopped at a red 1970s model Dodge Dart and lugged open the driver-side door. Quite a collectible car in the future. I thought about telling her to hold onto it.

"So where are we going, Columbo?" she said.

"Do you know how to reach Danny?" I said.

"Danny? Daniel Astrella? Why?"

I had to think fast. "My brother's friend Vinnie called from California. He needs to get in touch right away, but says the old number wasn't working. Says it's urgent, for Danny's ears only. Do you have Danny's number?"

Joanne revved the engine. "Not any more. The Astrellas got an unlisted number. I remember Danny saying his mom was sick of the middle-of-the-night calls from his father's drunk-tank friends."

"We could go to Danny's house. You know where it is, right?"

"I doubt he still lives at home, but we can try."

At least Danny hadn't met Carmen yet. I could help him avoid that misery. Maybe he and Joanne could get together. She would be good for him. She was kind, but strong enough to keep him in line.

We sang along as Pat Benatar's "Hit Me with Your Best Shot" blasted from the car speakers. Our friendship would have been this carefree the first time around, if I hadn't ruined it.

Joanne hung a left from Beachcross Boulevard into the lower income Sycamore section of Woodward. We drove past a large, fenced-off swampy area labeled with *No Trespassing* signs.

I remembered hearing stories of rapists dragging girls into that no-man's land. I got a bad feeling in the pit of my stomach.

Joanne lowered the volume on the radio. "If I remember right, his house is off Goines Street, a little way down."

That name rang a bell, but before I could answer, a vehicle rammed us from behind. Metal crunched and glass exploded. My head bashed into the dashboard.

Joanne screamed, "What the fudge?" She pulled over to the curb and parked beside the swamp. Her lip bled along a line where it had split. She was shaking.

The armored security truck that hit us screeched past. Tinted windows made it impossible to see in.

My head pounded—nothing new—but something wet stung my eye. My hand came away red and sticky.

"Holy Mother," she said, "you're a fountain of blood."

"A flesh wound," I said, hoping it were true. "How about you?"

"Fat lip. Otherwise fine, I think. I better go out and check how bad the damage is. My father's going to kill me." She stepped out of the car.

My perception of time slowed.

The armored car came roaring toward us, head-on, and mowed Joanne down. One minute she was there, and the next not. The vehicle screeched to a stop with my best friend crushed under its wheel. Her legs kicked out three times, then stopped moving.

A petite redhead in a purple bikini jumped out of the armored car's passenger side. She looked like she could have been Candy's younger sister. A young, red-haired man, attired in a security uniform, bounded out of the driver's side.

Still dazed from watching Joanne die, I had no fight left when the man dragged me out of the Dodge. He kneed me in the chest to hold me down.

Bikini woman whipped a hypo out of her cleavage and injected me in the arm with a clear liquid. "Sleep now, bitch," she said.

The last thing I saw was a giant pink bubble she blew with her gum.

TIME FLASH 5

YEAR 1991 — THE PAST

Time is the substance I am made of. Time is a river which sweeps me along, but I am the river; it is a tiger which destroys me, but I am the tiger; it is a fire which consumes me, but I am the fire.

— JORGE LUIS BORGES, LABYRINTHS: SELECTED STORIES
AND OTHER WRITINGS

CHAPTER 58

SARA, AGE 28

Friday, August 23, 1991, 1 AM
Gentry Research Laboratory
Fishburg Falls, NY

y brain wanted out of my skull. From the green gown covering my body, I assumed I was in the hospital. Every part of me ached as if I'd been run over by a truck.

No, that was Joanne, I remembered. The image of her death played over and over in my mind.

I looked for the nurse call button. Leather restraints prevented me from moving my arms. Cuffs strapped my ankles as well. This was no hospital after all, but another Domestic lab.

Fluorescent lights accentuated the antiseptic feel of the white-walled room. Against the wall loomed a stainless steel table crammed with medical devices. A vent over my bed blew cold air. In the corners of the room, speakers were mounted at ceiling height. The two beds across the room sat empty, one of them stripped of sheets the way they do when the patient dies.

Nausea possessed me. I barfed and barfed. My throat burned from the bile. Unable to sit up, the puke strangled me. I coughed until my airways cleared.

"Help!" the woman in the next bed shouted. "Somebody is dying in here."

Bandages covered her head and half her face, but I could still make out who it was—Elise, Dr. Gentry's long-time assistant.

"Elise," I said, my voice hoarse, "it's me, Sara García." I wasn't sure she could see me with one of her eyes covered and the other reduced to a squint. "How did you get here? We're in the Domestic lab, right?"

"I don't know you," she said. "They'll kill me for knowing you."

"Who will kill you and why?"

"When they brought you in last night, they said 'Here's the one who's all the trouble.'"

"Did you see who brought me in?"

"I can't help you," she said.

"I'm sorry. I don't want to bother you. Tell me one thing, please, what date is it today, what year? Do you know?"

"They must have done more to your brain than mine. At least I know it's 1991. Summer, but I've lost track of days."

"It isn't 1982? Are you sure?"

"I know what I know. Now, leave me alone. Nurse pencil bun tried to help. Now she's dead."

The fluorescents clicked off.

"Did the power go out?" I said. "Or do they put the lights out at bedtime like in a prison?"

Elise let out a low growl, and then went quiet.

I wanted to ask about *pencil bun* too, but it was hopeless. Elise didn't want to answer. She was too scared. I wriggled and contorted my left hand in an attempt to free it from the restraint. After a while, I gave up and tried to sleep. I kept having visions of Joanne getting run over in the accident. *No —not an accident—murder.*

CHAPTER 59

JON, AGE 34

… I fall in myself without touching bottom …

— OCTAVIO PAZ

Friday, August 23, 1991, 1:35 AM
Gentry Research Laboratory
Fishburg Falls, NY

*J*on tried the door to the patient room. Locked. Shadows prevented him from discerning if the room was occupied. He went to work on the lock, this one no tougher than the back door to the facility. He'd save the victims, get the evidence against the lab, and get out. Simple.

He entered, gun poised, just in case. His eyes adjusted to the darkness of the room, though it was much dimmer than the hall lit by exit signs.

Four beds in all, two occupied. He holstered his piece and got out the tiny flashlight.

He moved to the first bed, leaned over the patient, a woman with wild hair. Her eyes blinked in response to the direct glare.

"You okay?" he whispered. He had no idea how incapacitated the research victims might be. He'd heard some ended up paralyzed or mental vegetables.

"I'm strapped down," she said, her voice a rasp. "Let me go, please."

"I'm with the Department of Justice, here to help. You good to walk?"

"I think so," she said.

He moved to the foot of her bed, lifted the sheet to reveal the leather restraint. "What's your name?"

"Sara Rodríguez Bloom."

He undid the cuffs around her ankles. "Listen, I'm going to get you and your roommate out of here. But we need to be quiet." He freed her wrists.

She smelled acrid, like she'd been sick.

He held out his arm.

She wobbled a little, then straightened and stood. "My roommate's name is Elise. Elise Wells."

"Okay, Sara, wait right here for me."

He went to the other woman, leaned over her. "Elise," he said in a quiet voice.

One eye was bandaged. The other was open, but didn't look right, didn't blink.

He nudged the woman a little and said her name again.

She kept still.

He felt for a pulse in her neck but couldn't find one. He laid his head to her chest—no heartbeat.

He went back to the first woman. "Let's go."

"We can't leave Elise."

"I'm sorry," he said, placing his hand on her back, "she's dead."

Red emergency strobe lights flickered into the patient room. Alarms peeled. He'd been discovered. His priority was to get Sara to safety.

In the now brightly lit corridor, the woman said, "Jon, *mi sol*, it's really you. I couldn't tell in the dark. And you were whispering, so I didn't recognize your voice." She tried to hug him.

How could she know his name? He kept her at arm's length. Despite the stained hospital gown and frazzled, dark hair, she was something—honey-gold eyes, bronze skin, ample curves. He'd never met her. *A woman that beautiful I'd remember*. She must have mistaken him for someone else.

"I don't know how you know my name. You can explain later. Now, we've got to move. Fast."

Good thing he'd studied the building plans. He led her through the labyrinthine halls toward the front exit.

Footsteps echoed from behind. It had to be the security guard.

"Your people?" she said.

"No. Run for the door. Straight through the parking lot. Exit right on Twelfth Court, turn right onto Cole Lane. Look for my black Ford Econoline van."

"I won't leave you. Not again."

She was confused. *Domestic must have done a number on her.* When they got out of there, he'd be happy to get to know her for real. "I'll be fine. Key code to get in is ten, zero nine, fifty-six. Can you remember?"

"Your birthday. Yes."

"How do you know my … never mind. Go."

She raced past the empty lobby desk to the revolving glass door, slid a little, but made it outside and kept going.

He watched her for longer than he should have.

He needed to retrieve the mainframe computer tapes and get the hell out. He headed back to where he'd left the box of evidence. He moved in and out of the turns with ease, away from the sound of the guard's footsteps.

Vento would be proud. Maybe he'd get a promotion.

The carton was not where he left it. Someone had hauled it back inside the computer room and secured the door. No choice but to pick the lock again. He wasn't leaving empty-handed. Maybe the woman could testify against Domestic, but she'd probably been too mentally compromised to be much use.

The tumbler clicked, turned. Immediately, he heard another click followed by a shush—the tell-tale sound of a magazine being loaded into a nine-millimeter.

"Get up. No sudden moves or I'll shoot."

Jon stood. His heartbeat revved like a motorcycle. He could reach for his gun, pivot, and fire in the hopes the guard had slower reflexes. Or he could duck into the computer room and scramble for cover behind one of the big desks.

He opted for plan B.

The guard shot.

A bullet grazed Jon's ear. From inside the computer room, Jon spun and returned fire.

The guard, a moving target coming toward him, escaped being hit.

This guy's got balls of steel. And a red "1" tattoo on his arm—army trained.

The guard fired three more times.

The first shot sailed over Jon's head. He felt the second bullet rip into his temple. By the third, he felt nothing at all.

CHAPTER 60

SARA, AGE 28

Friday, August 23, 1991, 1:35 AM
Gentry Research Laboratory
Fishburg Falls, NY

I sprinted to the revolving glass door. My bare feet slid as I went, but I stayed upright and made it outside into a warm, summer night. Little rocks stabbed my soles as I ran through the parking lot. At the exit, I looked back, expecting to see Jon behind me.

He wasn't.

I wanted to go back for him. But he had a gun, and I had nothing to fight with. I kept running and turned right on Cole Lane. I hurried, grateful for my unhindered legs. I dashed into the gutter to get to the driver's side of Jon's van. My right foot landed on something sharp, and I limped the rest of the way, the pain radiating up my leg like a jolt of electricity.

My hand shook as I punched in the numbers one, zero, zero, nine, five, six. A red light blinked. I squeezed the door handle.

Locked.

My heart hammered. I tried again, punching harder. One, zero, zero, nine, five, six. Same blinking red light, same locked door. My hands tingled, going numb. I tensed and relaxed my fingers, then started again. I stopped.

I played over in my head what Jon had said. I punched the one and the zero at the same time, the zero and nine at the same time, the five and the six at the same time.

A green light blinked.

I pulled the handle.

The door opened.

I was safe.

Someone called my name.

"Sara, let me help you." It was Dr. Gentry.

What in the world was he doing here?

Before I could ask, he clamped his arm around my neck. "Sara, I don't want to hurt you, but you give us little choice."

As a doctor he'd taken the Hippocratic Oath, swore to keep me from harm and injustice. He was crushing my throat.

I couldn't breathe.

He meant to kill me. Was he in cahoots with Domestic? And if he was, did that mean Joanne was right about Steve being a bad guy, since Dr. Gentry had put me in touch with him?

I had no time to work out all the connections in my head. I was choking to death. My fingers tore at the flesh of his arm.

"This will calm you down," he said. The hand not choking the life out of me reached around and stabbed my arm with a needle full of clear liquid.

Instead of suffocating, I drowned in a sea of murky light.

REDO 4

YEAR 2000 — THE PRESENT

El tiempo da buen consejo.

— PROVERB

Time is a dressmaker specializing
 in alterations.

— FAITH BALDWIN

CHAPTER 61

SARA, AGE 37

Sunday, July 2nd, 2000, 8 AM
Fresh Crisp Supermarket
Hollymont, Queens, NY

y center of gravity feels off. The ear-piercing screams of a nearby toddler must be upsetting my balance. I am about to trip over my own feet, but the grocery cart keeps me upright.

The Godzilla-costumed boy tosses boxes of Captain Quackenbush cereal onto the supermarket floor. A tall, thin brunette in a tight white t-shirt dress, presumably the boy's mother, ignores the child's tantrum and studies her grocery list.

My dad goes over to the boy and offers him two quarters to put the boxes back.

The mini-monster is stunned silent.

His mother says, "Put those boxes back and you can use the money for the gumball machine, Eduardo."

Eduardo stuffs the cereal back onto the shelf and holds out his palm.

My father obliges.

The mother says, "Normally, we don't take anything from strangers. But thanks."

My father bows to her, then returns to me. His wrinkled hand wavers between the oatmeal choices on the top shelf. "The instant or old fashioned?" Dad says.

"Um …" I have no idea why we are at the market or why we need oatmeal. I notice the cart is over-filled with eggs, bacon, cheddar cheese, hamburger meat, buns, ketchup, pickles, and potato chips. Looks like he's having a barbeque for an army. The Air Force and Navy too. A wave of nausea crashes over me.

"For the cookies, which do you need?" His eyes widen with concern. "*Mija*, what's wrong? You're white as a *fantasma*."

"I don't feel well. Upset stomach." But that isn't all of it. I realize I have traveled in time again. Last thing I remember is Dr. Gentry trying to strangle me. My sweet Jon, who didn't seem to know who I was, came to rescue me. And Elise died there in the lab. Tears stream down my face.

"You're crying. Do you need to go to the hospital? Are you suicidal?" His lower lip trembles.

Suicidal—why is he asking that? "I'll be okay once we get out of here. Old fashioned oats, please." *Can't go wrong with the original.*

He touches my forehead with the back of his hand. "You feel clammy. It's the air conditioning. We go from sweating outside to freezing in here. Not healthy for anybody. No wonder you're sick." Dad goes to the shelf, selects the oatmeal, and sets it in the cart.

For a second, I wonder if his body will go limp and his consciousness will travel off somewhere else in time.

He studies his shopping list and ticks off items with his fingers. "That's everything. Good. Let's get you home." His hair is the shocking gray it went overnight after his heart attack in 1997.

I push the cart, wondering when in time we are.

"Where you going now?" he says.

"To check out."

"Registers are the other way." He commandeers the cart from me. "When we get back, I want you to lie down. Forget baking for the party."

I do my best to appear normal, but I feel as if I am dragging my body through water. I can't keep pace with Dad, who was never a speed-walker in my original life.

He wheels up to the shortest line, staffed by a young cashier with long dark braids. She bears enough of a resemblance to the male Domestic redheads that I cringe. The badge indicates her name is Weena.

Unusual name but familiar, though I can't think why. I browse the magazine rack.

TV Guide's cover with Judy Garland in the *Wizard of Oz* is dated the week of July 1st, 2000. I'm back to the future again, or my present year plus a couple of months.

I think I might be okay here with Dad. At least the toothless old man and the male redheaded clerks are nowhere to be seen.

~

Outside the grocery store, the day is hot and humid. I feel like a polar bear in Florida.

A couple of guys in pick-up trucks shout obscenities arguing over a space. A peroxide blonde, who looks a lot like Jon's ex-girlfriend Misti, stomps out a cigarette with her cockroach-killer heels. One of the shouting men eyes her up and down and loses the space to his rival.

An old man in a rumpled, stained, gray suit pushes a twin stroller. The identical toddler boys wear matching sailor outfits and sport heads of carrot-red hair. The old man flashes a toothless smile at me.

My stomach somersaults. At least if I need to hurl, it will happen before we get to Dad's car. Like always, it appears he's parked in the next state.

I lumber along, trying to tune into memories the way I have in other redos. My fourth alternate life comes to me in flickers of images, a movie on fast forward.

I live alone in Maine in a small cottage. I work as an accountant for the Washington county school system. Same as last redo.

Wait. Something's not the same. I stop dead in my tracks.

Dad goes on ahead pushing the cart.

I live all *alone* in Maine. *No Gallo.*

I search my memory. I never went to the shelter in Queens to get him. *Oh no, my sweet kitty.* He must be with someone else now. I'll have to go to see if they have the record of his adoption. Right—unnamed black kitten—I'll never find him. And there's the chance he didn't get adopted because he's black. Too many superstitious people.

"Bus is leaving," Dad calls.

I start walking again. I can't obsess over Gallo now. I have to fill in the rest of the blanks of my life.

I'm single, I focus on my job, and avoid social engagements. There's no Jon in my life. We've never met. Steve dumped me after we dated for only a week because he said he couldn't tolerate my lack of hygiene. The last time I saw Danny was at Adam's funeral. What happened between us in Maine feels like nothing more than fantasy.

The car accident happened. No one blamed me for Joanne's death except me. I couldn't face her family, so I didn't attend the wake or burial. I never told anyone that my time traveling was the cause. I feared everyone would think me crazy and I'd be institutionalized.

I planned on exposing Domestic. Instead, I went into a deep depression. I was sent to a locked psych ward a couple of times. Once for suicidal thoughts. Once for delusions. Under hypnosis, I told my shrink I used to be married, but I went into the past and broke the engagement.

So far, I've spent most of this redo on antidepressants and stronger meds. Baking Joanne's cookie recipes is the most effective therapy for me.

When I heave myself into the beat-up Civic, I realize the trouble isn't that Dad is a speed-demon. I can't keep up with him because of what's wrong with me.

There's an extender on the end of the passenger seatbelt that I need every last inch of to fasten it around my blubbery body. In the sun shield mirror, I say hello to my multiple chins. Cookie therapy has added up to me looking like a walrus.

Great. In this timeline, I am a fat, lonely spinster who got her best friend killed and didn't have the courage to try to stop Domestic. It's clear why this me is depressed. She has no Gallo, no Jon, no Joanne, no boyfriend, no friends. With each time flash, *another me* loses more.

Dad turns on the all-news station. The big story is the election in Mexico.

Do I feel defeated because the body I am in is depression-prone? Or because I make things worse for those I love? Maybe if I can, I should anchor my tugboat self here to this redo, go on with my pathetic life and not risk hurting anyone else.

Repulsed by myself, sweaty, and short of breath, I close my eyes.

～

I stared at the foreign object in my hand. Silver barrel and black handle. Like guns I'd seen in TV Westerns, but stubbier. For something so small, it was surprisingly heavy.

I sat on a white sofa in an unfamiliar, sparsely furnished white living room. A clear glass, rectangular coffee table, situated in front of me, held stacks of sheet music. A white grand piano occupied a quarter of the room. A small kitchen peeked through a cutout in one of the walls. Street noise trickled in through high windows, honking, sirens, muffled conversations.

Having a gun in my hand scared me. I needed to get rid of it, or at least hide it.

I thought about stuffing it under a sofa cushion. I worried if it were loaded, it might go off when someone sat. I gently laid the gun on the glass coffee table.

The moment the metal made contact, the glass shattered—the sound of a thousand clocks chiming at once. I jumped up.

Just then, John Lennon walked in.

That seeing him didn't surprise me, surprised me.

He wore a white t-shirt and blue jeans. He removed his round glasses and rubbed the bridge of his nose. "Like being in the eye of a hurricane," he said.

"I'm sorry," I said. "The table—it was an accident."

"There are no accidents, love," Lennon said. "You're a dreamer."

"I'm not the only one," I said. I smacked myself on the forehead for being a walking cliché.

"A shared dream is reality," Lennon said, "remember."

"Reality is that I caused the deaths of the people I love the most. And maybe my cat. I'm a screw-up. I don't know what to do now."

"I can't wake you up, love," Lennon said. "You have to wake you up."

"What about this gun?" I said.

"Years later ... I realized ... the walrus was the bad guy in the story," Lennon said.

What did he mean? I didn't know how to answer. I felt a searing pain in my mouth. I used a finger to hunt for the source. I found new teeth emerging above my upper, front-most incisors. Sharp and pointy like tusks, I pricked my finger on one of them and tasted the iron tang of blood.

CHAPTER 62

SARA, AGE 37

Sunday, July 2nd, 2000, 8:35 AM
Basement, Hector Bloom's condo building
Hollymont, Queens, NY

I wipe the drool from my chin.

The inside of the parked car smells like bread and perspiration.

"Are you awake, *niña?*" Dad taps my shoulder. "We're here."

Here is the underground parking garage of my dad's Hollymont condo.

"You shouldn't watch all those late-night monster movies," Dad says. "They give you bad dreams. You were yelling at something in your sleep." He frowns. "How do you feel now?"

"Better after my nap." I take a share of the grocery bags and walk with him across the concrete floor to the elevator. I'm breathing like I ran a marathon by the time we reach it. I have to stop eating cookies and start exercising.

~

"Speaking of dreams," I say as the elevator makes its slow ascent, "I had a dream about John Lennon."

"Oh," Dad says, "that's good luck. John Lennon is a good omen."

"You sound like Grandma with her omens and curses. How do you figure?"

"John Lennon was all about love. It must mean love is coming your way."

I smile. *A good omen.* I guess I won't mention the gun.

CHAPTER 63

SARA, AGE 37

Sunday, July 2nd, 2000, 8:43 AM
Hector Bloom's condo
Hollymont, Queens, NY

I hoped for the best, but unfortunately changing the past didn't change where Dad lives. Same miniscule apartment as in my original life, on the fourth floor with a view of the adjacent brick building. The furniture from our home in Woodward is crammed in. His kitchen isn't much more than an alcove. My parents' wedding photo dominates the mantle over the gas fireplace in the living area.

I help put the groceries away, but ask Dad to leave the oatmeal out on the counter. I have no idea whether touching the canister of oats will send me flying through time.

"Remind me who's coming to the party," I say.

"You know, our Woodward neighbors, the Bodells, the Norviks, the Nagles …."

All Dad's friends. *Should be a blast.* "How are all those people going to fit in this place?"

"We're using the community room. I told you. We have it reserved till midnight."

"I forgot."

"You forget a lot lately. We can start getting things ready up here at three.

Until then, you should go back to bed. You don't get enough rest. You looked so cute fast asleep in the car. It reminded me of when you were a little girl again."

There's nothing little about this version of me—I am probably twice the me *I used to be.* "I must have been deep asleep to have such a vivid dream."

"Grandma used to say, *for every pot there is a lid.* Thanks to John Lennon, you will meet your mate, and I am going to dance at your wedding." Dad smiles.

I haven't seen that expression of happiness on his face since before Mother died. Meeting my maker is more likely now than finding love. Those clear shots couldn't have been serum H-88, so my Penrose wave center clock is still ticking down. But I wish he could dance at my wedding.

In my real life, before redos, Dad couldn't even make it to the courthouse when the judge married Jon and I. Mother lay in their bed, the cancer eating away her cells. My father with her to the bitter end.

My marriage to Jon feels like the stuff of fiction now.

Dad could have remarried. He still can. A man his age has plenty of opportunities to find an available widow or divorcee.

"Maybe I'll dance at your wedding," I say.

"Nah," he says. "Those old ladies chase me at the senior center. But you know your mother was my one true love." He looks up at her in their wedding photo.

My mother beams with loveliness in an all-over Spanish lace gown with pearl-adorned veil.

"Dad, no offense, but Mother treated you like hired help. How can you call her lovable?"

"She gave me your brother and you."

"She was an ice queen. Wouldn't you have preferred an affectionate woman?"

"Come, let's talk in the other room. I can see this weighs on you."

The *other room* is a euphemism for the couch a few feet away. I sit kitty-corner from Dad on the green camelback sofa that resembles a caterpillar.

"Your mother did not believe in public affection."

"But she was a big believer in ordering you around in front of everyone and talking down to you like you didn't speak the language."

Dad shakes his head. "No, *mija*, it wasn't like that. Your mother put on an act. She radiated beauty and confidence in public. In fact, she was the most beautiful woman I ever saw. But away from everyone, she was unsure. She needed my strength, my reassurance. She gave my life purpose."

Mother should have won an Oscar if she was really acting. "I don't know what to say, Dad. I'm glad you got what you needed from her, but you deserved much more."

Dad licks his lips. "The things I could tell you about what went on behind closed doors."

"No, please don't." Sexual innuendo from my father is more than I can bear.

Dad's ordinary serene look returns. He leans forward, pats my knee. "You're her legacy, all she had left, especially after Adam died. That's why she was tough on you."

"Mother rated a diamond on the hardness scale. She couldn't accept that I was never going to be super-model thin like her, or care about social status."

"She loved you. In her own way she was proud of your education."

"Funny way of not showing it at all. I never saw—"

The doorbell buzzes before I can finish my thought.

"I'll get it, Dad." It takes me a minute to haul my bulky body up off the cushions.

"I'm not expecting anyone," Dad says. "Could be the postman with a special letter. Or maybe it's your pot lid."

Through the peephole, I see the back of someone's head. Liver-spotted skin shows through thin white hair. *If he's my future husband, kill me now.* "Who is it?"

The man turns.

I shiver.

"I need to talk," the toothless old man from the grocery store says. "Urgent. Shit. Piss. Please."

"Who is it?" Dad calls from the living room.

"Wrong door," I say.

"I have Tourette's. I'm sorry, you donut head. Now let me in. They're after me too. Rosy butt."

Did he call me by Steve's nickname for me? I leave the chain on and open the door. If need be, I can wrestle the old man to the floor and sit on him. I have heft now. "What do you want?"

"Too late for me, but not for you. Shit. Piss. I need you to blow job."

"Go away." I slam the door, but the old man's foot jams it.

He shrieks.

Dad rushes over. "Sara, what's going on?"

The old man pulls a card from his pocket and holds it out through the opening. His hand shakes.

My dad takes the card. "Tourette's Syndrome," he reads, "a brain disorder. I saw a special on TV about it. What can I do for you, sir?"

"Help," the old man says. "Please let me in. I'm not, shit, domestic, dangerous."

He said *Domestic. Not from Domestic or not dangerous?*

Dad opens the door and gives the man his arm.

The old man hobbles into the condo and drops to a sitting position on the sectional.

"Sir, do you need me to call someone for you?" Dad says. "Are you lost? Or having a medical emergency?" Dad turns to me. "Get him a glass of water, please."

"I have to talk with your daughter, mother humper. She's in deep shit peril."

"Calm down," my dad says. "My daughter will get you a drink."

I bring back a glass and set it down in front of the old man.

"Dad," I say, touching his shoulder, "maybe I should talk to him in private. Would you mind?"

"I don't know what's going on here," my dad says, "but anything that concerns my daughter concerns me."

I look at the old man. "Is this about Domestic?"

He gives a palsied nod.

"A domestic, you mean a maid?" Dad says. "My daughter's an accountant, not a maid."

"I think I know what he wants. Please, this is hard enough with his disorder. I promise I'll explain later. Maybe this gentleman would like some coffee or tea."

"Tea, yes. Thank you, spank your tart ass."

"Would you mind, Dad?"

"Sure," he says, and gets up.

"It would be easier," the old man says, "to penis, suck me, on paper." He wrestles a notepad from his jacket pocket. His hand quivers as he writes. He stops, takes a sip from the glass, but his violent tremor causes drops to splash all over his suit. He clears his throat, smiles a toothless smile. "Call me George."

"George, write faster please. I don't want my father to worry." I lower my voice. "He doesn't know anything about Domestic."

George writes a little more, then hands me the pad. The penmanship is full of scribbles, but I can make out what it says.

Domestic killed my wife in 1991. They dissected her brain to find out why the serum makes some of us time travel. They'll dissect my brain too. I have traveled into the past twenty times. I see you in the past and present. I recognize the fear in your eyes. There are only a handful of us travelers left. I tried to stop Domestic. I failed. Now you must do it. Before your body ages too fast like mine. Once the aging starts, you can't reverse it. I am too far gone.

"How can I remember your wife if she died in 1991?"

"Because you're part of the experiment, doo doo brain," he said.

Plausible, I guess. "How can I stop Domestic?"

George holds out his unsteady hand. "Paper."

I give him the paper, thinking he'll scratch out another answer.

Instead, with some effort, he returns the pad to his coat. "Go back far enough, hard on. Destroy the puss puss laboratory."

"How far back is far enough?" I say.

He shrugs his shoulders.

"You're a big help," I say. "There are government agents after Domestic. I think we should let them handle this."

"Too late, shit for brains. You know where the fuck face laboratory is, don't you?"

"I was there once or twice."

"Go there before you suck my ass, walrus."

There are no coincidences. "Did you call me a walrus?"

George winks or blinks, I can't tell which.

Dad comes with a tray of tea cups and a plate of the short bread cookies that come in a tin. Guess I haven't baked in a while. Or I ate all the cookies. *That's more likely.*

"What about the redheads?" I say.

"My grandkids, sausage lips."

"Redheads?" Dad says.

"Lard ass. I have to go." George wobbles to a standing position.

"Sir, your tea," Dad says. "Are you okay to leave?"

The old man smiles.

My dad appears taken aback by the toothless grin.

"Right as rain dung," George says. He limps toward the door.

"Dad, he's fine. I'll see him out."

Even with all my extra pounds, I am able to step ahead of the old man. I beat him to the elevator. When he catches up, I say, "Tell me about the redheads I keep seeing. Are they working for Domestic too?"

"Spit spies. You already know, jerk face. Act."

"Isn't there anything else you can tell me? How do I do this alone?"

"Don't wait, sugar tits." He reaches out a palsied hand and squeezes my breast. Hard.

I push his fingers off me. "Dirty old man."

"I'm fifty-one years old, you fat whore." He shuffles into the waiting elevator.

He looks more like a hundred and fifty. I block the door to keep the elevator from leaving. "You know something you're not telling me."

"Hurry up, blubber head, the end."

I let the door go. It is about to snap closed, when George shouts, "And follow the fluffy cat."

What the hell? I smack the call button, but the elevator stays shut. I head for the staircase at the far end of the long hall.

By the time I lug my lard body to the ground floor down the four flights of stairs, the elevator sits open and empty. I check the lobby.

George is nowhere.

Outside, I scan the parking area. No vehicles are leaving.

I can't believe how slow this *me* is.

CHAPTER 64

SARA, AGE 37

Sunday, July 2nd, 2000, 9:29 AM
Hector Bloom's condo
Hollymont, Queens, NY

*B*ack upstairs, I find my Dad at the sink washing dishes. "Where did you disappear to?"

"I walked George out."

"Strange fellow, that Mr. Wells. What did he want with you?"

The back of my neck prickles. "Mr. Wells? He only told me his name was George."

"George Wells. That's the name on the card he gave me." Dad turns off the faucet and dries his hands on a dish towel. He fishes the card out of his pants pocket and hands it to me.

Sure enough, the old man is George Wells—Elise Wells' husband. The one she said Dr. Gentry signed into a nursing care facility for early dementia. He must have gone AWOL.

Elise died the day Jon freed me. Those bandages on her head make sense if they were dissecting her brain. She told me it was 1991, but I didn't know for sure.

If she were correct, I somehow time flashed to 1991 from 1982 after the redhead from the armored truck injected me and told me to go to sleep. Then, I returned to the present from 1991 after Dr. Gentry gave me another shot to calm me down. They were probably giving me some kind of sedatives. But what if it is stress that makes me time travel, and not being drugged? If I time flash whenever I'm distressed, I'll never stop wending my way through the years.

I tell my dad that I need to rest, in part, to prevent him from interrogating me further about the old man. I feel guilty about adding to Dad's worry lines. But it's true I don't feel well. My entire right side smarts, from my shoulder to my toes, like someone's sticking pins into a voodoo doll of me.

The guest room door shuts behind me. I slump to the disheveled sleep sofa. Danny said average citizens can't win against a huge conglomeration. *Was he right?*

I try to rest, but behind my eyelids I see George Wells' toothless smile, more dismal now than scary. This depressive Sara has nothing in her heart but indifference. I can't unthink her dark thoughts.

I have to find a way to get back to another me. No—to the real me.

TIME FLASH 6

YEAR 1981 — THE PAST

"I was in '78 recently," he announced. "I brought you this."

He handed me a single by the Beatles. I didn't recognize the title. "Didn't they split in '70?"

"Not always."

— JASPER FFORDE, THE EYRE AFFAIR

CHAPTER 65

SARA, AGE 18

Friday, February 6, 1981, 4:30 PM
Flushing College Bookstore
Flushing, NY

A plethora of hearts and metallic cupid decorations hung below the college logo banners of the Flushing College bookstore. Light-headed, I steadied myself by grabbing onto a rack of sweatshirts.

No, not just lightheaded, but lightweight. I caught the reflection of my body in the nearby mirror—decked out in all black, I was my normal size. Hadn't I just been obese?

Yes. I stood in Dad's condo kitchen moments ago, reaching for a box of Berry Beary Crunch. I visualized time flashing back to Friday, January 21, 1994, the date of my first kiss with Jon. It happened at The Wishing Well Pub after work, an evening so etched into my memory, not even all those redos could erase it. He became not only my lover then, but my hero.

That was also the night of our first dance to Bryan Adams' "All for Love." Outside the pub, on that freezing Manhattan night, Jon took me in his arms to zip up my coat. He said he didn't "want such a beautiful woman to catch her death." When the zipper reached my throat, he leaned in. His hungry mouth tasted mine with bottomless desire. The cold, loud city around us took backstage to the perfection of the moment. All the smooches that followed became homage to our first blissful kiss.

While Jon was stealing my heart, a thief came along and made off with my purse.

Jon, not missing a beat, said, "Keep those lips warm for me," and lunged at the mugger. He overtook the guy, wrestled him to the ground, and put him in a choke hold until the police showed. I swooned as much from Jon's affection as from his action hero machismo.

If I had time flashed to my student days at Flushing College, I could be at least a decade too early for my special night with Jon. I'd have to find him somehow and convince him to help me take down the Domestic research lab.

Largely a commuter campus, the school didn't stock much in the way of actual groceries. They sold a variety of canned soups, sliced cheeses, peanut butter, and a few kinds of cereal. The Berry Beary Crunch bear, decked out in green fur, wore a Yoda-like toga. Looking at the box aroused me—as was the intended effect of the mind-control serum—but made me queasy at the same time. I assumed the queasiness had more to do with my consciousness surfing from body to body across the space-time continuum, maybe brain-wave motion sickness.

There were two things I needed to do right away—find out exactly when in time I'd landed, and get to a bathroom in case my stomach rejected its contents.

Given the black motorcycle jacket and biker boots I had on, it had to be my actual college days. At least I had youthful energy on my side. Plus, I didn't feel the mantle of depression weighing me down like a lead x-ray apron the way it had my last redo.

I went to the periodical aisle, located the *Daily Post*, and scanned the date. February 6, 1981. *Thirteen years before Jon's mouth on mine. Holy molé salsa*, maybe Joanne was alive. I didn't get her killed until 1982.

I wished I could tune into memory when I traveled back to the past the way I could peruse long-term memory when I returned to the year 2000. But time flashes back didn't seem to work that way. Steve had said the consciousness of the past me got suppressed. *Damned Penrose waves.* I needed to bluff my way through as if I knew exactly what was going on.

I'd landed squarely in my second semester of college. In my original life, during the first semester, thanks to Comp 101, I met and started dating Steve Ranger. Or rather, thanks to Professor Gumm, who played match-maker when he informed us we'd both turned in personal essays mentioning Godzilla as "a misunderstood monster." The professor called it coincidence, not plagiarism. Steve called it kismet.

Not love at first sight with Steve, but first love. And my mother adored his all-American name and Caucasian good looks. She urged me to try anorexia, or at least a steady diet of laxatives and water pills, to make sure I'd be skinny enough to keep him interested. She firmly believed in college for women as a Mrs. degree, rather than a means to independence and a career. But in my last redo, thanks to the Butterfly Effect, Steve had broken up with me after a week of dating due to my poor hygiene. I'd soon find out if he and I were still together in this version of the past.

I looked at the newspaper again to get an idea of what was going on in the world. The *Daily Post*'s headline caught my eye—*Paul, George, and Ringo Record Tribute to John.* Lennon had been shot two months before. Fresh grief made it hard to swallow.

If only I'd time flashed back earlier, I could have saved him. I would have warned him and informed the police about Chapman. But Danny, with all those science books in the back of his car, couldn't figure out a way to get his wife to remain faithful. *Did that mean there were certain occurrences that remained fixed on every possible timeline and couldn't be changed?*

I recalled a *Twilight Zone* episode where this time traveler planned to kill Hitler and prevent the bombing of Hiroshima. He ended up bungling everything and not making a difference. Yet Marty McFly altered his family's life for the better. Walker in *Timecop* saved his wife and unborn child. Of course, those were just stories.

And yet, with all the theories about time travel, there was so little actual fact. I had altered the past by accident and gotten my loved ones killed. I had to try to do better. It didn't seem I could do any worse.

But not until after I barfed. I hurried to the ladies' room in the cafeteria next door.

CHAPTER 66

SARA, AGE 18

Friday, February 6, 1981, 4:30 PM
Flushing College Student Union Building
Flushing, NY

ime travel made me sick to my stomach, literally. Cleaning up, I studied my face in the mirror. Eyes heavily delineated with liquid liner, a helmet of teased, dark hair, lipstick a matte scarlet red—the poster girl for teenaged angst. But what did I have to be tormented about?

Well, Reagan being president, for one. My brother lost to leukemia. My grandmother dying far away. And John Lennon murdered. That was a pretty strong list. Still, I wished I'd known my first go-round how ridiculous it was to obsess over my appearance.

When I got out of the bathroom, someone called to me.

"Sara, where have you been?" Under the hall spotlights, Steve's white-blond mullet and pale skin made him appear ghostly. "I've been waiting for you for over half an hour in Gunpowder Hall."

We were together after all. "I lost track of time," I said, sure he wouldn't get the irony. I had no idea why he was waiting for me in the Social Sciences building. Was I cutting class?

"No need to fret. Thanks to you, I am almost halfway through now. Best one yet." He held up a hardcover copy of *The Restaurant at the End of the Universe*. "Here, let me read you a line."

As I went toward him, my right leg gave out. I puddled to the floor.

Steve rushed over. "What happened?" He held out a hand to help me up.

Before I could grab hold, he snapped it back.

"Did you wash?"

I knew he couldn't help himself. Obsessive-compulsive disorder is a dictatorial disease. He must have been cursing himself for asking.

"With soap and hot water," I said. "My leg's asleep." It felt more like someone shot it with a high-speed nail gun.

Steve tucked the Adams book into his backpack, and rather than grabbing my hand, he lifted me by the armpits.

I hadn't washed there.

"Try taking a step," he said.

My right leg buckled under the stress. Maybe I had time flashed too many times and my motor skills finally paid the price.

Wiry, but strong, he caught me before I fell again. "Tell me if I am moving too fast." Supporting my weight, he guided me to a wooden bench at the closest cafeteria table. "Should I call an ambulance? No *Rocky Horror* for you tonight."

I'd forgotten we went to see that cult movie at least once a month. "I'll be all right in a sec." I leaned back against the cinder block wall. Worried but pretending otherwise, I winked at Steve.

He pursed his lips. Never one to argue, he said, "I will procure us some coffee, Rosy. That will perk you up." He set his backpack down on the opposite bench and left.

The disparity between his formal speech and rebel appearance was what charmed me when we had first met. I watched him disappear through the food line doors. Sinewy and sexy, he was an innocent playing at being a bad boy. Domestic may have destroyed his goodness in my original timeline, but history didn't have to repeat itself. Not if I could help it.

I kneaded my leg and the sting began to ease.

Blondie's "The Tide Is High" echoed inside the cavernous dining area. The campus radio station, airing twenty-four hours a day, played to a nearly empty room. Two guys in football jerseys argued over something in a *Legions of Superheroes* comic. In the far corner, an attractive woman in her thirties, no doubt a professor, shuffled through a stack of papers.

The two dorms on campus each had their own small cafeterias for breakfast and dinner. Commuter students like me cleared out by three in the afternoon. If evening events were scheduled, people didn't start showing up until seven or later.

AC/DC was belting out "You Shook Me All Night Long" when Steve returned. He carried an orange tray with two Styrofoam cups and a package of chocolate Twincakes. "How's that leg, Rosy baby?"

The junk food brought back a bittersweet memory—Danny glowing in the sun at the Maine gas station—a future that wouldn't happen. "My leg's awake." The rubbing I gave it had paid off.

He unwrapped the cupcakes and set one in front of me. "Sorry I did not prepare something from scratch to celebrate. It is impossible to bake a decent cake in a dorm kitchen."

I sipped the weak coffee to disguise the fact I had no idea what celebration he was talking about.

"You thought I forgot, did you not?"

"Um … no. You have an exceptional memory."

"For all things Sara." He moved in for a kiss, and I caught a waft of his Old Spice cologne.

The kiss was brief, warm, and sweet. I knew the 1981 version of me loved Steve, and he loved me as well as a college kid could. It wouldn't have been awful killing an afternoon making out with him.

But I had to focus. I wasn't there for Steve. I kept my mouth closed, not taking the kiss any deeper. I needed to find Jon and stop Domestic.

Steve pulled back and looked at me. He cupped my cheek. "You are my dark angel." From his leather jacket, he whipped out a canister of breath spray and doused his mouth and lips. He offered some to me.

I declined.

Steve being able to kiss me at all with his germ phobia was nothing short of a miracle. Love glinting at me from his soft blue-gray eyes made me more unbelieving that he could ever become the sociopath that Joanne described.

Danny had told me he didn't believe people were capable of changing their stripes. If that were true, Steve was as evil right then as he would someday become. But all I experienced were his kindness and affection. He had to have been brainwashed, or worse tortured, at the obsessive-compulsive disorder clinic overseas.

Though it was too late to save John Lennon's life, I promised myself I would save Joanne and prevent Steve from becoming a killer. Plus, with Jon's help, I'd save however many people Domestic's research hurt.

"A penny," he said, "for your thoughts. Though I am sure they will be worth much more."

Bob Marley's "Redemption Song" came on.

I started on my scheme to save Steve. "You are such a brilliant writer, it would be a tragedy for you to do anything but pen novels. You need to attend the Iowa Writers Workshop."

"A little premature, with three plus years until graduation. Anyway, I should consider something practical first, like seeking treatment for my disorder."

"The worst thing you could do would be to focus on your condition. Don't let it define you. You can't put your writing aside. I won't let you go to one of those experimental centers in Sweden. Who knows how they might reprogram your brain."

Steve's mouth made a perfect circle, showing his surprise. "How did you know I was thinking about volunteering for an experimental cure? However, the one I am considering is in Switzerland, not Sweden."

"Same difference. Bad idea, only with holier cheese. You can find treatment options in America. Even in Iowa among the cows."

"But how did you know? Ah, you sleuthed in my bag." He reached for the backpack on the bench.

"I know my man," I said.

He removed a brochure and handed it to me.

The pamphlet, decorated with serene blue skies, promised revolutionary success with the most complicated symptoms. On the back, at the bottom, in tiny print, the words "A Division of Domestic Global International Clinical Research." I tore the brochure into strips.

Steve protested. He grabbed for the pieces in my hands.

To distract him, I planted a kiss on his lips, this time giving it all the force I could muster. And then, some tongue. The situation required desperate measures.

Steve stopped trying to pull the papers out of my hands and kissed me back.

I made confetti of the rest of the brochure. When I ended the kiss, I scattered the pieces on the cafeteria tray. "I care about you too much to let you put yourself through anything potentially harmful."

"You love me." His whole face beamed with a smile that could make you do anything he asked—his killer smile.

My stomach ached. The burnt coffee wasn't sitting well. I didn't want to lie, but I saw no other choice. I looked into those guileless eyes. "I love you," I said, though *this* me didn't.

Our declarations to one another were over a week premature. Steve had first professed his love for me in my original life on Valentine's Day in a sonnet he composed. That I was sure of. I burned the sappy verse in a laundry sink three years after he left.

"I love you too, Rosy." He squeezed my hand. "Tonight, after the movie, I planned on showing you how much. I have a card and red carnations waiting for you in my dorm. My roommates are away for the weekend."

"Great." I'd lost my virginity to Steve the week before he professed his love. *Uh-oh*. I'd already been unfaithful to Jon with Danny. My husband and I were broken up at the time, but cheating was cheating. In my heart I'd always be married to Jon.

"Can I give you my arm or would you prefer I carry you?" Steve said.

I took his arm. Strained, but at least not dead, my right leg followed the left.

The buildings glowed in the dusk light, lending the campus an ethereal appearance. I zipped my jacket and slipped on my gloves to stave off the cold while I waited for Steve to get done washing up inside.

I wished I had my entire life ahead of me, instead of a few days until my Penrose waves went into stasis. I could do so much with another entire nineteen years to live over again any way I chose. I could change my major, maybe focus on music instead of accounting. I could stop going on crazy diets and live in the body I was given. I could take myself out hiking more often, do yoga to maintain my heart health and stay limber. Of course, even if I could survive my Penrose wave receptors' dormancy, Domestic would surely come after me.

But I was losing focus. I had to defeat Domestic, and to do that I needed Jon's help. I hadn't thought about what I'd do if I didn't end up in the year I intended. There had to be dozens of J. Garcías in the phone directory, if his number was even listed. Finding him would take time.

I stamped my feet to keep the blood flowing in my legs.

"Here you are," Steve said. The magical early evening light created a halo around his platinum hair.

I took his gloved hand in mine.

We walked west, toward the setting sun.

No matter how many Garcías there were in the five boroughs, and the greater New York area, I would locate Jon and we'd put an end to the mind-control experiment. I only needed to get through one night with Steve.

It occurred to me, if I pretended to be getting sick, I could beg off the evening and get out of sleeping with him. He'd steer clear of me and my germs. I started to feel pathological with all the lies I was telling. *Another me*, the original Sara, had been honest to the bone.

"Steve, would you promise me something?" I said.

"Anything," he said instantly. He stopped walking to face me. "You look serious, Rosy. Yes, I will marry you right after I get my Master's degree." He knelt down on one knee on the unclean ground. "Be mine forever."

Holy molé salsa. I was speechless. Not only had time travel enhanced my sex appeal and increased my self-confidence, but marriage proposals tripled. Well, maybe doubled, since Jon would never ask me again.

Steve pouted. "Say something, Rosy."

"I'm speechless."

"You are my soul-mate. I knew it on our first date to see *Somewhere in Time*. In the theater when you turned to me, your eyes glistened with the same pure love as the characters in the movie. You saw me for who I was, and you wanted me despite my shortcomings."

I'd forgotten we went to a time travel movie on our first date. Another weird coincidence. "Yes," I said, meaning, I remembered looking at him that way, feeling myself falling for him.

Steve jumped up and embraced me. "Should we tell our parents?"

Oops. He'd thought my affirmative was an answer to his offer of marriage. "It's going to be a long engagement. Let's wait till you start the graduate writing program."

"Whatever you want, my love." He kissed me on the forehead.

"I have to ask one more thing of you."

"Now, what do you want, the moon? I am no George Bailey."

"I want you to promise me no matter what, you will go get your Master's degree right after college, the Iowa Writer's Workshop, or somewhere else in the states, not abroad."

"That way we can be together. An easy promise." He stroked my hair. "We can get an apartment near the campus."

"If anything should happen to us, or to me, promise me you will pursue your writing. You're too talented to let it go to waste." That wasn't a lie. He was a gifted poet and storyteller.

"There is no power strong enough to break apart soul-mates."

Domestic had the power. And they did effect our separation. "We don't know what fate has in store," I said. "Promise, on your mother's heart." Steve had told me his mother's death when he was sixteen left him utterly bereft. I asked no small thing.

"If it means that much to you." He raised his right hand and placed his left over his own heart. "I swear an oath on the heart of my dear dead mother, I will pursue my Master's somewhere in the country immediately upon graduation from Flushing College."

"Thank you. Your oath means the world to me."

We walked toward the dorm again. He swung our entwined hands back and forth, obviously joyous.

I had no choice but to believe he would keep his promise. This *me* wasn't going to be able to stick around to find out.

It crossed my mind I should make love to him to seal the deal. Wasn't it foolish to want to be faithful to a husband I hadn't met yet, and would never marry again? After all, I was going to die soon. If one night of sex could prevent Steve from going to Sweden to be brainwashed by Domestic into becoming a killer, it would be a worthwhile sacrifice.

Young Steve appeared incapable of doing those terrible things, the least of which was drugging me. *Had Domestic convinced him that he eradicated germs when he burned corpses?* Despite his best efforts to look tough in black leather, he exuded a pussy cat vibe.

Or else, Joanne and Danny were both right about Steve, and I was deluding myself. Perhaps Steve was such an accomplished sociopath that I mistook his tenderness for goodness.

CHAPTER 67

SARA, AGE 18

Saturday, February 7, 1981, 8:30 AM
Q 200 Bus stop, Flushing College
Flushing, NY

*A*t the bus stop the next morning, I kissed Steve goodbye as if I would never see him again. Anyway, this *me* wouldn't.

An elderly woman waiting in line behind us, clearly not a fan of public affection, puckered and spewed a wad of spit at my feet.

Steve drenched his mouth with breath spray, then stuffed his penned declaration of love into my coat pocket. "You almost forgot my poem."

"Never," I said. He'd given it to me a week early, and not a love sonnet this time, but a villanelle. Maybe it had always been a villanelle and the Penrose waves wreaked havoc with my memories. Or maybe it was the Butterfly Effect again.

"I can escort you," he said.

"You have to work on your Chaucer paper. I can get home by myself. Done it a million times."

His brow wrinkled. "But not with a migraine."

"I'll be fine." I planned to leave him in the morning by begging off with a headache. I hadn't counted on actually waking up with one, and certainly not one so massive. My eyes ached. Fortunately, the overcast sky let only a modicum of light through the clouds.

The screech of brakes signaled the arrival of the Q 200 bus. I was sixth in line to get on, but the mass exodus of passengers onto South Main Street took time. I tried a little more reinforcement. "Never forget how much I love you right now. Nothing can change this moment." Another lie—*time flashes changed everything*.

"You are always accusing me of melodrama. You have a headache, not a brain tumor." He mimed hitting me in the head with the Douglas Adams book.

I smiled to reassure him. But Penrose waves could do the same damage as a brain tumor, probably worse.

The line surged ahead. My slightly rigid leg climbed the three stairs. At the change box, I pivoted to face Steve, stopping the flow of passengers and pissing off spit-lady in back of me.

"*Puta*," she said.

I ignored her, the scolds of the bus driver, and the rest of the grumbling hoard. "Promise," I said.

"On the heart of my mother." Steve placed his hand on his chest for emphasis.

"I see a Pulitzer in your future," I said.

The sign on the coin box showed the fare was sixty cents.

I paid, then settled into a window seat for the long ride.

Like a scene from a movie, Steve came to where I sat and laid his gloved hand against the glass.

I matched my hand to his. If it were a movie, the soundtrack would be something mournful like The Rolling Stones' "Wild Horses." Instead of him initiating our break-up as he did in my original life, this Sara would abandon him by dying.

The bus lurched away from the curb. I told myself *another* me loved Steve, but *this* me did once too. Tears streamed down my cheeks. I hid my face in my hands to avoid strangers' stares.

Losing my virginity was a big deal, even for the second time and with the same guy. Better than I remembered, Steve was generous and full of stamina. He told me he never would have guessed I was a virgin because I was such a natural. If only he knew he'd been bedded by a thirty-seven-year-old woman in a teenaged virgin's body.

With Steve being so inexperienced, I could have barked and he would have thought it erotic. I tried to make the sex memorable, thinking it would give him incentive to keep his promise about not going to Sweden.

He had insisted we take showers in the segregated dorm bathrooms before and after intercourse, but when we touched he didn't have any concern about germs. He let me kiss every part of his body, put my tongue wherever I wanted.

I rationalized that the sex was for Steve's sake. He'd stick with writing, wouldn't become a Domestic flunky. At least I told myself that, until my first orgasm, followed swiftly by a second, and third, and so on. *That* me was an appalling woman unfaithful to my once- and never-to-be-again husband. Spooning Steve in the twin bed, I laid awake all night, my mind raging with self-recrimination.

He slept peacefully through the night. Sex had a sleeping pill effect on men, I'd noticed. For me, sex was akin to a double shot of espresso. I always wanted to talk after or do a few laps around the block.

I closed my eyes, willing my headache away. Sleep deprivation and the movement of the bus proved hypnotic.

~

A warm summer night, the giant moon illuminates the backyard of my childhood home. I sit with Joanne on a blanket in the grassy area. She is a little girl, and I'm even smaller.

We lean back on our elbows and admire the sky. The stars are close enough to reach out and grab them.

"Your grandmothers are going to sing to us," Joanne says.

I am confused because I have only one grandma—my dad's mother Rosa. My mother's mother died in Argentina long before I was born.

I want to ask Joanne why she used the plural, but my grandmother steps through the metal gate and enters the yard. She is a vision.

Wearing a daffodil yellow taffeta gown decorated with matching sequins, Grandma sparkles more than the sun.

I run to hug her.

She hugs me back and says, "It's later than you think." She points a finger toward the gate.

Another Grandma comes in, indistinguishable from the first, except her taffeta gown glows bubble-gum pink. She brushes my cheek. "Shana maidela," she says.

Dumbfounded by Grandma's twin, I ask, "What's going on?"

Pink Grandma puts a finger to her lips, then points to the gate.

A third Grandma enters, absolutely identical to the other two. This one wears a dazzling sky-blue taffeta gown. She closes the gate behind her, comes to me and ruffles my hair. "¡Que linda!" she says to me.

317

Yellow Grandma claps her hands. Pink and Blue Grandmas join in.

Joanne calls to me to come sit by her.

I know I am inside a dream—the best ever. Three Grandmas mean three times the unconditional love. I settle on the blanket and get comfortable.

My Technicolor grandmothers hum in unison, a deep, melodious tune. They all turn toward the gate.

John Lennon comes through, dressed in blue jeans and a white t-shirt, his hair long and his glasses round.

He joins the Grandma trio and starts singing "Stand by Me."

My grandmothers provide harmony.

I wish for a way to capture the dream, record it to play back whenever I want.

When the song ends, my three Grandmas curtsy.

I cheer.

"Encore," Joanne says.

"I don't believe in yesterday," Lennon says, and takes a bow.

Lightning flashes. Rain begins to pour.

Joanne snaps up the blanket and holds it over our heads. We hurry through the gate toward the house. I look back to make sure my Grandmas are following.

No one is there. Not Yellow, nor Pink, nor Blue. John Lennon is gone too.

CHAPTER 68

SARA, AGE 18

Saturday, February 7, 1981, 9:40 AM
Beachcross Boulevard
Woodward, Queens, NY

*T*he bus rocked to a stop on Beachcross Boulevard in front of Wauldsons supermarket. The last time I'd made the walk to my childhood house from here was in a time flash with my grandmother, the summer of 1975. I think for a moment how long ago that was in real time—about two weeks since the time flashes began. I half-expected to see Danny come roaring by in his Firebird. But all I saw were Chevy Novas, Cadillac Eldorados and Dodge Chargers. And none of the drivers stopped to pick me up.

The smell of chorizo greeted me as I entered my childhood home.

Dad was cooking himself a breakfast feast. All four burners sizzled away. Mixing bowls, utensils, and plates cluttered every inch of the boomerang Formica countertop.

Since Dad had on his "Kiss the Chef" apron, I did.

"*Mija*, I didn't think we'd see you till Sunday," he said. "Hope you're hungry."

Mother came in, wearing the plush maroon bathrobe Dad called her "smoking jacket." Her long, black hair piled on top of her head in a messy bun, not a dot of make-up on her face and she looked lovely. When she rubbed the sleep from her eyes, she let out a disgusted sigh. "Ugh. He dumped you, didn't he?"

"Good morning to you too, Mother." I went to embrace her.

Her hands remained rigid at her sides.

"I told you if you didn't lose weight this would happen."

"Steve loves me the way I am. We both have papers to work on. That's all."

"Right. He's with another girl this minute."

That taunt should have stung, but didn't. My newfound self-confidence protected me against my mother's attack. "Thanks for believing in me, mother."

"Sit down and let me feed you," Dad said. He held out a pan of eggs scrambled with *Tetilla* cheese.

"Don't you dare, Hector," Mother said. "Black coffee is all she can have. She's on a diet."

"I already ate," I said. Time travel made quite the liar out of me. In truth, nausea claimed my appetite. Probably the aftermath of my faded migraine. "Do you know whether Joanne is home?"

"Why do you care?" Mother said. The unlit cigarette bobbed in her mouth. "Did you plead your way back into her good graces?"

I ignored the question. I had no idea whether we were friends or not.

"She's away on a buying trip," Dad said. "Won't be back for another month. I worry about her. A young woman traveling all over on her own."

He'd really have worried if I told him about me being haphazardly cast about through time. "I need to make some calls. I'll catch you later."

Mother had transformed my brother's bedroom into a den. She demanded we get rid of all evidence he ever existed—his books, his comics, his Godzilla figures. My father hid all the photographs of Adam in the attic to keep them from being tossed out. It was a wonder my mother let me keep my brother's Timex.

My parents, like Jon and I, had survived the loss of a child. But with them, no apparent rift appeared in their relationship. Whereas Jon and I disappeared into our own separate griefs.

The den was the only place where I could use a phone in private. I settled in the brand-new sleeper sofa. Only yesterday in my father's condo, the very same piece of furniture had been a ragged ruin. I thought of Steve's favorite poem where T. S. Eliot proclaims time past and time future are always present, and therefore, unredeemable. I counted on Eliot being wrong—redemption, the very mission I had in mind.

There were thirty-nine J's, Jons, Johns, and Jonathans in the Brooklyn phonebook. If unsuccessful with those, I would embark on the Queens, Bronx, and Manhattan tomes. Staten Island seemed to be missing. If I hadn't located Jon by the time I went through those books, there was always directory information. If need be, I'd try all of Long Island, as well as Westchester. I just hoped my voice held up.

CHAPTER 69

SARA, AGE 18

Saturday, February 7, 1981, 1 PM
Sara's childhood home
Woodward, Queens, NY

As it turned out, my being able to speak wasn't the problem. By the third call, my left hand became limp and useless, like it had in Maine with Danny. I wondered if seeing a doctor might help. But what if Domestic monitored medical facilities for patients with my symptoms?

I used my right hand to dial and cradled the phone on my shoulder. Over a hundred calls later, I had reached several J. Garcías, but none were mine. One invited me out to dinner. I declined. Another of the J's, a Jesus, requested I talk "filthy dirty" to him. I did not oblige. I'd also reached an elderly woman named Jimena who was hard of hearing and eager to chat, even with a stranger. She insisted I call her back on Sunday afternoon when she could tell me about the sermon at her church. I was non-committal.

When Jon and I met at Domestic in 1994, he had just moved to the studio apartment in Floral Gardens, Queens—the one we would later share. I tried to recall exactly where he lived before, but drew a blank. Many details of my life with Jon were hazy. Whether an indication of brain degradation from time traveling, or some backward Butterfly Effect on the memories of my original life, I didn't know.

I thought about trying to find a phone number for Jon's mother, who was living with a boyfriend in Mexico City at the time we met. The number of María Garcías there had to be staggering. Exhausted from all those wrong numbers, not to mention lack of sleep, I closed my eyes to clear my head.

The dream I had on the bus about John Lennon and three Grandmas came back to me. My third John Lennon dream—maybe the dream meant something other than me finding "a lid" for "my pot" as Dad had said. But what?

John Lennon's death was one of those life-defining moments. I learned about the event from television. On December 8, 1980, my father was watching Monday Night Football in the living room. I sat at the dining room table working on an Accounting 101 project when I overheard Howard Cosell announce the tragedy of Lennon's shooting. Even my parents, far from Beatles fans, had tears in their eyes.

The next day at school, people had shared memories of his music and where they had been when they heard the news. The college radio station played non-stop Lennon songs all week.

Jon possessed the most decisive Beatles album collection I'd ever seen, including a lot of imports and bootlegs I never knew existed. On our first date, he shared with me that he had been at the Yesterday Bar, downstairs from his place, watching the football game with pals when the news broke of Lennon's shooting. They hopped the subway from Brooklyn and rushed to the scene outside the Dakota in Manhattan. Other fans had the same idea. An impromptu, middle-of-the-night candlelight vigil arose.

Holy molé salsa—Jon had been at the bar *below his apartment* the night Lennon died. A few months ago. I took up the Brooklyn phone book again.

I begged off lunch with my parents by saying I had to go work on my paper at Peggy Sue's house. I told them not to expect me for dinner either, as I would spend the night there. Of course, I had no friend named Peggy Sue, and working on a college paper was the furthest thing from my mind. I hated how easily the lies came. But *this* me had to get things done and would stop at nothing.

CHAPTER 70

SARA, AGE 18

Saturday, February 7, 1981, 3 PM
Hedgehurst, Brooklyn, NY

*B*y the time I came up out of the subway station, the world was swimming in snow, everything hushed, or at least muted a few bars. Hardly any cars ventured out in the storm. A handful of pedestrians navigated the avenue of stores and restaurants. The layers of white morphed the over-filled trash bins into abstract snowmen. Nervous about finding Jon, the snow gave me the sense of inner calm I desperately needed.

I changed outfits several times before leaving home. When I met Jon in my pre-time-flash life, I was a thirty-one-year-old, no-nonsense business woman clothed in skirt-suits. I had no idea what kind of impression this eighteen-year-old self would make on him. I needed him to believe me about Domestic's experiments. I didn't think he would take me seriously dressed as a rocker chick. I kept the make-up to a minimum. No heavy liner. No multi-color shadow. A dash of mascara to make me appear bright-eyed. I ditched the red lipstick and applied some Vaseline as lip balm. Grandma Rosa would be proud.

After rejecting half a dozen black tops, I settled on a blush cashmere button-down sweater, a cast-off of my mother's. Tight, but clingy in all the right places. Around my neck, I clasped a simple gold cross that had belonged to a maternal aunt. I finished the outfit with dark denim jeans, so snug I had to lay down to fasten them. I hoped the overall effect of my outfit came off as mature and feminine, rather than slutty. But the more I contemplated seeing Jon, the guiltier I felt about spending the night with Steve.

~

The Yesterday Bar turned out to be located in Hedgehurst, a part of Brooklyn I'd never ventured into. I tramped along leaving impressions in the snow the way astronauts did in moon dust. Laced up in thin leather boots less clunky than my biker pair, my feet were damp, but ladylike. I moved quickly to keep the cold from penetrating.

After going five blocks without finding the bar, I turned around to retrace my steps. That's when I caught sight of a tall, redheaded man wearing a green parka and Red Sox ski hat. My blood turned to ice. Was he the Domestic agent I'd last seen in Maine? How did he find me this far back in time? Never mind, I knew—boundless resources.

As soon as the man saw me notice him, he darted into a deli.

Bouncing up and down on my toes to keep warm, I considered my options. Run for the subway and head back home. Go around the block, duck into a shop myself, and try to lose him. Head for the bar and pray Jon would let a total stranger into his apartment before Mr. Redhead came after me. All those options required my leg not to go numb again, which would slow me down at the very least.

I trembled thinking about another option—the toughest one—confront the Domestic agent. Go into the deli and get in his face. If he tried to overpower me, I'd need help. That plan depended on the shopkeeper to intervene on my behalf, not to mention my own bravery. Contrary to what some believed, New Yorkers would come through for you in a tight spot.

Waiting for the walk light, my resolve wavered. I stepped off the curb into the intersection.

A yellow cab sped around the corner. It swerved and missed hitting me by mere inches. The cab driver shouted at me in what sounded like Polish. He sounded like Adam's Polish doctor who had informed us the final chemotherapy protocol had been unsuccessful. His news broke my heart. That's when I stopped believing in God.

Maybe my nearly getting killed by a Polish cab driver was an omen that I'd chosen the wrong option. Then again, maybe my near miss meant I'd be rewarded for my risk.

In moments, I stood outside Sal's Subs, my hand on the door. Tinted windows prevented me from seeing what was going on inside. My teeth chattered. *Now or never.* I went in.

Aromas of tomato sauce and garlic permeated the small shop. A long sandwich counter took up most of the back wall, with a glass-doored drink refrigerator off to one side. Behind the counter, a plump man in an apron diced tomatoes. Five tables filled the middle of the room and a lunch counter with four stools hugged the front window. A couple of old men playing chess sat at the center table. One was bald, and the other had on a Yankees cap. Each wore thick glasses. They didn't look like they would be much help, should I need assistance.

The redhead sat on the corner stool at the lunch counter perusing the *Daily Post* newspaper. He sipped from the largest Pepsi cup I'd ever seen.

You can do this. I strode in his direction and hovered over him, which wasn't easy. Seated, he was nearly as tall as me.

It turned out that up close, his height was the most intimidating thing about him. He was young, maybe in his early twenties, and fine freckles dotted his face. Baby blue eyes, level with mine, peered at me over the paper.

Finally, he said, "Can I help you?" I never imagined that tall a guy would have such a nasal voice.

I tried to channel Humphrey Bogart, the diminutive actor from the thirties and forties who intimidated criminals twice his size. "You looking for trouble, buddy?" I said. "What are you doing tailing me?"

"I'm tryin' to read the paper. Beat it. Scram," he said, channeling a nonchalant movie gangster to match mine. He rustled the newspaper for emphasis.

"I'm not going anywhere until you give me answers," I said. I needed a threat fast. "Don't get wise with me, or I'll scream rape faster than you can blink."

He folded the paper and set it aside. "No need to holler, doll." He gestured to the stool next to him. "We should get cozy."

Doll? I suppressed a laugh. I wished I could identify which film we were borrowing dialogue from. Then I'd know how to crush him. I sat with my legs dangling into the aisle. If he tried to bolt, I'd trip him. "Talk," I said. "And make it snappy. I don't have all day."

"Well, I do," he said, "all day and all night." He smirked, revealing green-tinged teeth. It may have been an attempt at flirting. The effect, neither sexy nor intimidating, was plain icky.

I kicked his shin hard enough to show him I meant business.

He shook out his leg. "What'd you do that for?"

"You can't," one of the old men said from behind me.

Alarmed, I looked in their direction.

The bald man pointed at a piece on the board. "I don't play with cheaters."

The man in the hat said, "Fine, fine, I'll put it back. Stop shouting. You'll upset these nice youngsters." He smiled at me with a full set of pearly whites, likely dentures.

I turned back to the redhead. "Sing like a canary."

"I'm a delivery guy," he said.

"What is that supposed to mean?"

"I pick up wanderers and deliver 'em safe and sound."

"Safe and sound to Domestic Labs?"

"You mean Gentry Research Laboratory. Oops. Shouldn't a said that."

"Gentry as in Dr. Lance Gentry?"

"Nope. Claire Gentry, my aunt. Uncle Lance is her husband."

That explained why my own doctor tried to kill me. He and his wife were in it together. "You call running over my best friend with a truck a safe and sound delivery?" I kicked him again. Of course, that hadn't happened yet in this timeline.

He let out a shriek. "Stop that, will ya? You don't know your own strength. And I have a perfect driving record. I never crashed into nobody."

"If it wasn't you, it must have been your clone."

"Could a been my twin. But I'm the good one, I swear." He held up his left hand.

I didn't buy the evil twin defense. "What does Dr. Claire Gentry want with me?"

"Make sure you're A-okay. Not sick or," he lowered his voice, "contagious. Another Typhoid Mary. That happened you know. So I sniff out the ones who get away and haul 'em back there. Volunteers need to honor the contract."

"By sniff out, you mean kidnap?"

"I show up at the address I'm given and make a pick-up. It's a cinch."

"What contract is it I am supposed to honor? I never signed anything, and I sure as shit didn't volunteer for mind control."

"Watch your mouth," he said. "There's seniors here. A little respect. Besides, I seen the contract with your photo and personal information. Your address was in the file."

It rattled me to no end that Domestic could have been keeping tabs on me since the '80s. That's twenty years before everything went awry. "Show it to me." I stuck out my leg to kick him again.

He moved his appendages out of reach. "I don't have it with me. They keep records in the office."

"Why do they need a delivery guy? Why not phone me?"

"With the treatments, sometimes volunteers get confused. So, like in your case, they forget where they need to be."

"You sound like you really believe this bullshit you're feeding me."

"Hey, watch your mouth—the seniors."

For a second, he reminded me of Joanne, always correcting my cursing.

"Salami all the way," the man called, from behind the counter.

"That's me," the redhead said, and started to go.

Yeah, right, more like bologna. I clamped my hand on his sleeve. "Don't move. And don't even think about trying to scram." He could definitely outrun me, but I chanced it. Either he was a brainwashed dolt, or he played dumb better than anyone I'd ever seen. I kept one eye on the redhead as I went to the counter.

"*Bellisima,*" the man in the apron said. "Your boyfriend's a lucky guy. Enjoy." He handed me the long sub wrapped in foil with a few napkins.

"Thanks. We will." My hand shook as I took the warm package.

The redhead hadn't budged.

I gave my *boyfriend* a coy smile. "You know, I think we got off on the wrong foot. I don't know your name." I held out the sandwich.

He grabbed it, then my hand. "Murray O'Keefe. A pleasure to meet such a dish." His smile, though greenish, seemed on the level.

When he let go of me, I unzipped my jacket and sat. "Much better," I said, hoping he couldn't see right through my performance. Maybe a bit of my mother rubbed off on me. *Act like the confident woman you mean to be.*

Murray rubbed his hands together, then opened the foil.

Steam wafted from the sandwich. It smelled like Italian heaven—fried salami, onions, peppers, mushrooms, oregano.

"I'm so hungry I could eat a horse," he said. "Shadowing people sure works up an appetite."

"I'll bet it does." I tried a new tactic—flattery. "And you're good at what you do."

He wiped his mouth. "Thanks. My aunt's always threatening to fire me. She says I ain't got a brain in my head sometimes."

"That's terrible. You've got a knack for the delivery business. I'm sure the lab couldn't do important work without your help. What does Claire Gentry do there exactly?"

"My aunt's the scientist in charge of the whole shebang." He took a bite and talked while he chewed. "She's tryin' to come up with a vaccine for the common cold. Like Dr. Salk with polio. But you already know that."

"I do? How do I know that?"

"Because you're a research volunteer. Shoot. Don't tell my aunt I told you nothing. When the volunteers forget, it's dangerous to remind them. That's what my aunt says. Could cause a psychedelic break."

I think he meant psychotic. "Nonsense. I'm fine."

He looked me up and down. "Yeah, I can see that."

"How long have you worked at the lab?" I said.

"Since I got discharged," he said.

"Oh, you were in the military. That's very brave of you."

"Nah, nut house. I'm not supposed to say nothing about that neither."

Murray was institutionalized! My fear resurfaced, but I tried to hide it. I visualized my mother's erect posture, her shoulders thrown back. "Your secret's safe with me. You know, I'm glad I caught up with you. I'm having such a good time."

"Yeah?" He smiled, and set the sandwich down. "You know, me too. I stick 'em with a needle and get 'em back where they need to go. It's nice to talk to somebody for a change. 'Specially somebody pretty as you."

I returned his smile. "Sorry about kicking you earlier. I get carried away sometimes."

"Don't sweat it. I got the same problem. My nickname used to be *Jalapeno* on account I was such a hothead."

Great. I was speechless. I imagined Murray turning green everywhere, not just his teeth, and shouting *Hulk smash!*

"I'm sorry I told you to beat it," he said. He picked up the sub and shoved the remaining half of the sandwich into his mouth.

He was a lean machine who ate like there were no tomorrows. Why did men get to have such forgiving metabolisms? For a moment, I forgot to be anxious. I took a chance on another question. "What do you stick 'em with to make your job easier?"

Mouth full of sub, he said, "Aunt Claire calls it 'dream juice.' Sleep tonic mixed with muscle loosen-upper. But you and me can have a nice talk on the drive to the lab. That'll be swell. A real nice change. I mean, I always talk to the deliveries. They just never answer." His grin was nothing short of maniacal.

I worked hard to regain my composure. "Well, I'm afraid I can't go with you right now. I have to visit a sick friend. Nothing contagious. But if it were, I'm sure your aunt Claire could cure it."

His smile evaporated. "I can't let you go, Sara. You know that."

My heart skipped a beat. I took a deep breath and went on. "I know you work very hard, and you're underappreciated. Let me buy you another drink. You know, to say thanks."

"I'm not done with this one," he said. "And nothing doing, doll. I have to bring you back today."

"Or what?" My voice shook. I hoped he didn't notice.

He was lanky, but I would bet all muscle. I worried he could manhandle me back to his car. Screaming rape might be my best option after all.

"Or I'll catch heck," Murray said. "Don't make it harder than it has to be." He pushed the foil aside, then reached inside his coat with his right hand.

I stroked his left hand. "I promise to come with you tomorrow. Pick me up at my house."

"How can I trust you?" He locked his hand onto mine like a vice. "You might skip out on me."

"We're pals now. I give you my word."

He closed his eyes.

I tried in vain to wriggle my hand free, but he only clamped down tighter.

His lips started moving, but he made no sound. It looked as if he were praying.

I no longer believed in God, but I prayed too—for Murray to believe me.

He opened his eyes, then slid the hand out of his coat, empty. "What time?"

Phew. "After supper. Unless you want to eat with my parents and me."

"Supper," he said. His eyes got wide. "You want me to come for supper? No gal's ever asked me over to eat at her place before."

"Come at five. And bring your hearty appetite."

"Gee thanks, doll."

I stood, but he kept hold of my right hand. "I have to go visit my sick friend now. I'll see you tomorrow, Murray." I smiled like I meant it.

He squeezed my fingers hard enough to leave marks. "Don't make a fool out a me. I hate that worse than anything. I already know where you live."

After I kissed him on his cheek that reeked of onions, he let go of my hand. I wanted to flee, but I forced myself to walk away slowly. I stopped at the door and waved to him before I went.

Outside, the snow had stopped falling. People and cars filled the previously vacant Brooklyn streets. The peace of the storm had vanished.

I ran like hell to get away from Murray.

CHAPTER 71

SARA, AGE 18

Saturday, February 7, 1981, 2:30 PM
Jon's apartment
Hedgehurst, Brooklyn, NY

$\mathcal{M}$y boots, not designed for inclement weather, slipped and slid all the way to the Yesterday bar. To the right of the entrance, a locked glass door led to a flight of stairs for the second story above. While I waited for an answer to the intercom button I'd pressed, I scanned the block to see if my delivery guy had followed me. Murray was nowhere in sight. I crossed my fingers he'd stay that way.

"Hello." Even with crackling interference I recognized Jon's voice. Despite the frigid weather, heat rose in my cheeks. Perhaps the Penrose waves hadn't erased as much of my memory as I thought. All I had to do was get Jon to believe I was his time-traveling wife from the future come back to get his help. It would have been easier to try to sell him the Brooklyn Bridge.

On the subway ride over from Queens, I'd rehearsed about a hundred different things I might say when I saw Jon again. But right then all the words flew out of my head. "Hello" was all I could muster.

"Pizza?" he said.

"What?' I said. Oh, of course. He must have been expecting take-out. The perfect opening. "Pizza," I said.

The intercom buzzed and I pushed inside. My boot clops sounded like hooves as I raced up the steep flight, grateful both legs cooperated. I ended up with a stitch in my side and doubled over.

Three locks clicked, and the metal door squeaked open. The Beatles' "Anytime at All" blew across the threshold.

"You okay?" Jon said.

Winded, I held up my hand for a moment and straightened up. "Will be," I finally managed. That wasn't how I imagined our reunion. I'd hoped something in him knew me, and somehow he recalled our life together in my original timeline, like déjà vu.

Jon was younger than I'd ever seen him in person—twenty-four—and incredibly handsome, with his smooth olive complexion, proud chin, and kissable lips.

A faint parenthesis formed around his mouth. Those lines deepened in the future. "Where is it?" he asked, but nothing in his expression said *I love you*. Not even a look that meant *hello, cutie*.

"What?" I said, lost in lust.

"My large sausage," he said.

"Yes," I said.

"My pizza," he said, sweeping a hand through the air like a magician. "Where is my order?"

In my excitement seeing him, I forgot about pretending to be the delivery girl. I dropped his partner's name to get his attention. "I'm a friend of Joanne Vento." I searched his face for recognition of her name. I saw none.

"Just what is it you want?" Heart-melting dimples weakened his sternness.

I behaved boldly with the Domestic flunky, Murray. So why did I feel like mush around my own husband? "I'm a friend of Joanne Vento," I repeated.

He crossed his arms. "So what?"

Starting to panic, I rambled. "She was my best friend, we grew up together, next door neighbors. She taught me how to bake."

He didn't budge. "How nice for you."

"You're in danger from Domestic Global. Joanne is too. We all are. Let me in and I'll explain."

Recognition flashed in his eyes. "What did you say?"

"Domestic Global. They're experimenting on people without their consent. I'm one of their guinea pigs."

He uncrossed his arms. "Let me search you first."

I held out my arms. *My pleasure.*

He patted me down—thoroughly. I tingled at his no-nonsense touch. He unzipped my jacket to check inside for weapons. I was reminded of our first kiss accompanied by the zip-up.

Instead of smooching me, he steered me inside his apartment.

I dried my feet on his *Wipe Your Paws* welcome mat.

Two brown corduroy sofas consumed most of the space in the living room. Newspapers and magazines cascaded from tall stacks on the glass coffee table, jarringly similar to the one I'd broken in my dream of John Lennon's apartment. Open modular bookshelves bowed under the weight of encyclopedias, non-fiction hard covers, and record albums. A black stereo console, situated under the pass-through to the kitchen, gleamed with expensive-looking hi-fi equipment. His framed Peter Max Beatles poster hung next to the window.

No dirty dishes or beer empties anywhere. He'd always been tidy with everything but his clothes.

Jon turned the volume off as "I'll Cry Instead" ended.

I removed my coat and hung it on a rack behind the door. I tugged at my tight sweater so the scoop rode lower on my chest.

Jon straightened a few of the piles of periodicals. He took a book off the end table and shelved it—a pristine hardcover edition of Octavia Butler's *Kindred*.

By the time he took notice of me again, I had seated myself on the end of the sofa opposite the window.

"Make yourself at home," he said in a tone I didn't recognize.

From the nearly six years we'd been together between dating and being married, I remembered sweet, aroused, sleepy, excited, angry, sad, irritated, indifferent, even bitter. But never sarcastic. That was new. Or old, given the date was years before we first met.

"Fantastic Max poster," I said. "Is it an original?" I knew the answer. It hung in our Long Island condo in a position of honor above our stereo.

"Why do you want to know?" His voice oozed hostility—also new. "Casing the joint?"

Holy molé salsa. On the subway ride, I'd anticipated that seeing Jon again would be exhilarating. That he'd be falling all over himself to come to my rescue. I scoured my brain for something that would help me to connect with him. Something I'd seen in the newspaper on the way over seemed appropriate. "Did you know today is the seventeenth anniversary of The Beatles landing in America at JFK?"

He didn't answer.

I kept on jabbering. "I'm a big Beatles fan too," I said. "I've got a couple of bootlegs of the BBC sessions."

"Good for you," he said. "Are you going to tell me why you think Vento is in danger?"

He clearly had no interest in small talk. I couldn't believe how cold he sounded. *Where was the Jon who wanted me?* I stalled. "I'm a little dehydrated. Could I trouble you for a glass of water, *mi sol?*" The endearment slipped out.

"I'm not your sun." He stalked off.

Despite the room being chilly, I unfastened the top button of my sweater. Jon had always been a fan of my assets.

In a moment, he returned with a juice-sized glass. He set it in front of me and stood there.

I drained the water in a single swallow.

He snapped a fist to his waist. "More?"

"Not yet. *Gracias.*" I smoothed the top of my sweater to draw his gaze to my chest.

"Get down to it, then," he said, his posture stiff.

"It would be easier if you sat. My neck will get sore talking up at you." *No matter how amazing you look to me.*

He acquiesced and took a seat on the other sofa.

Just then the intercom buzzed.

He sprang to answer it.

"Pizza," a deep male voice said through static. Thank goodness it wasn't the nasal voice of my delivery boy, Murray.

Jon stepped out in the hall and in a few moments returned with a box. He disappeared into the kitchen and came back carrying a plate with two slices on it and a can of cola. "Are you hungry?"

"Actually, I'm starving." Watching Murray inhale his aromatic sub must have inspired my appetite.

He handed me the food and drink, then went back to the kitchen. Next trip, he returned with another plate of slices, soda and a few napkins.

"Eat," he said, "while it's hot. We'll talk after. Unless it's some kind of emergency."

"Not yet it isn't. Give it a few years."

He grunted.

I toyed with the second button on my sweater.

Jon was too busy chewing to notice.

CHAPTER 72

SARA, AGE 18

Saturday, February 7, 1981, 3:07 PM
Jon's apartment
Hedgehurst, Brooklyn, NY

At first the silence between Jon and I made me uncomfortable. But the taste of the pizza changed that. Each of New York's five boroughs always claimed to have the best. Brooklyn won my vote right there and then. And to think, in my original life, I had sworn off all the best foods to adhere to the granola diet.

After Jon finished a second helping of slices, he rose and cleared the plates.

I stood too. "Let me take those. I'd be happy to wash them for you."

"I got it," he said. "Chill. Your clothes are too fancy to do housework."

I flushed. Not quite a compliment, but it didn't seem a dig either. It gave me hope that hunger accounted for his earlier curtness. People get brusque when their blood sugar drops.

While he cleaned up in the kitchen, I started the *Hard Day's Night* album from the beginning. I adjusted the volume low enough to be able to hold a conversation.

Jon returned with two cans of beer and one empty glass. He set a can and the glass in front of me. "I thought this might make it easier to say whatever you came to tell me."

LANA AYERS

My heart beat a little faster. At least he didn't think of me as a kid, drinking age being eighteen then. I popped the top and poured.

A glimmer of a smile crossed his lips. "How about starting with your name and where you're from."

I laughed. I'd forgotten the year being 1981 meant he didn't know. "I'm Sara Rodríguez Bloom from Woodward, Queens."

He took a sip of his beer. "Go on." He fixed all his attention on me.

Holy molé salsa, with my faded memories I'd almost forgotten his eyes— smoldering raw umber. Feeling feverish, I unfastened the second button on my sweater, then gulped some beer to cool off. "Domestic Global is experimenting on people without their consent or—"

He interrupted. "People. How many and how do *you* know this?" He pointed at me to punctuate his question.

"I don't know how many."

"Can you name any names of the victims?"

I felt my face flush again. I was about to tell my husband the name of another man I'd slept with during a time flash. Except Jon wasn't my husband then or yet. "Daniel Astrella. My brother's best friend. Something about exposure to a certain radioactive chemical in the neighborhood we grew up in made us better test subjects."

"Woodward, Queens."

"Yes, but that's not important right now. What's important is that Domestic injected us with experimental serum." I stopped there and tried to gauge his expression.

Jon wore an impenetrable poker face. A good accessory for an under-cover agent. "And the purpose of the injections?"

"Mind control. To coerce consumers to buy their brands of cereal and cigarettes and every other product they make. With some people, like Danny and me, the drug had an unexpected side effect." I took a deep breath. "Time travel. I flash back in time."

"Look, maybe you should see a counselor. Get into a drug dependency program." He stood. "You knocked on the wrong door. You need to go."

Panic set in. My armpits went swampy. I needed Jon to believe me, to help me. "I can prove it to you," I said. "I'm not on drugs. Well, except for what Domestic pumped into me. Please, give me a chance. What have you got to lose by hearing me out?"

He rubbed his chin. "You may be deranged, but I'm sure I could take you down if you get out of line. Okay, I'll let you have your say. But when we're finished, I am going to call the county psychiatric hospital and have them send someone to pick you up."

I thought it best not to mention I'd already been to the nuthouse a couple of times in the redo where I lived with my dad. "I know I sound crazy, but I have evidence I'm not."

Jon sat. "How exactly are you going to substantiate time travel?" He spun a hand in the air over his head.

I thought a minute. "Well, you and I have never met, right?"

"Go on." He tapped his fingers against his thigh.

"But I know you because we know each other in the future. We meet in January 1994 when you take a job in the corporate accounting office at Domestic's Long Island headquarters."

"Now I know you're cuckoo. I'm no accountant, sweetheart."

"You're an operative for the undercover arm of the Department of Justice."

His eyes narrowed. "You know where I work. What does that prove?"

"If we've never met, how do I know you share a birthday with John Lennon?"

"What did you do, sneak a look at my driver's license when I was in the kitchen? You probably saw my badge in there too." He got up, went to the coat rack, and fished out his wallet and DOJ cover from his jacket. He riffled through the wallet. "Everything seems to be here."

"I swear I didn't snoop through your things," I said. "Isn't there any question I could answer that would prove I am telling the truth? Ask me something only a person very close to you would know."

He laughed. "Oh, now you're telling me we know each other intimately. Why not say you're having my baby too?"

His snippy remark cut me to the quick. I wanted to shout, *You loved me, you married me, I was pregnant with your baby before it died inside me. How can you look at me and not know me?* But instead I said, "We've slept together more times than I can count."

"Now, you're trying to seduce me. To what end? I don't know any state secrets."

I went to him and rested my hand on his heart. "I'm trying to save your life, Jon. We need to put an end to these illegal experiments. Please, ask me one question."

"Okay," he said, flicking my hand away as if it were an insect, "tell me about my scar."

I didn't hesitate. "You have a scar under your right buttock cheek from sitting on a Coke bottle when you were six."

He reached for his backside.

I continued, "You needed stitches."

His pupils dilated.

"Your mother, María García, forbade soda in the house afterward, not even in cans."

He slapped his side. "You've obviously spoken to my mother. Did she put you up to this?"

"Call her. Ask her if she knows me. She won't. We haven't met yet."

"You know about the scar. Maybe you talked to an ex-girlfriend."

"Come on, Jon. I answered your question. How about you give me the benefit of the doubt?"

"Okay, let's say you're a time traveler. How does that put my life, or anyone else's, in danger?"

"All I ask is that you hear me out. If you don't believe me afterward, then send me on my way." I hugged myself. "Or have me carried off in a straitjacket."

"Sure. Why not? I didn't have any plans tonight anyway. This might be entertaining. But I'll need another beer. Can I get you anything?"

For a skeptic, he was a decent host. I asked for water and went back to my place on the sofa. I had to figure out a way to win him over.

He came back with a tall glass of water this time, and two more beers. "You sure you don't want another?"

I declined. I needed a clear head.

"Just so you know, I phoned Vento. She's out of town, but when she calls back maybe she'll vouch for you."

"She will." At least I hoped she would, regardless of whether we were still friends.

He sat on the opposite sofa as before. "Time traveler, enlighten me, what's the future like?"

"Noisy, polluted, smaller phones, bigger TVs, nearly everyone owns a personal computer, and compact discs—CDs—have replaced vinyl and cassette as the preferred medium for music."

"What's a CD?"

"It's a metallic-coated plastic disc about the size of a bread plate. Instead of a needle, the music is played by a laser beam."

"Sounds far out, like something from *The Jetsons*. But I'm going to hold onto my vinyl anyway."

"True aficionados will always collect records." Music, a subject he loved, I went ahead and risked appealing even more deeply to his heart. I took a breath first. "And in the future, you and I are married."

He snorted. "Now I know you're delusional."

His dismissal irked me. "Is being married to me beyond the realm of possibility? Do you honestly prefer bimbos like Misti?" I regretted letting her name slip the minute I said it.

He smacked the sofa with a fist. "I knew it! You talked to my ex. She told you about the scar." Even the way he sipped his beer looked smug.

"Please, this is getting us nowhere. I need your help to shut down the lab. To stop them from developing the mind-control serum. As an agent, you have special skills. You're principled and brave enough to go after the bad guys."

His impartial expression returned. "Go on, I'm listening."

"If we destroy the lab now, before the experiment goes too far, we'll save countless lives."

"The DOJ has never come across any evidence of illegal experimentation."

"I've been there. I can show you where the lab is."

He squeezed the beer can. "Tell me."

"No. If I tell you, you'll go there on your own and get killed. Let me take you there."

He blinked. "Why do you think I'll be killed? You saw my future—you said we were married. They can't both be true, that I get killed at the lab and I'm married to you. Unless you think I'm about to pop the question and fly us to Vegas for a quickie wedding before heading to this lab."

"We were married. Then I went back in time, broke our engagement, and somehow when I got back to my present you were dead. Domestic killed you."

"Why would you break our engagement?" He actually sounded annoyed that I would ditch him.

"Too long of a story to get into that now. I made a mistake."

"A mistake by marrying me or by breaking up with me?" He was like a dog with a bone who refused to let go.

Or maybe I'd wounded his ego. "Letting you go was the mistake. But I need you now. You are a trained professional agent who can help me stop bad guys now. In the past."

"Are you taking me back in time with you?" He pointed to the wall behind him.

"Not exactly."

"Then what?"

"This is the past for me."

"Fine, future girl, when are you from?"

"My present is the year 2000."

"How do you expect me to wrap my head around that?" he said. "How can you be from nineteen years in the future? Do I marry you when you're a baby? Talk about cradle-robbing."

"My body doesn't travel in time, just my consciousness, my mind."

"Right, of course. I should have consulted Jules Verne. When am I supposed to die?"

I looked at my hands. "1995."

"And you know this how?"

"Because Joanne told me about it in the year 2000. She said you went into the lab alone. Without back-up."

"That's over a dozen years from now. My future." He got up and paced from one end of the living room to the other like a shooting gallery duck. "I can't call this in to the agency. 'Yeah, boss, a time traveler wants us to go take down a lab. Can you send a team?' I'll be the one shipped off to the loony bin."

"But if you go there with me, you won't be alone. Do you have explosives handy? We should blow up the place."

He stopped pacing and glared at me. "You expect me to keep dynamite in my nightstand, right next to the condoms? I'm a government agent, not an anarchist."

I bit my tongue trying to picture the parade of skanks those condoms were for. "Sorry. I know you're a good guy."

"Okay, let's do this," he said. "You give me the location of the lab. I won't go in. I'll check the perimeter. See what there is to see. If there's cause for me to call it in, I will."

"No address. I go with you and show you where it is. That's the deal."

"You are one stubborn girl."

"Thanks. That's the nicest thing you've said to me since I got here." I sprinted across the room and hugged him.

Instead of returning the embrace he patted me on the back.

I pressed my face into his chest.

He smelled clean, like the air after a rainstorm.

"We're going to take down those bastards," I said under my breath, "together."

CHAPTER 73

SARA, AGE 18

Saturday, February 7, 1981, 4:20 PM
Truck stop, Route I-87 North
Tarton, NY

I fingered the Holland county map in my pocket to make sure it was still there. I held off telling Jon where we were going until we had already driven half an hour north on route I-87. After we left the rest stop with a full tank of gas, I fessed up as to our destination.

Before leaving to find Jon in Brooklyn, I'd sorted through my dad's jumbled collection of New York state maps. It took me the better part of an hour to find a county that contained both Twelfth Court and Cole Lane. Holland County, in the town of Fishburg Falls. Back when Jon broke me out of the lab, I had no idea where I was. He told me to head out of the parking lot on Twelfth Court, then turn right on Cole Lane. I didn't take notice of the license plates on the few cars in the nearly empty lot. Fleeing for my life put me in kind of a hurry. Then Dr. Gentry caught me, stuck me with a needle, and I time flashed out of there.

This younger Jon had never heard of Fishburg Falls. He was skeptical anything that diabolical could be happening in such a small, out the way town, but he kept on driving north as I instructed, hands tapping the wheel to whatever tune played on the radio. Sweet dimples, he looked too innocent to be an agent of any kind. Had he any idea what chaos he'd go up against when he signed on to the undercover bureau?

CHAPTER 74

JON, AGE 24

... life which unlives us and makes us strangers ...

— OCTAVIO PAZ

Saturday, February 7, 1981, 5 PM
Jon's car, driving up I-87 North
to Fishburg Falls, NY

*J*on didn't know who was crazier—the beautiful girl who claimed to be a time traveler from the future. Or him, for almost believing her. He wasn't going to trust everything she said. Definitely not the part about the two of them being married. Or him being killed. But the compact disc music thingy sounded pretty cool.

If Sara was on the level, this Domestic lead could make the top brass take notice, get him a promotion. Sure, it was a risk investigating without going through proper channels. Officially off-duty, he could claim he went upstate for the weekend with a date. That way if the lead paid off, he would say they came upon the place by accident. But more likely, it wouldn't amount to anything.

Going for a drive with a beautiful woman wasn't the worst way to spend an evening. And there was something about Sara. Something more than her striking eyes, luscious lips, bronze skin, and plush curves. He felt a connection with her. *Now, that was crazy.* He'd never even met her before. *And yet.*

She looked out the back window for the hundredth time. She had to be checking for the redheaded delivery boy she told him about.

"Don't worry," he said. "No one's following us."

"How can you tell?"

"I've been keeping a close eye since we left the truck stop. I go by the style of the headlights, the distance, speed, and location. Besides, all this slush would make it more obvious."

"Oh, I see," she said. "Thank you for taking me seriously."

But what if she hoped someone was following them? She could be a clever double agent working for Domestic, sent to set him up. *No—she's too emotional to be a Mata Hari.* He needed to maintain a professional distance. He tuned in a news station on the radio to discourage further conversation. It worked for a while.

After a report about children dying at a circus fire in India, Sara began sobbing. A sad story, but she sure was sensitive. Jon turned off the radio. "Do you need me to stop? We could pull off the highway. Get some coffee."

"No, I'll be fine." She popped the glove box where he kept his Magnum.

"Don't touch that," he said. He reached across her and closed the box. "It's loaded."

"I was looking for a tissue."

"Here, take this." Finally, a use for the clean handkerchief his mother always insisted he carry.

She dabbed at her leaking eyes. Her lips sucked in.

He hated seeing her sad. "Would it help to talk about it?"

"I'm overwhelmed by how much I can't fix." She took a deep breath. "And I feel guilty focusing on my own problems. The world is full of misfortune."

No stranger to heartache, he tried to cheer her. "Full of good things too. Family, friends, music, art, nature. And a whole lot more."

"You left out love," she said.

"Sex," he said, "great sex."

"Ha," she said. "What about soul-mates?"

"I wouldn't know about that," he said. "But a good pizza and the Mets ahead in the seventh inning—that's the perfect pair."

"Not what I'd call romantic, but you're definitely a glass-half-full kind of guy."

"That I am." He had to be to balance out his mother's pessimistic world-view. She saw the cloud in every silver lining. *Even before his father was killed.*

"How can you be so optimistic when your job is carrying a firearm and chasing criminals?"

"I'm going after the few people who make bad choices. A lot more make good ones. And those few I arrest get a second chance to do the right thing. After they do their time, that is."

"You love humanity," she said. "Is that what made you want to be a government agent?"

"In a way, but I got my love from my father."

Tears stopped, she folded the handkerchief in her lap. "How so?"

A subject that meant everything to him, he ran off at the mouth. "A beat cop all his life. *Papá* got passed over for promotions because of his last name. Not a lot of our kind in his precinct. Regardless, he took the job to protect and serve seriously. Managed to save the lives of a school bus full of children hijacked by a known killer. The mayor awarded him a special commendation. My father was a real hero to those kids, to their parents. A hero to me, to the entire Spanish-speaking community. How could I want to be any less?"

"Your family must be proud," she said.

"My mother wanted me to be an accountant." Jon hoped *Papá* was watching over him from heaven and approved the choices he made.

"So how come you didn't become a cop like your dad?"

"The week I graduated from the police academy, the Department of Justice recruited me for their undercover investigative department. They were looking for young men with few attachments. The bureau has a reputation for killing marriages. I'd recently left a miserable relationship. But you know all about Misti, don't you?"

"Only her name and that she was a ditz."

He didn't want to talk about his ex-girlfriend, especially not with another woman. "When John Lennon was murdered. I knew I made the right choice joining the DOJ. As an investigator I hoped I could stop the worst crimes before they happened."

"To do that you would have to know the future," she said, "like me." She stuck out her tongue.

"If you're giving me a hard time, then you must be feeling better."

"Ready to take on the bad guys," she said.

"You're forgetting. I'm checking out the address you gave me to see if there's anything suspicious. Don't go all *Dirty Harry* on me."

"More like *Harry Met Sally*."

"What does that mean?"

"Another movie. You wouldn't know it. It's from the future." She smiled.

He liked the way her whiskey-colored eyes lit up when she challenged him. "Yeah, about the future … tell me about us. I'm not the marrying kind. How'd you trap me? I didn't get you pregnant, did I?"

She bit her lip and was quiet for a few moments.

Is that pain in her lovely eyes?

Finally, she said, "You couldn't resist my charm and good looks."

"You're not my type, you know." *That's a lie.* Except for her being *loca*, he liked everything about her. And that scared him.

"Plus the mind-blowing sex," she said.

He sat up straighter. She looked young. "You're at least eighteen, right?"

"You served me alcohol," she said, avoiding the question. "And what do you mean I'm not your type?"

"I prefer simple women." *That's the truth.* He'd dated a lawyer for about five minutes. All she ever wanted to do was argue.

"You mean dumb as a brick," she said.

He didn't want someone shallow either. Misti couldn't converse about anything but beauty products. "No. I mean uncomplicated. You'd be too much work."

"If you mean I'd want a man who can hold an intelligent conversation and treat me as an equal, then yes, I'd be too much for you to handle." She sounded miffed.

Now he'd gotten her upset. That wasn't his aim. "Truce," he said, and turned the radio back on.

"Please, no more news. It's all so depressing."

He fussed with the dial until he located a classical station. Haunting piano strains of Debussy's "Clair de Lune" filled the car. The superb music underscored a desire and melancholy he didn't know he'd been suppressing. He couldn't live for his job alone. He wanted a full life. He wanted to be with someone. *Someone like Sara.*

CHAPTER 75

SARA, AGE 18

Saturday, February 7, 1981, 8:45 PM
Jon's car, driving up I-87
to Fishburg Falls, NY

*D*ebussy, Mozart, Liszt, and Chopin buoyed us safely through the slick, descending night to our destination. Though we weren't being followed, I worried how things would play out. *Would the research lab even be there this early in time? Could Jon and I really stop Domestic?*

The brick structure at the corner of Twelfth Court and Cole Lane hunkered in shadows. A nondescript white van, like Steve's in the future, and two beat-up sedans occupied the parking lot. The building's walkway was unlit. Through the glass entry door, a dim lamp illuminated the lobby area. The only evidence of a security guard was an abandoned Styrofoam cup and newspaper on the vestibule desk.

Jon turned onto Cole Lane, and pulled to the curb, but left the car running. "I'm going to go look around. You stay here."

"I'm coming with you. You can't go in alone."

"No. You're safer here."

I opened the glove box and took the gun. It wasn't like the barreled weapon in my dream. This one had a more rectangular look to it, and considerably more heft. "I'll be safe with this."

"Give that gun to me before you hurt yourself."

"Not unless you let me come with you. I won't make a sound or get under foot. I promise."

Jon sighed. "I could be fired for coming here with you. I can't let this go any further."

"How about I shoot myself in the foot?" I said. "Then you'll have a lot more explaining to do. Like why there's blood all over your nice government car and why you shot an innocent woman."

"Go ahead," he said.

I couldn't believe it. *He called my bluff.* "How do you know I won't?"

"It's a chance I'm willing to take."

I got out of the car holding the pistol. "I'm coming with." My breath vapored in the cold air.

Jon turned off the engine and came around to the curb. "Give me the gun, and I'll take you with me."

I held out the weapon.

He tucked it in his coat pocket. "Stay behind me. And if I say 'run,' I want you to high-tail it back here to the car and drive off." He tossed me the keys.

I surprised myself by plucking them out of the air. "I'm not leaving without you."

"You sound like a broken record." He started up the block. "If you insist on being my shadow, at least act like one and stay quiet."

I didn't appreciate his gag order.

Instead of going to the wide-open parking lot entrance, Jon stopped at the fence along the side of the building, removed a wire cutter from an inside jacket pocket and sliced a vertical line down the chain link. He crept through the hole. "Careful, Sara," he said.

I followed.

Jon pulled a small flashlight from the well-stocked jacket. *More like a magician's hat. Maybe a rabbit was next.*

He shined light on the boundaries of the brick structure.

"Looking for a secret door?" I said.

He shushed me and kept searching until he found something—a small brass cylinder. He picked it up, examined it, and shoved it in his pants pocket.

"Is that a bullet casing?" I said. "I've seen them on TV."

"If you won't return to the car," he said, in a whisper, "make yourself useful." He pointed to a large dumpster. "Go look for anything suspicious— papers, body parts, whatever."

350

"You said I was too well-dressed to do dishes, now you want me to go dumpster diving?"

"Dumpster what? Just take the flashlight." He held it out to me.

"Where are you going?" Our whispered breaths mingled in the air. I had the sudden impulse to take his face in my hands and kiss him. I resisted.

"Never mind. If I'm not back in ten minutes, get in the car and leave. You can drive, can't you?"

"Promise me you won't go in the building alone."

He said nothing.

I watched him check the first darkened window. It didn't open. He continued around the building. I followed him.

He turned.

I knew he was glaring at me before I shined the light on him.

He pointed to the dumpster again.

I shuffled over to the trash and lifted the lid. The odor of rotting bananas assaulted my nose. I didn't see any body parts, but there was lots of paperwork. And old-fashioned computer printouts, the kind with a series of holes down the side. Papers were hardly suspicious for any kind of office. Perhaps some of these held the secret formula or the names of test subjects. There was really too much to go through there in the parking lot. And I wasn't about to dive in for real.

I sought out Jon to ask him what to do next.

Around the back of the building, a single bulb illuminated a metal door. A man's pocket comb jammed between the door and hinge prevented the door from closing all the way.

Jon had to be inside. *Alone*. A chill climbed up my spine. Grandma used to say that sensation meant *somebody is walking on your grave*. Jon's grave worried me more. Joanne said he had died doing exactly this—going into a Domestic lab alone, without any back-up. But he had me this time. I went in after him.

The flashlight illuminated a long corridor. There were doors on both sides of the hall. A soda machine to my left made a dripping sound. The snack machine on my right hummed softly.

The place was quiet otherwise. I tiptoed forward, willing the balls of my feet to take my weight and prevent my boot heels from clopping.

The first set of glass doors was locked. On one side, the flashlight beam revealed mainframe computers with reel-to-reel magnetic tapes. The other room held a conference table with a dozen chairs.

The second set of rooms was also locked. An examination space like in a doctor's office was on the left. There were four patient tables with sanitary paper stretched across them. The room on the right appeared to be an operating area, complete with shiny, sharp instruments. If this facility really carried out research on the common cold, how did surgery play a role? I shuddered at the thought that maybe they had cut open Elise Wells' brain in that room.

The third set of doors was made out of metal. I put my ear to the one on the left and heard a whir of some kind of machinery. Behind the right-side door, a sound like a cough startled me. *Could it be Jon?* I listened again. Nothing there. Maybe my mind was playing tricks.

But a steady thump approached from down the hall, along with the jingle of keys. The sound kept getting louder.

Definitely not my imagination. I killed my flashlight and tried the door on the left. Locked. The door on my right whooshed open as I turned the handle.

I dashed into a dark, frigid room and looked for a way to secure the door. It had no lock on the inside. I wondered if I should have run for the back exit of the building instead.

The footsteps and jangled keys passed by and kept going.

Was it Jon? As I leaned out, my right leg went numb. I struggled to keep my balance.

A thinner man than Jon stood in front of the soda machine, his back to me.

I closed the door and switched on my flashlight to look for another exit. Instead, I saw six gurneys—all occupied. *Holy molé salsa—I'm in a morgue!*

Footsteps approached the room again and halted.

Despite the freezing cold, I sweated like a sumo wrestler in the Sahara.

Keys clattered.

Certain I was being locked in, I scanned the perimeter for another way out. None.

I clambered up onto the gurney closest to me, dragging my numb leg under the cloth. I covered my mouth and held my breath. I snuggled a corpse. At least it didn't smell like anything but formaldehyde. Still, I had to will myself not to retch.

The room's overhead fluorescents buzzed on. Enough light bled through the sheet for me to see the small blanched face next to mine was a little girl's, maybe five or six. Queasiness gave way to anger. *What kind of monsters would experiment on a young child?* Experiment and kill. They had to be stopped.

Footsteps echoed in the morgue.

My heartbeat thudded loud enough to give me away.

"Hello sweetheart," a man's voice said.

Definitely not Jon.

"You're too pretty not to have a date on a Saturday night."

Was he talking to me? I might shiver to death waiting for him to pull the cloth off me.

Instead, I heard the rasp of metal from another table, then squeaking.

I sneaked a look.

A pudgy, blond-haired man had his pants and underwear down around his ankles. He was staring at a naked dead woman while touching himself.

I threw off the shroud, jumped down, and tried to run. My right leg wouldn't cooperate.

The man fell back against the table with a loud thud. "Oh my god, oh my god," he said. He either thought a dead body had come to life or he'd climaxed.

While he was tangled up in his pants, I hobbled out and headed into the long hall.

All the lights had been turned on. More footsteps echoed behind me.

I turned to see Jon running in my direction, gun in hand. I called to him.

"Are you hurt?" he said. He raced toward me.

It all happened so fast.

The tall, thin guard rushed out of another hall. He had a gun too.

Shots rang out. At least four, maybe five.

I don't know if Jon returned fire or initiated. His arm stopped mid-aim. His face wore a look of surprise. His body froze for a second, and then folded. He collapsed in a heap on the floor right next to me.

Blood gushed from a head wound and another at the base of his neck.

I turned his face to me. I said his name.

Jon's eyes stared blankly. He didn't see me or anything. He was dead.

It was my fault, as sure as if I'd shot him myself. If I hadn't led him to the lab ....

The anger I'd felt over the dead child converted into rage. I stripped the weapon from Jon's hand. I'd never used a gun in any of my lives. I squeezed the trigger hoping to hit the guard. My hand lurched.

The guard fired.

The right side of my body burned. I didn't know if the blood that covered me was my own or Jon's.

The tall guard ripped the gun from my hand. "You're gonna wish you died with your friend," he said. "I'll take a turn with you before we call the doc. You look like a cushy ride." His upper left incisor, much longer than the right, bit into his lower lip as he talked. And he had long ears.

I must have been in shock, because all I could focus on was how much this man who had just killed my husband, and who threatened to rape me right there in the hall, resembled a cartoon bunny.

But the rabbit was partly right. I wished I'd died. Instead of Jon, not with him.

"Already called it in," the pudgy guard said. He bent over me. "Quite a looker. She ain't stiff the way I like 'em, but I can go either way."

He moved some hair out of my eyes.

The butt of a gun came at me.

CHAPTER 76

SARA, AGE 18

Sunday, February 8, 1981, 1:03 AM
Gentry Research Laboratory
Fishburg Falls, NY

I smelled urine—maybe my own. The too-bright fluorescents ticked in the otherwise quiet room. I'd been awake watching the clock for nearly two hours, over the course of which my vision shifted from blurry to sharp focus. Bound to an examination bed, my wrists and ankles were secured with duct tape.

I had no memory of being raped and no pain down there. My clothes had been replaced by a diamond-patterned hospital gown. Blood seeped through a bandage on my right side. The wound stung. My head ached.

Crying made the hurt worse, but I deserved to be in pain. *My love's blood is on my hands.* Jon died because of me. I made him take me to the lab. When Domestic dissected my brain, sorrow and regret would be all they'd discover there.

But I didn't want to die. I wanted revenge.

A door opened behind me.

"Awake, dear? Sorry to keep you waiting," a woman said in a sing-songy way. I heard her opening cupboards and drawers. Finally, she came around and faced me. The voice belonged to a short-haired redhead, extremely thin, with a gaunt face that gave the impression she'd been starving for months. Probably in her thirties, she wore a lab coat buttoned over a long, filmy nightgown.

"You didn't have any identification on you, but you resemble the photo we have on file. Is it safe to assume you are Sara Bloom?"

"Who wants to know?" I said, all bravado.

"I'm Dr. Claire Gentry." She held out her hand, then withdrew it, seeing I was in no position to shake. "I believe you've already met my nephew, Murray. He can verify your identity for me."

"Get me out of this tape," I said.

"It's the middle of the night, and you caught us unaware. Murray told us not to expect you until Sunday evening."

"Your guards threatened to rape me."

Her eyebrows shot up. "We're all professionals here. The security people may be a bit primitive, but I assure you this is a research facility, not a penitentiary. No one molested you."

"How do you know?"

"I tended to your gunshot and examined you. I'm a doctor as well as a scientist."

"And a prison warden. If you won't let me go, how is this not a jail?"

"Tut, tut." She moved out of my field of vision, but instantly came back with a needle filled with clear liquid.

I strained against the duct tape as she stabbed my arm.

"This will make you feel more sociable," she said.

A wave of relaxation coursed through my body. "Well, if it's sociable you want, let's go to the mall." I tried to rage against the sedation and lost.

"Good. We've already taken a blood sample for analysis, but it would help us if you could tell us something about the testing you've undergone."

"I have no idea what you're talking about."

"The serum, can you tell us about color, odor, texture, anything?"

"You killed Jon and now you want my help? You must be insane."

"The dead man was a spy trying to steal our secrets. Tell me what you know about the experiment."

"I don't know anything." Suddenly exhausted, I closed my eyes and tried to shut out Claire and her third degree. The blow to my right cheek prevented that.

"There now, don't make me slap you again. It hurt me more than it did you." She giggled as she flicked her wrist. "Stay with me, dear. I only gave you something to relax your muscles, not put you to sleep. You got me out of bed in the middle of the night. If I'm up at this ungodly hour, you should be too. Besides, there will be plenty of time later to rest." She smiled wide. Her teeth were oddly greenish, like Murray's. And the whites of her eyes were yellowish. She resembled June Lockhart, if June Lockhart had been a heroin addict.

I couldn't let Domestic win. I had to find a way to make Jon's death mean something. Maybe I could get information out of her. "How about you tell me what you know, and I'll fill in any gaps I can?"

She tapped her cheek with her forefinger and rolled her eyes. "You're going to be our guest at this facility for the rest of your days. So, I can accommodate your request."

I lost my composure for a minute and tried to kick my legs free to no avail.

"Dear, you are volunteering for scientific research. There is no more noble cause. Think of all those indigenous people who died in order for the polio vaccine to be perfected. Their deaths advanced medicine, and saved innumerable lives."

"Murder is not science." I wanted to scream, but my sedated body didn't comply. If not for the restraints, I would have punched her in the mouth.

"As a young girl, all I dreamed of was making great scientific discoveries, like Marie Curie. Can't you see, I am an explorer? And I intend to be one of the greatest."

"Murray told me you're working on curing the common cold."

When she laughed, the taut skin on her face pleated, accordion-like. "Murray is my flesh and blood, sweet as sucrose. But he thinks we turn lead into gold. Fortunately, his twin brother Malcolm has the O'Keefe brains intact. After the accident, all poor Murray was left with was brawn. Hard to believe identical twins could end up as different as H_2O and H_2O_2. But that's another study."

Holy molé salsa—Murray wasn't lying when he said he had an evil twin. If I flattered her ego, maybe I could outsmart her the way I did with her nephew. I tried to sound attentive, even for a captive audience. "What are you studying here, Dr. Gentry?"

"As a disciple of Wilder Penfield, the remarkable neurosurgeon, I am unlocking secrets of the human brain."

She meant mind control. I tried to smile, but it didn't feel like my face muscles were cooperating.

She continued, "Like Wilder, I have discovered much by trial and error."

By error, she meant brain damage. "Very noble, but what does that have to do with me?"

"We have learned about certain subjects undergoing drug trials in this lab years from now who have experienced unprecedented episodes of chronic consciousness transference. Your name was given to us as a volunteer in a future study. That's why I sent Murray to fetch you."

"In layman's terms, please, doctor."

"A woman came to this lab claiming to be a test subject from the year 2000. She believed the experiment somehow transported her back in time—her mind, not her body. Naturally, we interviewed her thoroughly, ran all kinds of assessments. We've been studying her. She's had projective visions with statistically significant accuracy."

I played dumb. "She told you she's from the future. Sounds nuts. Could you have her give me the winning lottery numbers?"

"This woman recalled your name and a list of others as being part of the same study. She worked for my general practitioner spouse before volunteering for the experiment herself. And she told us that you will be a patient of my husband's a dozen or so years from now."

The *she* Claire was speaking of had to be Elise—Dr. Lance Gentry's assistant and George Wells' wife. I hoped Danny's name was not on that list Elise produced. "How can you justify statistical significance? You need a bigger sample than one test subject. Or are there more of these insane folks who claim to be time travelers?"

"We're hoping to get a good sample population, but these consciousness transfer subjects have not proved to be resilient thus far. I'd forgotten you are a Mathematics major, Miss Bloom."

Whoever else they'd captured must have already died. My heart sank. *Please not Danny.* "I'm studying accounting," I said, to keep my head in the conversation.

She sneered.

I guessed she didn't appreciate being corrected.

"Tell me, why did you break in here with that spy?" she said. "What's your connection to him?"

"Spy?"

"Our studies are underwritten by a private corporation who want us to help them understand the nature of desire, particularly what makes one product more attractive than another to potential consumers. We refused government funding opportunities. We didn't want to share our results with Uncle Sam. Since our government isn't a fan of privacy, they try to steal all our discoveries. That's why they send spies. We can't have that. But I was surprised to discover you were with him."

"Jon came to find out why Murray wanted to bring me here. I didn't sign up for any medical study. He was only looking out for me as a friend. You didn't have to kill him." I tried not to show weakness, but my tears flowed.

"Did you know he was a spy?"

"He's an accountant."

She snorted. "And I'm the Queen of England. What do you know about the year 2000 experiment?"

"I'm a student at Flushing College. I don't know anything about experiments. Now or in the future. You're talking science fiction."

"Our brain studies are potentially quite lucrative, Miss Bloom. But do you realize what it means if I have unlocked the secret of time travel? Not only will I make the corporation even richer than it already is, but with my royalties, I'll become one of the wealthiest women anywhere. More than that, I'm going to change the future of the human race and win a Nobel Prize."

I'd already changed the future—I'd gotten Jon killed in the past. Time flashing was not a precise skill. I couldn't bear to imagine all the damage that could be done to the world if more fools like me had the ability to time travel.

"You look skeptical, Miss Bloom. But I think you're hiding the fact that you are from the future. Who is president right now?"

I answered without hesitation. "Ronald Reagan." The first election I'd been eligible to vote in, and my candidate, the incumbent Jimmy Carter, had lost.

"And our last president?"

"Jimmy Carter. Look, I'm in pain and exhausted. Could we pick this up later?" I needed time to strategize. Plus, I was afraid I might give myself away if she kept questioning me.

"Bus fare?" she asked.

I'd paid it only yesterday. Losing my virginity a second time to Steve seemed a lifetime ago. "Sixty cents in New York City." She'd be shocked at the fee in my present—a whopping dollar fifty. "Please, this tape is cutting off my circulation. Could you remove it?"

"Attendants will be in to transfer you to a bed later on. We can make you reasonably comfortable, Miss Bloom, but that all depends on you. We've invented some rather unique techniques for extracting information. I'm afraid some of them might be quite agonizing if you fail to cooperate."

The doctor walked around the exam table and out of my line of vision again. In a moment, she came back with another needle filled with clear fluid. She stabbed it into my thigh.

I yelped at having become a human pin cushion. "What did you inject me with?" My blood felt tingly in my veins.

"That's enough for this evening." She yawned. "I need to get back home to bed." She walked behind me. The door slammed.

I was left alone with my own thoughts—my guilt over getting Jon killed —a more effective torture than Claire Gentry, with all her innovations, could ever envision.

CHAPTER 77

SARA, AGE 18

Sunday, February 8, 1981, 3 PM
Gentry Research Laboratory
Fishburg Falls, NY

I'd been awake and unattended for what felt like hours. No matter how much I strained against the leather restraints, they held.

The stark room's ceiling-mounted speakers produced continual static. Three other beds sat empty. Scents of applesauce and ammonia hung in the air. Without a clock or window for reference in the new room, I didn't know how long I'd been unconscious. From the hallway, footsteps echoed and muted voices drifted in.

When my delivery boy Murray showed up, I was almost glad to see him.

Dressed in a dark green suit that accentuated the redness of his hair and highlighted the tint of his teeth, the words *Hulk smash* came to mind once more. His eyes blazed like blue flame.

When he spoke, the toothpick stuck in the corner of his mouth bobbled up and down. "I told you I don't take kindly to being made a fool of."

I needed to give an Oscar-worthy performance, like my mother had done for years according to Dad. I had to convince Murray once again that I was sweet on him. "I'm so glad you're finally here. I thought you would never come."

"What are you jabbering on about?" He pulled the toothpick from between his lips and pointed it at my right eye.

The restraints made it impossible to use my hands to flirt. And I was sure I looked as awful as I felt. At least someone had cleaned the gunshot wound and changed me into a clean gown while I was out. Maybe stroking Murray's masculinity would do the trick.

"I told my sick friend about the lab, and then he dragged me here with him. He said he needed to see for himself. I didn't want you to think I stood you up. I was excited about our dinner date at my parents'. I couldn't wait to see you again."

Murray cleaned gunk out of a fingernail with the toothpick and flicked it onto the bedcover. "Supposed to be a date, huh?"

"I didn't get a chance to tell my mother about this great guy I met. She would have loved you too," I said.

"I knew you went for me." He thumped his chest with his fist. "And I already met your old lady. Decent cook. I had second helpings of everything. She was as miffed at you as I was when you didn't show for supper."

I hadn't thought about the possibility of him actually going to my house. "How did you leave things, with my folks, I mean?" I was worried the answer might be *in body bags*.

"Told them you musta got held up by your sick friend. Your pops invited me for supper next Sunday too. I said I'd be there with bells on."

Thank God for Dad, always a soft spot for stragglers. We would have taken in a million stray cats if Mother let him have his way. "I'd really like to be there with you."

"What about your steady, the college boy with the fruity hair?"

Murray must have been stalking me for a while if he knew about Steve. "He's a real nice kid," I said, "but I need a man. The genuine article. Now how are you and I going to get cozy with me handcuffed to this bed?"

He blushed, and his freckles filled in like connect-the-dots. "I could climb in there with ya."

The very idea made me want to heave. "Sounds swell, but your aunt might walk in on us."

"Right. How 'bout I ask Aunt Claire when she'll be through with you?"

"How about we grab some food right here? Like a picnic. I got the blanket already."

"What do ya want?"

"Would you be a sweetheart and grab me some cold cereal?" I fluttered my eyelashes. "I'm famished. But you'll have to free my hands so I can eat."

"Sure thing on the eats, doll, but I can't uncuff you. You're tied down for a reason."

"I guess you'll have to feed me with those strong hands of yours. I'd be ever so grateful."

"How's about a down payment on the gratitude?" He leaned in and held his mouth over mine.

I kissed his lizard lips until bile billowed at the back of my throat.

"Good start," he said. "Back in a jiff."

Maybe I'd be able to convince him to set me free if I flirted some more, or bragged about the things I could do with my hands and toes. But mostly, I hoped that eating cereal would activate the Penrose waves and I'd time travel the hell out of there.

Murray returned before too long with a ceramic bowl and a lidded coffee container. "Hope you like Berry Beary Crunch."

"Tops," I said.

Murray arranged the bowl and cup on the bedside table. He gathered up the pillows from the spare beds and tucked them under my head to angle me more upright. *Thoughtful, even for a homicidal maniac.*

"Thank you, handsome sir," I said.

"I got manners." He sat on the bed facing me.

"I could feed myself, Murray. And after, I could do some other things with my hands you might really like." I wiggled my fingers. "I know how to make my guy happy."

"South paw, eh?" he said, completely ignoring my sexual insinuation. "Did you know John Dillinger was left-handed? I got respect for the guy. He's sorta my hero."

That explained a lot. "You remind me of Dillinger."

"Thanks, that's awful nice." He scooped up some cereal and held the spoon to my mouth.

I took the bite of cereal. My heartbeat ratcheted up, drowning out the crunching sound in my mouth.

The last I saw of Murray O'Keefe, as the room dwindled to thin air, was his green-toothed scowl.

TIME FLASH 7

YEAR 1970 — THE PAST

Time moves in one direction, memory in another.

— WILLIAM GIBSON

Time stays long enough for anyone who will use it.

— LEONARDO DA VINCI

CHAPTER 78

SARA, AGE 7

Wednesday, March 11, 1970, 3:30 PM
Sara's childhood home
Woodward, Queens, NY

The kitchen smelled like toast and crayons. Seated at the round, boomerang-patterned Formica table, it seemed like I was falling through my chair. A giant bowl of Berry Beary Crunch loomed in front of me. My tiny hand clasped an empty spoon.

All of it felt wrong. *Why was my hand so small? Why was all of me stuffed in a tiny body?*

I knew.

I'd done it—time flashed and escaped the lab and Murray. But I had traveled from the past to further back into the past. I remembered Danny's horrific experience of doing so. The spoon slipped from my grasp and clattered to the table.

At the sound of the metallic clink, my brother Adam, a kid himself, peered up from the newspaper. He was so thin, his face mostly cheekbone and bulging eyes. He didn't say anything, just went back to reading about the Knicks on the back page of the *Daily Post* and munching Berry Beary Crunch straight from the box. The Crunch Bear, dressed in a NASA astronaut's suit, floated above the moon's surface.

I lifted the newspaper up off the table to see the date.

"Bug off, spaz," my brother said, and tugged the paper out of my reach.

Given how sick he looked, his excellent reflexes surprised me. I'd managed to see anyway—March 11, 1970. The year his battle with leukemia began. A terrible time all around, with Paul McCartney confirming The Beatles' break-up.

At seven and a half years old, I was too young to fight Domestic. I worked out in my head the number of days I'd lived since having green serum pumped into me. My Penrose wave receptors would go dormant in a week or less.

Maybe I could enlist Danny's help, but like my brother, he would be only eleven or twelve. And my record of getting people killed in time flashes didn't bode well.

I had to figure out some other way or I was doomed to fail.

Adam set the paper aside. "Wanna go swing?"

"You mean it?" My brother never asked me to do anything with him. I was the tag-a-long kid sister.

"Why not?" He swiped his jacket from the hook by the side door and held out my poncho. I stepped into it.

A balmy March afternoon, the air smelled like freshly turned earth. The grass had greened, but many of the trees remained bare of leaves.

Adam shed his jacket right away and set it on the fencepost.

The swing set belonged to Joanne's family, but we were allowed to use it any time we wanted. I took the lowest seat, which happened to be in the middle.

My brother sat to my right.

"Let's see who can go the highest," Adam said. No contest—being older, he always won.

We both pushed off, flexed and straightened our legs.

Adam's bell-bottoms scraped the ground.

I vaguely recalled a competition like this one, in my original life, where he accidentally kicked me in the head. I ended up needing stitches over my right ear.

I pointed my toes, then pulled back my heels, as Adam had taught me to do. I flew higher and higher. Way above my brother.

Instead of filling me with the thrill of finally beating him, I felt miserable. I didn't want to win if that meant him being ill. I dragged my legs to slow down and dug my Mary Janes' heels into the dirt.

He stopped too. Eyes fixed on his Keds, he said, "I don't want you to be scared for me."

I was astonished. My brother—who spat in my hair on a regular basis, used my Barbie dolls for BB gun target practice, and pinched me on the arm in the back seat on family trips for entire car rides—wanted to talk to me seriously about hard things. If that ever happened in my original childhood, I either forgot or blocked it out.

"I'm sad." Though we'd never been super close, I loved him with all my heart. His was the first death I ever experienced.

"It's going to be okay." He patted me on the head. "Grandma told me there are some children who come to earth for a short time. They visit people they loved in a life before and get to say goodbye. That's me." He stamped his feet, raising a cloud of dust.

A lump at the back of my throat, I said, "Grandma told you you're going to die?" That didn't sound like her at all. She was a glass half-full kind of woman.

"She said not to be frightened because I will come back again and have a whole new life. But for now, all I have to do is have fun. I don't have to do anything I don't want to, not even homework. So, don't you be sad."

That explained why a smart kid like him got C's in school. His courage amazed me.

Though I'd developed a talent for it of late, I couldn't lie and reassure him he'd be all right. "Adam, I don't want you to die. I love you."

The idea of reliving his slow demise, his failed treatments, and multiple hospitalizations felt unbearable. I cried until I realized, with my Penrose waves receptors' going inactive, I'd be the one to die first.

"I'm not going anywhere right now. Quit your bawling."

I wiped my face with the back of my hand. If Grandma's beliefs had merit, Adam was a kind of time traveler too. "When you live your life over, what would you wish to be different?"

He stroked his chin, considering my question. "Everything's been pretty good so far. Can't think of anything."

The grace of his answer misted my eyes again. I wanted to throw my arms around him, but I knew he'd be embarrassed by public affection from his kid sister.

He got up, grabbed his jacket, and headed back to the house.

I toddled after him.

He stopped at the stoop by the side door and said, "You know, maybe there is one thing I'd want different." He scanned the cloudless sky.

"What?"

"I'd like to be taller." He smacked the back of my head with the flat of his hand, and then darted inside. That was the feisty brother he had been when he was well enough. Always looking to sneak-attack me.

I stood there dazed and aching, but strangely cheerful. It didn't last.

Mother, wearing a black halter dress, stepped from a cab onto the curb in front of the driveway. Her shiny, black hair dangled above her bare shoulders. She glowed with health. Cancer wouldn't bloom inside her for a long time. Her newly manicured nails matched the tip of the lit cigarette in her hand. "Don't you have chores?"

I had no idea, so I kept quiet. Opening my mouth to her always got me into more trouble.

She grabbed me by the arm and dragged me into the house.

"Is this your doing?" she said, indicating the open box of Berry Beary Crunch and the half-eaten bowl of cereal. "Clean up your mess. And how many times have I told you we never waste food in this house? Don't make me get the paddle."

Instead of an ordinary spanking, which could damage her manicure and hurt her hand, my mother employed an old wooden toy. The paddle had once been a favorite of mine, when it had its orange ball attached by a long rubber band. Soft wood and softer strokes, the punishment didn't smart much.

But *holy molé salsa*—my mother wanted me to finish a meal. Baffling, since she's the one who forced me to go on the first of many starvation diets when I turned eight. She wanted me piously thin for my First Communion. I didn't know if I would ever see my mother again, so I took a chance. "Mother, why do you hate me?"

She took a step back, as if I'd punched her. "What makes you say an awful thing like that? I love all my children."

"You can't seem to accept me the way I am. I'm darker than you, and I will always be rounder. But that doesn't make me worthless."

She crushed her cigarette in the sink. "Of course not. It's just that I want the best for you. I'm trying to spare you pain. The world is a hard place, and men are shallow bums. I know from personal experience."

She couldn't mean my father. "But if that's true, shouldn't our family be a place of love? Home shouldn't hurt."

Her eyes looked damp—the closest I'd ever seen her to tears. "I'm sorry," she said, meeting my eyes for a moment. "I don't mean to hurt you, *mija*." That was the only apology I'd ever gotten from Mother, and the first endearment.

I went to hug her.

But the emotion of the moment must have been more than she could handle. She turned away. "Please straighten the table," was all she said over her shoulder before heading down the hallway to the bedrooms.

To oblige her request, I lifted the box of Berry Beary Crunch to put it away. My heartbeat clanged inside my head like a bell, and the dim kitchen granulated away to nothing.

REDO 5

YEAR 2000 — THE PRESENT

Time is a cruel thief to rob us of our former selves. We lose as much to life as we do to death.

— ELIZABETH FORSYTHE HAILEY, A WOMAN OF
INDEPENDENT MEANS

CHAPTER 79

SARA, AGE 38

Saturday, September 23, 2000, 1 AM
Hector Bloom's condo
Hollymont, Queens, NY

The nightlight illuminates the tiny galley kitchen of my dad's condo. A "Twelve Months of Monkeys" calendar, hanging next to the wall-mounted phone, shows the month of September, year 2000.

Just once in all my redos, I wish Dad could live in a nicer place.

I grab the edge of the counter and puke my brains out in the sink. Maybe literally, given the damage the Penrose wave transfers cause. I try to throw up without making a sound so as not to wake Dad.

Bad idea. I end up swallowing the vile upchuck and choking some more. I hold my face under cold water to wash away the smell of rancid meat. Maybe I'm rotting on the inside. I hope my teeth don't fall out like George Wells' did.

Heading toward the guest room, I get about three steps before my right leg gives out. I land chin first on the floor. The thin carpet doesn't soften my fall.

I keep trying to get up, but my leg won't stay steady enough. I panic and scramble, only to end up on my back. Struggling to right myself, I wonder if this is what Gregor Samsa went through when he awoke to discover he had transformed into a cockroach. I curl into a ball, roll over onto all fours, and slog to the sectional. Using its arm for leverage, I manage to stand. All my weight on my left leg, and dragging my right, I hobble the rest of the way.

The guest room is more crammed than in my last redo. An armoire blocks half the window. Shelves of paperback books and movie videos take up the wall space. The pull-out couch, open and made up, has an inch clearance from a large dresser. I throw myself onto the bed and close my eyes to recollect this redo timeline.

My altered life rushes back to me in pictures. My brother's funeral, my grandmother's. Taking a correspondence course in accounting. Working at my Dad's firm. Caring for my mother on her deathbed. Her telling me to get gastric bypass surgery. *Some things never change.* Moving with Dad to the new condo after he sold the family home in Woodward.

I recall the rest as a long series of nevers as compared to my original life —never went to college, never met Steve, never made up with Joanne, never met Jon, never dated much, never married, never went to pick up Gallo at the shelter. As in Schrödinger's thought experiment, there can be no certainty whether my cat is alive or dead.

My life consists of ledgers full of numbers. *How depressing.* At least I don't seem to be whale-sized and can't recall any time in mental institutions. So, this redo is a step up from that last one.

But I can't stay here. I have to get back to destroy Dr. Claire Gentry's research to be sure serum H-88 never gets developed.

I wonder if there's a computer with an internet connection in the apartment. No memories come to me of an America Online account. As soon as it's morning, I can head to the local library. I close my eyes and see myself on a first-name basis with Hollymont's head librarian, Mrs. Railly. The recollection comes with a crushing pain in my skull. I should sleep. I'll need all my wits about me to come up with a plan to take back the past.

Adam and I were seated in maroon-colored cushy seats in a crowded, circular auditorium. An electronic, wordless version of "Yellow Submarine" played over loudspeakers.

My brother looked different—healthy. Dressed in a black suit and tie, he was a grown-up, older than he lived to be.

But I was so young, my feet didn't touch the ground. I had on a pink skirt, but instead of the usual poodle dog, this one was embroidered with a fluffy black cat.

I looked around, but didn't see anyone else I recognized. From the giant projector in the center of the room, I guessed we were in the Hayden Planetarium in Manhattan. One of my favorite places ever since a third-grade school field trip there.

"What are we doing here?" I said.

Adam loosened his tie. "We're going to see the universe being born,"

The lights dimmed. The music stopped. The voice of Leonard Nimoy came over the loudspeaker. "Get ready for the big bang. Out of the first colossal flare-up, the greatness of time begins."

I looked up as the domed roof exploded into a fiery blaze that sent out waves of light. The flames' heat scorched like a blow dryer set too high. The explosion wasn't a projection.

People around us screamed and fled the auditorium.

Adam stood, lifted me from the seat, and held me in his arms. "It's your time, Sara. Be brave. I believe in you. And tell Danny, I say hi." He winked, then set me back down. He sprinted for the exit and disappeared through the double doors without looking back.

I wanted out of there, but I couldn't leave the seat. I was harnessed into it somehow. There were no buckles to open. I screamed for Adam, but he was long gone.

CHAPTER 80

SARA, AGE 38

Saturday, September 23, 2000, 8 AM
Hector Bloom's condo
Hollymont, Queens, NY

*A*wake for a while, I'm trying to recall my dream—something to do with Adam and me. Seeing my brother for a few minutes in my last time flash makes me miss him all the more. At least now I understand why he was smiling in Danny's photo. Thanks to Grandma, he lived his life for joy, even while dying. *My brave brother.*

The door opens and smacks against the pull-out bed.

"Morning, birthday girl," Dad says. "Ready to celebrate?"

Now I know the date. I shimmy to a sitting position. "I had a dream about Adam," I say, "but I can't remember it."

Dad looks wistful. "I see him in my dreams too. He's always so healthy. We should go visit the family tomorrow. Okay?"

I know Dad means the cemetery. "Sure. But I'd like to spend today at the library. They open at ten, right?"

"What about your birthday?"

"You can take me out for dinner after."

"I have to run errands. And I need to stop by the library anyway to see if they got the new translation of Paz I asked for." Dad closes the door.

I'm thirty-eight today according to the calendar, but I feel more like a hundred. I hope I don't start rapidly aging as George Wells did. With all the flitting around in time, I wonder just how old my consciousness is.

Determined to extricate myself from the phone-booth-sized room, I swing legs over the side of the sofa bed. My right leg feels weak, the knee tender. Once vertical, I stay that way, but I have to put most of the weight on my left side. I limp along. Whatever plan I come up with to defeat Domestic, running away probably won't be an option.

The condo bathroom feels spacious compared to the cramped bedroom. I study myself in the mirror, recalling that I cut off all my beautiful long curls so it would take less time to get ready in the morning. What remains of my hair resembles a lamb's wool muff. At least I am not a blonde, and I don't look as old as I feel. It's hard to know how I should appear after bouncing around timelines.

CHAPTER 81

SARA, AGE 38

Sunday, September 24, 2000, 10 AM
Pinebough Cemetery
Easthaven, Queens, NY

A warm, but cloudy morning, my father pulls a few weeds from my mother's plot. I should be helping him, but bending hurts my right knee. As it is, I'm hobbling. Dad wondered earlier today if my arthritis was flaring up. Guess I am old before my time after all.

I run my hand across the top of Adam's granite headstone. The surface is cool.

Adam, I should have been more like you, I say to him in my head. *Lived life for joy and put the rest aside. Now, I'm ready to risk everything for the greater good. I think you'd be proud of me. I need some of your courage. Send it along to me from wherever you are.*

"You about ready?" Dad says. There is straw on his jacket.

I pick it off. "Just saying goodbye."

"You'll see Adam again. We'll all be together in another life."

Short of time travel, I don't see that reunion happening. But the universe being a grand mystery, I suppose anything's possible.

Dad puts his arm around me. He smells like sweat and the Blue Moon aftershave he always used when Mother was alive.

As we turn to go, I see Danny plodding toward us, puffing a cigarette. He looks the same as he did when I saw him in my third redo—a scarred face, bald, and paunchy.

"Hey, Squirt. Hey, Mr. Bloom." Danny stamps out his cigarette on the stone walkway. He shakes Dad's hand, then comes in close to hug me.

I'm not surprised he smells like beer this early in the morning, but I am sorry. I hold onto him a long time. *Does he even remember our time flash together?*

Danny pushes me away and turns to my dad. "Came to shoot the breeze with Adam. How's retirement, Mr. Bloom?"

"I haven't dropped the reins completely, but Sara's taking over more and more of the business. It's nice to see you, son. Thanks for visiting Adam."

"He's still my best bud," Danny says.

Danny and I are two friendless, sad specimens.

"You ought to come around to our place and have dinner," Dad says. "We celebrated Sara's birthday last night, but there's leftover cake. Why don't you join us?"

"Wish I could, but I have other plans. Happy birthday, Sara." He covers his mouth with his hand, as if he's muffling a comment.

Maybe he is my time flash Danny. I'm both relieved and disappointed that he declined the invitation. Thanks to me, he followed in his father's alcoholic footsteps.

But if my next trip back in time goes how I hope, maybe I can help Danny too. Of course, I won't live long enough to find out.

TIME FLASH 8

YEAR 1977 — THE PAST

Time is the fire in which we burn.

— DELMORE SCHWARTZ, "CALMLY WE WALK THROUGH
THIS APRIL'S DAY"

They always say time changes things, but you actually have to change them yourself.

— ANDY WARHOL, THE PHILOSOPHY OF ANDY WARHOL

The time is always right to do what is right.

— MARTIN LUTHER KING, JR.

CHAPTER 82

SARA, AGE 14

Friday, August 19, 1977, 5:25 PM
Sara's childhood home
Woodward, Queens, NY

*T*he window box air-conditioner unit going full tilt did nothing to lessen the humidity.

I sweated like a slug in salt. I wished I could go shirtless like a boy and at least feel the breeze blowing everywhere on my skin.

On the jumpy black-and-white picture on the TV screen, Captain Kirk flirted with Edith Keeler.

"Can you adjust the antenna?" Adam said. My brother lay on the couch, his hair a quarter inch of peach fuzz, his skin gray. An upended copy of *Slaughterhouse-Five* rested in his lap. Despite the heat, he had a thick plaid blanket tucked in around him.

I got up from the rust shag carpet to adjust the rabbit ears and vertical hold. But I'd lost my own vertical hold. I prevented my fall by grabbing on the sturdy wooden TV cabinet.

A commercial came on for Kodak film, using "The Times of Your Life" song to punctuate family memories.

Like Dorothy in *The Wizard of Oz*, I realized where I wasn't any more—not in my dad's year 2000 condo kitchen reaching for a box of Berry Beary Crunch. But when was I?

I could tell from how wasted away Adam was, that I'd time flashed to somewhere in the final decline of his health. I'd been aiming for 1980 to get to the Domestic lab the year before I managed to get Jon killed.

From the dining room, a familiar voice startled me.

"Need anything?" Danny was young and adorable again. He wore a King Kong t-shirt from the version with Jessica Lange. "I'm getting a snack," he said. "Anyone want some iced tea?"

"Nah, I'm too cold already," my brother said.

"What about you, Squirt?" Danny said.

"I can get it." I followed him, still feeling unsteady.

Danny had his head in the fridge. He pulled out a full pan of meatloaf. "Your mother said this is supposed to last us the weekend. Split it with you."

My stomach somersaulted. "No thanks," I said, hoping I wouldn't throw up in front of him. "Where are my parents?"

"Heat get to you? They're in Toronto for the weekend. What's the matter, don't trust me to babysit you?" Not waiting for my answer, and clearly at ease in my family's kitchen, he set about getting a plate and utensils.

"What is the date today?" I said.

He reached into a cupboard and got out a bag of potato chips. "I wish your brother would eat more than a few crumbs."

"Danny, please. I'm serious. I need to know the date and year."

He stopped pouring chips and studied me. "You're worried about him too, aren't you? Come sit down." He guided me into the chair with his hand on my upper arm.

I remembered how gentle his touch could be from our mutual time flash to 1994. *Was he my time-traveling Danny?* I hoped the hurt I'd caused him would be erased when I succeeded in destroying the lab.

We sat at the Formica table.

"I know this is hard for you, with Adam sick. Try not to worry. He'll get well again, you'll see."

Wrong. Once Adam's skin took on that weathered barn-wood tone, he never fully recovered. He had a few good days here and there. *Time-flash-Danny would have known that.*

I guessed from the heat, it had to be summer. "This summer has been a blur with everything going on. I don't even know what day it is."

"Today is Friday, August 19," he said.

"1976?" I asked, based on how ill my brother seemed.

He mussed my hair. "1977, Squirt. Heat getting to you? You have two whole days with me and Joanne to boss you around." He blinked his dragonfly green eyes. "Can you dig it?"

Adam had only one year left. But at least I'd arrived years before I got my best friend killed. "I dig it," I said without conviction.

My grandmother always used to babysit when my parents went anywhere. But my mother shipped her off to an old-age home in Florida in 1976 with the excuse Grandma wouldn't have to suffer New York winters. Grandma suffered, missing us.

I calculated my age—a few weeks shy of fifteen. Being a young teen made my mission more difficult. But I looked older because of my large breasts. On my fourteenth birthday, dressed up and out to dinner with my parents, the waiter asked if I wanted to order a cocktail.

What was going on in the summer of '77? A big city-wide blackout in July. Elvis died sometime around then. NASA launched the Voyager space probe with a record of humankind. The first *Star Wars* movie debuted, but I think that was spring. My brother quoted "These aren't the droids you're looking for" weekly after seeing it at the Baycross Theater on one of his good days.

Police tracked down and arrested Son of Sam, the forty-four-caliber killer. Brunettes no longer had to dye their hair blonde to avoid being the serial killer's type. Joanne never had to worry. Her golden-brown hair sun-bleached in summertime to honey blonde with the aid of lemon juice.

"Is there anything else, Squirt?" Danny said. He mussed my hair again.

I saw a chance to make things better for him and I took it. "About Joanne," I said. "I know how she feels about you."

"And how is that?" He fished a potato chip out of the bag and crunched it.

"You can't tell her I said so, but she likes you. I mean likes you—likes you. You should ask her out."

Danny snorted. "Right. Not gonna happen. Can't eat just one." He munched a second chip.

In our time flash back to 1994, he told me he wouldn't have asked her out because he didn't want to hurt my brother's feelings. "It would make Adam happy to see you two together," I said.

Danny dropped the bag of chips, but caught it before it hit the linoleum. "He tell you that?"

I lied for the greater good. "Yes, but not in so many words." Seeing my brother last time flash, not long after the leukemia diagnosis, I believed Adam would feel that way. "You and Joanne belong together. Adam knows it, and so do you. Tell me you'll ask her out"

"Pushy little thing, aren't you?" He grinned. "I'll think about it."

I hoped he'd do more than think. "Well, there is one reason I can see she would turn you down."

His smile faded. "What's that?"

"She hates smokers. Swore never to date one. You need to quit."

He breathed a sigh. "You're not supposed to know about that, Squirt. Anyway, I quit three days ago with my mom. We're trying to keep each other honest. Uncle Isaac died of lung cancer. Ugly death. She promised him we'd stop. Not my dad though. He's puffing his head off." Danny patted his stomach. "Quitting's tough on my girlish figure though. I'm so hungry."

He looked hot to me, but I didn't say it. "Ask Joanne for a kiss every time you get the urge for a cigarette."

Danny chuckled. "You're quite the little schemer."

"I'm sure Jo's a great kisser." I recalled how attuned his mouth became to mine after some practice. My cheeks burned. "When is she coming over?"

"Any time now. But don't get your hopes up."

I felt as optimistic as I had in a long time—days, hell, years, considering alternate timelines—that I could make things better for the people I loved.

I had no idea about the status of my friendship with Joanne. If time rippled backward as well as forward, maybe she still liked me. But if things were the same as my original past, she hated me for the boyfriend debacle I caused.

Another me, in another timeline, won back Joanne's friendship. If I didn't have much time left in 1977 or anywhere, it couldn't hurt to try.

Adam's snores filled the living and dining rooms. It dampened my spirits to know he didn't have the energy to watch his favorite TV shows.

When I reached for the cabinet door on the credenza, my fingers wouldn't close around the knob. I tried again and failed. The muscles refused to work. Already sweating, drops trickled into my eyes. I tried one more time. My hand didn't work. At least it wasn't my dominant hand this time, but my right. Still, being one-handed would make everything I had to do to defeat Domestic twice as difficult. "Shit," I said aloud.

"Better not talk that way when Joanne gets here," Danny said, his arms loaded with food and drink.

Joanne's abhorrence of swear words was legendary, even when we were kids.

Danny set down a glass of iced tea and a dinner plate piled high with food. "What gives?"

Penrose wave induced motor-skills damage. "Nothing," I said. "My hand fell asleep."

"So did Adam," Danny said. "Poor guy. Chemotherapy treatments are almost as bad as the disease." He came over to me.

I told him I needed the Manhattan phonebook and he got it out for me, no more questions asked.

I hauled the enormous tome down the hall to my parents' bedroom by squeezing it to my chest with my forearms. It felt like a workout. But I'd always had excellent upper body strength for a girl. Maybe it had something to do with taking on all my brother's chores once he became ill, like lugging overloaded trash barrels from the backyard to the curb. Anyway, I was grateful to be strong. I was going to need to be, physically and mentally.

I dialed radio station WPLJ and made my double-header dedication request for seven o'clock. Next, I called information for Amtrak to set the rest of my plan in motion.

CHAPTER 83

SARA, AGE 14

Friday, August 19, 1977, 6:15 PM
Sara's childhood home
Woodward, Queens, NY

y brother still snored away on the couch. *Better to sleep than to be in pain.*

Joanne hadn't come yet. If she still hated me after the songs, I could die knowing I tried to win her back.

I asked Danny to put the radio on and tune it to WPLJ and he obliged. Jackson Browne's "The Pretender" came on.

We played checkers, a game I could easily manage with one hand.

Joanne finally showed up at a quarter to seven carrying a plate of brownies. She had on a purple tube top and jean shorts. With her small chest, the top looked modest rather than slutty. Barefoot, her petal-pink painted toenails matched her fingernails.

I suspected Danny and I had the same thought about her—beautiful—or maybe in his vernacular, "smokin'." Her nineteen-year-old flawless complexion glowed. Her sun-blonde hair, cut in a short pixie style, brought out the warmth of her hazel eyes.

"Glad you're here," Danny said to Joanne, getting up to pull out a chair for her. "Sara's clobbering me at checkers. Lost four straight and on the way to a fifth defeat." He picked up a paper napkin and waved it in the air. "I surrender."

Joanne nodded to me instead of saying hello.

I didn't rate a smile. *She hated me.*

She gawked at Adam asleep under the thick blanket. "He looks like a wrung-out mop head in a spaghetti factory," she said. "I could cry. I could bawl my eyes out."

"Me too," I said. "It's so unfair. He's my only brother. He deserves a long, healthy life."

She turned to me. "Aw, this is hard on you, isn't it, sweetie?"

Encouraged by the endearment, I said, "I did something for you, Jo. Please pay special attention to the radio at seven PM."

She shook her head at me with an expression that said *what have you gone and done now?*

"Ready for a rematch, Miss Card Shark?" Danny said to Joanne.

"Sure thing," she said.

I wished for Danny's sake that she would be his sure thing.

He went to the credenza, got out a deck of playing cards, notepad and pen, and gave everything to her.

She dealt two hands of rummy.

Clearly not invited to play with them, I perused my brother's Batman comic books. Too bad I hadn't held onto them—they became highly collectible. As I read, I kept sneaking peeks at Joanne and Danny. It struck me as wrong that two healthy, attractive nineteen-year-olds of the opposite sex had to babysit on a Friday night instead of going out.

But they weren't there only to watch over me. I understood that. Both of them wanted to be near Adam. They loved him as much as I did.

With Joanne and Danny focused on rummy rather than flirting, I needed to intervene further to cement the pair as a couple. Joanne, compassionate but tough, could be his incentive to avoid alcohol and cigarettes, until doing it for his own sake became enough.

In a few minutes, the disc jockey Vic-the-Voice, announced "Our first double-header dedication of the night, coming up after this message from our sponsor."

I trudged over, turned up the volume, and stared at the radio, too anxious to watch Joanne's reaction.

My brother snored louder.

Vic said, "*These next two tunes go out to Joanne from her thoughtless best friend Sara. Sara says, 'I need you in my life now more than ever. Please forgive* me.' *Joanne, if you're listening, Sara sounds pretty sincere. Enjoy the Beatles' 'Two of Us' and 'We Can Work It Out,' and make peace not war."*

I turned to face Joanne.

She stood and held out her arms.

Happy as I'd ever been at any time in any of my lives, I hugged my very much alive best friend.

We embraced and cried for what felt like ages.

Wiping my tears, I asked if we could go in my room and talk.

Walls painted institutional green, twin bed with a faded, pink-striped bedspread, and a stark white dresser made the space seem more like a hospital room than a young teenager's domain. A *Sergeant Pepper* poster hanging on the wall—a gift from Joanne on my tenth birthday—was the one cheerful thing.

We sat on opposite ends of the bed, mirroring each other with legs tucked under.

"I am sorry about Ronald Gott. I should have kept my stupid trap shut."

"Water under the bridge," Joanne said. "Ron was a user in more ways than one."

"Drugs?" I said.

"Don't you even go there, but yes."

"Besides," I said, "Danny likes you. You should go out with him."

"He doesn't like me that way." She examined a thread on her top. "I'm just one of the guys to him."

"Not true," I said. "He wants to ask you out, but he's afraid you don't like him."

She looked up. "He said that?"

I had her hooked. *Time for another lie.* "And it would make Adam happy to see you two together." *And one absolute truth.* "You're the two people Adam loves most in the world outside of family."

"Okay, I get it. But Danny needs to make the first move. I'm not chasing him. Enough about that. How are you?"

"Sad," I said, honestly. "I wish I could make my brother well. But there isn't anything I can do." *No matter where I go in time.*

"It's in God's hands," Joanne said. "All we can do is pray."

"And in the doctors' hands," I said. Maybe I could take out a little insurance on my mother's future as well. However slim, I gave it a shot. "I hope

393

my mother is as willing to put herself in the doctors' hands should anything happen to her."

"Aunt Reya is fine."

I told another lie. "She had a breast cancer scare, didn't she tell you?"

Joanne's hand flew to her chest. "No. When was that?"

"A while ago. Benign. But Jo, if it had been cancer, she wouldn't have taken treatment. You know how she is about her looks."

"Yes, but she'd put her health first."

"She likes you. She'd listen to you. Promise me you'll talk to her, reason with her, if the scare ever becomes something real."

"Bite your tongue," she said. "But of course, I'd help. You know my aunt Agnes had breast cancer. She's fine now."

"It means the world to me. You should get back to Danny."

"What about you, do you want to play cards with us?"

"Maybe later. I want to read for a while." I reached with my good hand for the copy of Philip K. Dick's *Time Out of Joint* on the window sill.

Joanne stood. "I don't know what you and all the boys see in that crazy science fiction stuff." She kissed me on the forehead. "I'll be around until you fall asleep."

After she left, I looked around for some paper. Thank goodness it was my right side that had trouble. At least I was still able to write.

Dear Mother,

I'd called her "mother" my whole life, but that seemed too formal for the purpose I had in mind. I started again on a clean page.

Dear Mom,

We haven't always seen eye to eye, but I want you to know I appreciate you always looking out for my best interests. I will try to be more like you and be confident.

I am writing because it is hard to say these things face to face. With Adam being sick, I can't bear the thought of losing you too. I know you feel fine now, and I want that always to be true. I do not wish anything bad to happen, but seeing how Adam went from being a happy child to a sick boy made me realize how quickly things can change.

Maybe I am being silly, but you must do everything in your power to be well. Dad and I need you and love you. Dad loves you for the person you are. He says you will always be the most beautiful woman on earth no matter what.

Remember when you had a gigantic pimple in the middle of your forehead and Dad never noticed? He sees you through the eyes of love.

Your life and health are worth more to me, to our family, than any body part or physical scar. Promise me, Mom, should you ever be ill, you will accept every possible treatment option.

This promise is all I will ever ask of you.

Your loving daughter,
Sara

The note seemed like a long shot. More of a gamble were the anonymous letters I wrote to John Lennon and Yoko Ono, to the administration of the Dakota apartments, and to the New York City Police Department warning them about Mark David Chapman.

I had to believe that not only could Joanne and Jon be saved, but my mother and John Lennon too. I held onto the hope that the death and damage Domestic caused—and that all the versions of me had caused—could be undone.

In bed, trying to get some rest for my big day, I tossed and turned. The details of my plan, and the many things that could go wrong, played over and over in my head.

There was enough light from the hall for me to see Joanne steal into my room while Danny waited in the doorway.

I closed my eyes and pretended to be asleep.

I heard Joanne whisper, "She's out like a light."

"She looks like an angel," Danny said.

"She does," Joanne agreed.

"But she's more like a matchmaker," he said.

"Oh yeah," she said, "why's that?"

I opened one eye.

Danny took hold of Joanne's shoulders. "Sara thought I should tell you how I feel." He leaned down and kissed her on the lips.

A pang of stupid jealousy hit me. But I knew I'd done the right thing.

Joanne moved out of the kiss for a second and smiled up at Danny. "Finally, you noticed I'm a girl."

"I've been noticing for quite a while," he said.

They kissed again.

I tried to sleep for real. I needed rest to make my last days on earth count for something.

CHAPTER 84

SARA, AGE 14

Saturday, August 20, 1977, 8 AM
Sara's childhood home
Woodward, Queens, NY

When I woke from dreamless sleep, the fingers of my right hand still wouldn't obey my commands. With great effort, I managed to wash and dress in black stretch shorts with deep pockets, a navy sleeveless top, and flip flops. I had given up on trying to put on a bra after it flew across my bedroom like a slingshot.

No time to waste, I set about gathering the things I needed for my plan.

I searched my mother's closet for a pair of heels I could wear without breaking my neck. After I secured some beige platform shoes, I chose a tight pink corset blouse that would showcase my D-cup cleavage. In the pocket of a mini-skirt, I discovered her prized beauty pageant silver cigarette lighter. I flipped it open and pressed the igniter button to make sure it worked, then filched it along with the skirt. I selected a floppy straw hat to shade my face.

From Mother's cosmetics area, I swiped a pair of dark-lensed sunglasses, sturdy hair pins, and a tube of peony pink lipstick. I raided her jewelry box for cash, as well as silver hoop earrings.

In my brother's room, I searched for a box of large paper clips. I could always buy those on the way if need be, but I got lucky.

I stuffed the clothes and shoes into a backpack, then packed that and all my spoils into a duffel. It was time to find Danny and tell him I was leaving.

~

Sunlight filtered through the damask drapes into the living room.

Danny snored away in a sleeping bag on the carpet in front of the TV.

On the couch, Adam sat up reading *Slaughterhouse-Five.*

Vonnegut's book was a favorite of mine and his. Only a Tralfamadorian could look at my brother now and see the pain-free moments. *Shit.* It would be hard to lie to my sick brother. But I'd honed my acting chops with Murray and Danny and Joanne. I could pull it off.

"How are you feeling?" I said.

"Better," he said. He appeared skeletal.

"When's the last time you ate?"

He glanced at his Timex. "About an hour ago, I made peanut butter toast. Didn't save you any. Did you hear Groucho Marx died last night? He was 86."

"That's sad. At least he lived a good long life." I wanted to smack myself for saying that to Adam.

He didn't react at all to my putting my foot in my mouth. "Where you going with a giant bag?"

"I have a sleep-over at Diane's." Diane, a friend from school, lived conveniently near the stop for the express bus to Manhattan, where I needed to go to catch a train to Fishburg Falls.

"Did you ask Mom?"

"Um ... no ... it kind of came up last night. It's not like Diane lives on the moon, just the other side of Woodward."

Adam stared at me, his once-bright eyes cloudy.

Did he see through my lie?

"And when would you be home?"

"After dinner Sunday. Around seven." *I hated to think how he'd feel when it got later than that and I still wasn't home.*

"Okay. Leave the phone number. But Mom wouldn't want you walking all that way on your own. Danny will drive you."

"Somebody call?" Danny sat up and rubbed his nose.

"Yeah, my sister needs a ride to her friend's house."

"Okay, give me a minute to piss." Danny climbed out of the sleeping bag, except for socks, fully dressed.

Relieved not to have to ogle him in front of my brother, I headed out the door. "I'll wait on the stoop," I said. I still needed to collect a few things from our garden shed.

~

Gentleman that he was, Danny took the duffel from me and tossed it into the backseat. He didn't ask why it was so heavy. The gas can alone had to weigh ten pounds.

Already uncomfortably warm outside at nine AM, the day would be another scorcher.

Danny rolled down the windows and peeled away from the curb.

Riding in his Trans Am again, like I did the first time flash episode, gave me the feeling my journey had come full circle.

We drove along the lazy summer Saturday morning streets of the neighborhood. The manicured hedges and well-watered front lawns, the modest ranch homes, and more sprawling split-levels gave the impression of a place where childhood shone wholesome and uncomplicated. *Where brothers don't die young.*

I observed Danny's face. His scars internalized, no one would ever guess the tortures he suffered at his drunk father's hands.

The radio blasted Springsteen's "Thunder Road."

I turned it down to find out if the seeds I'd planted had sprouted.

"So how did it go with Joanne last night?"

He didn't answer, but his cheeks reddened.

"All right," I said, genuinely excited. Last night's jealousy had evaporated. "Now hold on to her."

"She's special," we both said at the same time. We laughed simultaneously too.

"Adam and I talked," he said. "He gave me his blessing."

"My brother wants you to be happy," I said. "He loves both of you."

"Me too," Danny said in a quiet voice.

I didn't know what else to say. He had to realize my brother didn't have much time left. Maybe it was too hard for him to admit not much else could be done after years of Adam being in and out of hospitals.

Danny turned up the radio. The Bee Gees' mysterious, some would say bizarre, "Edge of the Universe" played.

A few dads mowed lawns. One mom with a couple of kids loaded beach gear into a station wagon. An old woman walked a dog that looked like the offspring of a Dachshund and a rabid squirrel.

We arrived at Diane's house and Danny pulled over to the curb. He left the engine running and charged around the front of the car to open the door and help me out. He grabbed my duffel bag from the back and set it on the sidewalk next to me.

Good thing he did all that, since struggling with my one good hand would have revealed something was wrong with me. I threw my arms around him and squeezed him hard. "I want you to have a good life." I sounded melodramatic.

"C'mon, Squirt. You won't be gone that long." He hugged me back.

Sweet guy, he smelled like gasoline and the sea. Like a friend you could always count on. I let go of him and said, "Take good care of my brother and Joanne. Be excellent to each other." It was a dozen years before he would get the Bill and Ted reference.

"I will," he said. "Pick you up at seven sharp tomorrow night." He trotted back to the driver's side and sped away.

I was lucky he didn't wait for me to be let into Diane's house. I didn't know if her family was off on one of their Disney vacations. When the Trans Am turned the corner out of sight, I cried without knowing why.

Maybe because I was certain I wasn't, and never had been, in love with Daniel Astrella. But he was a good guy who deserved to be loved.

Maybe because if my plan succeeded, I'd never see Danny or anyone I cared about ever again.

Maybe because I was tired of all the time flashes and redos, tired of wasted opportunities, tired of my mistakes.

Or maybe, I was just plain used up.

CHAPTER 85

SARA, AGE 14

Saturday, August 20, 1977, 11:20 AM
Grand Central Station
Manhattan, NY

I ducked out of the soupy air into the air-conditioned station that was every bit as grand as its name. It was my last chance to set things right because my Penrose wave center had only a few days left of activity. I thought about a line from *The Matrix* about no turning back, "You take the blue pill, the story ends …." My story was about to end, whether I succeeded in defeating Domestic or not.

Unlike the people plodding in the streets outside, travelers inside the depot hurried to and fro, lugging too much baggage. I located a ladies' room and locked myself in a stall to complete my transformation. The place reeked of vomit and urine. Changing clothes one-handed, and in such a tight space, required considerable contortions. How Superman managed it in a phone booth was beyond me. Too bad I couldn't spin on my toes and be done with it, like Lynda Carter's Wonder Woman.

Fifteen minutes later, I exited the stall wearing my mother's revealing corset blouse, a black pull-on miniskirt, platform sandals, big dark sunglasses, and a floppy hat. I hoped I appeared old enough to be traveling on my own and set off to buy passage upstate.

I needn't have worried. The clerk at the window didn't look up when I said one-way to Fishburg Falls. I handed him the cash, and he gave me a ticket. Everything went according to plan, which in itself, made me nervous. Something else had to go wrong.

Adam had no reason to be suspicious of my sleep-over claim. But if he tried calling Diane, he'd learn there was no sleepover and might call the police. That could derail my plan. But even if I succeeded in my mission, my face would appear on flyers, APBs, and perhaps on the back of milk cartons.

I wished the Walkman had been invented sooner to distract my nerves on the more than four-hour train ride. I brought the Philip K. Dick book with me, but turning the pages one-handed was awkward. Being anxious made it hard to concentrate, anyway. I watched the scenery roll backwards out the window—the train yard, graffiti-covered walls, tall apartment complexes, the Hudson River, trees, industrial sites, more trees.

By the time I was one station away from my destination, I looked up to see a thin, redheaded man approaching from the far end of the train car. I held my breath until I confirmed it wasn't Murray from Domestic or any of the red-haired supermarket clerks. This redhead, dressed in a beige polyester leisure suit, had sunken cheek bones and a crooked nose. Though there were plenty of open seats, he plopped down next to me.

"Where you headed, hot pants?" he said, his raw garlic breath an assault to my nose.

"Off." I got up, duffel slung across my body, intending to head to the next car.

Garlic breath followed me. "Hey baby, be cool," he said to my back.

I slunk into a seat next to a woman knitting a pink baby sweater. If need be, I'd grab one of those needles and skewer his testicles. It didn't hurt that she was as substantial as an offensive lineman.

The woman sized up the situation and said, "This jackass bothering you, honey?"

"Following me," I said. "I don't know him."

She pointed her needles at his crotch. "Listen here, dirty old man," she said. "You want a piece of me?"

"Be cool, sister," he said, and headed into the next car.

"Thanks," I said.

"We fine birds got to flock together." She whooped a great big laugh, which made me smile.

But hoping to discourage any conversation that could lead to questions I didn't want to answer, I wrestled my book from the duffel and pretended to read.

Profoundly observant, she said, "What's wrong with that right hand of yours? I see you're not using it."

"My fingers are stiff," I said.

"I got terrible arthritis, but you'd never know it." She put down the knitting and flexed her fingers. "I can make two sweaters a day now. You want to know how?"

"Lay it on me," I said to be polite.

She reached into her giant macramé bag and removed what looked like a vinegar bottle. "My own remedy—cod liver oil, borage, turmeric, ginseng, a couple of things I like to keep secret, and cayenne for kick. Fixes my joints, keeps me regular as a Timex. And look at my face. I'm sixty-seven."

Her smooth, mahogany skin glowed. "You look so young," I said. Except for white hair, she could be in her thirties.

She produced a yellowed plastic cup from her bottomless bag. "You're gonna take some of this elixir right now."

Steve's vitamin infusions came to mind. *What if she meant to drug me?* "I couldn't take your medicine."

She unscrewed the lid, poured out the murky brown liquid, and took a swig. She refilled the cup and held it below my lips. "Can't do you a bit of harm."

I chugged it. The stuff tasted worse than it smelled, and it reeked of dead fish. I wished I had a piece of gum.

As if reading my mind, the woman set down the cup and handed me a stick of Juicy Fruit. "I'm gonna give you this bottle, but you want more, you have to ring me up." She took out a pad, jotted down her name—Ella Williams—and her phone number, then stuffed the paper in my duffel along with the bottle.

The conductor announced the next station, and the train slowed.

"This is my stop," I said. "Thank you for everything."

She hugged me close to her chest. She smelled of mothballs and oranges, like someone's grandmother. "You drink the tonic and be well, dear. Promise."

"I will," I said, though I wouldn't live long enough to do so.

CHAPTER 86

SARA, AGE 14

Saturday, August 20, 1977, 4:35 PM
Fishburg Falls, NY

I stepped off the train onto the Fishburg Falls platform in the early evening haze. Every bit as humid upstate as in New York City. At least the air up there smelled fresher. Brick buildings and store-fronts with picture windows lined the quaint downtown. On the walk to the Seneca Hotel, I passed the local grocery store, a movie theater hosting an Elvis retrospective, and a diner called Milliway's.

I didn't want my plan to bring shame on my family, so I had booked a room under a false name. I said the first thing that popped into my head when I was on the phone—Sara Smith. I realized later that it might lead to a *Doctor Who* conversation.

Despite the Victorian exterior, the hotel lobby consisted of an austere cinder block reservation desk and chrome and leather chairs. The clerk's enormous eyeglasses made him appear insect-like. He located my reservation and checked me in without comment or small talk. The seventies being a more trusting time, he didn't ask for identification. I paid cash and accepted my room key—another actual metal key.

It seemed a good omen that the room number was thirty-seven—the same as my real age. In fact, I would have tried to turn any number into an auspicious symbol. I needed all the luck I could get.

I rode the creaky elevator up to the third floor. The room was modest but clean, with a double bed, dresser, and TV. I dropped my duffel on the bed and left by the rear stairwell to verify that my key opened the building's back door. *So far, so good.*

Up in my room again, I removed the paperclips, hairpins, and needle-nose pliers from the bag. In my last redo, I used the library's internet to study how to make simple lock-picking tools. While he dozed, I practiced on every lock in Dad's condo. Too bad I couldn't bring the tools I had already fashioned back in time with me. Creating the tension wrench and lock-pick rake one-handed seemed an impossible feat.

After much trial and error, I realized that the pliers could be locked and I could bend the clip with my left hand. I made half a dozen tension wrenches and rakes to be safe. I dumped the failed parts back into the bottom of the duffel.

Unsure how to pass the next few hours, I turned on the TV and tuned into a game show. I found a take-out menu for Milliway's Diner in the dresser, and decided to order Swedish meatballs. Not exactly my idea of the best choice for a last meal, but at least it wasn't cereal.

I watched variety shows and a tribute airing of *A Night in Casablanca*, without laughing once. Whether from nerves or Penrose wave sickness, I'd thrown up half a dozen times.

I decided it wise to repack the duffel to remove things I wouldn't need, like Ella's tonic and my backpack. I inventoried items as they went back in —the gasoline can, paint thinner, moth balls, a bag of saw dust, matches, and a box of sparklers stolen from the backyard shed at home. The lock-pick sets and toothpicks I tucked into the bag's outside compartment. I wanted my mother's pageant lighter, my father's utility knife, and the flash-light close at hand. I dumped all those, plus some toothpicks, in my shorts pockets. I donned Dad's navy sweatshirt, so big it came down to my thighs. With the hood covering most of my face, I exited the hotel by the back stairs.

CHAPTER 87

SARA, AGE 14

Sunday, August 21, 1977, 12:10 AM
Fishburg Falls, NY

The post-midnight streets of Fishburg Falls were quiet enough to hear your fingernails grow. On the eight-block walk to the lab, I passed a couple making out in a parked car and a wino sleeping it off on a bench. I didn't know if they saw me.

No fence surrounded the lab at Cole and Twelfth. Except for the street address, the building had no identification as a research facility. Through the glass front door, all I could make out was an ill-lit reception desk. No one seemed to be behind it. I went around to the back. A few plastic trash receptacles stood in for the car-sized dumpster of the future. Moths flitted around the dim bulb over the rear door like a real-world illustration of my anxiety.

I knelt down in front of the lock and used my mouth to work the rake, while my left hand managed the tension wrench. The rake dropped out of my mouth a dozen times. I nearly swallowed it once or twice too. Finally, the lock pins gave way, and the tumbler turned. I was in.

Anxiety converted into adrenalin.

The inside of the building looked similar to the way it would in nineteen eighty-one. In the red glow of safety lights, I could see a long hall ahead with doors on either side. Coffee and snack machines flanked the back door. I had no idea about security guards—if or how many.

The air smelled metallic, like spilled blood. My heart hurt remembering my last visit to the lab and Jon's death. I tapped the utility knife in my pocket for reassurance. It wouldn't do much against bullets though.

The exam room, operating theater, and future morgue were currently set up as a conference room, a lounge, and a desk area, respectively. A jumble of sealed cartons filled the area that would be the computer room.

I counted on my theory that destroying all the research prior to serum H-88's creation would prevent the drug from being invented. I believed the nineteen seventies' lack of digital and computer sophistication would keep the experimental data from being easily recreated. The innocent state of the facility seemed to bode well.

I didn't know where I'd find the actual research part of the lab, or if it would be one room or many. I reached the end of the long hall and turned left. That wing consisted of restrooms, a kitchen, and a cafeteria. I took note of an alarmed fire door at the end of the hall.

A noise startled me as I headed into the next wing. *Water flowing through pipes?* I flattened myself into the wall as best I could.

I heard footsteps coming, louder and louder.

I stifled my breathing.

The footsteps got quieter. Whoever it was had turned down one of the other halls.

I chanced a look. No sign of anyone. I checked each of the halls.

A tall, thin figure stood in front of one of the snack machines.

Was he the security guard who shot my Jon in the future? I couldn't tell in the low light. I had an urge to charge at him with the utility knife. I wanted to hurt that long-eared guard about as bad as I'd ever wanted anything in my life.

But my mission had to do with saving lives, not taking them. And somewhere out there in this earlier time, Jon was alive.

I took a deep breath and went back to investigating. I found nothing resembling a laboratory yet. Finally, in the last wing, through glass wall panels, I came upon a large area filled with beakers, test-tubes, Bunsen burners, centrifuges, and other equipment I didn't recognize. One side of the room held stone and metal tables, sinks, and shelves of chemicals.

Pay dirt.

I checked sightlines. The lab door was not visible from the front reception area where the guard likely spent most of the night, but it was close by.

Footsteps Dopplered toward me again.

I crouched in the far corner of the hall, hoping my dark clothing blended me into the shadows.

The thin guard passed by with a slew of snacks and sodas cradled in his arms. To eat so much junk and stay that skinny, he must have been blessed with the metabolism of a hummingbird.

From my vantage, I didn't get a good look at his ears. I might never know. I counted to a hundred, removed the lock picking tools from my pocket and went to work on the lab door.

A series of coughs sounded from the lobby followed by low voices. *More guards?*

My heart beat outside my chest. I listened intently. Something about *farm team* and *ERA* and then letters. *A radio station.*

When I let out my held breath, I blew the lock-pick rake out of my mouth. Not wanting to waste time searching for it, I grabbed one of the spares.

After a few more minutes, I heard the click and turned the knob. Before going into the lab, I got toothpicks out of my pocket and broke them off inside the keyhole. That way, I could lock myself into the lab and someone on the outside couldn't fit a key in. I grabbed my gear and set the lock. The toothpick crunched in the process, but hopefully the splinters would be enough to prevent the tumbler from turning. I dragged a metal chair and angled it under the doorknob for insurance.

The room was rectangular in shape and about the size of the entire Bayfront condo in my original life, maybe 800 square feet. There didn't seem to be a sprinkler system in the ceiling. However, smoke detectors blinked periodically. If I disabled them, they might send an "out of order" alert to the guard before I got down to business.

In one corner of the room stood a dozen cages filled with rats. *Holy molé salsa!* I hadn't counted on live animals. I had no desire to harm them. They'd suffered enough. I decided to get the place doused first, set the lab rats free, and then light the fire.

I hoped I brought enough incendiaries to get a good, roaring fire going. I poured dollops of fuel or paint thinner over the machinery, notes, and desk areas. I tried to be strategic with the sawdust and mothballs, sprinkling them in areas that looked less flammable. Not knowing what the lab chemicals even were, I spread those liquids around liberally as well. I kept going till I had nothing more to spread or pour.

With all the fire extinguishers stuffed under the wooden desk at the far end of the room, I heaped the empty gas and paint thinner cans on top.

I unlocked the lab door, possibly destroying what was left of the toothpick I'd jammed in, then propped it open with a chair. I snapped open all twelve cages and shooed out the animals. Using my flashlight, I guided the rodents toward the closest fire exit down the hall and held the door open with my foot. No alarms sounded. Luck was on my side.

Rat paws tickled as they ran across my toes. The thought crossed my mind that I might be setting off a plague by freeing these test subjects. Only if fate possessed a sadistic sense of humor.

Back in the lab, I secured the door again. Before I lit the first sparkler, I closed my eyes and uttered a silent goodbye to everyone I loved.

With the sparkler in my mouth, I flipped open the lighter and depressed the button. The lighter glowed and the firework sizzled to life. I lit the first work area, which blackened then burst into flame. When I had all the work tables burning, the smoke detector went off. But I was only halfway done. Red lights flashed in the hallway.

I raced along, lighting sparklers and setting new fires.

The thin guard shouted from the other side of the glass panel and pounded on it. He was the bunny-looking murderer who killed Jon in the future. He ran from the panel. Keys rattled in the lock, but the door remained closed. There must have been enough toothpick left inside to keep his key from fitting. Back at the glass panel, he shouted for me to get out.

I held up my middle finger.

He scuttled away.

The quantity of incendiaries turned out not to be a problem. Fires roared everywhere around me. A couple of booms went off. Even if the guard came back with fire extinguishers, he wouldn't make a dent.

Finally, I opened the gas valves under the half dozen Bunsen burners.

My plan was to die in the lab rather than let the Penrose wave braincenter stasis kill me. Having been blessed with few cavities, I hoped my body could not be identified with dental records. I didn't want my family to bear the shame of me being an arsonist.

Would I die from smoke inhalation before the fire scalded me? My eyes already seemed like grilled cheese, my lungs like the inside of a barbeque pit.

A vat exploded near the front of the room, cracking a round hole the size of a basketball in the glass wall. The fires blazed higher with the sudden backdraft.

"Mrow, mrow, mrow."

Is that a cat? With my head filled with boom and alarms, I had a hard time believing my ears.

"Mrow, mrow, mrow."

In the library research, in addition to lock-picking, I'd studied up on fires. Apparently, oxygen deprivation could cause hallucinations.

"Mrow, mrow, mrow." There it was again, a deep meow that sounded like my Gallo's.

I unlocked the lab door and surveyed the hall. Not much smoke out there yet.

"Mrow, mrow."

Holy molé salsa!

A long-haired, black fur baby who could have been Gallo's twin appeared at my feet. He licked my big toe with his raspy tongue, then dashed to the nearest fire exit. The cat jumped and scratched at the door, clearly wanting out of the burning building.

The guard was nowhere in sight.

I wheezed my way to the fire door. As soon as I reached it, the cat did a one-eighty and sped the opposite way. He took a left toward the back of the building.

I chased after him, choking.

The cat sat by the back door where I'd come in. *"Mrow, mrow, mrow."*

I cracked open the door.

The cat stopped on the threshold.

"Go on, kitty," I said. "You're free."

The cat remained there, statue-like.

I nudged him with my foot.

The kitty clawed onto my calf and held on. I hopped out the back door with the cat clinging to me. I shook my leg, but the cat held on. I took a few more steps and shook again.

The cat let go and ran away down the street.

I turned to go back into the lab just as the door snapped shut.

My lock-picking tools were sealed inside the building with my duffel bag.

No choice. I followed the fluffy cat down Cole Lane.

CHAPTER 88

SARA, AGE 14

Sunday, August 21, 1977, 1:02 AM
Seneca Hotel
Fishburg Falls, NY

I trudged back to the Seneca Hotel, coughing most of the way. I took no notice of anyone on the street. I'd automatically tucked the room key in my hoodie pocket even though I wouldn't be needing it. That was dumb, considering it would have helped identify my body as Sara Smith's. I slumped up the backstairs.

Fully clothed, I shivered under the shower's cold flow. I stayed there until the water washed away the smoky odor.

With great effort, I peeled off my wet clothes. I wrung everything out as best I could one-handed and shoved my wet things into the hotel's courtesy laundry bag. Using leverage, I managed to wrap a towel around me.

I never expected to live through the fire. I had no idea what to do next. Trembling and exhausted, I lay down on the bed and closed my eyes. A sudden realization opened them.

My mother's pageant cigarette lighter hadn't been in my shorts when I squeezed them to release excess water. I must have lost the lighter in the lab. My mother's engraved prize would connect me to the crime. I wondered about the food in the women's prison. *Probably lots of Berry Beary Crunch.* Not that it mattered.

I would die when the Penrose wave center in my brain went dormant. I thought about turning myself in to the police. But I had wanted to keep my family's name out of the news. I got up and paced.

That's when I heard a small tapping sound.

Maybe the police had found me out. I went to the door and looked through the peephole. *No one there.*

The tapping continued.

I checked the bathroom shower and faucet. No water dripped.

The tapping turned into scraping.

I followed the noise to the window and pulled back the curtain. *Holy molé salsa!*

There on the fire escape sat Gallo's look-alike, scratching his claws on the glass.

Another hallucination maybe, but I opened the window anyway.

The cat hopped into my room.

"How did you find me?" I said, as if the cat could answer.

He spit out something that looked like a brick of charcoal and said, *"Mrow."* He circle-danced around my ankles arching his back.

I bent down to stroke his fur, but he leapt up to the open window and out over the sill. I leaned out the window. "Kitty, come back."

He flitted down the fire-escape stairs two at a time. Like a trapeze artist, he clung to the top rung of the ladder, then flipped himself onto the ground, landing on all fours. He looked up at me, issued another *"Mrow,"* and blinked three times, before tramping off down the street and out of view.

I decided to leave the window open in case he might fancy another visit. When I stepped away, my foot landed on something flat and hard—the object that the cat dropped from its mouth.

I picked it up. The coating of soot rubbed off under my thumb to reveal silver beneath—my mother's pageant lighter. Both elated and stunned, I felt like I'd crossed over into the *Twilight Zone.*

The cigarette lighter felt warm and solid in my hand. So it wasn't a mirage. I sat on the edge of the bed and flipped the lighter open. I depressed the button with my thumb and nothing happened. I tried again. No flame came. Maybe it was out of fluid. I was certainly out of steam.

I wondered for the second time that day what death would feel like. I wished Jon were there with me to hold my hand, as he had been the day surgeons removed our dead baby from my womb.

Steve stands on a brightly lit stage in front of a large audience. He looks to be in his late thirties, his blond hair shoulder length, like a rock star's. He wears a black suit and shirt with a rose-colored tie.

Misti, dressed in a gold lamé gown, hands Steve a silver statue.

The audience applauds and cheers.

I watch from the wings.

Steve steps up to the microphone stand.

Before I hear what he has to say, the scene changes.

A dark-haired little boy, maybe four or five years old, dumps a plastic pail full of water onto a mound of beach sand. The boy has lovely rosy-brown eyes that match his copper skin.

The ocean, a hundred feet away, sparkles under blue skies.

The boy holds out the empty, yellow pail. "Mama, water please," he says.

He means me. I am his mama.

CHAPTER 89

SARA, AGE 14

Sunday, August 21, 1977, 7:45 AM
Seneca Hotel
Fishburg Falls, NY

*L*ight streaming in through the window, I woke remembering the sweetness of my dream-child's face. Somehow that felt like a good omen. I gathered my things into my backpack, donned my sexy clothes, and checked out without a hassle.

Smoke hung in the humid air like fog. The town reeked of cheap cigars.

As I walked to the train station, several older women, dressed in their Sunday best, gave me the stink eye. I figured it had to do more with my provocative attire than being an arsonist.

I checked the station board to see when the next train to New York City came through. As luck would have it, the Southeaster was due in less than half an hour. Then, not another train until three PM. I could head home and die in my own bed.

If I'd been killed in the lab, my family might never know where I'd disappeared to. I supposed the not knowing might hurt them worse.

The ticket office was closed until eight. I stepped into the railway café, a hole-in-the-wall establishment with two ice-cream parlor tables. At the glass case counter, I ordered a coffee and an egg sandwich to go.

The Fishburg Falls Gazette caught my attention. A photo of the burning

Gentry Research laboratory splashed across the front page. I bought the paper too.

I took a seat outside the office, set down my coffee, and read. The headline said "Arsonist Burns Down Gentry Lab, Head Scientist Dies in the Blaze."

Holy molé salsa—I was a murderer. *How can that be?* The guard had been the only other person on site. I had walked through the entire facility.

Night security guard Russ Weylin, aged thirty-nine, was on duty when the fire alarm sounded at a little past one AM. Upon further investigation, he discovered that a short man wearing a hoodie, possibly a teenager or seaman, had locked himself into the lab where all the experiments were conducted, and started multiple fires. Weylin attempted to unlock the door to save the intruder, but the lock had been jammed. He called the fire department, and Dr. Claire Gentry, head of the facility, to apprise her of the situation. He then exited the building.

I couldn't believe the guard thought I was male. I looked down at my cleavage. Sure, I had on a hooded sweatshirt, but wasn't it obvious? Then again, there had been a ton of smoke. Maybe long-ears was near-sighted like my grandma. I read on.

According to Weylin, Dr. Gentry arrived at the laboratory shortly after the call. She insisted on going in to save her research notes. Weylin attempted to physically detain her, but she bludgeoned him with her briefcase and ran inside. Unconscious, he was unable to follow.

Police arrived on the scene within fifteen minutes of the call. Captain Matthew Fuller deemed the situation too lethal to risk sending in any of his men to rescue the head scientist. Several small explosions went off.

The Fishburg Falls Fire Department, out assisting at a four-alarm fire at the soybean processing plant in neighboring Bedford Falls, arrived on the scene at the research facility approximately three quarters of an hour later. By then the facility was completely engulfed in flames. It is not known at this time if the same individual who set the soybean plant fire, a known arsonist, is also suspected of setting the laboratory fire.

When the blaze was finally extinguished three hours later, firemen discovered

the charred remains of a person believed to be Dr. Claire Gentry. Dental records
will be sought by the Holland County Medical Examiner's office for verification.

Mortified that I had killed a human being, I looked up from the paper to see
a police officer a few feet away showing a sketch to people waiting on the
platform. Long-eared Weylin came up next to the cop, and the two men
approached the railway worker opening the ticket office. After a brief
discussion, and handing off copies of the sketch, the men approached me.

My good hand shook, and I spilled most of my coffee attempting to set it
down on the bench. My first instinct was to strangle Weylin. But I knew
with the lab gone, he wouldn't be killing Jon.

"Buy you another java, baby?" Weylin said.

I tugged at the hem of my too-short skirt and crossed my legs at the
ankles.

"Good morning, Miss," the officer said. "We're looking for the arsonist
you've been reading about in the paper. Have you seen anyone who fits this
description?" He held out the sketch to me.

Dr. Claire Gentry did evil in the name of science, but she didn't deserve
to die. I wanted to confess. Instead, I took the drawing. It looked nothing
like me. The male in the picture had a very round face, heavy eyebrows, and
a bulbous nose. "Haven't seen this guy," I said. When I looked up, I caught
the policeman and Weylin eyeing my breasts. I returned the sketch.

"Thank you," the officer said, speaking to my chest. "Have a pleasant
trip." He dismissed me and walked on.

Weylin adjusted his crotch, then followed the policeman.

Stunned that the cop hadn't asked my name, business in town, or where
I was headed, I went in his direction. Also the direction of the trash. I tossed
the empty coffee cup and counted to ten. If the officer turned around, I
would give myself up. My fate lay in his hands.

The policeman did not turn.

But one second after I finished counting, long-eared Weylin spun
around. He winked at me, then went on ahead to talk with an older woman.

Did he wink because he knew I set the fire, and if so, why did he let me
get away? I had that *Twilight Zone* feeling again. I wouldn't have been
surprised if the train left the station on a Mobius track only to arrive at
Fishburg Falls over and over again.

CHAPTER 90

SARA, AGE 14

Sunday, August 21, 1977, 8:30 AM
Train from Fishburg Falls
to Grand Central Station, NY

Once aboard the crowded train, I nearly collapsed. I threaded my way on shaky legs to the only available seat next to a girl who looked like a teenaged version of Candy Starr—complete with Raggedy-Ann fake-orange hair and matching lipstick. Her chest, however, once much bigger than mine, could have doubled as an ironing board.

She scrutinized me, then stretched a strand of bubble gum out of her mouth. "I'm Candy," she said, without a trace of fake southern accent. "Candy Stein, but I'm changing it to Starr."

That's not all you'll change. I nodded, but didn't introduce myself. I wanted to wring her neck. But I told myself some other version of Candy was responsible for injecting me with serum H-88. Not this one.

"You know," Candy said, "I'm going to beauty school. I could fix that dreary hair of yours. Give you a groovy blonde hairdo."

"No thanks on the hair. I like it dark brown." Maybe I could prevent her from becoming Red Cross. I thought a minute while she blew bubbles and popped her gum. "Ever consider going to Hollywood?"

Her face lit up. "I'm not surprised you asked me that. Everyone tells me I should be an actress with my foxy looks."

"Well, of course," I said, "but if acting isn't your bag, you could be a hairdresser to the stars, work for movie studios. Actresses know all the best gossip and give out fancy jewelry and furs as tips."

"Righteous, sister. That's the best idea I ever heard. I may do that. Thanks."

I removed my book from my backpack and tried to read. My mind was reeling with the events of the last twenty-four hours. I couldn't concentrate.

Candy filed her nails and continued popping her gum.

Fifteen minutes later, at the first station stop in Briarton, Candy stood. "Have a good trip," she said.

I watched her queue for the exit, waggling her non-existent ass all the way.

Before she stepped down, she turned to me. "See you on the flip side, Sara."

My blood went cold. I hadn't told her my name. I was sure of that. *Has Domestic outwitted me after everything I went through?* I didn't want to believe it. I couldn't. It meant everything I did would be for nothing.

What we've got to do is keep hope alive, John Lennon famously said. I would. I could, for the last few hours of my life. What choice did I have?

When I tried to read again, I figured out how Candy knew my name.

She must have seen the personalized bookmark Grandma had made for me years ago.

On it, the name Sara was embroidered in large pink cursive. *You don't have to be wise to be lucky,* Grandma used to say.

CHAPTER 91

JON, AGE 20

… in the foundering cities rooms, and streets … names like wounds …

— OCTAVIO PAZ

Sunday, August 21, 1977, 2:25 PM
Shea Stadium
Flushing, NY

Tom "Terrific" Seaver was back to pitch against the Mets for the first time after his trade on Black Tuesday to Cincinnati. Jon's father had bought them tickets. It was the first game they'd been to together in almost a decade.

Papá stood up and jeered as the Reds took the field.

Jon booed right along with him. Seeing Seaver up there on the mound with a "C" on his hat was just plain wrong.

The crowd seemed to agree. A guy in the seats behind home plate held up a sign that read *We Come To Bury Seaver* on one side and *Not To Praise Him* on the other.

Papá flagged the beer seller and bought a couple of cups. He handed one to Jon.

It was the first time his father ever bought him a drink. He raised his beer and said, "To my son, the college graduate. *Salud.*"

A lump at the back of his throat made it hard for him to say, "*Salud, Papá.*" He embraced his father and held on for half a minute.

His father hugged him back.

When they broke apart, Jon thought *Papá's* eyes looked damp. Maybe the tears were because their former hero Seaver was making quick work of the Mets' batters. But he hoped the emotion meant his father was proud of him.

Before Jon's teen years, they had been so close. More like best friends. But Jon's love for The Beatles and other rock-n-roll music, plus his refusal to get a haircut, had driven a wedge into their relationship.

Jon signaled the hot dog vendor and bought two dogs for each of them. *Papá* ate them with gusto. So Jon bought another round of beers.

At the end of the third inning, Seaver headed toward the Mets dugout. He only got a few feet before he veered toward Cincinnati's side.

Seaver would always be a Met at heart.

And though the Mets lost, it was the best afternoon of Jon's adult life.

CHAPTER 92

JON, AGE 20

… a ghostly king rules over your heartbeat …

— OCTAVIO PAZ

Sunday, August 21, 1977, 9:55 PM
The García family apartment
Harbor Ridge, Brooklyn, NY

The tiny kitchen still smelled of the *sancocho* his mother cooked for the Sunday dinner. Jon had been too full of hot dogs and beer to eat.

He paced. Of hiring age in a couple of short months, he was determined to attend the police academy, follow in his father's footsteps. He didn't need his mother's approval to become a cop. But he'd wanted it nonetheless.

"Dad's fine with it," he said. He sat next to her at the table and patted her arm. Crying women, above all his own mother, made him uneasy. Even these crocodile tears, meant to manipulate him, had set him on edge.

"*Mijo*," his mother said, "I don't want you to be in danger. Try something else for a couple of years. *Tío* Congrio can get you a job in the office where he cleans." She dabbed each eye seven times with an embroidered handkerchief. She crossed herself, then dabbed another three times.

"You want me to be a janitor? I have a college degree."

"Yes, with college he can get you a real office job." She pronounced "office" like the entire word required capital letters. "Congrio says the accountant department has openings."

"Accountants are square. That's not me. Tell uncle, no thanks."

"Square?" She held up the handkerchief, unfolded it. "What do you mean, like this?" His mother dressed like girls his own age—tight t-shirts and jean shorts—but she didn't know how they spoke.

"Square means dull." He dropped the antacid tablets into the glass and watched them fizz.

"You shouldn't eat that *basura* the baseball house gives you," she said.

"I don't want any favors from *tío* or anyone. I need to prove myself. Make my own way, like *Papá. ¿Entiendes?*" He downed the bubbling antacid.

She wrung her hands in the handkerchief, but didn't answer.

This argument is pointless. He was never going to make her understand how he felt. "It's late, *Mamá*. You must be tired. I can pick up after myself."

She snatched his glass and stomped to the sink. With the hot water turned on, the pipes banged inside the walls of the apartment.

Jon tramped into the living room to watch the news.

An interview came on with Elvis's cook. She said the only thing that the King enjoyed in life was eating. "He'd have butter running down his arms." The commentator concluded the dialogue with the obnoxious platitude, "The good die young, especially the good eaters."

Jon shifted on the couch to get away from the sprung coil that dug into his backside.

Next, a short segment came on about the golden record to be launched into space with Voyager.

"Dark Was the Night" by Blind Willie Johnson and Chuck Berry's "Johnny B. Goode" seemed decent choices. *"A Day in the Life" or "Strawberry Fields Forever" would be better.*

The story was interrupted by late-breaking news about a shooting at a bar on Manhattan's Upper East Side. One police officer had been killed, another injured. Names were being withheld until the families could be notified. That location happened to be within his father's beat.

Before he finished dialing the precinct, someone pounded on the apartment door.

Jon didn't recognize the two uniformed men.

The one closer to his own age said, "Are you related to Officer Luis García?"

"Don't tell me my father—"

"Son," the older man said, "I'm sorry to inform you ..."

Jon didn't hear anything after the words "... died bravely in the line of duty." Always a possibility, but he never believed it could happen.

Papá was Jon's hero. He was gone forever. Bewildered, like Seaver when he headed toward the wrong dugout, Jon thanked the uniformed officers for the bad news.

The thud of *Mamá*'s platform shoes announced her arrival in the living room.

Jon raced and caught her by the waist as she crumpled. He hoisted her up.

She released her grief in wordless shrieks.

There wasn't anything he wouldn't do for her now. His mother was all he had left in the world. He vowed to himself at that moment to fulfill all the duties of a devoted son—bury his father, speak at the funeral, and take care of *Mamá*.

He'd even become an accountant if that were truly her wish.

CHAPTER 93

SARA, AGE 14

Saturday, August 28, 1977, 11 AM
Twin Elms Rest Home
Valentine, Florida

I searched for my grandmother in the sea of gray-haired ladies. She was my only hope.

The half dozen fans spinning overhead in the large day room spread out rank odors of mildew and burnt toast. Residents sat playing cards or bridge. Some clustered around a television tuned to cartoons.

One stranger held out her arms for a hug and called me "Rita, my baby."

I bit my lip, touched by her hope and sorry to dash it. "I'm not Rita. Forgive me."

A familiar turquoise polka-dot dress caught my eye. Grandma looked much older than when I saw her less than a month ago, in my first time flash. Even her wrinkles had wrinkles. At least those raisin-brown eyes shined.

"*Oy*, what a treat, *amorcito*," she said in an excited mishmash of Yiddish, English and Spanish. "What are you doing here?"

"Dad and I got on a Greyhound Bus yesterday." I leaned in to embrace her in the wheelchair. I pressed my face into her cheek. She smelled of her familiar vanilla and baby powder scents. My eyes gummed up with tears.

"Where is your father now?"

"Talking to someone in the office about how you're doing. How are you doing?"

"How about giving me a ride to my bedroom? I can hear better there."

As she directed me through the building, residents waved to us. We stopped a dozen times for Grandma to introduce me. "This is my beautiful granddaughter from New York."

Most folks nodded and responded with the usual pleasantries. At the rate we were stopping, it might take a week to get all the way to her room. And I didn't have a week. My Penrose waves were on borrowed time.

A stooped man, ambulatory, with translucent blue eyes that reminded me of Steve's, said, "You get your looks from your granny. Rosa's a knockout too. Will you please tell her to marry me? I lost track of how many times I've asked."

"Get in line, Harry," Grandma said. "I keep telling my suitors, I don't want to be tied down. They never listen."

Despite tangerine-colored walls and avocado carpeting, Grandma's room was sunny, clean, and spacious. From atop the small chest of drawers, a potted jasmine sweetened the air.

Dad, seated in the wing chair, looked up from the newspaper. "I wondered where my two best girls got to."

Mother wouldn't like it that she wasn't on the list.

He got up and gave Grandma a kiss and hug. "You look well."

"You could use a shave," Grandma said. "Your cheek is sandpaper."

"Need to get to the motel to freshen up. We had a long bus ride, but wanted to say hello first. How about dinner out at Steak and Ale tonight?"

"I have to cancel my date." Grandma winked at me. "But sure."

Rumpled as I was, I begged off checking into the motel in order to have more alone time with Grandma.

As soon as Dad left the room, I said, "Are you happy here?"

"Happy as I can be without my family around."

"I'm sorry Mother won't let you live in our home."

"This is a good place. And I do love the weather. I can go outside every day. Not like New York. People are nice, food's so-so, and there's a lot to do. Besides, I never had so many boyfriends. Imagine that. Me, who only ever had one man in her bed before this place."

My cheeks burned. "Grandma, are you saying what I think you're saying?"

"There's a lot you should know. You're old enough." She stood. "Let me get over there first."

Short, but shapely with an hourglass figure, and a beautiful face, it was easy to see why men her age would be attracted.

She sidled from the wheelchair to the bed on her own, but I hovered to make sure she didn't fall. Once she sat, I positioned pillows behind her back to make her more comfortable.

She pointed to the walker in the corner of the room. "Some days, poor circulation makes me too slow for my bicycle. I use my race car instead." She indicated the wheelchair she'd just vacated.

At least she had a sense of humor about her situation. I pulled the wing chair close to the bed and sat. "So tell me about all these marriage proposals."

"People say men want only one thing. But it isn't sex. What men really want is respect. You give them that, you got them. But make sure you want them."

Danny came to mind. "Already made that mistake."

"Me too. But when the right one comes, don't mess it up playing hard to get. I almost lost your Grandpa being a cold fish."

I couldn't imagine Grandma being anything but warm. "I'm sorry I never got to meet him." *Too bad I couldn't time flash to before I was born.* My consciousness would have nowhere to go.

Grandma fussed with the gold locket around her neck. She opened it to reveal a tiny, yellowed image of a stocky man in his twenties, one I'd seen many times. Light brown eyes and hair, my dad resembled him, though Grandpa possessed a sharper chin.

"A good singing voice, a jokester, and a great kisser," Grandma said. "No other boy made me weak in the knees like Ramón did."

"How did you know he was the one you should marry?"

"Easy. My bunions didn't hurt. Being with him made the pain in my feet go away."

Dr. Scholl's could have done that too. "But Dad says you two liked to holler at each other."

"We both had strong opinions. But in the bedroom, we agreed on everything."

"Grandma, I'm not sure you should be telling me this."

"You should be so lucky to find a man like my Ramón. And he would have loved you and your brother the way he loved his son. He wanted a crowd of kids, but my womb went *kaput* after one."

I hadn't realized she wanted more than one child. *Poor Grandma.* Maybe I'd inherited my uterine issue from her, but I felt fortunate to have gotten her good looks. "Sounds like your advice is to find a man who doesn't aggravate my aches and take him to bed."

"Don't forget respect. That doesn't mean you can't give a man a hard time. A squabble keeps the blood moving."

"Mother argues. Dad gives in."

Grandma coughed.

I poured her a glass of water from the pitcher on the side table.

She gulped it down. "Your mother doesn't respect your father, not the way she should. I said that to her face more than once. And she's all hush-hush. A husband and wife shouldn't have secrets."

"What secrets could my mother have?"

"Hector didn't find out till they went for the marriage license that Reya had been to the altar before. I don't know more than that, but I know there's plenty else."

Holy molé salsa. My mother had a life before Dad? A life that went wrong. My father was a second chance for her. *Like a redo.*

"Don't tell her I told you," Grandma said. "She won't let you come see me anymore."

"Don't worry, I won't. And I think she and I are getting along better." The note I wrote to Mom had thawed her frosty exterior and prompted her to give me an actual hug. *Major progress.* Her interior ice core, however, seemed to be intact.

"What's that gloomy face for?" Grandma said. "You look like your heart is hanging down."

"I have a long story to tell you, and you're going to think I am completely *loca*."

"Never, not my granddaughter. Now, you tell me everything."

Finally, I got the whole story off my chest. I told her about my life in the year 2000 before time flashes, about all the excursions into my past, and all the redos. I left nothing out. Not the part about sleeping with Danny in the past. Nor losing my virginity to Steve a second time. After Grandma's candidness, I figured that would be okay. I needed to confess my sin to someone before I died. If anyone could help ease my conscience, it would be Dr. Vaseline.

During my full disclosure, Grandma's expression was impassive. She nodded every once in a while, but didn't stop me, even to protest or ask questions.

I got to the part about burning down the lab and the scientist who died. "The guilt is eating me up. I am a terrible person."

Grandma patted the bed.

I settled next to her.

She wrapped her Vaseline-greased arms around me, and I broke down. I cried for all the mistakes I'd made and all the people I'd hurt.

She smoothed my hair and sang "Tra la la, it's later than you think. You are in the pink." When my tears subsided, she said, "What happened to the man that set the soybean plant fire? The one they think also set your fire?"

"I read he was killed in a shootout with police two days later."

"Then it's over," she said. "Listen, a black hen can lay a white egg. A bad thing done for good, for the welfare of others."

"A woman died because of me."

"Only a *meshugge* runs into a fire. You can't blame that on yourself."

"But I started the blaze."

"*Silencio*. Enough." She'd never shouted at me before. "We all have a burden to bear. I killed your grandfather."

"That's not true."

"True as you killing a crazy person. You have a good heart, *shana maidela*. Your whole life ahead. I know your mother raised you as a Catholic, but you are Jewish too. Live for our people who died in the war. You have to thrive so they didn't die for nothing."

I expected to die days ago. I could expire at any minute. At least I got to see Grandma one more time. "But why do you say you killed Grandpa?"

"He had a heart attack when we went walking. He didn't want to go, fought me, said he didn't feel well. But I forced him. A few steps from our apartment, he fell to the ground. Heart stopped. Dead. I wanted to be dead too. My insides burned like from Hell."

"He would have had the heart attack anyway. You didn't cause it."

"I thought I did. For years nothing helped. Then a book, a writer named Viktor Frankl, who survived the camps, the Holocaust. He said something I never forget. 'What is to give light must endure burning.' Sara, me and you, we burn so the people we love, they see, they get warm by us."

She wasn't to blame. I had no idea how much pain she endured when Grandpa died. Just as Dad suffered when mother died. Like Jon and I when we lost our baby.

Grandma cherished her life, cherished me. She found a silver lining in every cloud. I wished I had the time to grow up to be like her—not only a survivor, but a *thriver*.

FINAL ALTERED TIMELINE

YEARS 1980 THROUGH 2000 — THE PAST BECOMES THE PRESENT

And I asked myself about the present: how wide it was, how deep it was, how much was mine to keep.

— KURT VONNEGUT, SLAUGHTERHOUSE-FIVE

Life is what happens while you are busy making other plans.

— JOHN LENNON

CHAPTER 94

SARA, AGE 18

Monday, December 8, 1980, 10:45 PM
Outside the Dakota Apartments
Manhattan, NY

*A*ll my lives, redos, and time flashes led me here, to this night where I will change history.

I didn't anticipate surviving the fire I set in the Domestic lab. And when I did, I expected to die within a few days' time, when my Penrose wave brain receptors went inactive.

Instead, I drank Ella Williams' fishy tonic and got better. I've had no trouble with my hands or legs since. Everything works fine. I even sent the recipe I got from Ella to Grandma, and it helped her to walk easier.

Reliving high school wasn't as bad the second time around because I knew how little the cool kids really mattered in the scheme of things.

Losing Adam again—there are no words. But, oh, how he loved life to his very last breath.

In the back of my mind, there's the nagging fear that Domestic will develop the serum anyway. But no one can see the future. Not even me in this alternate timeline I created. Still, I keep watching for Candy or Murray or some other redhead from the corporation to come after me. I tense up when I see tall, thin, red-haired men. In the three years from 1977 until now, I've had no close calls.

I'm attending Flushing College like I did in my original life. Instead of Accounting, I'm a Biology major. I'm also training as an EMT, but maybe later I'll attend nursing or medical school. I need to save many, many lives and clean my karma.

But tonight, there is one important life I have to save, and I am willing to give up my own in the process if it comes to that.

I'm a couple of yards from the entrance to the Dakota apartment building with Steve Ranger. Having turned him down when he tried to date me, we became best buddies instead. He doesn't understand why I dragged him out on a freezing night to walk the streets of Manhattan. Or, why we continue to circle the same block. I keep checking my watch, looking around. There are no police in sight. No one suspicious either, except for us, I guess.

"Want to get something warm to drink?" Steve says, his pale skin bluish in the night air.

"A few more minutes and we can go home."

Shots ring out and echo from somewhere nearby. I spin on my heels. I tell myself the sound could be a car backfiring. *I know better.*

All the letters I sent over the years—warning the police and everyone else I could think of—have come to nothing. I collapse, wailing.

Steve hoists me up and holds me. He'll need to disinfect his coat later from my tears and mucus.

Sirens keen.

I make Steve go with me, toward the sound.

A block away sits a sideways limo with shattered passenger windows, one wheel up on the curb.

Yoko Ono, terrified, screams, "John's been shot."

I have no idea how much time passes, maybe seconds, maybe minutes, but the next thing I know, Yoko accompanies a gurney being loaded into an ambulance.

The cloth is pulled up over Lennon's head. He is already gone.

I failed.

Another version of Steve told me the universe favors certain patterns. But why did a good man's death have to be one of those?

Steve's eyes are filled with tears, too. "You knew, did you not? That is what you dragged me out here for."

"I wanted to prevent it, but it happened anyway," I said. "I was in the wrong place at the right time."

Steve holds me until I stop crying. He's always been a good shoulder in every timeline.

CHAPTER 95

SARA, AGE 18

Monday, December 8, 1980, 11:30 PM
A-train heading east
Manhattan, NY

The lights flicker as the subway car passes into a tunnel.

I wish I had one more time flash in me so I could try again.

As if reading my mind, Steve says, "It is not within your power to change another man's destiny. But sometimes, I do believe you are preternatural."

"A freak of nature," I say. "Blame it on my amygdala."

"Remember Rosy, Jim Morrison said, 'Love cannot save you from your own fate.' And no one had more love to give the world than John Lennon."

CHAPTER 96

SARA, AGE 18

Tuesday, December 9, 1980, 9:00 PM
Yesterday Bar
Hedgehurst, Brooklyn, NY

alf expecting to be accosted by Murray, I race all the way from the subway to the Yesterday Bar. Once inside, I catch my breath and scope out the pub's intimate setting. Several booths occupy the back wall, half a dozen tables take up the center of the room, with a foosball game off to the left side and jukebox off to the right. The place smells like beer, popcorn, and oddly, pine resin. A few of the tables are occupied and there are a couple of guys at the bar watching the TV.

I order a draft and throw my coat in a booth. Armed with quarters, I peruse the jukebox. A lot more country tunes than I'd have guessed for a tough Brooklyn neighborhood. Two thirds through the choices, I find three Beatles forty-fives—A and B sides— "My Bonnie" and "The Saints," "Nowhere Man" and "What Goes On," and "She Loves You" and "I'll Get You." I'm about to make my selections when someone taps my shoulder.

My glance connects with the vintage Liverpool t-shirt before I see who's wearing it.

Holy molé salsa. As I'd hoped, it's Jon—alive and whole again. I want to throw my arms around him. But I've learned a thing or two about patience from all my time flashes.

"Can I buy you a tune?" His dimples flirt with me.

"I bet you say that to all the girls."

He looks around. "I would, but you're the only one here right now."

His deep voice resounds everywhere in my body. "Very flattering. What will you say next, 'Want to come home with me, I have a sink full of dishes that need washing?'"

He laughs. "Now that you mention it …. What were you thinking about playing?" He leans in. He smells like baking bread and freshly brewed coffee with a hint of cinnamon.

I show him the songs I selected.

"Whatever your name is, you've got great taste."

"I'm Sara Rodríguez Bloom. And who are you?" I don't want to make the mistake I did last time and freak him out by telling him I know him from the future.

"I'm Jonathan García," he says. "Jon to my friends. Let's play all six." He slides his own quarters into the jukebox. "A terrible day, yesterday."

"I would have given anything to change it," I say.

"Me too." He twirls a lock of my hair between his fingers. "Have a drink with me, Sara?"

"Why else would I be here?" I say, flirting for all I'm worth. I indicate the booth where my coat is.

He waits for me to sit down before doing so himself. "Where were you when you heard about it? I was right here watching the game with some buddies. This very bench."

"A friend and I were out walking near the Dakota when we heard the shots."

"How awful to be that close. My friends and I went down there after Cosell announced it. Paid our respects. Did you stick around?"

"After I saw Yoko's face. I couldn't."

"I'm sorry," he says. He lays his hand atop mine.

Despite the tragedy, his touch gives me tingles.

The bartender comes and Jon orders.

Showing up here tonight, I didn't know for sure if I'd get to see Jon. Now I find myself tongue-tied. It doesn't help that he's not saying much either.

He keeps looking into my eyes like he's watching a pair of goldfish swim. Maybe he's focusing on the music—on the ghost of John Lennon's voice.

After his beer arrives, he says, "Now this is going to sound like a line, but have we met before? I mean, I feel like I know you from somewhere."

"You should know me," I say.

"I will," he says. "How about right now? I live over the bar. And there's not a dirty dish in the place."

"I believe you." I feel like I'm winning the love lottery all over again. Finally, I can lose my virginity with Jon. Maybe not tonight, but soon. Three times is a charm, after all.

CHAPTER 97

JON, AGE 24

… if two kiss / the world changes …

— OCTAVIO PAZ

Tuesday, December 9, 1980, 10:00 PM
Jon's apartment
Hedgehurst, Brooklyn, NY

The Paz line *You and your hair unhurried lightning* comes to mind. She has marvelous hair. He knows it isn't a guy thing to notice. He always sees short, long, dark, light. But this girl, her hair is a quilt of soft wool he wants to pull up all around his chin, tuck himself into. Not only her hair. She's got a body built for caressing.

She's next to him on the sofa, real and impossible, like a genie rubbed from a bottle about to grant him three wishes—on top of her, on top of him, on top of her again. *God, I want her.* And he wants to stare into her big eyes, golden ale-colored irises with sexy dark rings around them.

There are two of him in this moment in time. The one who hungers to take her to bed where it will be remarkable. And the other one who needs nothing more than to stay inside the moment of perfect desire. *I don't stop falling / and I fall.*

She tilts the wine to her lips.

He wants to be the glass, be the curved edge touching the inside of her mouth.

Her hand trembles when she sets down the wine.

Nervous? That can't be, she's so self-assured.

"Tell me about you," she says. "What do you do when you're not hitting on women in bars?"

Did she mean it as a dig? He isn't a Lothario. "Anything specific you want to know?" he says, hoping his openness will change her mind about him.

"Work?"

This night deserves a soundtrack. He goes to the stereo and drops the needle on *Abbey Road*, notching down the volume enough to keep conversation flowing. "I started at a law firm in the accounting department, but decided to take a more hands-on approach to the law. I'm about to graduate from the police academy."

She knots her fingers in her lap.

He imagines untangling them, sucking them one by one.

"You're willing to put your life on the line every day for people you don't know?" she says.

"My father did. He died on the job. I'm not half the man he was, but I'm going to try."

"Your father would be proud." She unlaces her fingers and brushes his forearm.

A current of exhilaration pulses through him at her touch. *Does Sara feel the electricity too?* He steadies himself. "What do you do when you're not picking out Beatles tunes on a jukebox?"

"Not the family business," she says. "My dad's an accountant—like you were. I nearly went in that direction too. But now I'm training to be an EMT, and I go to Flushing College part-time."

His admiration for her deepens. "Talk about facing death every day. Intense."

"I wanted to give something back," she says. "I'm grateful for this life, this new chance." She wipes nonexistent sweat from her brow with the back of her hand.

He can't resist any longer and takes her into his arms. He kisses her.

Her lips respond fervently, but as soon as he deepens his kiss, she draws back. A chasm opens between them.

"Maybe I should go," she says. "It's late."

"What's wrong?" he says.

"I don't want to push my luck." She bites her lip like she wants to say more, but stops herself.

"You're not making sense," he says, and immediately regrets that it sounds like a criticism.

She stands. "I want to see you again."

He rises and takes her hands in his. The words leave his mouth before he can stop them. "I want to see you now and later and tomorrow and the next day. Stay."

"How do you know?" she says. "What if tonight is all there is?" Her eyes look so sad.

"Sara, you move my heart the way the moon moves the tides. Eternally."

She wriggles her hands free. She won't look at him. "I should tell you ..." she begins but doesn't finish.

If she wants to drive him crazy, she's succeeding. "Whatever you need to say, *mi luna*, I'm listening."

Sara sinks back to the sofa.

He sits too, facing her, his legs touching her knees. He fills the stillness with his anxiety. "It's like I started to say at Yesterday's. I know you. Déjà vu, I mean ... I know I sound like an idiot here ... I know we—"

"I know you too," she says. "I've lived other lives with you, *mi sol*. I've gotten you killed."

"You're killing me now," he says, "but I don't believe in past lives. Somehow I know you like I know my own face."

She leans in, finally meeting his gaze. She says in a throaty voice, "Make love to me."

Talk about doing a one-eighty. She goes from leaving to loving in no time flat. His heart races, but he pretends calm as if women say this to him all the time. "You have only to ask." He leads her by the hand to his bedroom, uncertain which of them trembles more.

CHAPTER 98

JON, AGE 24

… I travel along the edge of your thoughts …

— OCTAVIO PAZ

Tuesday, December 9, 1980, 10:32 PM
Jon's apartment
Hedgehurst, Brooklyn, NY

*H*e's been kissing her a long time, when she reaches for him. He's already hard, but her fingers working his zipper thrill him. Despite wanting nothing more than for her to continue, he stops the kiss, moves her hand away.

She blinks her dazzling eyes.

"I want you to know," he says, "and it isn't macho of me to admit this, but I've never had a one-night stand. I don't plan on starting now."

"I'm a virgin," she says, "this time."

The word "virgin" buzzes in his head like an alarm. She's young, but he didn't consider he would be her first. She must truly trust him. He has to take it slow, show her everything he feels for her.

When her hand goes back to his zipper he doesn't stop her, nor when she takes him in her mouth. Immersed in warmth until it is nearly too much, he eases himself out to focus his attentions on her.

He removes Sara's clothes piece by piece, kissing his way across her body. He loves the fullness of her breasts, the berry-stain nipples that tighten between his lips. He wants his hands to be everywhere on her at once.

When she lets out a moan, he brushes the fleecy hair from her forehead, away from her blood-rouged cheeks to see how pleasure looks on her beautiful face. Her mouth is an 'O,' her eyes glow amber as if lit from within. He likes seeing her that way, how much she flares beneath his touch.

"I want you inside me," she says, not in the husky voice of earlier, but in her plain-spoken voice, which is even more arousing.

He moves on top of her.

She guides him with her hand and lets out a guttural sound.

He does too, when her flesh surrounds him, slick and close. His first time with a virgin, and he's nervous about hurting her. His shallow thrusts deepen when she arches into him, her face taut with pleasure.

Their rhythms together take him out of his head. He loses track of time. Everything is sense and sensory, perfect verve.

She cries out, her muscles throbbing around him, sending him over the top.

When he eases out of her, tears spill from her eyes.

Did I hurt her after all?

As if she reads his thoughts, she says, "Tears of joy, big boy."

He laughs, then licks away the salt from her cheeks.

"I'm glad I waited for you this time," Sara says.

"Me too," Jon says, though he has no idea what she means by "this time." *Probably that past-life stuff.*

Their legs entangled, he notices how the shade of her skin perfectly matches his own. But more than that, how they belong to each other. He recites from memory, *"There is no you, no I, no tomorrow, / no yesterday, no names, the truth of two in a single body, a single soul, oh total being …"*

"Octavio Paz," she says. "You're well-read for a cop."

He moves to kiss her belly. "I can't tell where you end and I begin."

"I know," she says. She kisses the top of his head, then quotes Paz back to him, *"because two bodies, naked and entwined, leap over time."*

CHAPTER 99

SARA, AGE 38

Saturday, December 23, 2000, 6:15 PM
Sara & Jon's House
Bayfront, Long Island, NY

*T*he kitchen is a potpourri of beef roast and sweet potato scents. The holidays are my favorite time of year, bringing the opportunity to celebrate with the family and friends I love the most.

"Sara," Jon says, "your mom's on the phone."

"Keep your eye on the pie," I say, closing the oven door. "It's on the verge."

"So am I." He brings me the phone and nibbles my throat. He covers the mouthpiece. "Make it quick. I need to have my way with you again before company comes." He play-bites my neck some more.

I take the phone and spank Jon on the rump. "Mom, how was the cruise?"

"I was voted Mrs. Bahamas in the passenger pageant," she says.

"Of course you were." *Some things never change.* And then some things do. She's alive eighteen years after having a partial mastectomy, along with chemo and radiation, and has been cancer free ever since.

"I'll be wearing the tiara when you come over for Christmas. It's impressive. How's my grandson?"

My mother turned out to be a doting grandmother. "Len is great.

Looking forward to seeing his grandparents. He missed playing one-on-one with Dad last week. But he's been practicing free throws with Jon."

"Put Len on the phone," Mom says.

"He's not here right now. He's at a friend's house. How's Dad?"

"We danced every night. You should see him Salsa."

"I'd like to. I hate to cut this short, but we have company coming."

"Okay. Give my love to Jon and have Len call me later."

"Will do. Bye, Mom."

Jon has my jeans undone as soon as I hang up.

CHAPTER 100

SARA, AGE 38

Saturday, December 23, 2000, 6:45 PM
Sara & Jon's House
Bayfront, Long Island, NY

I check my brother's Timex again. I'm worried I won't be finished getting dressed before our guests arrive.

Jon and I took advantage of the last twenty minutes of dinner's cooking time with a swift, but satisfying romp between the sheets. Our second love-making session of the day. Pretty good for a couple married sixteen years.

When our new toddler arrives in January, there won't be time for double-headers. We're adopting a second baby from the same orphanage in Mexico City where we got Len. We've already decided the child's name will be Luis or Luisa, after Jon's *papá*. My husband wants a girl, but I will be happy with either. Hard to believe our son is ten already.

At the mirror, I pin up my hair and apply red lipstick to match my red satin cocktail dress. Another me, stuck in diet hell, bought a sale dress two sizes too small. *Some fortnights ago and several lifetimes.* This *me* paid full price. Not a day goes by, I don't count my blessings.

"Mrow," Gallo says, hopping up onto the sink counter. "Mrow, mrow, mrow."

I turn on the tap for him to drink and pet his fluffy fur. I can't help but wonder if he's the same cat who saved me from dying in a fire in 1977.

Maybe felines are just natural time travelers. Or maybe Gallo is simply one magical kitty.

Jon comes up behind me, strips the towel from around his waist and tosses it in the hamper. He's as tan and toned as the day we met this redo, or final time flash. I'm not sure what to call this amazing life I'm living now.

Perhaps a time flash that turned into my redo as I remained in one time-line, and the years unfolded with me staying put.

"Let's go back to bed, *mi luna*, I'm not finished with you." Jon nuzzles my neck.

"*Mi sol*, if only there were time. Our guests will be here any minute. You need to get dressed."

He straightens up and pouts. "Okay, but where the *bejezzus* is my talcum powder?"

My husband still doesn't know where anything is, especially in our roomy, three-bedroom, Long Island, split-level home.

Jon spins me into an embrace. He smells like soap and aftershave and true love.

CHAPTER 101

SARA, AGE 38

Saturday, December 23, 2000, 7:05 PM
Sara & Jon's House
Bayfront, Long Island, NY

The Beatles' "In My Life" croons from the stereo. Scents of balsam, bayberry candles, and pine fill our living room. Stockings hang above the fireplace and holly decorates the mantle. I plug in the blinking colored lights on our tree to complete the festive scene.

There's a special ornament on the tree for every Noel we've been together, my Christmas Eve present from Jon. Two weeks and one day after we met at the bar, Jon offered me a silver ornament that turned out to be a box in disguise. Inside was a diamond ring that had been his paternal grandmother's. His mother was about to sell it since she never got along with her mother-in-law. But he stopped her just in time.

Jon asked me to marry him Christmas Eve 1980. He told me it was love at first sight for him. More like *ten-thousandth* sight, with all the time spent together in our original life and redos.

Before I said yes, I confessed about Domestic, the serum, my time travel, and all the other versions of me. I left out the parts about sleeping with Danny and Steve. *No need to upset him.*

After my crazy, rambling revelation, Jon took both my hands in his and said, "I love you, and I'm grateful you found your way to the Yesterday Bar, however you got there."

Four years later, we were married at the Hayden Planetarium on New Year's Eve. Our wedding portrait hangs above the fireplace. In it, my hair is naturally brunette, and I am wearing an understated A-line silk gown. Jon has on his dress blues.

I never spoke to him of Domestic again. And I swore off lying.

As in my original life, Mom wasn't happy about my choice of husband, with his distinctive ethnic last name and Latin appearance.

Jon turned down the job with the DOJ's special undercover investigative bureau when it was offered, and joined the Bayfront, Long Island, police force.

Our doorbell rings, and the door flies open. Len runs in ahead of his friends, Adam and Kaylee, and their parents. He rushes into my arms.

Gallo circles Len's legs. "*Mrow, mrow mrow,*" he says. It sounds like *I love you.*

I kiss the top of Len's head and muss his dark hair. He smells like baby shampoo, chocolate and snow. "I missed you, *mijo.* "How was the sleepover?"

"Great, Mom." Len's cocoa-colored eyes sparkle. "You're gonna love the present I got you and Dad. It's by that bug guy you named me after."

"You mean The Beatles' John Lennon."

"Un-hum," he says, peeling off his coat.

I look to Danny for some explanation. "Where did my son get the money to buy this gift?"

Danny brushes snow out of his full head of honey-brown hair, ignoring me. His face is free of all scars, the years having been much kinder to him in this life.

Joanne hands me a shopping bag, brimming with wrapped packages. She places a plate of her homemade gingerbread men on the glass coffee table, next to my deviled eggs.

Danny helps his wife out of her puffy down coat, then removes his own bomber jacket.

Jon gathers everyone's outerwear and hangs them in the entryway closet.

Joanne has on a jade silk blouse that matches her husband's eyes. "Don't look at me," she says. "The present was his idea." She pokes Danny in his abdomen, obviously flat beneath his red plaid shirt. "Only my true love would want to go to the mall this close to Christmas."

"Don't worry about the money, squirt," Danny says. He comes and gives me a hug. He smells like cloves and ginger and happiness.

"You're too generous," I say.

"Nah, it's really for your husband. He whispers in my ear. "It's an import of the 'Borrowed Time' single." He goes and shakes Jon's hand, then hugs him too.

Joanne and Danny's ten-year old twins, Adam and Kaylee, rifle through the wrapped boxes under our tree.

"Hey, kids," Jon says, "how about we open one present each before dinner?"

Cheers all around from the three children.

I cross my arms. "What about the tradition of one present each after dinner?"

"We'll do one after dinner too," Danny says, clearly in cahoots with my husband.

"A conspiracy," Joanne says. She gives Jon a hug and kiss on the cheek.

"You can take these into the playroom and open them," Jon says, dealing out a present to each child.

"Dinner's almost on the table," I say to the kids' backs.

Gallo gallops after the children.

Danny, already munching a deviled egg, goes to the bar and pours two glasses of sparkling cranberry juice. He takes out a pill bottle. "Almost forgot to take my allergy stuff. That darned cat of yours." He shoves the pill bottle back into his pocket and extracts a camera. "Hey, I should take pictures of the rugrats with their presents. Take these," he says to his wife, thrusting the glasses of juice into her hands. "Wait for Daddy," he calls, and dashes off.

"Can I get you a drink?" Jon says to Joanne.

"Already have more than my share." She carts the glasses over to the coffee table, then relaxes on the overstuffed sectional. "How did date night go, you two?"

"*Family Man* was really good. The plot was a reverse of George Bailey in *It's a Wonderful Life*," I say. "Danny should take you to see it."

"I'm sure he will. But I don't go in for that science fiction, alternate time-line, nonsense the way you guys do."

"It's much more real than you think," I say, unwrapping her plate of gingerbread cookies.

"The movie's romantic," Jon says to Joanne, heading over to the bar. "You'll love it,"

"Better than *Frequency?*" Joanne says.

"Almost no violence," I say. "It's a comedy."

Jon fills two cups with his signature rum-spiked eggnog and brings me one.

We sit across from Joanne.

"Let's have a toast when Danny gets back," she says, patting her belly. Face flushed, her creamy complexion glows more than usual.

Danny didn't give her the spiked eggnog, which she's always raved about in years past. I put two and two together. "I think I know what we should be toasting," I say.

"To best friends," Jon says, "and family."

"Jo, do Danny and the twins know?" I say.

"Know what?" Jon says.

"They do," Joanne says.

"When?" I say.

"June," she says. "I'm going to be the oldest pregnant lady in Lamaze class."

Danny, who's just returned, sits and kisses his wife's cheek. "You heard my Jo's pregnant?" His eyes twinkle like emeralds.

"Congratulations," Jon says to Danny. "Well done. And how'd the kids like their presents?"

"X-Men figures are a big hit," Danny says. "Thanks, bro."

And then it happens.

When he says *bro*, I think of my brother Adam, who I could not save through all the time flashes and redos. I blubber like an idiot, though I am grateful for this remade life that came about because of serum H-88—the drug's invention and annihilation. Grateful for this me who has almost everything she ever wanted.

Jon puts his hand on my back and rubs. "What is it, love?"

I get my emotions under control and say, "I'm sorry. I was wishing my brother Adam could be here with us."

"Me too," Joanne says.

"I know how you feel," Danny says. "I went to see him at the cemetery this morning."

"To Adam," Jon says, lifting his glass, "in heaven watching over us." My husband never met my brother, but he knows how much I miss him. He feels the same way about his *Papá*.

We all clink glasses and drink.

"How about we open up a present each?" Danny says. "The kids shouldn't have all the fun." He jumps up and starts shuffling through boxes under the tree. He hands me a small, rectangular package expertly wrapped in paisley paper with a velvet bow. "Hostess first," he says. "Here you go, Blondie."

This takes everyone by surprise—no one more than me. Especially since I've never had blonde hair in this timeline.

"I ... ah ... I," Danny says, stammering.

All these years, I had no idea *this* Danny is my time-traveling Danny. The same one I slept with in Maine. No time to figure out how that is even logically possible, I try to help him out of the inexplicable hole. I say to Jon, "I guess you're next, Dagwood."

Joanne chuckles, seemingly unaware.

"Might as well live up to my reputation," Jon says. He stuffs an entire deviled egg in his mouth at once.

Relieved Jon doesn't seem suspicious, I get back to the present. The tag says *To Sara*, but there's no from. I open the paper to reveal a hardcover book titled *Time Travel with Cornflakes* by Steve Ranger. I hold it up for everyone to see.

"That college friend of Sara's," Jon says. "Still carries a torch for her. Good thing he lives in Switzerland."

"Sweden," I say. "Is he the one who sent it?"

"Check inside," Joanne says.

Gooseflesh rises on my arms as I read the book's formal dedication:

For Sara, my Rosy, the one who got away, again and again, with all my love for all time.

I show it to Jon.

"Uh-huh," he says. "Torch, told ya." He takes the book from me and passes it to Danny.

"Dibs," Danny says. "I get to read it when you guys are done."

"I should get dinner on the table," I say. My words are swallowed up by the doorbell ringing.

"Expecting anyone else?" Danny says.

"Not that I know of," Jon says. He goes to see who it is.

"Hello, son," Mrs. García says, coming in. My mother-in-law's hair is a new unnatural shade of yellow I haven't seen anywhere but on a Barbie doll.

"María," I say, "to what do we owe this pleasure?"

"Lance and I are having dinner with some friends of his a few blocks away. I wanted you to meet him, but we can only stay a minute."

I've lost track. Lance is either the fifth or sixth in a string of widowers Jon's mother dated this year.

"Where is he?" my husband says.

"Parking. It's as hard to get a space near your house as it is for Sara to pick up the phone and call."

Not a dig about my weight at least. I am the same size as before, and haven't been on a diet since my original life.

"Good evening," a tall man shouts from across the street. He's waving an extremely large hand. And in a moment he's in through the door, in the entryway, holding out his huge appendage for me to shake.

I don't. *Holy molé salsa.* My heart is in my throat.

My mother-in-law's boyfriend is Dr. Lance Gentry, the physician from my original life who worked for Domestic all along. Scientist Claire Gentry's husband. *The man who I made into a widower.*

I never signed up as his patient in this life, and steered my own mother away from him.

Jon shakes Dr. Gentry's extended hand. "Pleased to meet you."

There isn't enough air in the room. Suddenly, I'm on the ground, with five concerned faces looming over me.

Dr. Gentry takes my pulse. "Is she diabetic?" he says. His voice sounds far away, as if from a dream.

Or from a nightmare.

"No," Jon says, stroking my hair. "But she hasn't eaten much today."

"I could give her a B-12 injection," Dr. Gentry says. "That would perk her up."

"No shot," I say. I struggle to get up, but it is like my legs are swimming in sand. The Christmas tree lights appear to jiggle in my hazy vision.

"The hypos are in my bag," Dr. Gentry says. "I'll go fetch it."

"No," Jon says. "Sara is an EMT. If she says no shot, then no shot." He sits me up, then lifts and carries me to the couch. "Are you all right, *mi luna?*"

I sip from the glass Joanne offers me. "Fine," I say. "Low blood sugar. The juice is already helping."

Jon's brow wrinkles. "Keep drinking it then."

"This will help too," Dr. Gentry says. He reaches into his coat pocket and pulls out a small box wrapped in silver paper. "Anniversary edition. Going to be a collector's item. I thought your son would like it." He extends the box toward me.

I reach for his gift. The air goes dead around me as if I've been struck deaf, as if time itself has stopped. I look down and realize what the doctor is bestowing—a single-serving package of Berry Beary Crunch, cardboard coated in foil, with the bear wearing an embossed Santa hat.

Jon stopped eating that sickening cereal in favor of eggs, and Len prefers bagels for breakfast. I never touch the stuff.

I tell myself the cereal is just cereal. That cereal no longer has any power over me. I remind myself there is no Domestic mind-control experiment. No serum H-88.

My hand quivers. The Berry Beary Crunch slips through my fingers.

I stare at the box, commanding the silver bear to stay solid, willing every molecule of the wooden floor beneath to maintain cohesion. I implore my consciousness to stay docked in my cozy home filled with my family and friends.

The clock of my heart ticks on and on. The second stretches to infinity.

Yet nothing happens. The box *is* just a box.

I remain in the present, in the life I forged from my bungled, mostly wrong-headed escapades. I don't know if I deserve this happiness, but I will do anything it takes to keep it.

Sound returns to my ears with the sputter of a spark in the room's crackling fireplace and John Lennon's "Happy Xmas (War is Over)" playing on the stereo.

The chaos of Domestic's experiment is over. Once and for all. I am the *me* I always will be. I swallow the last of the sparkling cranberry juice. "I'm much better now," I say.

"*Mi luna*, you scared me," Jon says. "You look like yourself again." He kisses the tip of my nose, then goes to see his mother and Dr. Gentry out the door.

As they make their hushed farewells, I say to Joanne and Danny, "Let's eat."

"I'll help you carry everything," Danny says. He supports me as I stand.

Joanne takes me by the hand.

The three of us meander toward the kitchen. We pause in front of the cabinet that holds my most beloved books and displays a framed photo from twenty-two years ago. There we are together, glowing with late-summer tans. In the photo we're linked—Joanne, Danny and I embracing each other's shoulders, and holding up my brother. Adam's smile outshines us all.

I tuck a few loose curls behind my ear. "You know, if I were to write the story of my life, I'd call it *Feast with Family and Friends* or *A Steady Diet of Love*."

Danny says, "Speaking of feast …" He heads toward the stove and digs a finger into to the glass baking dish.

"I can't let that man out of my sight around food," Joanne says, letting go of my hand. "He'll wolf down half the stuffing before it gets to the table."

Danny sticks out his tongue. "Spoilsport. Stuffing is my favorite thing besides you and the kids, babe."

My favorite thing is this moment in time.

∾

AUTHOR'S NOTE

Stories have always been my favorite mode of travel to other places, times, universes. Until time travel or teleportation become widely available, I'm sticking with stories.

My author heroes—Margaret Atwood, Octavia Butler, Ursula K. Le Guin, Marge Piercy, Ray Bradbury, Harlan Ellison, Stephen King, Kurt Vonnegut, H. G. Wells, and so many more—inspired me to want to tell stories of my own.

I am so grateful to each and every reader for picking up this book and traveling to the alternate timelines along with Sara and Jon and Gallo. I hope it was as much fun to read as it was for me to write.

So many wonderful people helped me bring *Time Flash: Another Me* into this timeline—

I wept for joy when author Karen Joy Fowler said she believed this was a story worth telling. My Seton Hill mentors, authors Heidi Ruby Miller and Barbara Miller, nurtured and nursed me all the way through the writing of this tale. My "unofficial" Seton Hill mentors, Timons Esais and Jason Jack Miller, generously gave their time and feedback. My Tribe traveled with me and buoyed me throughout the Seton Hill journey, especially Valerie Burns, Jeff Evans, Crystal Kapataidakas, and Patricia Lillie. My critique partners, Alex Savage, Matt O'Dwyer, Penny Thomas, and Tom Connair were not only excellent critics, but friends as well. My dear friend Linda Warren read with an enthusiastic heart and a sharp pencil. Michael Dell of EditOneNine aligned my wayward ducks. Thanks to the Cedar Circle Writers who welcomed me into their sun-dappled grove. Author Dean Wesley Smith's online workshop forced me to face my fear of putting my story into the world. Author Mary Buckham cheered me on.

Heartfelt thanks to artist Marie Fox for granting permission to use her glorious painting *Cat Nap*. The cover perfectly captures how I imagine Sara and Gallo.

This adventure in words would not have been possible without the loving sustenance, endless back rubs, and keen technical acumen of my husband Andy.

And of course, this story only exists because of my brother Alan, who exposed me to the limitless realms of *what if*.

ABOUT THE AUTHOR

Lana Ayers is a poet, novelist, publisher, and time travel enthusiast. She facilitates Write Away™ generative writing workshops, leads private salons for book groups, and teaches at writers' conferences.

Born and raised in New York City, Lana cemented her night-owl nature there. She lived in New England for several years before relocating to the Pacific Northwest, where she enjoys the near-perpetual plink of rain on the roof. The sea's steady whoosh and clear-night-sky stars are pretty cool, too.

Lana holds an MFA in Writing Popular Fiction from Seton Hill University, as well as degrees in Poetry, Psychology, and Mathematics.

She is obsessed with exotic flavors of ice cream, Little Red Riding Hood, TV shows about house hunting, amateur detective stories, and black & white cats and dogs. Her favorite color is the swirl of Van Gogh's *Starry Night*.

www.LanaAyers.com

ALSO BY LANA AYERS

FICTION

"Sideways" in Hazard Yet Forward

POETRY

The Dead Boy Sings In Heaven

Red Riding Hood's Real Life: A Novel in Verse

Four Quarters: An Homage to T.S. Eliot's *Four Quartets*

The Moon's Answer

What Big Teeth

A New Red

Dance From Within My Bones

Chicken Farmer I Still Love You

Love Is A Weed

Made in the USA
Columbia, SC
02 September 2020